ALSO BY JAY SINGH

Mythologika
Mortazarro: Opera Hero
The Little Samba Boy
The Epic of Stick-Guy
Maya's World: Dragoonies Make Chaibars
Maya's World: Total Word Domination
Maya's World: Picasso's First Love

Once upon a time in
a forest far away

Note for Librarians: A cataloguing record for this book is available from Library
and Archives Canada at www.collectionscanada.ca/amicus/index-e.html

Printed in Victoria, BC, Canada.

ISBN: 978-1-4251-9122-1 (Soft)
ISBN: 978-1-4251-9124-5 (e-book)

*We at Trafford believe that it is the responsibility of us all, as both individuals
and corporations, to make choices that are environmentally and socially sound.
You, in turn, are supporting this responsible conduct each time you purchase a
Trafford book, or make use of our publishing services. To find out how you are
helping, please visit www.trafford.com/responsiblepublishing.html*

*Our mission is to efficiently provide the world's finest, most comprehensive
book publishing service, enabling every author to experience success.
To find out how to publish your book, your way, and have it available
worldwide, visit us online at www.trafford.com*

www.trafford.com

North America & international
toll-free: 1 888 232 4444 (USA & Canada)
phone: 250 383 6864 ♦ fax: 250 383 6804
email: info@trafford.com

The United Kingdom & Europe
phone: +44 (0)1865 487 395 ♦ local rate: 0845 230 9601
facsimile: +44 (0)1865 481 507 ♦ email: info.uk@trafford.com

10 9 8 7 6 5 4 3 2 1

The Butterfly

The Brutal

ℰℐ

Everything's in a smile. Or at least that's what my Mother used to say. She used to say that there was nothing more beautiful than a genuine smile. Those genuine smiles of youth where the simple riches of the Forest always suffice--the sun, the moon, the stars, the misty mornings just after a night of rain, the Forest when it first greets the spring, the sun that breaks through the canopy, the blissful buzz of a passing bee...

Riches, ah yes, I will forever cherish.

And then my Mother would ramble on about the forced smile-- those horrible little half-smiles born of vanity, trickery, and the social need to make things happy. She used to say that there was nothing more despicable; and she used to say that it made its owner look more ugly than pretty, more scary than friendly, more deadly than lovely. A smile that instantly turned its owner into a smelly old prune, not to mention darkened any room.

She used to say that there was nothing like a smile to teach you everything. That a smile was worth a thousand words, and that no matter how hard you tried your smile would never lie. "Can't hide the color of your soul," she would say, "in your smile." And then she would look at me and smile a smile just as pretty as heaven and say, "It's your signature...the one we feel."

And, sure enough, I'd be lost--lost in her smile.

I loved my Mother's smile and always hoped I would one day smile like her.

And still I hope.

And still I respect and observe her teachings.

And never have I found reason to take issue with her. She was right: a soul had its color, a unique color, and that color was a signature. The kind you couldn't forget. The kind you couldn't forge. The kind you couldn't buy. A signature, it's true, born of your life, how you lived, what you lived and what you took from those experiences.

And till this day I agree: there is nothing more smothering than a genuine smile. A smile born of respect, understanding and a deep respect for the Forest and everything in it.

And till this day I agree: there is nothing more disgusting than a false smile--a motivated smile--the muddy smile of greedy want. "This despicable hue," my Mother would tisk-tisk-tisk and say, "is more obvious than a screaming baboon on a bullhorn and--and--and smellier than a string of dead fish on a hot summer day."

Yes, Mother liked to exaggerate.

She would exaggerate everything and say if it wasn't worth exaggerating it wasn't worth mentioning.

And she liked to speak of things as if they were alive. It was her way of exaggerating the importance of a thing. And she did this with smiles. She would say of the genuine smile:

"If ever you trap one...don't you harm it. Keep your fangs to yourself! You hear! You just look at it. Appreciate it. Learn from it. And then you let it free. Hear?!"

"Hear."

I would answer and look her straight in the eyes. It was what she required of her children. For she always said there was something shady about a spider who couldn't look at you straight in the eyes when he spoke.

"No matter how delicious looking!" she would continue.

"No matter how delicious looking," I would answer, a little annoyed as I had heard this speech a babillion times.

"Just leave it be--hear?"

"Yes..."

"Even if you're hungrier than an ocean of--of--of starving fleas!"

"Yes Ma, even if I'm hungrier than an ocean of starving fleas."

"Just set it free!"

"Yes."

I would answer with a sigh, and she would continue:

"Some things are just sacred--sacred--not meant to be touched."

She believed the genuine smile was sacred. She believed it belonged to the Forest and not my belly. And she believed that these sacred smiles were becoming rarer and rarer as more and more bugs traded in the infinite number of reasons there were to smile in the Forest for one or two.

And every night before bed she would gather all my brothers and sisters, she would pull out the "Trapper's Guide To Game", and she would

The Butterfly

flip over to the smile section where she would go through each and every smile--sly, social, blissful, lovesick, clumsy, clueless, idiotic, arrogant, genuine--as to make sure we'd be okay when she was gone. To make sure we wouldn't make the horrible mistake of eating a smile she deemed worthy of the Forest. Smiles she believed the Forest needed more of. Smiles she was sure, like the Dodo-bee, we would never again see.

I could not, in the little time I have, express the profound knowledge my Mother had about smiles. It was too much. Even annoying at times. Smile this. Smile that. Smile here. Smile there. Smile everywhere. Be careful of this smile. Be cautious of that smile. Look out for this smile. And be weary of that smile.

Sometimes--to give you an idea of her obsession--we would spend an entire day hiding under a leaf playing a game she liked to call "Hit or Dud." We would hide and simply bug watch. We would watch them crawl by and, staring at their faces, my Mother would whisper "Hit" if a bug could smile with the Forest and "Dud" if the bug seemed to be trudging around with some sort of a permanent frown.

Yes, indeed, my Mother could go on and on and on about her theories...if you let her. And I did. After all, she was my Mother.

And, no doubt, after talking to her for about half a nanosecond, you got a whole new appreciation for smiles. You started to look at them. And I mean really look at them--as a critic might look at a painting or sculpture--trying to unravel and decipher all the many mysteries and intricacies and ideas the artist may have, knowingly or unknowingly, put there.

Well, overbearing as she was, her constant badgering paid off. The other night, hungry as I was--and I was hungry--I let one go.

A bug, that is.

A fuzzy pink thing with a smile worth a thousand lazy Sunday sunsets.

Or at least that's what my Mother would have said.

And this fuzzy critter was so calm it hardly made sense. She wasn't scared. Not in the least. And they're all scared. They all plead and beg and cry for their lives like lost children in a game they thought would last forever.

But not her.

Nope!

Calm.

Iceberg-calm. As if she knew something I didn't. As if she were but a mere spectator of a movie she had so enjoyed, but always knew would end. And that to despair over that end, for even a second within the movie's duration, was to allow that end a double victory.

And there would be no double victory! Not for her. She was going to enjoy her every last breathing moment.

And as I approached, she stared at me as a child would a rainbow--in awe, in absolute awe, as though she had never seen a spider before.

But she had. And I knew she had. And I thought she was just trying to make me feel inadequate. And I thought she was doing a pretty good job.

So I did what I could to feel adequate again. To feel a spider again. To be feared properly, as all spiders should be.

And so, I put on my best act--my very best act.

I slowly crept up to her, making sure my approach was dark and deathly. I analyzed her puffy pink face and snarled like a crazy old dog.

She grinned.

Deeply insulted, I narrowed my gaze and made horrible hissing noises with my mouth, making sure to sound weird and crazy. And guess what? Right. She grinned.

I barked.

She grinned.

I neighed.

She grinned.

I even cockadoodledooed.

And she--she--she--grinned.

And she drove me clear-nuts with that--that--face! That fearless face. And I felt about as scary as a flea.

But I wouldn't bow down to her act. To that disturbing indifference.

And so, I polished my fangs and warmed up my spinnerets, and I did so right in front of her, hoping all this would scare her.

Not a chance.

I circled her. And as I circled, I hummed the spookiest tune you ever heard.

And still, not a shake.

I grabbed her and stared deep into her eyes and hoped my rather imposing gaze would help her realize both the severity and certainty of her situation. And, with no such luck, I said in a rather cool, nonchalant, matter-of-fact tone, matching that cool, nonchalant face of hers:

"Now, just so you know, as I do fear ignorance may be the cause of your really, really juvenile and most unwarranted courage, I will immobilize you, crunch into you, and--and--and..."

And that's when I lost it:

"SUCK-THE-LIVING LIFE-OUT-OUT-WHHHHY AREN'T YOU SCARED? WHY? WHY? WHY?"

And I was puffing and panting and cursing under an exerted breath.

And she held her head high and smiled.

She did.

And I was lost.

Confused.

Dazed.

Bedazzled.

And it's hard for me to explain, but right there and then I felt something jump out of that smile and lodge straight into my soul. I don't know what it was or where it came from, but it was there. It was definitely there. And it calmed me. Or rather, it smothered me. There was such understanding, such forgiveness in the color of her soul--for what she seemed to acknowledge I had to do rather than enjoyed to do--that she, with but a mere flash of her smile, devoured me.

And I swear her smile, like some sort of divine skeleton key, opened the most casehardened casket of my soul and let me see in her all

The Butterfly

I ever needed to see: her friends, her family, her dreams, her ambitions, her passions, her pains--her life.

And that's when I knew: it was a smile that belonged to the Forest and not my belly.

And so, with my soul now open to hers, I chose to starve and listen to her story rather than binge and later feel sorry.

The first thing I discovered, strangely enough, was that she wasn't always able to smile. That there was a time when she couldn't smile at all. When smiling was a horrible struggle to keep up a life of appearances. For how could she smile, she sadly confessed, when all she had ever wanted to be was a butterfly, a real butterfly, and all she had ever done was give herself every excuse for why she would never be one.

And I was surprised.

For my Mother had told me long ago that there were no more real butterflies and that the only butterflies that existed were but diseased caterpillars in perfectly woven butterfly suits.

Which as a youth I found quite amusing.

But my Mother would give me a gentle smack on the back of the head, look at me with that look only a Mother can give, and tell me that it was no laughing matter and that forgetting ones nature was really quite serious.

See--from my Mother's version of the story--caterpillars were once creatures of the Forest. And like all creatures of the Forest, vulnerable. Maybe more so than others. In any case, one day this caterpillar gathers all the caterpillars together and tells them he's been thinking and observing and thinking some more. That he thinks they need not fear the birds, the bugs or the featherless chickens no more. That he's got a plan. And that his plan is fool proof. And that his plan far exceeds anything any ant or bee or termite has ever built before...

And then he shows them his plans.

A Silk Palace.

And with thunderous applause they all go for it.

And so millions of caterpillars worked together, day and night, spinning incredible quantities of silk until they could spin no more. And then, with all this silk, they resurrected a palace, a Silk Palace, a palace which outshone anything ever created by ant or bee or flea or any other insect for that matter. Thick and impenetrable, with only one gate, the caterpillars had succeeded where others had failed; and now they were safe and secure from birds and bugs and beasts and little bratty boys who were often referred to as Featherless Chickens.

Now the caterpillars lived in a new world. They lived in a modern world. A gray world. A sunless world of stations and glitter, fake flowers and smiles, butterfly suits and butterfly boots. A world better described as a Monster. A gigantic silk Monster which had, in a most arrogant way, turned its back on the Forest, looking onto itself and only itself with its millions and billions of little beady greedy caterpillar eyes. And the caterpillar who had thought of the Silk Palace was right. The Silk Palace was stronger and more efficient than any other hive or hill or mound ever built. Moreover, it was self-sufficient, self- reliant, self-contained.

The caterpillars never had to leave.

They printed their own currency, which they called glitter. And with this glitter they, the founders, paid caterpillars a fixed monthly salary to subdue their chance to go out in the Forest and find their food plant (the unique plant by which a caterpillar becomes a butterfly) and work in stations whose sole purpose was to mimic and make better all things found in the Forest. Things they once had for free, but now, because they lived in a palace; because they walked instead of crawled; because they had complicated their language to a point where language defeated itself; because they had light bulbs instead of the sun, moon and stars; and, because they were civil, refined and well-defined, they paid for their food, water and fun.

But, as intelligent as they were, they couldn't mimic the food plants. There were just too many. And so, fearful the caterpillars would one day leave the palace in search of their food plants, thereby weakening their soul-sapping scheme, killing their Monster, destroying their most beloved Silk Palace, they, the founders, had done a most impressive job at deflating the whole idea of becoming a real butterfly.

First they instilled within their population an unwarranted kingly attitude. They convinced them that they were above the Forest and that a caterpillar's search for a food plant was but a silly pursuit of their primordial past. Then they complicated their lives to the point of insanity with so many unnatural wants and desires that they no longer had the time to even think about their food plants.

Food plant?

What was that?

14

The Butterfly

They had forgotten.

And finally, the founders worked extra hard and were extremely creative at distracting their unsuspecting slaves to the point of anxiety, with all their posters and stories and songs which preyed on fears and insecurities and which imprisoned the unsuspecting populace in an inescapable labyrinth coated in sticky green want.

And so just being a caterpillar was no longer enough. Had to have a definition. Had to have a station. The better the station, the better the definition. And the better the definition, the more the glitter.

And so, in the end, sad but true, there existed no more real butterflies. Only caterpillars in butterfly suits. Caterpillars who had thinned all their passions, pleasures and desires with glitter. Caterpillars whose sole purpose in life seemed to revolve around owning and wearing the most fashionable butterfly suit of the time. Which, sadly, took a caterpillar's entire life to save for.

And after an anxious life of hard saving, these withered and old, gray and dull, fake but proud butterflies, grown feeble with age, barely able to walk, inspiring envy and anxiety in the young with their perfectly-fitted butterfly suits, would strut their stuff around the Silk Palace saying in a barely audible grating voice:

"Look at me caterpillars--I'm a butterfly."

And if by chance a young caterpillar would challenge:

"Then fly!"

The fake butterfly would nobly retort:

"Flying--young one--is for the birds."

And so, as my little friend made me realize, caterpillars lived in a constant contradiction: it took as much time to search for ones food plant as it did to spend ones life in a station. Only the first seemed slow and without measure while the latter seemed quick and rewarding.

And it was with a sigh and deep conviction that she said to me, "Those stations--they make a caterpillar's day too long and life too short."

I agreed. And right there and then I knew I had been fortunate. I had been given the chance to speak to a creature once thought lost to the Forest. And lucky for me she loved to talk. And when she talked she always looked me in the eyes. That is, when her bulky blue hat wasn't covering them.

When I asked her about the hat, I knew it was more than just a clumsy-looking, oversized, broken up cap. For in the mere mention of it her eyes began to swell, her gaze narrowed and she bit her lower lip, which trembled under the strain of letting her memories get the best of her.

But she didn't cry.

She kept strong.

She was proud.

And when she felt composed enough to talk, she spoke of her pottery teacher. And she did so with such respect that I immediately knew he had been a marking figure in her life. For it was he who had given her the necessary strength and courage to leave the Silk Palace when, noticing she never smiled anymore, he asked her:

"Why don't you smile anymore? Always miserable. Always sulking. Always this frown."

And she put her head down and didn't answer. For she loved her teacher too much to lie to him or even pretend she was okay when really she wasn't. She loved and respected him so much for having taught her so much. And not, as you might think, in pottery, which she really didn't care for, rather, for all those life lessons her parents, both very consumed in their pursuit of glitter, had failed to teach her.

So, often needing his gentle guidance and understanding, she had spent all her free time at his school. She would pretend to be interested in pottery but was really only interested in his stories, his mannerisms, those little wisdoms that only come with age and experience. He was an older caterpillar who had lived a full life and who had a deep love for chocolate. He had an air of what she called, "a creature of the Forest."

"Kid," he said again, wiping his hands of wet clay, " why don't you smile anymore? When you were younger you used..."

"Does it matter?" she quickly interrupted, as if to hint the issue was not open for discussion.

"Does it matter?!" he repeated and laughed in utter disbelief, tossing the dirty rag to the earthen floor.

The Butterfly

"Sheeesh! My smile! My business! My problem!"

"Well I would say it's a problem..."

"Good! Fine!" she quickly interrupted. "Let it be then! It's a problem! My problem! I don't care! Bother someone else!"

"Bother someone else!" he exclaimed in disbelief, and then looked at her wide eyed with surprise. She had never spoken to him in such a disrespectful manner--so roughly, so curtly, so unapologetically.

And she put her head down in shame, realizing what she had done. He hadn't deserved that. Anger, anxiety, and inner turmoil were taking their toll on her heart. "I'm sorry," she whispered.

"Miserable about something else," he said shaking his head and tutting under a disappointed breath, "so you'll take it out on me. Just like a caterpillar. Ha! Just like a caterpillar! Instead of dealing with the actual problem you'll give everyone else a problem. Instead of shouting at the one who deserves your shout, you'll stay silent for the sake of keeping a station--then you'll shamelessly take it out on the ones you love...just like a caterpillar." And then he shook his head, tutted some more, put his hand on her shoulder, and said, "Kid...that's not the way to go."

"I'm sorry..."

And she looked up at him and tried to explain why she couldn't smile anymore, but her throat was all choked up with hurt and her eyes were all wet with tears. It was true: she couldn't smile anymore, and yet he had been the only one who had noticed.

He continued, "Tell me kid...what use is a station when you have no smile to show for it?"

And tears began to slip down her puffy-pink cheeks, down her trembling lips and, one by one, off her chin.

He put a comforting arm around her, pulled her closer, and, sensitive to her pain, said in a voice on the verge of tears, "Hey pretty pie-- don't cry."

He hated to see others sad, especially those he loved. But her tears were streaming down fast and now he had tears in his eyes. He held her tight and offered her some chocolate, " Have some chocolate."

And for a long while they were silent. They just ate chewy dark chocolate and stared at each other with mutual respect and understanding. And then her teacher, chocolate rimming his mouth, broke the silence, "I too had once lost my smile."

"It's not lost!" she exclaimed, loud enough to disturb his wife who was making a vase in the far corner of the studio.

"Kid," he said, looking at her and shaking his head, "It's lost."
And she sprang into his gentle arms and wept.

"Ohhhhkid!" he said as he patted her back and shook his head
sadly. "You think you're the only one who's ever wanted to be real?"

But she didn't answer.

"So why don't you just go? Really! Just go!"

But she didn't answer. She knew why she wouldn't leave.
Cowardice. She was too scared to leave the Silk Palace where she knew
she could live a long and safe and most comfortable life.

"Jeeeze Kid," he continued, "I know you're not happy here. You
feel trapped like I once did. But you know what...I'll tell you what...as
soon as I felt my smile beginning to fade...I left!"

She shot him a surprised look, and he nodded reassuringly.
"Yeah I left!" he said. "This place just wasn't for me. Some need a near
death experience to wake up and smell the smelling smelly...while others
just need to be half decent fortune tellers. Now I'm no fortune teller or
anything, but when I looked deep into my crystal ball...this is what I
saw...this is what it told me: a life without a smile, well, a life without a
smile is no life at all." He took two bites of chocolate and then he continued. "So I left! Gathered a few buddies, five of us, and together we said
goodbye to the Silk Palace, and went off to find our butterflies..."

"Butyournotabutterfly!" she interrupted.

"Never said I succeeded!" he added and took another bite of
chocolate.

And her head fell in a slump and, without looking at him, she
grabbed the chocolate from his grasp and stuffed it in her mouth.

She chewed softly, slowly, and sadly.

He put a comforting arm around her and said, "Kid, Kid, Kid--my
dream died as dreams often do. That's okay. That's life. Dreams die as
you pursue them...no sin in that."

And she looked up at him curiously, chocolate dripping from the corners
of her mouth. He smiled and continued, "Jeeeze Kid...it happens all time!
There's nothing you can do about that. Nothing. Cause you know one day
you think you got a dream and you go after it and as you go after it you
learn new things about yourself and as you learn all these new and wonderful things about yourself you begin to change and as you change so
does your dream. That's okay. That's life."

The Butterfly

He paused, looked at his wife and, his eyes wet with love and his voice crackling with happiness, he said as though speaking to himself, "See I found my smile."

And she immediately understood.

"See Kid," he continued, his eyes still on his wife, "I can live without being a butterfly, I can. No big deal! Not a problem...but I wouldn't last a second without her."

And they were silent.

"Kid," he broke the silence. "You have one chance at this. One! Don't mess it up by bowing down to your fears...don't...don't let your fears stand in the way of your hopes...don't..."

She beamed at him with shame, for she knew she was doing just that. She was letting her fears stand in the way of her dream: to leave the Silk Palace and pursue the one real butterfly who supposedly lived amongst the hermit fleas; and, who, she was sure, would teach her the ways of the old.

"Kid," he said, his voice gentle and genuine. "Have the courage to fail, for it's only when we..."

"But I don't want to leave you," she interrupted. "I don't..."

"I don't think you understand," he interrupted in a firm voice. "No, you're not understanding me. See, love you as I do, and I do...I don't, and it pains me to say this, I don't want to see you tomorrow, or the day after that, or the day after that...not like this...no...not like this...find your smile...it's the only thing that matters--all else is bunk--absolute bunk."

"Bunk..."

"'Cause Kid, if you don't have a smile, if you slump around like this any longer, you'll turn into a smile-hole. And you don't want that. You don't wanna be a smile-hole."

"Oh dear!" she exclaimed. " A smile-hole!" But realizing she didn't know what a smile-hole was, she asked, "What's a smile-hole?"

"Worse than a bitter black-hole! Only instead of sucking planets and stars you'll end up sucking smiles!"

"Sucking smiles?!"

" Yup," he confirmed. "You'll be sucking the smiles straight out of everyone--the ones you love--me."

And her head fell. She knew he was right. She had known many smile-holes. Their happiness, sadly, fed upon the smiles of others. She shook her head and looked up at her teacher with determination.

He smiled a knowing smile, as though he had seen something ignite in her. He took off his old blue hat, gave it a little tap, placed it on her head, and, with all the happiness and success a teacher can wish upon a student, he said:

"Find your smile--it's the only thing that matters."

ॐ

And so, the next morning, while her family was still asleep, after a night of heavy crying and deep thinking--of which she hadn't done in a long time--my friend, who I will proudly call the brave little caterpillar, put on her favorite blue t-shirt, her favorite blue shorts, and her favorite blue hat, and set off to find her smile.

And as she made her way through the narrow roadways of the Silk Palace, she thought of the hermit fleas. She wondered if they were really as she had read in the books: weak, soft-spoken, and humble. How she couldn't wait to see a real flea. The very thought sent shivers of excitement through her whole body.

She soon came to the gates. They were the only way in or out of the Silk Palace. Two excessively overweight caterpillars in undersized armor guarded them. In one hand they held a long silver spear, in another a fat green leaf burrito and in the others dirty napkins and magazines.

"Leave the Silk Palace you say?" one guard said while stuffing his mouth with a gooey green burrito, when she politely asked them to open the gates.

"Leave the Silk Palace she says!" repeated the other who was licking his fingers clean of the green paste. And then he burped.

Now they were making her feel nervous.

"No, no, honey, you don't want to leave," said the guard without looking at her, focused only on the food he was breathing down his throat, greenish slime dripping down his chin.

"I don't?" questioned the brave little caterpillar.

"No! You don't!" exclaimed the guard. He gazed at her with irritation and then went back to his slop. He chewed, swallowed in chunks, chewed some more and then swallowed everything in one huge gulp. "(gulp)It's much too dangerous out there."

"Yes, much, much too dangerous(gulp)," repeated the other.

"That's okay," she said proudly, "I'm not scared."

At these words, they stopped chewing. They stared at each other and then her, exposing the yellowness of four full circles. Then they

21

stared at each other and laughed. When they stopped laughing they questioned her.

"You're not scared you say?" questioned one.

"She's not scared she says!" repeated the other.

There was a short silence. Soon they were both eating and chewing rather pensively and the only sound that could be heard was the sound of their mouths now taking the time to first mince, then grind, then liquefy, and finally swallow.

"Of course you're scared," said one guard, shaking his head as if to shake her words off as a dog would fleas. "(gulp)We're all scared."

"Not I," said the brave little caterpillar in a firm voice. " Not I. I have the courage to fail. Yes...I do!"

"What the who! (gulp) " exclaimed the guard, looking at her strangely. He laughed a hissing laugh. "Is that supposed to be some kind of a joke?!"

"A joke!" repeated the other in a howl, food dripping down his dull gray armor.

"No," answered the brave little caterpillar strongly. "It's not a joke. I do. I have the..."

"Tell me honey(gulp)," interrupted the guard, "do you want to be, like...mantis food!"

"Mantis food!" repeated the other with a laugh, holding a burrito up to her and then taking a huge aggressive bite(chomp).

"No," answered the brave little caterpillar, her mouth now slightly turned downward at the corners. She had never really considered the possibility.

"Tell me sweetie(gulp), do you want to be, like...baby food! For some hatchling!" asked the guard with a smirk.

"Baby food!" repeated the other with a laugh.

"No," answered the brave little caterpillar softly.

"Or tell me--oh please tell me (gulp), if you wish to be torn bit by bit, leg by leg, hair by hair, by some bored little featherless chicken?" And he made awful noises with his mouth imitating the noises of a body being torn apart.

"Bits! Legs! Hairs!" repeated the other in a shout.

"No," whispered the brave little caterpillar, now fully aware of all the many things that could happen to her. Maybe, she thought, she didn't have the courage to fail after all.

The Butterfly

"Courage to fail!" laughed the guard. "Pahhhhh--why don't you scoodaddle outta here!"

"Scoodaddle!" repeated the other brushing her away with his slimy fingers.

Filled with things she hadn't even considered before, she felt her courage seeping, draining, leaving--gone. She pulled her hat over her eyes and let her head fall in a slump.

"You see!" yelled the guard in a cool authoritative voice, staring down at her. "You're better off staying here(gulp), where you're safe."

"Very safe!" added the other.

"Out there you will like...suffer!"

"Yes," added the other, nodding his head reassuringly.

Gloomy and upset, she dragged herself away. She would go back home and act as though nothing happened. Her family was right, her dream of becoming a butterfly was absurd and foolish and sought after only by bottom dwellers with little or no grasp on reality.

She turned around to catch just one more glimpse of those gates that kept her from her dream...her butterfly...her smile.

And the guards howled with laughter.

They waved her good-bye with their fat gooey fingertips. And then they raised their burritos to her, scoffed at her and yelled:

"To safety! To conformity! And to luxury!"

"And, like, let's not forget butterfly suits," said one to the other.

"No, no! Let's not!"

And they shouted:

"To big beautiful butterfly suits!"

"Which by the way," said one guard in an overly excited voice, "have you seen the new Monarch by Doo Doo Dadel?"

"No! Is it out?"

"Is it out?! Is it out?! Like where have you been?"

"It's out!"

"Oh honey! The purples! The blues! The yellows! One word: Gorgeous!"

"Really?"

"Really!"

"Oh, and have you seen the new Pigmy Blue by..."

"The Pigmy Blue! You are, like so five minutes ago."

"I am?"

Once upon a time in a forest far away...

"Are."

At that very moment a shout came thundering from a short distance:

"NOOOO!"

Their arms fell. They dropped their burritos. And they stared at the brave little caterpillar, chewing like a cow, slow and circular.

"Open the gates now!" demanded the brave little caterpillar. "Right now!"

Her hat was up. Her eyes were fierce. And her mind was set. There was something in her. Something that overwhelmed her. Something that took control of her. Something dark and angry and determined.

They took a step back and whispered concerns to each other.

"NOW!" she yelled. "NOW! NOW! NOOW!"

And with a deep sense of urgency, struggling with their excessively fat blubbery bellies, they unlocked the gates and pushed the doors wide open. There was something in her that scared them. And they stared at each other in disbelief as she held her hat by her heart and stomped away with her chin up and eyes focused.

Once beyond the gates the brave little caterpillar was taken aback by the newness of everything. She stood there dazed and bedazzled, squinting at the sky and simply not believing. She had never seen a sky without the foggy distortion of the silk ceiling. She had always thought, and the books confirmed, the sky was gray.

But the sky was blue! Definitely blue. Blue and beautiful. And she thought it looked like an unending magical blue rose expanding leaf on leaf dotted here and there with little hints of white.

"Blue!" she shouted and then began to laugh hysterically.

And then she saw real grass.

"Green!" she shouted for the grass they made in the Silk Palace was white. Then inspired by the blueness and the greenness of everything she began to twirl and jump and swish through the humongous strands of grass all the while shouting, "Blueandgreen! Blueandgreen! Blueandgreen!" And then, exhausted, she collapsed on the ground and twirled around a blade of grass still wet with morning dew.
The sun fell lightly over her soft pink belly and the glory of the sky filled her little heart with a joy that made her laugh out incessantly. She just lay there on her fluffy pink and green back, laughing at the sky and saying, "It's blue. It's really, really blue."

But her happiness was short lived. She had no time to waste. She had to get a move on. She had to move quickly if she was ever going to find the real butterfly. And so she began to get up and as she rose she noticed a dark thing with wings swooping down toward her. "Ahhh...a bird," she said to herself as if a bird were no real threat, frozen in spot, pointing toward the sky. " A bird," she repeated to herself pensively and she put a wondering finger to her lip. Then, with a shudder, the threat registered, and she shouted, "Birrrrrd!"

With a screech, she ran for cover.

The bird, dark and princely, landed with a thump and charged. And the ground shook. And just before he could snatch her up, the brave little caterpillar wiggled under a huge gray boulder.

And the raven chirped angrily, and he pecked at the rock, trying his very best to get to the brave little caterpillar who was pale with fear.

The raven patiently waited by the rock, his beady black eyes fused with her tiny green eyes. And there was a dark silence between them. And with one final chirp, the raven flew off. There was no question: she would out wait him. He was waiting for food. She was waiting for her life.

It was a long fearful while before the brave little caterpillar summoned up the courage to leave the shelter of the rock. But she did and now she was walking toward the river where, regardless of the fish below, she would have to swim across.

As she walked on, thinking about what kind of butterfly she would be and how everyone in the Silk Palace would be jealous, a beautiful buttercup, yellow and grand, caught her attention.

She had never seen a real buttercup before. It was tall and bright and it had a soft sweet hypnotic smell. Hardly had the brave little caterpillar stared at it before she began to wobble toward it, wanting to lose herself in the beauty of those soft golden petals. Beauty had hypnotized her and had done so as beauty always does. Without warning. Without mercy.

"Boooooteeeefuuul," she said as she walked toward the flower's stem. She crawled up the thick green pole, and, once on the flower, she curled up and fell asleep.

"Young! Green! Not very keen!" said the buttercup, and then she cleared her throat.

"Oh--heavens!" woke the brave little caterpillar. "Where? Who? What?"

"Wow!" exclaimed the buttercup. "A caterpillar! A real caterpillar! I thought you were all too good for the Forest. At least that's what a bee once told me...well, it's no wonder you're so young and green."

"Young and green," questioned the brave little caterpillar. "What does it mean?"

"It means be careful," answered the flower. "Lured by my beauty. Understandable. So understandable. So so very understandable. I am beautiful aren't I?"

"Yes, oh yes!"

"But be wary," said the flower. "Had I been a Venus flytrap...well, you don't want to know..."

26

The Butterfly

The brave little caterpillar was lost in her thoughts. She couldn't remember how she ended up on the buttercup. "How did I get here?"

"Insects," continued the flower, ignoring the question, "think there is happiness wherever there is beauty. Wrong. So wrong. So so very wrong. This is a mistake you know...a terrible mistake. Just because a flower is beautiful doesn't mean..." And the flower laughed an absurd laugh to illuminate the absurdity of the belief, paused, and then continued. "See all flowers are beautiful--but not all flowers are beautiful...and that's what insects seem to forget..."

The brave little caterpillar was confused. She had never seen a real flower before or any other insect for that matter and so she had no idea as to what the flower was talking about.

"You don't know what I'm talking about--do you?" asked the flower.

"No," answered the brave little caterpillar softly.

"Suffering beauty! Young! Green! Not very keen!"

And the flower let out a sigh of irritation. "Ask when you don't know...okay! No shame in that..."

"Okay..."

"So listen," continued the flower, "a flower's beauty is dependant."

"Dependant?"

"Sure dependant," answered the flower. "...dependant on nature. A flower's born beautiful and that's nothing more than cosmic luck."

"Cosmic luck..."

"Nothing more than cosmic luck being born a flower. That's all. All flowers are beautiful. All of'em. Gotta really go out of your way to find an ugly flower. But do you want to know a secret?"

The brave little caterpillar didn't answer. But her eyes answered. And so the flower continued in a whisper, as though revealing a secret deeper than the sea. "Not all of'em are beautiful. Some are ugly. Really ugly."

"But you said all..."

"Looking and being aren't the same thing!" interrupted the flower. "They're not. They're two very different things. You can look beautiful and be ugly. And you can look ugly and be beautiful. Being beautiful...well that comes from how you look at others. Looking beautiful...well that's just cosmic luck. Got to find that beauty within. And once found, help others find it. That's being beautiful. That there is a beautiful

27

flower. A rare and truly beautiful flower. Not dependant on the beauty bestowed upon it by the great celestial garden keeper--which most flowers settle with--looking and being aren't the same thing."

"Sheesh-that's kinda heavy stuff to think..."

"They don't think and that's the problem," interrupted the flower. "And so most flowers are just sad and alone, only slightly happy when praised. And then there are those who are just mean and angry. They're angry cause they know their beauty won't last. They know their petals will fall; and they can't smile cause this thought of a future without beauty overwhelms'em. It robs'em of all their worldly joys. It picks at their happy heart as a woodpecker would a tree. It makes'em do the most absurd things to cling to that beauty--the joke of it all-flowers making themselves ugly trying to keep themselves beautiful--sick trying to look healthy."

"Ugly, angry, sad, and alone," said the brave little caterpillar in a whisper.

"And deadly," added the flower. "Don't forget deadly!"

"Deadly!"

"Oh yes, deadly!" said the flower. "They use that beauty not to help but to destroy. To make others lose themselves in their beauty. See if I were a Venus fly trap, and be glad that I'm not..."

"Venus fly trap--what's that?"

"I'm proud, pink one--you're a quick one!" exclaimed the flower, happy she had asked a question when she didn't know. "Suffering beauty...you may just have a chance..."

And the flower fell into a reflective silence.

"Well," said the brave little caterpillar, "What is it?"

The flower, shaking itself from her thoughts, answered, "The most beautiful plant you will hopefully never lay eyes on."

"Ohhhh..."

"Oh yes, beware!" exclaimed the flower. "Beware! Beware! Beware caterpillar! If ever you do see one, turn away. As fast as you can. Even if she lies and says she's a rose. They often do that. A notorious liar the Venus fly trap. Notorious! Good at it too. Don't be fooled. They just want you to look and fall under a trance..."

"Ohhh..."

"Don't! Don't stare no matter what you do! For if you do, you'll fall under her spell. Her soft inviting smell. Her brilliant colors. Those

28

The Butterfly

awe inspiring leaves--hypnotizing and luring one and all to find happiness...but there is no happiness there, caterpillar. Misery. Only misery."

The brave little caterpillar listened with religious respect.

And the flower continued, "Flower? Doubtful. More of a temptress weed! A cunning, green, temptress weed who'll quickly weaken your will with her soft narcotic words...words that confuse, cloud and clutter...then once incapable of rational thought, she'll melt you and assimilate you with all that ugliness...all that ugliness you mistook for beauty."

"Suffering beauty!" interrupted the brave little caterpillar.

And the flower laughed. "Suffering beauty is right," said the flower suddenly turning serious. "Everyone thinks there is great happiness wherever there is beauty. This is a mistake. Always a mistake."

But now the brave little caterpillar wasn't listening anymore. She was pacing up and down the flower wanting to get a move on. She couldn't spend her whole day talking to a flower. She needed to get on her way. She needed to find the real butterfly. She needed to show everyone back home that she could become a butterfly, a real butterfly. And so, in a moment of great anxiety, she thanked the buttercup and was quickly on her way.

It wasn't long before the brave little caterpillar reached the river's edge. As far as she could see the river was lined with lush green trees and bushes and huge round dots of white and yellow and purple--daisies and dandelions and violets. On the other side of the river, the forest seemed darker and wilder and less colorful. And there was a leafless tree amongst the many thriving evergreens. She wondered why this tree had lost all its leaves and thought the tree might have been sick or something; and then she hoped it wouldn't spread its disease to the other trees.

She moved toward the water and stared at it with mingled awe and curiosity. She had never seen fresh water before. In the Silk Palace, all water came from hyper-safe taps--as exposed bodies of water were considered a hazard--and all water was brown and thick and expensive.

The brave little caterpillar moved closer to the river. She admired the mirror-like surface before her.

She tried to smile.

But no sooner had she tried to smile than she pulled away. There was no smile in her. Not yet.

It was time for her to cross.

She took a deep breath and prepared to dive in. The river seemed silky and friendly and it flowed rather smoothly.
She could swim across, she was sure. And so she dipped a toe to feel the temperature. And then she lowered her entire foot. She found the water pleasingly warm.

"Caaaaaarrrefffuul!" wailed a voice form beyond a bush.

She pulled out her foot and searched for the owner of the voice.

Glancing over the bush, she saw a giant Siamese cat. He had a blemish of brown on his otherwise tanned body. On his head was a hook-ridden fisherman's hat, which jiggled every time he moved. Sitting on a lawn chair surrounded by harpoons, hooks, and an orange tackle box, he looked as ancient as the moon with his long white eyebrows, which dipped over his cheeks, and his long white beard, which he twirled around his free paw. The other paw held an old fishing rod. The line pierced the middle of the river.

"I wouldn't do that if I were you," continued the cat in a long drawn out voice without looking at her.

"Pardon me," said the brave little caterpillar.

"I said," said the cat briskly, "I wouldn't do that if I were you."

"Do what?"

"Swim across," said the cat staring at his line where it pierced the water. "I wouldn't do that if I were you."

There was a short pensive silence.

A soft breeze riffled the cat's whiskers.

"I see," said the brave little caterpillar. "And if you were me and I were you, who would I be?"

"A shark hunter."

"A shark hunter!" bellowed the brave little caterpillar with a laugh. Although she had never seen a river before she had learned many things about them in school. For one, she knew that sharks didn't live in rivers but oceans. "I don't mean to..."

"Then don't!"

"Sheeesh, that's rude."

The brave little caterpillar said to herself.

There was an awkward silence.

"Well," said the brave little caterpillar, "like it or not...sharks don't live in rivers."

"Ohhhhh?" questioned the cat, now looking at her. "Then where do you suppose they live?"

"Oceans," she answered.

"Oceans!" laughed the cat. "Silly caterpillar, these, like it or not...are shark infested waters!"

The brave little caterpillar stood silent. She didn't want to argue. He was old and maybe a little naïve and he had lived his entire life a certain way. And so she certainly didn't want to hurt his feelings by undermining his life. Her teacher had taught her better. She said quite politely:

"Well then I thank you for saving me from the sharks."

"Silly caterpillar, shows how much you know," laughed the cat. "I didn't save you from no sharks...I saved you from the current. Besides sharks don't care much for no caterpillars. Your small body. Its huge stomach. It just wouldn't work. It would be like giving a pea to an elephant."

"Oh," she said and felt rather insignificant.

She looked toward the water where everything seemed calm and welcoming.

"They love cats though," continued the cat. "Sure do! That's all they eat."

The brave little caterpillar thought he was very absurd now. But he was serious and he was staring deep into the waters as though watching his past unfold on its silvery screen. He let out a stressful sigh and, without tearing his gaze from the surface, he continued:

"Twenty years ago, my friend and I were experimenting with our consciousness...twirling...heard about it?"

"Read about it..."

"Read!" the cat said with a sarcastic laugh and then continued. "Well my friend and I didn't care much for book-learning...more into doing...twirled we did--around and around as fast as we could until finally we reached that careless state of laughs and giggles, smiles and flying pickles."

There was a moment of silence. The cat's eyes were inward. Then he shook his head and asked, "Ever talk to the moon, count the stars, feel so free?"

She didn't answer.

"Well it feels good!" he said. "There on the ground with a new way of seeing things. Not a single worry or regret or bother. Just you and the world. "

"Just you and the world?" she questioned.

"Just you and the world," he confirmed. He was silent for a thoughtful moment and then he continued. "This one night we twirled way too much. Way too much. And too close to the bank. And I told my friend. I told him! 'Don't get too close to the water.' 'Don't get too close to the water!' But did he listen?"

He shook his head gravely, sighed a painful sigh, and then a hurricane of emotion shook him. "NOOO! BAM! BOOM! RAAAH! Out of the blackness came this, this, this SHARK! This awful, monstrous yellow shark..."

"A yellow shark," interrupted the brave little caterpillar with a questioning look, her hands on her hips, not believing a word.

"A Great Yellow!" asserted the cat, his mouth quivering at the corners, his forehead tightening at the center, his gaze hard on the water.

The Butterfly

"A Great Yellow," she questioned and suddenly realized why twirling had been banned in the Silk Palace. She stared at him carefully and then at the water.   "Shark?"

"I've been here ever since," said the cat, still lost in his memories. "I'll get that damn Great Yellow if it's the last thing I do!"
Now the cat was staring at the water with mingled anger and sadness. He sniffled every now and then.

"Sharks don't scare me," said the brave little caterpillar.

"No," said the cat, turning toward her, "but a current should."

The brave little caterpillar moved toward the edge of the river. Looking down she could see its rocky bottom. Everything seemed so calm and peaceful. She questioned, "Current?" And then she looked at the giant before her and shook her head in disappointment. "Sheeesh," she muttered to herself and felt silly for having almost believed a crazy old cat.

Feeling her doubt, he let out a sigh, put down his rod, and slowly moved toward her. She took a few steps back. He looked at her, bent down and picked up a rock. He held it where she could see it. It was three times her size and ten times her weight.

She stared at the rock with mingled interest and wonder.

He suspended the rock over the water and, when she was focused on the water, he let go.

The rock pierced the water, sunk a little bit, and then--ripped away faster than the thought that could perceive it--it was gone, a gray smudge, taken by the great current of the river.

"Current," asserted the cat, and he went back to his fishing.

The brave little caterpillar stood scared and bewildered by the fate that could have been hers.

"Silly caterpillar," said the cat now sitting down. His eyes were on the water where he patiently searched for a yellow fin. "All is not what it seems."

The brave little caterpillar lumbered up and down the river's edge thinking of a way to cross. All she could think of was flying. But she couldn't fly. She had no wings. And as she had no wings she felt helpless. And in her helplessness she felt hopeless.

She sat by the water and sighed at her reflection, and then she began to weep.But no sooner had she begun to weep than she abruptly stopped. She heard a ruffle in the bushes and stood bolt upright. She stared toward the swaggering bush and saw a cryptically colored walking strand of grass pushing its way through the shrubbery and leaf litter. Only this walking strand of grass had a gaze that could pierce marble, a mouth more vicious than a piranha, and razor sharp arms as intimidating as a pair of samurai knives. "Mantis," she mumbled to herself in a calm voice, frozen in place. "Mantid...Praying Mantid...preditor...Mantodea...named Praying Mantis for its strange habit of standing still with its forelegs held folded up before it...carnivorous and deadly..."And then the threat registered, "Creepers! Carnivorous and deadly!"

With a screech she quickly hid behind the stem of a sunflower, and all at once she turned to ice and became quiet and still.

As it approached, her knees began to knock. She didn't know much about the Forest, but she knew this: the mantis was no friend of the caterpillar.
She had read all the books on the mantis and she was sure: the mantis was a ruthless, unforgiving, cannibalistic carnivore. And she knew that if this mantis would find her, she would be nothing more than a caterpillar casserole.

She trembled. She bit her lip. She stopped breathing altogether. All was silent except for the mantis marching toward the river's edge.

At the edge, the mantis surveyed the area. She then dipped her long lanky arms in the water and gazed at the other side.

The mantis prepared to dive in.

She swung her arms back and forth and as she did the brave little caterpillar scrunched her eyes shut. She wanted to warn this mantis but knew that to do so would mean her own life.

Then for a short moment she overcame her fear. She stepped forward and almost warned the mantis. Her hands were extended out and her mouth was open in warning, but no sounds poured out. And then she dashed back behind the stem and hid.

The mantis, hearing something behind her, turned around and surveyed the area. Finding nothing, she turned back toward the river and prepared to dive in again. She swung her arms back and forth and just when she was about to jump...there was another ruffle. And she turned around.

Nothing.

The brave little caterpillar fought with her fear.

The mantis went back to her preparations, occasionally glancing over her shoulder with deep suspicion.

The brave little caterpillar struggled with her thoughts. Would she let this mantis dive into certain doom? Or would she chance her life to save another. And do so knowing full well that this mantis would not do the same for her.

The mantis bent down as far as her knees would take her and she bobbed up and down ready to blast away. But there was another ruffle, and so she turned around and blasted toward the sunflower. Now she searched her surroundings methodically, pushing around grass, flowers, and weeds. But she found nothing. And not finding anything she stomped back to the river's edge where, without any preparations, without a second to lose, she assumed a diving position.

This time, forgetting all her fears, the brave little caterpillar yelled, "You'll die!"

And the mantis froze in place.

"Ahhh!" screeched the brave little caterpillar as she realized what she had done and dashed back for the stem where she hid and shook uncontrollably.

The mantis turned around. Her eyes searched frantically. And then, pronouncing every syllable and pausing after every word, she shouted, "Who said this?!" And she stomped her feet on the ground as she searched under leaves, rocks, and a rusty old can.

"Who said this?!"

The voice echoed in the can.

Then the mantis marched toward the sunflower, now shaking violently. "Come out now and be spared!"

Once upon a time in a forest far away...

But this meant nothing to the brave little caterpillar who had read that the mantis was never to be trusted. But she also knew that the mantis would eventually find her as they were persistent and stubborn. And so she crawled out in the open.

The mantis looked her over and said:

"Well I'll be jammed! A caterpillar! A true-to-life caterpillar!"

The mantis surveyed the caterpillar like she had never seen one before--she hadn't.

Lips quivering with fear, the brave little caterpillar couldn't speak.

The mantis continued to scan her. She was amazed. It took courage for a creature to surrender itself to a mantis. Lots of courage. Something she would have never expected from a caterpillar. Their eyes met for a long moment, then the mantis approached the caterpillar, pounding each step, and she shouted, "What is this!"

The mantis felt inadequate. Maybe she wasn't mantis enough to be feared.

"Th...th...this?" stammered the brave little caterpillar, retreating backward until she was pinned against the sunflower's stem and could go back no more.

"What is this!" the mantis grabbed the brave little caterpillar and lifted her up to her face. "What is this! A caterpillar! A caterpillar! The nerve!"

The mantis brought her closer and closer to her mouth and the brave little caterpillar moaned in fear. And soon the mantis felt adequate again. And now she just stared at the brave little caterpillar.

"Oh...de...de...dear," stammered the brave little caterpillar. She closed her eyes. She moaned through closed lips. And then she begged for her life.

Then a sudden realization came over the mantis. The brave little caterpillar didn't have to come out. She could have stayed hidden and safe and let her dive in. So reasoning, she asked, "Why did you come out? Did you say, 'die'?"

At this the brave little caterpillar's eyes flashed opened.

"Da...da...dangerous," she answered.

"Dangerous!"

The mantis recoiled in mock horror and laughed. When her laughs stopped, she dragged the brave little caterpillar to the river's edge.

36

The Butterfly

She pointed to the water, where all was quiet and still, and said, "That! Dangerous! I don't think so! No, no come now...do you take me for some kind of a fool?"

And the mantis brought her closer to her mouth.

The brave little caterpillar moaned with fear.

Then the mantis was taken by another realization. "You could have conceivably let me jump in?" The mantis thought a short while. "How then? How is it dangerous?"

"I...I...I can show you."

"Do!"

And the mantis put her down.

The brave little caterpillar, with all her strength, picked up a stone, dangled it over the water, and said,   "Wa, wa, wa, watch."

"Proceed," said the mantis.

And the brave little caterpillar released the stone.

The stone penetrated, sunk a bit, then suddenly, faster than the thought that could perceive it, the stone was snatched away.

The mantis stared in horror where the stone had vanished. She looked at the brave little caterpillar. She looked where the stone had vanished. And then she looked back at the brave little caterpillar. When the truth of the situation finally sunk in, she said in a soft pensive voice:

"You saved my life caterpillar. You risked your own life to save mine. You? A caterpillar? It doesn't make any sense. It doesn't at all."

And she shook her head in disbelief, trying to believe something that just didn't go with all she had ever learned about caterpillars.

The mantis began to walk away shaking her head, still disbelieving and mumbling under a confused breath, " a caterpillar...a caterpillar... how...from...where..."

And then the mantis froze in her tracks.

"My mother," said the mantis, turning back to the caterpillar, " always said that caterpillars were cowardly parasites that clung to their lives stronger than fungus to fruit. But not you. Not you. You risked yours for mine. Why? It doesn't make any sense..."

The mantis paused and seemed perplexed.

She began to walk away again.

Then, remembering something, she stopped in her tracks.

There was a short reflective pause, and then she quickly turned to the brave little caterpillar and charged. She grabbed her little soft hands

and shook them and said, "I must reward you...I must reward you...
somehow...I must..."

And the brave little caterpillar was scared. She knew not to trust
the praying mantis. Some way or another she felt the mantis was testing
her, searching for an excuse to gobble her.

"What can I do?" asked the mantis, still holding one hand and
shaking it passionately.

"N...n...nothing," answered the brave little caterpillar.

"No. No. You don't understand. I must help you."

"Th...th...thank you," said the brave little caterpillar, "
but...but...but saving your life was reward enough."

"Courageous and smart," replied the mantis, " contrary to all I've ever
been told...but caterpillar, you don't understand, I must reward you."

And the mantis let go of her hand.

"Th...th...then not eating me," said the brave little caterpillar, " is
reward enough."

The mantis thought a short while and then said in a firm but non-
threatening voice, "Look here caterpillar, I must reward you. Must. You
may or may not know this but the forest has a book," and she paused to
gather her thoughts. "A book...a book in which she meticulously records
everything that happens--good or bad. And if you leave...if you leave
without letting me help you--you'll upset the balance of things. And I'll
forever wander the Forest owing a caterpillar." And she looked at the
brave little caterpillar with a rather powerful gaze, shaking her head slowly. "And I don't want that. Not now, not ever. I'll have to repay you sooner
or latter...whether in this life or another."

"Another?"

"So really," continued the mantis, "my helping you has more to do with
me than you."

"Oh..."

"So now caterpillar," demanded the mantis, "how can I repay
you?"

And the brave little caterpillar thought a short minute before she
answered. "A blessing," she said smartly. " Yes. A blessing would be just
fine."

The mantis narrowed her eyes judgingly. She let out a little sigh
and said, "Fine. A blessing it shall be."

And the mantis blessed her. She wished for the Forest to guide

The Butterfly

and protect her. To guide and protect her from the worst. And, learning her predicament, she suggested that the brave little caterpillar take a few days and make a really strong boat out of a leaf, some twigs and mud.

And the brave little caterpillar thanked the mantis and was on her way.

It took the brave little caterpillar less than a day to finish her boat. "Days!" she muttered to herself with a laugh as she pushed her boat into the water. But as soon as the half-finished boat slid in, it sank with a loud, "Blub-Blub-Blub."

"Ahhhno!" she shouted and began to kick around leaf litter.

When she had exhausted herself, she fell to the ground where she lay on her back and wondered if she would ever cross. And the thought of failure filled her heart with a sudden pain that made her moan out sadly. She began to mutter over and over again as if trying to convince herself of something she now scarcely believed, "Ihavethecourage!"

Suddenly she stopped.

She took in a deep breath and exploded:

"I don't! I don't have the courage!"

And then she began to sob. But no sooner had the tears begun to fall than she made them stop. She couldn't give up so easily. She needed to find the real butterfly. She needed to show everyone in the Silk Palace that her dream was real, very real, and that she could do it. She just needed to figure out a way to cross the river. Without wasting too much time.

She moved to the riverbank and stared at her reflection.

Staring at herself with tear-filled eyes, she lost herself in a reverie, one of success. In her mind she was a butterfly. A beautiful butterfly, a graceful butterfly, a colorful butterfly. And in her mind she could fly, really fly, and when she fluttered home she made everyone envious for having never believed in her.

A tear rolled down her cheek as she regained control of her thoughts. She felt something staring at her. In a flash she turned around, looked up into the flowers and bushes, and called out, "Who's there?"

There was no answer.

She gazed for a while and, finding nothing, said, "Must be my imagination."

3

The brave little caterpillar spent the entire day dragging her tired legs up and down the river's edge searching for a safe place to cross. But there was no such place and all was hopeless. She would never cross. The river was too wide wherever she went.

Sulking toward the horizon, where the sun fell lightly through white pillowy clouds, she no longer cared for the sky's beauty. All she cared about was finding the real butterfly.

Then, suddenly, staring absently toward the horizon, she saw something descending toward her. The silhouette of a bird fell from the sky at an incredible speed.

She sat up, squinted, and admired. "Bird," she said in a calm voice. "Bird making its descent...bird..." Then it registered. "Bird!" she shouted and ran for cover. But it was too late; when she looked over her shoulder to see if the bird was still after her, all she saw was a pair of claws, outstretched and ready to snatch.

At the sight of those claws she fainted.

⚮

When the brave little caterpillar woke, she found herself in a glass terrarium beside a plump gray mouse who was running on a treadmill. Wearing torn blue overalls, he looked worn and exhausted. He puffed and panted but never stopped.

She gazed around the room: baby turtles in gray pots; birds of all shapes and sizes and color in big or small cages; bright tropical fish in a gigantic aquarium; and, a snail cleaning the aquarium's dirty glass walls.

She wondered if she was in heaven.

"About time," said a young featherless chicken staring down at her. He had short blond hair, small blue eyes, a dirty white shirt, muddy blue jeans, and a pair of untied sneakers a little too big for his feet.

"Where am I?" asked the brave little caterpillar.

"Not in a bird's belly, if that's what you mean." And he looked toward the mouse and let out a little laugh. Then he said to the mouse, "You never cease to amaze me mouse."

"Can't get enough, sir!" exclaimed the mouse, running and panting.

The featherless chicken grinned. Then he turned around, grabbed his knapsack, and left for school.

With a slam of the door, the featherless chicken was gone. The mouse immediately jumped off the treadmill and collapsed to the floor where he gasped and whimpered and wheezed.

"I thought he'd never leave," said the mouse without looking at the brave little caterpillar.

"What? You don't like running?"

The mouse shot the brave little caterpillar a queer look. And then he stood up and went about his own business.

The mouse ignored the brave little caterpillar for days. She often tried to start conversations, but he moved about as if she didn't even exist.

There grew a cold silence between them.

Everyday the mouse would jump on his treadmill and the brave little caterpillar would watch him begin his absurd race. And she would think, "How absurd--work from nowhere that goes nowhere."

And then she would sulk over to the other side of the terrarium where she would watch the snail clean--incredibly slow and meticulous-- the aquarium window. She thought it would take the snail forever to clean the entire aquarium. She figured she could do the job in less than an afternoon.

At times she would become so upset at the snail's slow and careful movements that she would turn her attention to another terrarium where another caterpillar sat wrapped in a badly made butterfly suit pretending to be a real butterfly. But this false butterfly enraged the brave little caterpillar even more and so she would quickly turn her gaze back to the snail.

Once she became so enraged by the false butterfly's arrogance, she gazed at him, pointed an accusing finger and yelled, "FRAUD!"
And then she pointed at the snail and yelled, "And you! It doesn't take that long to clean!"

And the mouse looked at her and shook his head disapprovingly.

She stared at the mouse and her anger turned to sadness and her eyes filled with tears and she began to weep. And then she began to sob so ridiculously that the mouse, unable to withstand her sadness, moved toward her, put a comforting hand on her shoulder and said, "No use crying. Yeah? There are worse things in life."
"There are also better!"

"Yeah," answered the mouse, "there are better."
And the mouse thought a short while, and then he continued:

"Sure there are better...but this is your life now. Yeah? Now. So now, you must give in to your life now."

Once upon a time in a forest far away...

"What does that mean?"

"You must give in to your current situation," continued the mouse, "so that you may live until you can change your situation. Give in gracefully--yeah? Find something to do. Make the boy think you're useful. Cause if he thinks you're useless...you'll soon find yourself lifeless..."

"Heavens!"

"Yeah...and you'll never be real..."

"How did you..."

"It's in your face," interrupted the mouse. "And how you look at him..."

And the mouse pointed toward the false butterfly.

Then he continued:

"The boy thinks she's real and that's all that matters. Yeah? Yeah. He came in here a caterpillar and made himself a suit. No one knows how he did it. He just did. Out of necessity. And now he just needs to sit there and be admired..."

"FRAUD!" interrupted the brave little caterpillar.

"Call him what you will, but he's alive and for some...that's enough."

The mouse scarcely began to walk away before he turned around, pointed toward the false butterfly and said, "What you fail to realize is that most caterpillars don't want to be real. Yeah? Some caterpillars just want to be content. And that over there is a content caterpillar." He lowered his arm and then continued, "Everyday he gets a little food, a little water and a little compliment; and that's all he needs to move on to the next day. Yeah? He's alive and content whereas you will soon be dead. Unless of course you zip yourself a suit."

"Never!"

"Yeah? Well then my advice to you would be to find something to do."

"I will," she said sadly. "But how do I get out..."

"You don't and you won't."

"I will!"

"No... you'll plot and think for a while and then you'll get comfortable and forget."

"I won't!" said the brave little caterpillar.

"You will," said the mouse. "I see it all the time...I've seen it happen to the best."

"Not me!" she said with all her dreams storming through her

The Butterfly

eyes. "What's a little food? A little water? A little compliment? For what? All your time! "

"Still...you won't get out," said the mouse with a sigh. "But then again, yeah, there's always hope."

And the brave little caterpillar began to weep.

"Crying, yeah, won't help you," said the mouse. " Submission will. Got to give in to the cat."

"Give in to the cat?" asked the brave little caterpillar, not fully understanding what a cat had to do with anything.

"Yeah," said the mouse. "You got to give in to the cat."

There was a short silence. Then the mouse broke the silence:

"Serve a purpose or be squished."

"Squished?"

"Yeah! That's what little boys do with insects who serve no purpose."

"Well, well, why don't they just set us free!"

"Laziness."

"Laziness!"

"Your life isn't worth the time it takes to fling you outside."

At that very moment the mouse heard the boy at the door. And without another word he rushed to his treadmill where he continued his absurd jog. And the brave little caterpillar shook her head and said, "Work from nowhere that goes nowhere--can't do it!"

ॐ

Contrary to the mouse's advice, the brave little caterpillar did nothing to
make herself useful. All she did was stare at the snail who always
annoyed her. She would say to herself, "Sooooooo annoying! Sooooooo
long! Does it take that long to clean!"

And one day the mouse interrupted her idle gazing and asked her:
"You want to be a butterfly?"
"More than ever!"
"Then..."
"What?"
"Then..."
"What?"
The mouse looked toward the snail and pointed:
"Learn from that snail!"
And from that moment on the brave little caterpillar began to
observe the snail with interest and curiosity. But still, she didn't under-
stand what it was in the snail she was supposed to see. Everything it did
was done with long, slow, meditative movements. Movements she was
sure she could do quickly and without a second's thought. All the snail
did, she was sure, was turn a short and easy task into a long and hard one.
And there was nothing remarkable in that.
The brave little caterpillar did nothing with her time. All she did was
watch the snail. One day the mouse made her a certificate out of a piece
of wrapping paper. It read:

FOR HAVING DONE NOTHING LONGER THAN ANYONE
ELSE

"You want to be a butterfly," the mouse warned. "Make yourself useful. Give to the cat what belongs to the cat."

"Cat!" exclaimed the brave little caterpillar. "Why always cat? I'm not afraid of no cat!"

The mouse was silent and thoughtful for a while, and then he cleared his throat and said, "If say, a cat should catch me, yeah?"

"Yeah..."

"I would squirm and put up a fight," he continued, "like my life depended on it. Yeah? Because it does."

"Yeah," said the brave little caterpillar.

"But after a while, yeah, if I saw my situation was hopeless, I would give in gracefully."

"Give in gracefully," questioned the brave little caterpillar.

"And smile..."

"And smile!" she interrupted.

After a thoughtful silence the mouse continued, "A pretty powerful thing a smile. And yet you'd never guess it."
And she tried to smile.

"Yikes!" exclaimed the mouse.

The brave little caterpillar frowned like an ancient prune.

Then, staring at her drooping mouth, the mouse said, "Look don't worry, yeah. You've got one in you. I see it. It just has to come out. How? I don't know. That's for you to figure out."

And she was silent. Now she thought of her smile. It would appear, she was sure, as soon as she found her butterfly. Until then, she was doomed to frown.

And the mouse, as he sometimes did, spoke as though he had already begun a story, "So there I was face to face with this drooling cat...dangling by my tail over his mouth..."

"Really!" she exclaimed, forgetting her inability to smile.

"Yeah, really!" confirmed the mouse. " And I gave to the cat what belonged to the cat."

Once upon a time in a forest far away...

"I don't--you're--well..."

" I smiled. Yeah. It's that simple. And I went completely limp. And in his grasp, in his mercy, he was puzzled, puzzled yeah, but he knew, he knew...I looked at him and I understood him. I forgave him. After all, he's a cat and I'm a mouse! Yeah? Way it goes."

"Yeah. Way it goes."

"And in return he...well I'm here aren't I?"

"Because of a smile?!"

"A pretty powerful thing a smile," he smiled and she remarked it as a beautiful smile, " and yet you'd never guess it."

And she thought about the story. And she was confused. She had read in many books that all cats hated mice and that all mice hated cats. She was beginning to lose faith in caterpillar books. And now she even wondered if it was true that caterpillars were the only creatures in the Forest that were capable of thought, graciousness, and feeling. And that maybe her kind needed to believe that so as to justify their abuse of the Forest and other creatures.

"Turns out yeah," continued the mouse, "he needed a little under-standing..."

At that very moment the mouse heard the featherless chicken at the door, and before the brave little caterpillar could say anything else, he was on the treadmill. And as he began his jog, he turned to her and, fin-ishing his thoughts, said, "And we all need a little understanding."
And the featherless chicken slammed the door, fell over his bed, buried his face in a big fluffy pillow and sobbed violently.
Days passed by in much the same way. Contrary to the mouse's constant badgering, the brave little caterpillar did nothing to make herself useful. All she did was stare at the snail. And all that snail did was annoy her. Once the mouse--fearful the featherless chicken would one day squish her, and wanting her to realize her dream--made her another certificate to motivate her. It read:

FOR HAVING DONE NOTHING LONGER THAN ANYONE ELSE AND SURVIVED

But when the brave little caterpillar wasn't watching the snail, she was watching the featherless chicken. And it wasn't long before she became completely accustomed to his habits--of which crying seemed dominant, more so than bathing.

And it so happened that one day his tears were so overwhelming

The Butterfly

that she too began to weep.

Over his cries the featherless chicken heard sniffles and sighs and snorts that were not his own. And so, he looked to the turtles. They were heavily involved in a debate over nothing, which made them look very useful and interesting. Then he looked to the fish. They raced each other round and round a little gray castle each trying to beat each other in a race that seemed to have no end. And then he walked over to the terrarium where he looked at the mouse. The mouse shrugged his shoulders and pointed toward the brave little caterpillar who sobbed violently in the far corner.

Wiping his cheeks, the featherless chicken asked, "Why are you crying?"
Her throat filled with tears, she couldn't answer.

"How peculiar," said the featherless chicken. And he picked her up and began to pet her. "I always thought insects couldn't cry." He looked her over and caressed her gently. "How peculiar," he said to himself. He stared at her with curiosity and again asked, "Why are you sad?"

She huffed and puffed and sniffled; but still she couldn't bring herself to answer.

"Did the mouse hurt you?"

"Oh, heavens no!" she said and calmed herself down.

"Then why are you sad?"

Her voice rising and cracking, she turned the question around, "Why are you sad?"

The featherless chicken tried to answer but failed. Tears were caught in his throat and he closed his eyes and tried his best to hold back his pain. Then he took a long labored breath and said, "My cousin..."

He paused. He opened his eyes. And then he continued:

"He ridicules me so that others may laugh."

And he started to cry again. Calming himself down, speaking quick and without pause, he continued:

"Theotherdayatschool! I was running through the hall. And he stuck his leg out. And I went flying through the air. And everyone laughed."
The brave little caterpillar began to sob with the featherless chicken.

"I don't UNDERSTAND!" the featherless chicken yelled with his throat drowning in tears. "Those he tries to impress will never love him even...even...even a milli-fraction of how much I love him. And yet"--

49

his voice fell soft and sad--"he would hurt me to make them laugh. I don't understand." He sobbed for a while, and then he shouted, "I hate school!"

All the insects and reptiles were taken aback. They had never seen the featherless chicken so upset. They stared at him and the brave little caterpillar who were both sobbing and crying, exhausting their souls of heavily accumulated pain.

The mouse smiled.

The next day, when the featherless chicken was at school, the mouse tore those certificates he had made her, and he told her that she had found her purpose. He explained that some souls merely existed for the sole purpose of making others feel good. That sometimes whether we know it or not, like it or not, want to or not, we exist to bring peace and tranquility to those around us, and sometimes, that was purpose enough. And the mouse went on to explain how the featherless chicken really needed to talk, and that it was a really good thing that he had opened up to her. For anger and pain would have thickened his heart until, so thick and heavy with bitter blackness, it would have anchored his soul to a pit of solitude where it would have been left to rot and wither and fester. And then, the mouse was sure, the featherless chicken would have made life miserable for all those in his kingdom. He would have been what the mouse called: "The Angry King." A king whose sole happiness came from the misery of his subjects.

At the thought, the brave little caterpillar touched her heart and hoped it wasn't the heart of an "Angry King". And she was sure, it wasn't. But then she thought that after she had found her butterfly she would talk to someone about those things that upset and hurt her about the Silk Palace. She also needed to talk.

For several days the brave little caterpillar and the featherless chicken became very close. But the more time she spent in captivity the more depressed she became, until one day she couldn't even get out of bed. All she wanted to do was sleep. When she slept she forgot. And she liked to forget.

Once the mouse sat beside her and nudged her and tugged at her. But she wouldn't wake. "You never get up anymore!"

"Is the boy back?"

"No..."

"Shheeesh. Then let me sleep."

"Get up."

"Why?" asked the brave little caterpillar in a sad groggy voice, "what's there to get up for?"

"There's always a reason."

"I'll get up when the boy arrives. Till then...I sleep."

"And what of your need to be a real butterfly? "

"Paaah! Realshmeal!" she yelled. "Only free caterpillars have the chance to be real. So long as I'm a little boy's prize, I will never! Ever! Schmever! Be real."

"So sleeping will help?" questioned the mouse.

There was a short silence, and then the mouse continued:

"Do you know what I would do if I were you?"

"No."

"Ask!" he answered. "Yeah. Just ask."

"Ask for what?"

"For your freedom! Of course!"

"Ask?"

"Yeah," said the mouse with a smile.

The brave little caterpillar began to rouse.

"The way he looks at you," the mouse explained, "the way he smiles at you, I'm betting you ask for your freedom, he gives you your freedom. That's what I'm betting."

Once upon a time in a forest far away...

The brave little caterpillar was silent.

"You've got something on him none of us have," continued the mouse. "He sees you, yeah, and his face lights up like he's been given a glimpse of paradise. I've seen him. He comes home, runs to his room, and, without a word to any of us, he sits with you...and you guys talk the night through..."

She was silent and thoughtful.

"What are we?" continued the mouse after a short reflective pause, twirling slowly with his hands outstretched toward the aquariums, terrariums, and cages. "Turtle spit! At most!"

"Ask?" questioned the brave little caterpillar. "Just ask?"

"Yeah, oh sleepy one, crazy as it may seem, sometimes it's just as simple as that."

Those words left her with a newborn energy and she vaulted out of bed and smiled a half-smile at the false butterfly who pretended not to see her. And she said, "I will ask!" And the fake butterfly turned his back on her.

&

As though an unthinkable disaster had struck his world, the featherless chicken's face turned pale with horror at the request and he immediately refused her freedom. Instead he bought her gift after gift after gift. And he bought her all these gifts hoping she would forget her need to be free. But the golden terrarium, the jeweled bed, and the gourmet meals were all in vain. All she desired was her freedom.

Then one day, so overwhelmed with grief, the brave little caterpillar remembered the cat and how he had twirled to escape reality. And that's what she needed. She needed an escape.

So she took to twirling.

And did it often.

And she forgot she ever wanted to be a butterfly.

Once the featherless chicken caught her twirling. "Stop that!" he yelled.

"Stop that!" mocked the brave little caterpillar. She wouldn't stop. She had already started. And once she started, she could never stop. And so, she just twirled and staggered around her golden terrarium in a very successful attempt to forget herself.

"I said stop that!"

"Whaahaawhhhy!" slurred the brave little caterpillar as she twirled around like a ballerina.

"Why are you doing this?!"

She stumbled and moaned and fell to the floor. Now she was lost in a world of fast-moving stars. "Why?" asked the brave little caterpillar with a laugh, trying her best to catch some of those imaginary stars.

"Why!"

"Pelican pie!" she shouted and then her shout receded into a drunken laugh.

The mouse, watching from her old terrarium, shook his head and his eyes filled with tears. He had grown very fond of her.

"What?" asked the featherless chicken.

"Cricket butt!"

Once upon a time in a forest far away...

And the brave little caterpillar laughed a horrible drunken laugh that stung his heart.

"What? What? What?" questioned the featherless chicken.

"A big fat nut--nut--nut!"

"A big fat what?"

"Cricket butt!"

Another horrible twisted laugh issued from her lips.

"You're being silly!"

"Okay willy!"

"Stop it!"

"Little twit!"

"Goodnight!" the featherless chicken yelled.

"Not without a fight!"

He walked away and jumped into his bed.

And she began to kick and punch the air as though she were sparring with some invisible demon. She stood and began to twirl again. She flung her arms everywhere and screamed, "HIYA! KYA! YA!" Then, sadly, she hit her head against the glass of the terrarium and fell to the ground unconscious.

౪

In the morning the brave little caterpillar awoke to the sound of a steady flowing hiss. When she cleared her eyes she found herself staring at the river.

"I think, yeah, you reminded him of his mother," said the mouse, startling the brave little caterpillar into reality. "You made him think, yeah, still young...still has that ability."

"I'm soooo dizzzy," moaned the brave little caterpillar, and she put a hand to her forehead.

"I should say so!" exclaimed the mouse. "Never saw anyone twirl so much in my life."

"I hardly remember a..."

"He let me go to take care of you," the mouse interrupted. "And the others, too!"

"The others? He let the others go?"

"That's the funny thing, yeah," said the mouse, looking off into the distance. "He gave them the option of leaving, and, well, nobody left." He paused, reflected, and then abruptly continued, "In any case, no more spinning, yeah?"

"Yeah!" she answered with a pain-filled moan.

"You'll be okay caterpillar," the mouse said as he patted her on the back. "Somebody somewhere is looking out for you."

And she thought of the mantis.

The mouse began to walk away, but just before he was out of sight, he turned to her and said, "You didn't learn from the snail, yeah?"
"Yeah..."

"Then find a honeybee."

"A honeybee?" she questioned and shot him a queer look.

"Yeah--a honeybee."

And the mouse was on his way again.

But then, remembering something he wanted to tell her, he stopped mid-track, turned around, and said, "Also, never forget to thank those who help you."

Once upon a time in a forest far away...

The brave little caterpillar already knew the importance of appreciation. Her teacher had taught her well. And so she smiled and said, "Thank you mouse."

"No caterpillar," the mouse said with a smile, "Thank you."

And he was gone.

She went back to sleep and had a dream.

In her dreams she was back at the Silk Palace. She was beautiful and she was real and everyone was jealous and begging for forgiveness for having never believed in her. But she was unforgiving and she was proud for she had made it on her own. Then suddenly, in the chaos of her dreams, the cat materialized. He held up a harpoon that shone in the sunlight and smiled. And although she was a butterfly, try as she did, she couldn't return his smile. The cat smiled and said, "Smile!" But she couldn't. "Smile!" He demanded, his smile shining beyond his beard. She looked at her wings for inspiration, but still she couldn't bring herself to a smile. Then, oddly, the cat said, "Harpoon." And she repeated, "Harpoon." Then he smiled. And she tried as hard as she could to return it, but just as the corners of her mouth struggled upward, her lips suddenly turned to cement and they cracked and shattered and crumbled to the floor.

She woke suddenly, touching and searching frantically for her lips.

Then, with her bulky blue hat, she mopped the sweat off her forehead and, remembering those very last dreamy images, she sprang up with an incredible sense of urgency and set off to find the cat.

ॐ

As she approached the cat, the brave little caterpillar felt something strange shrivel up inside her. There beyond the bushes she saw the cat holding up the mouse by the tail. He was hovering over a mouthful of sharp white teeth which sparkled in the sun.

"Don't you dare!" shouted the brave little caterpillar with a violence that shook the trees and bushes around. "You let him go now!"

Both mouse and cat stared at her in mute disbelief. They couldn't believe such strength could come from such a tiny creature. There was something within her that scared them both.

"Did you hear me!" she continued. "Let him go!"

She charged the cat like a bull would a matador. She rammed his leg. Her hat flew off. And she sprang back, falling to the ground, dizzy and distraught.
She scuffled to her feet and charged again.

Again, she fell.

Again, she rose.

Again, she charged.

She repeated the routine over and over again--she charged, she fell, she rose--until, exhausted, she tumbled to the ground where she lay on her back staring at the cloudless blue sky, trying her very best to catch her breath. "Don't you dare," she said and then drifted into sleep.
The cat and mouse stared at the caterpillar, then each other; and, after a moment of silence, they howled with laughter.

"Wow!" shouted the mouse now staring at the flattened caterpillar.

"Wow!" agreed the cat, still laughing.

The cat let go of the mouse and he fell to the ground, landing on his feet. He toddled over to the caterpillar and towered over her, looking for signs of life.

"Crazy caterpillar," said the mouse, "if he didn't eat me the first time…why would he the second?"

"Are you following me?" asked the mouse, still towering over the brave little caterpillar who was flat on her back drifting in and out of consciousness. She had been unconscious for a long while; and now the sun was already making its descent.

"No," answered the brave little caterpillar rather curtly, and then she turned her dizzy head to face the cat.   "I came to see the cat."

And she stood and felt a little silly.

"About what?" queried the cat.

"About helping me cross the river."

At the mere thought they both laughed.

But she wasn't kidding.

"I'm not kidding!" she shouted over their laughs. "I'm not!"

"No," laughed the cat, "Then I think you've been twirling!"

"I haven't been twirling! And I don't see IMAGINARY yellow sharks!"

Abrupt as a sneeze, the laughter ceased.

"And how!" asked the cat, looking her over judgingly, "Oh how! Do you propose I help?"

"Well--I was hoping, well I was thinking, well, maybe..."

"Maybe what?" interrupted the cat. "Carry you across like some angelical feline god?"

"Good heavens no!" said the brave little caterpillar.
"Swim you across?"

"No! No! Heavens no!"

"Fly you across like..."

"Yes!" she interrupted. "Exactly! Fly me across."

"Oh, sure, fly you across!"

The cat looked at the mouse. The mouse shrugged his shoulders. And the cat let out a little laugh.

"You'll fly across," commented the mouse, "yeah, when pigeons fly backwards."

"And fish dance in trees!" added the cat.

The Butterfly

Her head fell in a slump.

"Do you see wings caterpillar?" asked the cat and he jumped to his feet and began to flap his paws as though trying to catch air for flight. And then he began to caw like a crow.

She listened until she could take no more and then she yelled:

"No! No wings! I see no wings! But a harpoon! I do see a harpoon!"

And she pointed toward a harpoon that lay by the cat's lawn chair.

The cat stopped his teasing and thought.

"Fling me across," she said.

She gestured as though throwing a harpoon.

"Fling you across?" thought the cat, as though actually considering the idea.

"Are you mad!" yelled the mouse.

"Heavens no!" she answered and then explained. "I grip on to the harpoon, he flings me into that tree."

And she pointed toward the leafless tree on the other side of the river.

"She is mad!" the mouse turned to the cat.

"Could work," said the cat.

The mouse looked toward the cat, searched for signs of a joke, and, finding none, yelled, "You're mad!"

"Quite," replied the cat.

"You speak madness!" the mouse yelled and threw his arms in the air.

"Fluently," smiled the cat.

The mouse nodded his disapproval. He turned to the caterpillar and said, "You'll slip, yeah, and drown."

"No I won't!"

The mouse stared at her deep and hard. She was unwavering.

"Fine," said the mouse, "but let's sleep on it."

"No!" yelled the brave little caterpillar.

"Patience caterpillar," said the mouse, " it's dark, let's wait until morning--Yeah?"

"No--please!"

"I'm afraid he's right," agreed the cat, "we should wait."

And the cat curled up on the floor and said, "I will need all the strength a good night's sleep will afford."

Once upon a time in a forest far away...

"You can do it now, I'm sure you could," she begged, impatiently. "Look at you big and strong and--and--and you can do it..."

"You learned nothing from the snail," commented the mouse as he made a pillow of the cat's furry belly.

"Pleeeasenoooow..."

"Patience," said the cat, his eyelids falling.

"Pleeease..."

"Patience," said the mouse in a sleepy voice.

"Pleeeeeeease..."

"Patience!" snarled the both of them, their eyelids shut, their voices annoyed.

"Patience! Patience! Patience!" mocked the brave little caterpillar several times and then she pouted and made faces and kicked dust in the air, until, tired, she fell to the ground with a twirl and a thump. But she couldn't sleep. All she could think about was her butterfly. And all she saw in the stars above was her butterfly.

ॐ

Through the pearly essence of night the brave little caterpillar examined the mouse's face to see if he was awake. Feeling some awkward presence towering over him, the mouse opened his eyes.

"Ahhhh!" he jumped back, startled, nearly jumping out of his skin and they almost awoke the cat. The cat turned in his sleep.

"AHA!" exclaimed the brave little caterpillar, "I knew you were awake!"

"Go! Back! To! Bed!" muttered the mouse under an angry breath. He closed his eyes and returned to sleep.

"Aaaaaaagh," mumbled the brave little caterpillar, and continued her pouting throughout the night.

ៜ

In the morning the brave little caterpillar examined the mouse's face to see if he was awake. Again, feeling some awkward presence towering over him, his eyes sprang open and, frightened by her anxious face, he shouted, "Ahhhh!" He pushed back into the cat and this time the cat woke.

"Good!" yelled the brave little caterpillar. "You're both awake..." And she ran toward the harpoon.

"Ahhhh!" yelled the mouse, annoyed and rubbing his eyes of sleep.

The cat's eyes opened and closed with fatigue.

Without a second to lose, she crawled up the harpoon, held on tight and, with a cocky grin, turned to the cat and said, "Come on now!--time's a-wastin'!" And she hugged the harpoon tightly.

Slowly the cat stretched toward the big blue sky in a half-dream. He took in a deep breath and then walked over to the harpoon. He grabbed it, lifted it, drew it behind his head and, in a sleepy voice, asked, "Ready?" And he staggered back, almost falling asleep.

The mouse, worried for his friend, said, "You could fall--Yeah?"

"I know," answered the brave little caterpillar, staring at the leafless tree on the other side.

"You could drown," said the mouse with concern.

"I know."

The mouse thought a short while. He nodded a respectful nod. He smiled at the thought of a caterpillar whizzing through the air on a harpoon. And then he said, "Then I bid you farewell!"

"Farewell," repeated the brave little caterpillar.

And with one quick jolt the cat flung the harpoon toward the tree, and then he fell to the ground sound asleep. The mouse watched the harpoon zoom away.

The brave little caterpillar had never felt so free in her life. It was the most exhilarating experience of her life. She whooped and hollered and screamed as the harpoon sliced the cool crisp morning air. She looked down at the fast-moving glassy water and yelled sure as sure can be, "I'm gonna make it! I'm gonna really make it!
Yee--ha! I'm really, really gonna make it!"

Feeling invincible, she sang over and over again:

"I'm gonna make it la,la,la...I'm gonna make it la, la , la, la..."

She began to laugh and scream and holler over and over again:

"I'm gonna make it! I'm gonna really, really make it!"

Then an unexpected gust of wind caused the harpoon to slow and sway downward. And then another gust followed with the same result. And now it was obvious: she wasn't going to make it.

Headed straight for the shiny surface of the water, she whimpered:

"I'm not gonna make it! Oh, oh, oh--I'm not gonna make it!"

Then she shouted fast and fearful:

"I'm not gonna make it! I'm not gonna make it! I'm really, really, really not gonna make it..."

She looked toward the brilliant surface where everything looked calm and peaceful. She screamed and closed her eyes. At that very moment another gust of wind, fiercer and wilder, blew her straight off the harpoon.

She fell into a downward spiral and as she fell she screamed until she landed with a loud thud.

When she opened her eyes, all she saw was the tail end of the harpoon sinking into the crystal-clear water. And then she noticed something strange: she was being carried back to the shoreline where she could see the mouse staring at her with concern and the cat sleeping with heavy snores.

Luckily, an old and grimy turtle had been swimming below her. Not so lucky, he was swimming the wrong way.

"Aaaaaah...excuse me," said the brave little caterpillar to the turtle. "Where are we going?"

"Nowhere really," answered the turtle in a long monotone voice, not diverting his gaze from the shoreline. "Funny though," he continued in a mumble, as if talking to himself. "Everyone thinks they're going somewhere...really, they're going nowhere."

She moved up toward his head and said, "Well I'm going somewhere you see--over there." And she pointed toward the leafless tree. "Not over there." And she pointed toward the mouse and cat.

"Emmm...but really you're going nowhere," said the turtle dragging his words.

"Aha, well, fine, be that as it may, I would like to be nowhere over there," she said and pointed toward the tree. "Not over there." And she pointed toward the cat and mouse.

"Soon," said the turtle. "I must do something over there, and then, when I am finished, I will take you over there."
"Aaaaagh!" said the brave little caterpillar.

She crawled up and down the shell sick with anxiety. She swayed on her feet while the turtle bucked the waves. Then regaining control, she ran up to the edge of his shell, where his neck stuck out in fat folds of green flesh, and said, "Maybe you could, if you would, be so kind, as to turn around, and leave me behind--over there."

"Gladly..."
"Oh thank you, thank you, thank you! Thank you green head!"
She jumped up and down in sheer excitement.
"After I'm finished over there."
And her head fell in a slump.
"One must be patient," continued the turtle.
"One must be patient," mocked the brave little caterpillar.

Then she mumbled under an angry breath as she staggered back and forth over the turtle's shell.

"What is over there?" asked the turtle in that same long drawn-out voice. "What is the rush?"

"Nooooottthhhhing."
"Nothing--emmmm...how very interesting."
"Nothing interesting in nothing!"
"Then why do you seek nothing?"
"Joking," said the brave little caterpillar. "I was joking. There is nothing in nothing. Let alone anything interesting. Sheeesh! All you turtles do is

The Butterfly

bicker over nothing!"

"Well," said the turtle. "I have been thinking about nothing for twenty years now. Which...which is not a long time when thinking on something as mind boggling as nothing."

"Twenty years!"

She laughed.

The turtle thought a short while, and then he continued.

"Takes a long time to understand nothing. A long time. Specifically: how to make something of nothing. That is boggling. Where does something come from? First there is nothing, then there is something...strange...is it not?"

"I was joking!" she yelled, annoyed. "Turtles have a lot of time to think about nothing. A lot of time. Most barely have time to live. I, on the other hand, have maybe twenty caterpillar years left to find my butterfly" --and she exploded--"and you are--robbingmeofmytime!"

The turtle slowly turned his gaze to her. He looked at her from the corner of his eye and asked, "You are in search? Of your butterfly?"

"Yes!"

"Oh my," said the turtle. "There it is. Nothing. Nothing with the potential of being something."

"What are you yapping about?" she asked. "Sheesh! You turtles-you're so annoying with your philosobees!"

"Philosophies," corrected the turtle.

"Whatever..."

And at that moment the turtle, without an explanation, began to veer.

"Where are you going!" demanded the brave little caterpillar.

And, for some reason or another, the turtle spoke quicker and with a lot more life. "Could be days before I finish what I have to do."

"Days!"

"I am a slow worker," said the turtle. "Besides, I did not know you were going somewhere."

"Somewhere?"

"Most go nowhere," continued the turtle. "They go many places but they never really go anywhere. But...but the one who travels within is always going somewhere. And a turtle, by virtue, by constitution, and by all that is sacred, must help all those creatures going somewhere."

And then he proudly recited part of the turtle's constitution, as though reading the words from a scroll in his mind:

"We turtles of the world, in order to form a more perfect forest, ensure good luck to all seekers in search of themselves in the form of assistance no matter what that assistance may be so long as that assistance does not infringe on the happiness or welfare of another seeker."

"Good heavens!" said the brave little caterpillar.

She had read much about turtles, but had never known turtles to live by a constitution. And as he made his way toward the leafless tree, she ran up to his ears and showered him with little caterpillar kisses. "Thank you green head," she said, "Oh thank you, thank you, thank you!"

And then she swayed back to the middle of the shell where she sat down staring at the sky. She pondered deeply over the white puffy pillows moving across the blue abyss. And there she questioned each and every one of them: wondering why they were there; what purpose they served; and, where they were going. And then she thought about nothing. Which confused her more than anything.

&

The brave little caterpillar thanked the turtle and crawled away from the river's edge, stopping for a moment to admire her surroundings. Everything near the water was colorful, appealing, and animated, everything but the leafless tree, which looked like the end of a long violent storm. She stared at this dark and dreadful, stark and pitiful tree and wondered why all its leaves had fallen. All the other trees were lush and green and teeming with life.

"Don't you dare crawl on me!" yelled the leafless tree, staring bitterly at the brave little caterpillar.

"I wasn't..."

"You just leave me alone," continued the tree, interrupting the brave little caterpillar. "These branches are for my own. Let alone some worm."

"I'm not a..."

"Worm!" exclaimed the leafless tree. "I know that. You're a caterpillar, and an ugly one at that. I look at you and I see one thing: bird food."

"Bird food?" questioned the brave little caterpillar.

And with an old withered branch the leafless tree gestured toward the other trees. "Look at those trees letting all those horrible birds fondle their branches. Dreadful! Simply dreadful!" And then he pointed to the brave little caterpillar and said in a menacing voice, "They see you and you're as good as bird poo!"

The brave little caterpillar looked at the other trees, and then she was suddenly taken by a sharp and profound fear. Hidden under the big green leaves she could see moving and shuffling about big beautiful birds of every color and size. They were singing and chirping and tweeting and swooping and resting and playing.

At the sight, she swallowed a breath and became white with fear.

There was a long fearful silence before the leafless tree, with a twisted laugh, continued. "Worm...please tell me your secret."

"Of what?" said the brave little caterpillar, frozen in place, staring at the birds, her voice and body shaking.

"Perpetual foolishness!" yelled the tree. "I don't really like you, true. But the birds...horrible and happy birds! Useless creatures. What has a bird ever done for the world?" And the leafless tree pointed at the birds, mumbled angrily, and continued. "Them with their songs! Their tweets! Their happy-to-be-alive sonnets! The last thing I want is to see them enjoying a good old caterpillar meal--your meat is prized I'll have you know--the bragging, oh the bragging I would have to endure--dreadful! Simply dreadful!" And the leafless tree shook with the thought. "So go, vamoose, scat, get outta here! Or I'll be the one who points you out--at least then I'll have the satisfaction of knowing they owe their bragging to me."

And the leafless tree's words receded into a series of angry mumbles and curses.

The brave little caterpillar looked at the leafless tree with a sort of half-pity, and then, quiet as a dreaming stone, she crept away.

Once out of harms way, further up the mountain, she stopped to gather herself and as she did she gathered quick impressions. She noticed that things were a lot different than the other side. Now the Forest was dark and dangerous and all around there were droopy webs, tangled weeds and wild wicked wasps threatening above.

She shuddered and felt a cold wind against her pink cheeks. The wind whirled and whimpered and whined and rose and sighed with the trees, trees so fat with thick green leaves that they blocked out the sun and left her in almost darkness. She gazed from left to right and things seemed to move soundlessly in the underbrush. Things were becoming worse and worse and she had never felt more scared in her life. For a moment she wished she were back at the Silk Palace.

Frightened and bewildered, she closed her eyes and, in an attempt to curb her fear, imagined herself a butterfly. In her mind's eye she was beautiful and graceful and most important she could fly. And in her mind's eye she returned to the Silk Palace and made everyone feel foolish for having never believed in her.

When she opened her eyes, there was no more fear, only anxiety. She needed to find the real butterfly. She needed to prove everyone wrong. And, although she wished she could just rest a bit and recuperate, she knew she needed to get a move on. There would be no idle dreaming for her. And so, she gathered her thoughts, stood upright, and, regardless the winds and weeds and wilted flowers swaying in the wind, took one giant step forward.

And at that very courageous moment, a honeybee buzzed by.

She stared at it with curiosity, for she had never quite seen a real honeybee--especially one with a long black top--hat and round thick spectacles.

"Bee! Bee!" she yelled, remembering the mouse's advice. "Wait for me!"

And she ran after the honeybee, screaming and waving. She followed the honeybee out of the darkness and to a tree where

Once upon a time in a forest far away...

perched high up on its uppermost branch was a hive buzzing with bees. She stared at the hive and knew she would never get in.

ಬಿ

"You'll never get in," said a young honeybee while sucking on a honey candy. The honeybee sat on the curved end of an old discarded spoon beside a humungous mound of sticky, half-chewed honey candy. The mound was an unusual and glorious sight. It was golden and slimy and in the sunlight it glowed like a star.

The honeybee savored her candy, and then she added, "Not only is it too high for you to climb, but there are guards--huge, vicious guards--too many wasps, you see, pretend to be honeybees…they try to steal our honey--they're sneaky parasites." The honeybee paused to savor her candy and then continued. "I'm afraid they may mistake you for a spy and throw you in a pit of honey alive. It's not a pretty sight. Really, it isn't."

"I believe you," mumbled the brave little caterpillar. She stared at the golden mound of cracked candy with much curiosity, and the honeybee savored her candy with much concentration.

But then a bird tweeted and the honeybee lost her focus. She looked toward the skyline, and, in a brief moment of distraction, she unwittingly bit into her candy. Red with rage, her eyes opened wide, her lips tightened, and she let out a huge sigh of disappointment. She spat the candy into the pile beside her and yelled, "Phooeey! Phooeey! Phooeeeey! I'll never get this! Never!"

Then, slowly calming herself down, she reached into a humungous yellow bag, which lay in between her four little legs, pulled out another candy, held it up in the sunlight, and, staring at it as if it were the greatest obstacle in the world, she proceeded to toss the golden candy into her mouth.

"What are you doing?" asked the brave little caterpillar, alternating her gaze between the golden mound of candy, the yellow bag of candy, and the honeybee sucking on candy.

"Practicing," answered the honeybee.

"Practicing what?" asked the brave little caterpillar.

But just as the honeybee was about to answer, she bit into the candy. Her mouth froze. Her eyes closed. And she sighed. Then her eyes sprang open

71

and she spat the broken candy in the golden mound, and, as if stating the obvious, she said, "Patience. A test of patience. Why else would I be savoring candy? It's not that easy, you know, to finish one whole candy without biting into it."

And the honeybee tossed another candy into her mouth and added, "Really, it isn't."

"I believe you."

But the brave little caterpillar, not able to make the connection between candy and patience, stared at the honeybee and asked, "What does candy have to do with patience?"

But the honeybee didn't answer. She was too involved with her candy. But soon, in the distance, there was a howl, a gunshot and then a cry, and, from the honeybee's mouth, a loud crack.

She spat. She shouted. She cursed. And then she tossed another candy into her mouth and said, "I can do it, I can."

"Patience?" questioned the brave little caterpillar, still wondering what sucking on a candy had to do with patience; or why this honeybee would have it as her goal to finish a candy without biting into it.

"And concen-phooeey!" said the honeybee, turning to the brave little caterpillar with a crack.

She spat. She shouted. She cursed. And then she tossed another candy into her mouth.

"Concenphooeey?" questioned the brave little caterpillar.

"Concentration," corrected the honeybee with much concentration. " Not concenphooeey...concentration."

"Oh," said the brave little caterpillar, concentrating on the honeybee's mouth.

"Can't seem to finish one of these without biting into it."

"Why would you want to?"

"A test of pa-pooeey!"

And the honeybee spat the broken candy in the pile beside her.

"A test of papooeey?" questioned the brave little caterpillar.

"Not papooey," said the honeybee. "A test of patience--which--which--I'll never pass!"

"Must you?"

"Of course!" yelled the honeybee with a laugh. " Hello, wake up please. Do you know anything about honeybees? All aspiring Combers must."

The Butterfly

"Ohhhhh, I see, a Comber."

"Yes," said the honeybee, looking up at the hive, "I wanna be a Comber." And then she lowered her gaze to the brave little caterpillar and said in a voice more convincing than a gunshot, "Correction! I will be a Comber."

The brave little caterpillar thought a bit, and then, realizing she didn't know what a Comber was, asked, "What's a Comber?"

The honeybee let out an absurd laugh. "Hellooo…you don't know?"

"No," answered the brave little caterpillar. "I don't know."

"You don't know?"

"No--I don't know."

"You really, really don't know?"

"Noooo--I really, really don't know."

The honeybee shot the brave little caterpillar a disappointed look and said, "Fine then, let me explain. Combers are the best of the best, the cream of the cream--the creators of the hive. The select few who create the most perfect, and I mean the most perfect honeycombs! Gotta be patient, you see, to create something as perfect as a honeycomb. Else, and this is sad, you're doomed to the Boo Squad."

"Oh dear, the Boo Squad!" said the brave little caterpillar. And she thought a bit, and, realizing she didn't know what the Boo Squad was, she asked, "What's the Boo Squad?"
The honeybee took a short while to answer. "The Boo Squad…well…the Boo Squad…I don't really know…"

"What do they do?"

"Do?" thought the honeybee. "They, well…they don't really do anything. No, that's right, they don't do anything." The honeybee paused, thought, and then continued. "Well, what they do do is undo. That's something they do. They find mistakes and whenever they find a mistake, so happy are they, that they grab their boo-poms, do a little boo-dance, and break into a little boo-cheer. You know they've got many boo-cheers…I'd recite one but I can't ever manage to remember one. They have a boo-cheer for everything."

The honeybee tossed another candy into her mouth. "I don't want to be a booleader. Really, I don't." And then she exploded: "But these candies are freaking me out! Why can't I just finish one?! One! Just one! That's all I ask! One without biting into it. Why?!"

73

Once upon a time in a forest far away...

It was a while before the honeybee calmed herself down.

The brave little caterpillar looked at the bag in her hand and said, "Come on now, it can't be that hard. Can it?"

"Oh it can. Believe me, it can. Most aspiring Combers never pass this stage. Really, it's true."

"I believe you."

"You could not imagine how frustrating this is."

"Can I try?" asked the brave little caterpillar, pointing to the bag.

"Sure," answered the honeybee with a laugh, and she tossed a candy into the brave little caterpillar's mouth.

Scarcely had the brave little caterpillar sucked on the tiny piece of candy before there was a loud crack.

"Phooeey!" yelled the brave little caterpillar.

"Not so easy, is it?" smiled the honeybee.

"Again," said the brave little caterpillar, opening her mouth.

And the honeybee tossed another candy in.

"Phooeey!" yelled the brave little caterpillar, spitting the candy in the golden mound that was steadily growing to be a golden mountain, now almost higher than both the brave little caterpillar and the honeybee.

"Not so easy, is it?"

"One more!"

And the honeybee tossed another candy into the brave little caterpillar's mouth. And this routine continued for some time, and all that was heard in the forest was one loud "Phooey!" after another.

The both of them emptied the bag in vain. A mountain of golden bits shining in the sun lay beside them.

"I'm not very patient," admitted the honeybee.

"Neither am I," added the brave little caterpillar. She reflected and then said, "Thank heavens I don't need to pass this test to be a butterfly."

"You're lucky," said the honeybee.

"I know," said the brave little caterpillar.

And at that very moment there came a thundering shout from above:

"NOT ENOUGH COMMITMENT!"

And a honeycomb came soaring from out of the hive and, with a thud, landed right in front of them.

The brave little caterpillar shot the honeybee a questioning look.

"The hats-off honeybee," answered the honeybee. "She's judging the honeycombs. She's ruthless. Everything has to be perfect. Not a flaw.

74

The Butterfly

She doesn't care if you take forever to create a honeycomb so long as you pour your heart into it. A lot of Combers rush their work. And, well, this is what happens." And the honeybee extended her arms to the deranged honeycomb before them. "But," continued the honeybee, "if you've created something perfect, something worthy, worthy of the hive, she bows before you, she tips her long black hat, and she says with the respect one gives a master, 'Hats off.'"

"Hats off," repeated the brave little caterpillar.

"Hats off," confirmed the honeybee.

Then, after a moment of complete silence, another shout came thundering from above:

"NOT ENOUGH COMMITMENT!"

And another honeycomb came soaring out, landing right beside the other one.

There was another moment of complete silence, and then the honeybee said, "Eventually I wanna leave the hive."

"Leave?" questioned the brave little caterpillar. "Bees don't leave."

"It's rare, I know, but sometimes they do."

The brave little caterpillar found this strange, for all her schoolteachers had taught her that bees never left the comfort and security of the hive. But, then again, she had heard the same about caterpillars.

"A few bee years ago our Queen left."

"She did?" said the brave little caterpillar, her eyes wide with interest.

"Yes--she fell in love with a Drone," said the honeybee. "She's not supposed to do that."

"I imagine not," said the brave little caterpillar, who had read a lot about honeybees and knew the Queen had to love many and not just one.

"You see," continued the honeybee, "she was supposed to love many and not just one. It's always been like that. It's our way. It's been our way for millions and millions of bee years. So the bees tried to force others on her. And she wouldn't have'em. She simply wouldn't. And when it was obvious she would have no other, they threw the Queen and her lover out...or they escaped...I can't really remember--one of the two--no one likes to talk about it..."

"So you're in love then?" said the brave little caterpillar with a broad smile.

"No way!" answered the honeybee, as if love were the plague. Then she thought a bit and quickly corrected herself, "Well wait--yes--yes--I do love, I love to create. And you can very well love what you do. Really, you can."

"I believe you."

"And I love to create flowers and trees. I make them out of beeswax. I want to leave because I want to create beyond the comb. That's real creation--beyond the comb--beyond the demands and expectations of the hive--when what you created is done just to be done and not to please or satisfy some norm. The hive is good and all, don't get me wrong--I mean it's a great place to learn--but here, sadly, I will never truly create, I will always have to create honeycombs. There's no utility, you see, in wax flowers or trees."

And another thunderous shout came from above:

"NOT ENOUGH COMMITMENT!"

And another honeycomb came soaring out, this time landing out of sight beyond the bushes.

And the honeybee continued as though nothing out of the ordinary had happened. "Not allowed to sculpt flowers and trees, you know."

"Ohhh..."

"Here I can learn," continued the honeybee. "Here I will learn. Yes, I will learn. Then, I will leave. And I will create. Really create. And there is no real creation without freedom. Really, there isn't. There's only imitation. And that's what a comb is: a perfect imitation. We're a hive of amazingly skilled copycats, not creators." And she paused, but then, as if a thought had suddenly fallen from the sky and into her head, she quickly added, "Still, you have to be able to imitate before you can create."

The brave little caterpillar nodded her understanding. She stared at the honeybee, and then at the golden mountain beside her. She wondered what it was the mouse thought she could learn from a honeybee (honeybees and snails didn't seem to know anything about being a butterfly).

"Do you know anything about butterflies?" asked the brave little caterpillar.

"Afraid I don't...well wait, don't they all live in that thing, what was it called, it was that thing all the bugs were raving about fifty or so bee years ago. What was it, what was it, what was it--dear me, you know,

The Butterfly

if it happen five years ago, never mind fifty, it may as well have never happened..."

"The Silk Palace."

"That's it! The Silk Palace. I remember now, it's why we never see you guys anymore, rumor is you all have the Prince Disease."

"The what?!"

"Hey," said the honeybee in great excitement. "Here's another rumor that just amazes me: is it true you guys can make flowers and trees just like the Forest."

"Nothing like the Forest," answered the brave little caterpillar, bitterly. "Now, I can see that most clearly."

"I heard you guys could make..."

"It takes three real trees to make one pretend tree and seven real flowers to make one pretend flower. And everything is gray."

"Euhhh--why? Why gray?"

"No one really knows," answered the brave little caterpillar. "But my teacher thinks it's because gray is a thoughtless color--won't provoke thought, argument, or criticism against the founders."

There was a short silence, and then, anxious to leave, the brave little caterpillar said, "I would like to stay and chat, but I must go now."

"Nice to know ya caterpillar," said the honeybee.

"Nice to be known," replied the brave little caterpillar, and she began to walk away. But hardly had she taken three steps before she paused, thought a short moment, turned around to face the honeybee, and tipped her blue hat and said, "Hats-off-honeybee."

And the honeybee smiled a dreamy smile and said, "Thank you caterpillar."

And the brave little caterpillar was on her way.

ဆ

It wasn't long before the pink and green leaves of a Venus Flytrap caught the brave little caterpillar's attention. Hardly had she admired them before she was hypnotized and moving toward the plant's captivating presence. She stared at those leaves and thought she knew a place where she would find unconditional happiness.

"Booteeeeefuuul," she said as she moved closer and closer to the plant, her four hands extended in front of her like a zombie. Slowly she crawled up the stem, but before she set foot on the rather comfortable-looking leaf, a yell in the distance snatched her from the plant's spell.

"Hello!" boomed the voice. "Hello! Anybody there? Can somebody help me?"

Realizing she was on a Venus Flytrap, she sped down the stem and tried to get as far away from the plant as she possibly could.

"Where are you going?" asked the Venus Flytrap, in the sweetest voice the brave little caterpillar ever heard.

"Don't you talk to me in such a sweet voice!" answered the brave little caterpillar, without looking at the plant. "You're untrustworthy!" "Don't say such things," said the plant. "You don't know me! Just look at me and you will see...I am trustworthy."

"Ha! If only your exterior mirrored your interior," answered the brave little caterpillar. "Then I would see--I would see how ugly you'd be!"

"Ugly," cried the Venus Flytrap. "I am kind--gentle--I have done nothing to you--I have done you no harm--and you call me ugly? How rude! How very, very rude!" And the plant began to sob. "I am but a simple rose who has offered you a petal for..."

"You are most certainly NOT a rose!" interrupted the brave little caterpillar. "Roses are red. RED. And you are green."

"Am not!" said the plant.

"Are so!" replied the brave little caterpillar, looking at the ground.

"Am not!" said the plant. "Look at me and you will see. Come

The Butterfly

now, no wrong could it do."

And the brave little caterpillar thought she could sneak a peak without falling under beauty's spell. But as soon as her eyes lay rest on those gorgeous green leaves, she was under the plant's spell and was soon climbing the stem toward those leaves where everything seemed deceptively peaceful and happy. "Boooooteeeefuuuul," she said as she climbed in a trance.

"Hellooo!" boomed a voice in the distance, awakening the brave little caterpillar, saving her one more time. "Methinks I heard talking...anyone there? Help please. I really need some help here! How nice it would be to have some help!"

The brave little caterpillar, realizing where she was, about to step on the fuzzy leaf, yelled, "Creepers!" And she stormed down the stem faster than a jackrabbit with its tail on fire.

"Damn Ant!" yelled the plant. "Please don't go caterpillar. Pleeease!"

"Don't you talk to me!" yelled the brave little caterpillar, without looking at the plant.

"I have done nothing wrong," pleaded the plant.

"Deception! Lies! All hidden behind a voice sweeter than, than, oh I don't know, just sweeter than something really, really sweet."

"Deception!" said the plant, "Violets never dec..."

"You are NOT a violet!" interrupted the brave little caterpillar. "Don't even try it. Violets are blue. BLUE. And you are green. GREEN. And as much as I can remember, green is not blue."

"Yes it is!" assured the plant.

"No it's not," said the brave little caterpillar.

"Yes it is!" assured the plant.

"No it's NOT," yelled the brave little caterpillar.

"Listen caterpillar," said the plant, "I've been green all my life and I assure you: blue is green. Look and see, no wrong could it do."

"Lies! Deception! Trickery!"

"Trickery!" cried the plant. "That's what you think of me?"

"Most definitely," answered the brave little caterpillar.

"You don't even know me..."

And the plant began to sob.

"I believe your tears, Your Incredible Falseness," said the brave little caterpillar, " as much as I believe in, in, in a tree-climbing fish who,

who, likes to dance with birds!"

"They exist," said the plant after a short pause. "You said it and I saw it."

"Oh--stop!" said the brave little caterpillar. "Just stop."

"You conceived it--now believe it!"

"Just stop..."

"Fine--I will," said the plant. "But not because I'm trying to trick you, sweet caterpillar, who I wish would look at me, but because I don't think your little caterpillar mind can grasp the idea that the universe is infinite."

"Ahh-duh, I know that!" said the brave little caterpillar, who had read many books on the infinite.

"But did you know," continued the plant, "that the infinite includes everything. And that which includes everything includes all that your little mind can conceive of--somewhere, sweet caterpillar, in this vast universe there existed, exists, or will exist that fish. And that fish is probably wondering if there existed, exists, or will exist a pink caterpillar who talks to a blue violet."

"Green plant!" corrected the brave little caterpillar.

"You're sooooo wrong caterpillar--so wrong!"

"I am soooo right GREEN PLANT," said the brave little caterpillar. "Soooo right!"

"To think you would mistake blue for green, a plant for a flower..."

"I know what you're trying to do and just stop! Okay. I'm not going to fall for your trickery."

"Dear me!" said the plant, and she started to cry.   "Maybe it is I who is wrong. The horror. To live a life and not know who you really are! The hoorrorrror!" And she bawled and a stream of plant tears flowed passed the brave little caterpillar's feet. She calmed herself and continued, "Do me this one favor sweet, tender caterpillar, look at me, look at me, just once, please, just once, tell me what you see."

"Trick me once, your fault. Trick me twice, my fault. My teacher used to say that. And with that--I say farewell, OH GREEN PLANT."

"Look at me," said the plant in a softer, sweeter voice.

"And be lured by your deceptive beauty," answered the brave little caterpillar. "Not today plant. Not today. But comfort yourself with this thought: maybe in some other universe, in some other world, a world where fish climb trees to dance with birds, your lies succeeded. And I'll

The Butterfly

comfort myself with this thought: it wasn't this one."

"Please look at me," begged the plant, in a soft seductive voice.

Just then a voice full of distress came booming from beyond:
"I can hear you! I need help here! You up there! Hellooo!"

And the brave little caterpillar moved toward the voice.

"Look at me!" exclaimed the plant in a sudden harsh voice, harsh as a scorned demon.

But the brave little caterpillar continued on.

And the plant yelled as loud as she could:

"Looooook aaaat meeee!"

But the brave little caterpillar was gone.

"Right-oh!" said an ant stuck in a ditch, looking up at the brave little caterpillar, who stared back down in mute amazement. "Would you be so kind as to drop me a line? I seem to be stuck in a ditch." He was an older ant judging by his wrinkled face and long bushy white hair; but he was young in spirit judging by his constant pacing and his quick and sudden movements. He wore a gray robe stained with splotches of yellow and orange and green paint; and around his shoulder was a green satchel filled little paint containers.

"Wow!" exclaimed the brave little caterpillar, admiring the depth of the ditch. "So wide, so deep, so, so, so obvious! How'd you manage this? I mean really, how could you have possibly not seen this?"

She extended her arms, pointing out the obvious.

"Yes, yes--I know," said the painter, "Obvious. So, so obvious. Thanks. Appreciate the observation." He paused, shook his head, and then continued. "Look here caterpillar, I need help, not a lecture. Not an 'I told you so.'"

"Wait a minute," said the brave little caterpillar, and she left in search of something with which to pull the painter out, and she soon returned with a long scroll tied-up by a thick yellow ribbon.

But as soon as she began to lower the scroll, the painter yelled: "Dear no! My life! Not that! Something else, please! I beg you. Should it tear, forever and ever I would despair!"

The brave little caterpillar looked at the scroll with wonder. She placed it down gently, and she searched for something else. She soon lowered a long branch and pulled out the painter.

"Much thanks," he said and let out a heavy sigh of relief.

"Your life?" questioned the brave little caterpillar, staring at the scroll.

"Magnum opus," answered the painter in a well-spoken voice. "My life's great work--which amounts to the same--I suppose." And the painter reached for his scroll and held it in his arms and closed his eyes. "I've painted many sunsets before, but none like this--I've been working

The Butterfly

on it my whole life. And believe me when I tell you this: a life isn't too long a time to work on a single project."

"A life," said the brave little caterpillar. "Sheeesh, that's a long time."

"Well--half a lifetime," corrected the painter, opening his eyes. "I spent the first half just trying to figure out what I wanted to do. Then, once I figured that out, once I realized how much I loved to paint and that painting was where I 'lost' myself, I spent another good part of my life trying to figure out what--exactly--I wanted to paint...and then, once I figured that out, that I loved to paint sunsets, well, I spent another good part of my life trying to paint them like a master. And now, and you're going to laugh...after all this figuring out, I've figured something I wish I had known long, long ago..."

And the painter laughed to himself.

"What?" asked the brave little caterpillar.

"There are no masters," answered the painter, untying the ribbon. "Only amateurs. Some amateurs better than others, true, but still, all amateurs. And I can't tell you how liberated I've felt ever since I figured my work didn't have to be masterful, only heartful, and that so long as I emptied my heart into it, well, that would always be enough."

"So just heart," commented the brave little caterpillar.

"Caterpillar, trust me, you can go a long way with heart."

There was a short reflective silence.

"Can I see it?" asked the brave little caterpillar, breaking the silence, pointing to the scroll.

"Yes, yes! Of course, of course!"

He proceeded to unroll the scroll, and as he did he smiled a breathtaking smile. She examined his smile and thought she had never seen such a splendid smile. And then she lowered her gaze to his unfinished painting and examined it with great detail. It was a sunset, which she thought resembled a pink and orange jellyfish that had exploded over a violet horizon. And for a moment she lost herself in the painting and felt a great joy and satisfaction for sunsets recently experienced and deeply remembered. She felt sad for the caterpillars stuck under the gray filter of the Silk Palace who would never in their lives experience a real sunset.

"And so," said the painter, snatching the brave little caterpillar from her thoughts, "I merely do my best and let the world take care of the

83

rest."

"I do my best," repeated the brave little caterpillar, lost in the painting, " and let the world take care of the rest--I like that."
"It's yours!" exclaimed the painter, giving her a hearty tap on the back. "Say it when you like. No problems here. Modeling is, after all, the most sincere form of compliment."

There was a short silence, and then the painter smiled and asked, "Where are you going?"

"To the Temple of Fleas," answered the brave little caterpillar, proudly.

"So you should follow the stream, up the mountain," advised the painter, pointing to the stream that twisted and turned up the mountain.

"I know..."

"I suppose you seek the one they call the butterfly," said the painter. "You seek a master...I suppose to teach you the ways of the old. Though, be warned, he's no master. A...a...well you'll...my brushes!" Realizing his brushes were missing, he forgot the brave little caterpillar and yelled, "Oh-dear-oh-me! Oh-dear-oh-my! My brushes! My brushes! Where are my brushes?!"

And then he was frantic, searching for his brushes.

"Hey crazy old prune!" yelled a young ant sitting atop a blue and green mushroom. "Looking for these?" He extended his little arms, showing three weathered paintbrushes.
"Oh-dear-oh-me-yes, yes, yes!" cried the painter.

And he ran to the mushroom and extended his hands upward.

The young ant lowered the brushes and the painter stood up on the tip of his toes, stretched out like a rubber-band ready to launch. But as soon as the brushes were in reach, the young ant pulled them away and exploded into a loud devilish laugh and the painter, losing his balance, went tumbling to the ground.
The young ant then stopped his musing, smiled a devious smile and lowered the brushes. The painter rose, brushed himself of dust, and then reached for the brushes again. And again, the young ant pulled them away. And the painter went tumbling to the ground.

This routine continued for some time until the young ant, bored with a game only he seemed to be enjoying, yelled, "Borrrring!" And he stood up, drew his arm backward, smiled a sickly smile, and, with one incredibly wicked thrust, launched the brushes skyward.

The Butterfly

The painter let out a deep cry and ran for his brushes.

The young ant let out a wicked laugh and ran away.

The brushes scattered in the air, and, the painter, trying to save them all, didn't save any. And, one by one, they landed with a loud crack. And with each crack something seemed to crack inside him, for he twitched and shook and only stopped when the last brush hit the ground.

Eyes brimming with tears, the painter gathered his broken brushes and held them tightly. He slowly walked to a fallen acorn upon which he sat solemnly and wept silently. The brave little caterpillar, baffled by the young ant's utterly mean actions, put a hand on his shoulder and consoled him.

"My teacher gave them to me," sobbed the painter.

And the brave little caterpillar touched her hat and understood.

After a short silence, she asked, "Why so mean? Why would he do that?"

"It's not his fault," said the painter, "Don't blame him, poor fella, he's really sick."

"Oh?"

"Yes, he has the Hemilia Princilia Vastixia disease," said the painter, wiping his tears.

"The what? Hemilia Pina Prina--what?"

"The Prince Disease," said the painter.

"Ohhhh...the Prince Disease."

The brave little caterpillar thought a moment, and when she realized she didn't know what the Prince Disease was, she asked, "What's the Prince Disease?"

The painter looked toward the sky, as though searching for an answer. "Hard to explain."

"Do your best," said the brave little caterpillar. "And let me take care of the rest."

The painter smiled, thought a bit, and then said, "It's a terrible, terrible, terrible disease. One, not surprisingly, most common amongst the Nobliantae, the nobles. It's passed down by your parents--sometimes knowingly, sometimes unknowingly."

"Knowingly?" said the brave little caterpillar, confused, not fully understanding why parents would knowingly give their offspring such a terrible disease.

"By giving you everything you want," said the painter, "without

85

ever deserving anything. A terrible, terrible thing to do."

"Doesn't sound so terrible to me," interrupted the brave little caterpillar.

"Oh but it is!" exclaimed the painter, thinking of the many symptoms of the Prince Disease. "Everything comes too easy. Way too easy. And, because everything is given without having to be earned, nothing holds meaning anymore; everything bores you; you only smile when you're buying or receiving stuff; you make others suffer because you think you're the only one who suffers; you walk around with this terrible, terrible attitude that the world owes you everything, when, in reality, it is you who owes the world everything..."

"Parents do this!" interrupted the brave little caterpillar, disgusted by this Prince Disease.

"Oh yes, you can be sure they do."

"And this is how you live, as if you owed the world everything?"

"As if!" exclaimed the painter with a laugh. "I do. You do. We all do. But you wouldn't know that. Right? Not to come down on you or anything, but you're a caterpillar. It's not in your mental program to have such an attitude. And, quite frankly, I don't blame you for it. I've read your books. Caterpillar books are required reading for ants. And let me tell you, not impressed, not impressed in the least."

"Required reading for ants?" questioned the brave little caterpillar, in a voice full of surprise.

The painter let out a laugh, paused, and then continued, "One day, our leaders assure us, we will outdo the caterpillars. We will build something greater than the Silk Palace. In essence you caterpillars have infected us with those books. But don't feel guilty...most of us already had the disease to begin with. It's so awful at the Ant Castle you could conceivably catch the disease by merely talking to an ant. I had to leave just to keep my mind clean."

"I understand," said the brave little caterpillar, who was now thinking of her teacher and how he would probably like this ant.

"So I keep to my philosophy," continued the painter. "To liberate or elevate--there is no other reason to create. To hopefully lessen the pain and suffering of all those I meet along the way. And, let me add, to make extra sure that I am not the cause of another's suffering. For if there is one sin--one terrible, terrible, terrible sin-it is to make others suffer--unnecessarily, that is. Sometimes you just can't help it. Sometimes your very

86

presence causes suffering, especially if you're unhygienic...anyway, I'm getting beyond myself now and I have this sneaking suspicion that I'm preaching to the choir, right? Or I don't think you'd be out here, right?" The brave little caterpillar nodded and there was a short silence between them. Then the painter broke the silence. "Come then brave little caterpillar, follow me. You'll love this!"

"Now?" interrupted the brave little caterpillar, in her usual rush to get to the Temple of Fleas.

"Caterpillar," sighed the painter, " when you're my age, now is pretty much all you have. In any case, what I have to show you is worth your while. Trust me, you'll thank me."

"What is it?"

"What is it?" repeated the painter smilingly. "What is it? Well, it's a secret."

"Sheeeesh, a secret, I'm sorry, really I am, but I have no time for secrets..."

"Come on," said the painter pulling her arm. "You'll thank me!" And it didn't take much more convincing.

She followed him up the stream, finding him quite amusing. He was in the habit of talking to himself, and, more often than not, forgetting she was there, he would fall into huge debates with himself. He would laugh, tisk, and nod his head briskly. Sometimes he would laugh out loud, as though a balloon of giggles just popped. Other times he would tisk and shake his head angrily, as though a teacher grading a failing paper. But most of the time he would just mumble to himself, as though a spectator at a chess game, evaluating each and every move made. The painter was so distracted by the inner workings of his mind that the brave little caterpillar would often have to warn him about rocks, litter, shrubbery, anything that lay in his way. Once she even had to yell and warn him about a ditch.

"There's a ditch!" she yelled, pointing.

"Oh...right-oh!"

They avoided the ditch, and he thanked her with a wink.

It was dark when finally the stream led them to the mouth of an abandoned burrow, which glowed and flickered with torchlight. At the entrance stood two beautiful statues made out of beeswax. They represented a bee who, standing upright and proud, looked very humble and handsome. They were so perfectly crafted that they almost looked alive.

The brave little caterpillar let her hand caress them and she said in a low admiring voice:

"Beeswax...wow...I never thought it possible..."

"That's art," commented the painter. "'Art' in the heart. If one has the 'art', one can make a masterpiece of anything--a grain of sand even. But if one lacks 'art', well then, you can be sure as day, the best materials in the universe will be of no use."

And the brave little caterpillar was sure: her teacher would really like this ant.

ॐ

Inside the burrow they walked by statues and statues similar to the statues they had found outside. The brave little caterpillar admired them and thought the artist had been obsessed. They walked and walked toward a room that glowed and flickered with orange light.

Now the brave little caterpillar looked at the statues without really seeing them--all she could think about was the Temple of Fleas, the real butterfly, and how she felt she was wasting her time with this ant. And then she thought about being a butterfly: in her mind she was beautiful and graceful and everyone back home envied her and felt especially foolish for having never believed in her.

"What are you thinking of?" asked the painter, who had been studying her face for a while now, noticing the strain in her lips, the wetness of her eyes, and how she happened to be missing all the masterpieces about her.

"Nothing," answered the brave little caterpillar, shaking her head, suddenly snatched from her thoughts.

"Right," said the painter, staring at her frown. "Well 'nothing' seems to be anchoring your soul down like a sack of bricks."

"Nothing," she said curtly, picking up the pace.

"No room for art," mumbled the painter, " in the bitter heart."

And they were soon at the room.

As soon as they entered the room the brave little caterpillar forgot everything--her dreams, her despairs, the things she felt she had to do. There before her was the most awe inspiring sculpture she had ever seen in her life. And by this statue sat an albino bee gazing at the apparition with watery eyes.

"Beeswax?" questioned the brave little caterpillar, not able to tear her gaze from the sculpture.

"No," said the painter, never taking his eyes off the artist. "Marble--the purest kind."

And they sat in the orange glow of the torchlight and admired the statue for a long while. The sculpture was of the same bee they had seen in the entrance, only this time he was perched up on a flower, lying on his back, his hands behind his head, admiring the vast universe above.

And admiring this work of art, the brave little caterpillar thought the ant was right: the detour was worth her while. She had never felt so lost in a work. There was something in the sculpture that elevated her from all her worries.

"It's perfect," she said.

"Yes," agreed the painter. "And she never needed it to be perfect...she just emptied her heart into it...a tear of love, they say, turned marble."

And they were silent.

Beside the statue was another statue. It was much smaller in size and it was a representation of the albino bee. She was on her knees with her arms outstretched to the heavens. Tears were running down her cheeks and, with her mouth slightly open, she seemed to be locked in an eternal scream.

Staring at this statue, the brave little caterpillar felt tears welling up within her.

"Is that you," she asked the albino bee, in a sad muffled voice. "Is that you? You look...angry...sad..."

"She can't talk," interrupted the painter.

90

The Butterfly

"You're an incredible sculptor," continued the brave little caterpillar.

"She can't hear you," added the painter.

"Oh," said the brave little caterpillar, turning to the ant.

"Nor can she see you," added the painter.

"She can't?"

"All she sees is that," and he pointed to the statue, "And all she hears is his voice. She's dead to the world, you know. Dead. They say she really loved him."

And there was a long reflective silence.

"They used to sculpt together," the painter said, breaking the silence. "They used to do everything together. Then, one day, they got into an argument over the most mundane thing, things were said, she left in a rage, and when she returned…and when she returned, a day later, he was dead. Died, they say, of a broken heart."

"Heavens!"

Now there were tears in the brave little caterpillar's eyes.

"They say she collapsed and turned white overnight…"

The brave little caterpillar stared at the statues, silently.

"And when she woke," continued the painter, "she grabbed him in her arms, carried him outside, and, on her knees, she screamed at the heavens until she could scream no more. They say that's how she lost her voice."

"At the heavens?"

"Yes, for having blessed her with something so beautiful only to snatch it away."

Conscious of her own mortality, the brave little caterpillar began to sob.

"And now," said the painter. "Great works. Nothing but great works."

The brave little caterpillar nodded, agreeing.

"Works sprung from the deepest sadness," continued the painter.

And they both gazed at the statues.

"And the most profound sense of exile," continued the painter, and then he turned his gaze to the brave little caterpillar. "Everybody thinks they're going to live forever…that's why they allow themselves to say things they don't mean…they think they have tomorrow to make up…"

"Tomorrow," repeated the brave little caterpillar, lost in a thought.

"Tomorrow," said the painter with a laugh. "You want to know about tomorrow?"

The brave little caterpillar didn't answer.

"Ask her," continued the painter, and he pointed toward the albino bee, shaking his head. "Ask her about tomorrow."

There was a long meditative silence, and then the painter continued, "I come here to watch. To watch nothing transpire into something. It's the greatest miracle there is." And he turned to her and asked, "Don't you think?"

"Well..."

"Well it is," said the painter. "What was never there before is now there because of her. That's as big a miracle as a miracle gets."

The brave little caterpillar altered her gaze from the painter to the statue.

"Think about it," continued the painter. "Kind of odd, isn't it? First there is nothing, then there is something, an idea, which comes from where? Nowhere. Really? Where do ideas come from? Who knows! Not me. Though, I'm told, they come from an endless river of nothing above and beyond the stars deep in the universe of universes where everything that has, does and will exists..."

"Has, does, and will exist!" laughed the brave little caterpillar. "You've been talking with a certain green plant."

"Right-oh," answered the painter. "Talking, sure, all the time, she's fun to talk to, but always with a blindfold. I'm smart enough to enjoy her company without losing my life to her."

"She's a tricky one," commented the brave little caterpillar.

"Oh you can be sure," agreed the painter.

There was a reflective silence between them.

"So anyhow," continued the painter, "a speck of an idea comes from this river and it floats through your mind like a puff of smoke where it is beaten and kneaded and then shaped into something by all those many little things and experiences that make you you...and then you make something of it ..."

"Or you don't," added the brave little caterpillar.

"Right," agreed the painter. "But if you don't, I'm told, you'll never connect to the river again. What once flowed so smoothly and easily will never flow again. Rivers don't like dead-ends, you know. They soon learn where to go and where not to go. That's why the river flows so freely through the young--their minds and hearts are boundless, they don't

The Butterfly

care to please or displease, they just act. An idea from the great river of nothing and...BAM!" The painter clapped his hands. "Something! Like magic. No apologies and always ready for the next idea. I love the young. Boundless, I tell you--boundless."

The painter paused, reflected, and then added, "You can learn a lot from the young."

And the brave little caterpillar nodded her agreement, for her teacher used to say the same thing.

"You want to make something out of nothing?" continued the painter, "surround yourself with the young and"--the painter smiled and pointed to himself--"listen to the old."

At that very moment the albino bee exploded into a fit of cries, sobs and tears; and they couldn't take her suffering. The painter grabbed the brave little caterpillar's arm and said, "Come on, let's go, this is the part I can't take." And he led her out of the cave and they sat by the stream, which reflected a luminous star-stuffed sky. Cries echoed from the cave and for a second the brave little caterpillar felt something staring at her. Quickly, she turned around and searched, but, finding nothing, she returned her gaze to the water.

For a long time it was just moonlight and silence.

"A butterfly!" said the painter, breaking the silence, slapping the brave little caterpillar's knee proudly. "Now that's something. Good for you. Good for you caterpillar. Leaving the palace. Tell me, then, have you found your food plant yet?"

"Food plant?" questioned the brave little caterpillar, with a queer expression.

"Yes, food plant," said the painter, as if speaking the obvious.

"I eat many..."

"No,no,no," interrupted the painter, " caterpillars seeking to be butterflies must find their food plant--that one plant that suits their soul. It's the plant that will help you transmorph into the butterfly you have the potential to be. It's different for every caterpillar. Tell me you've heard of the term 'food plant.'"

"Never heard of it," said the brave little caterpillar, who had read every book on being a butterfly.

"Well...you've got to find your food plant," said the painter. "You've got to try as many plants as you can, and, as I've been told, through the process of elimination, you'll come to know your food plant, and, I've also been told, once you've found it, you'll never want to stop eating. It will be like food from heaven. But eventually you'll stop; and guess why?"

The brave little caterpillar shrugged her shoulders.

"Because you'll feel the changing within," answered the painter.

"The changing within?"

"Oh yeah. It will do things to you. Strange but good things. You'll feel a huge tiredness sweep over you like night over day. And you'll do your very best to find yourself a hiding spot where no bird or predator will ever find you. Then you'll spin yourself one of them chrysalis things, and, once that's all taken care of, you'll fall asleep...and when you wake up, when you wake up from your long, long, long slumber, you'll wake up a butterfly."

The brave little caterpillar let out a little laugh laced with doubt.

The painter, placing his hand on her shoulder, nodded his sincerity.

"Just find your food plant," said the brave little caterpillar, her voice full of disbelief. "You make things sound so easy."

"They are," said the painter. "It's you caterpillars who have complicated everything."

"You make things sound so easy," she repeated, talking to herself, pondering the painter's words, staring at the moonlight shimmering down over the stream.

"Just find what you love," said the painter.

"You make it sound so easy."

"It is," said the painter. "Just takes time. See you're one of the lucky ones. You have the gift of youth and knowledge, and that's luck. Most aren't that lucky. Most don't even know they have to find their food plant, until, well, until it's too late."

"Too late?" questioned the brave little caterpillar.

"The body just can't do it after a certain point," answered the painter, "The mind is willing, but the body just can't do it. A caterpillar must respect the rites of time. And so must an ant for that matter."

The brave little caterpillar and the painter fell asleep by the stream. One dreamt about butterflies and home, the other of sunsets and creation. When morning came, she wiped the dried tears from her swollen cheeks, thanked the painter, placed her hat, and was soon on her way.

In spite of the painter's advice, she didn't search for her food plant. He was an ant and couldn't possibly know anything about butterflies. Also, she had never heard of food plants or anything of the sort and she was a caterpillar and she had gone to the very best schools. And so, if there were such a thing as a food plant, she would have known about it ages ago.

No, her mission was to find the real butterfly. It was the only way. Only the real butterfly could help her. And so, she continued on her journey toward the Temple of Fleas.

She had not proceeded far when, mumbling angrily and thinking of home, she heard a shout so loud and fierce it could have easily humbled a thundercloud:

"THIS IS NOT WORKING!"

Suddenly snatched from her daydreaming, she detoured to investigate, and she soon came across a red-faced dragonfly fuming at the ears. The first thing she noticed was that he walked with an incredible slouch. Something in his chest was pulling him down, and that something was pulling him down hard.

The dragonfly, too preoccupied with cursing to notice the brave little caterpillar, pounded his each and every step with a huff and a puff, and he dragged himself to a gigantic green plant, which he climbed to the highest leaf, mumbling and moaning and cursing and groaning. At the top, he heaved a deep breath and closed his eyes. Then, suddenly, his eyes sprang open, and, like a sprinter, he dashed across the leaf, as if the glossy green surface were a runway, and dove straight into the air with his two arms stretched out in front of him. He soared like a plane for about a second, tried to fly, then suddenly, with a scream full of panic, his chest, regardless of how hard he beat his wings, stopped him in midair, and pulled him straight down to the ground. There was a loud thump, followed by a huge cloud of dust, followed by a:

"I WILL NEVER FLY!"

Concerned, the brave little caterpillar approached the fallen dragonfly. "Oh heavens! Oh dear! Are you okay?"

"OKAY? JUST GO AWAY!"

The dragonfly dragged himself to the plant mumbling to himself, "Are you okay? Are you okay? Who can be okay here? I need to go away! That's what I need. That's all I need. I need to go away. That's all I need. I just need to go away. And then yes...I will be okay!"

The dragonfly climbed the plant and, once on top, took a deep breath and ran across the leaf, plunged into the air, and then fell with a loud scream.

There was a loud thump, followed by another dust-cloud, followed by another:

"I WILL NEVER FLY!"

He coughed once, twice, thrice, and then cleared his throat of grime. "I HATE THIS PLACE!"

The brave little caterpillar couldn't see how this place had anything to do with his not being able to fly. "Are you okay?"

"YOU STILL HERE!" roared the dragonfly, his eyes bulging, his forehead tight, and his veins throbbing. "JUST GO AWAY!"

The dragonfly dragged himself to the plant, mumbling under an angry breath. He climbed, breathed, ran, leaped, soared, and fell.

And there was another loud thump, followed by yet another dust-cloud.

But this time he just lay there staring at the clouds roll across the sky. "I'LL NEVER FLY!" he yelled in great disappointment. "NOT HERE! NOT WITH THIS AIR!" He let out an incredibly loud scream filled with frustration. He stood and began to feel the air with his fingers, as if judging the texture. "TOO THICK!"

The brave little caterpillar felt the air, and she thought it was the same as anywhere else she had been. She was sure the air had nothing to do with why he couldn't fly. She studied him, and then she studied the odd protrusion in his chest and said, "I don't think..."

"I DON'T THINK WHAT!"

The dragonfly interrupted, turning to the brave little caterpillar, his eyes bulging, his veins throbbing, his lungs gasping, his jaws quivering.

"Nothing," she said, and she put her head down, realizing he didn't want her help.

"NOTHING!" yelled the dragonfly. "THEN GO! AND LEAVE

The Butterfly

ME ALONE! I CAN'T FLY BECAUSE, BECAUSE, BECAUSE
YOU'RE WATCHING... UNDERSTAND!"

And the dragonfly climbed the plant, mumbling, "I'll show them!
Oh I'll show them! I'll fly! Oh, I'll fly! They'll see! They'll see!"
And the brave little caterpillar went away thinking that no matter where
this dragonfly would go he would never find the right air; but, maybe,
always the right excuse.

଼ଇ

Crawling along the stream, the brave little caterpillar soon heard a loud gurgling and rumbling and snoring sound, which sounded as if the world were coming to an end. She searched for its origin. In the distance she could see an old rotten log, surrounded by pillows, shaking with every gurgle and rumble.

Curious, she decided to investigate.

She walked toward the log, and, once there, she stood on a pile of pillows and peered inside. There, to her surprise, she saw the body of a sleeping cricket. He was mumbling strange things in between heavy snores:

"Oooooh-Chickeepoopoo…you are…oh yes you are…my chick-eeepoopoo…I'm not…no you are…no you are…I'm not…no, no, no you are…you are my chickeepoopoo…"
And this babbling continued for some time.

The brave little caterpillar climbed into the log and tried to shake the cricket awake. But nothing she did could wake him. She shook him. She shoved him. And she screamed at him. But everything she tried was in vain. When finally she gave up, the sweet sound of tweeting bird woke him with a start, and, rubbing his sleepy eyes, he yelled, "BLASTED BIRD!" And he immediately reached behind his head, grabbed his pillow, and threw it out of the log, hoping to hit the bird. Then he stood up and slumped over to a pile of pillows by his kitchen sink, picked one from the top, and returned, zombie-like, to his bed.

"Oh--excuse me," said the brave little caterpillar, moving out of his way.

"Oh hello there," said the cricket, pulling his night hat over his eyes. "Oh goodnight thenZZZZZ…"

And he fell asleep.

Again, she tried to wake him.

Again, her efforts were in vain.

Again, the bird woke him.

"BLASTED BIRD!" he yelled, and a pillow flew out of the log. Then he

rubbed his sleepy swollen eyes, stood up, slumped over to the pile of pillows, pulled one from the top, and dragged it back with him.
"Oh--pardon me," said the brave little caterpillar, moving out of his way.

"Oh hello there," said the cricket with a yawn. "Oh goodnight
then..."

But just as he was about to sleep, the brave little caterpillar said,
"No, no! Wait!"

"What! What!" said the cricket, forcing his eyes open with his
fingers. "Wait?! Wait what? I can't wait. I must catch up on my sleep...I
must practice...practicing ones legs takes energy, lots of energy might I
add, and so, I must sleep."

"Legs? Practicing legs?"

"Yes, my legs," said the cricket with a yawn. "I'm going to be the
best leggist that ever existed, the best might I add...but for now...I
mustZZZZZZ..."

And now the brave little caterpillar waited for the bird.
Sure enough there was a tweet, a shout, and a helter-skelter pillow. And
the cricket rubbed his sleepy eyes, stood up, slumped over to the pile, and
soon returned with another pillow, all the while mumbling, "Blasted bird.
She knows I'm sleeping. She knows--and the racket! How rude! How
positively rude! And might I add how positively rude! If I weren't a
cricket, if I weren't ten times smaller than that nut-brained feathered turd,
I'd be all over her like ugly on a frog-blasted bird!"

"Oh-please," said the brave little caterpillar as the cricket walked
by her.

"Oh hello again," said the cricket, his eyelids already beginning
to fall. "Oh goodnight then..."

"Wait! Wait! I..."

"I can't wait," said the cricket, "I must sleep."

"But I just want to hear you play," said the brave little caterpillar.
"I've never heard a cricket play his legs before."

"You would?" questioned the cricket, struggling to keep his eyes
open. He thought a bit and then said, "Then you must wait until
IZZZZZZ..."
And the cricket was fast asleep.

Having had its fun, the bird was gone; and so the brave little
caterpillar, anxious to hear the cricket play, waited until the bird returned
the next day. She had never heard a cricket play before but had read that

they were great musicians. In the morning the bird returned to annoy the cricket. At first tweet, sure enough, the cricket was up and irritated. "BLASTED BIRD!" he yelled, and a drool-covered pillow blasted out of the log.

The bird laughed and tweeted and said, "Missed again!" And the cricket swore and sluggishly rose to his feet. He slumped over to the pile, and soon returned with yet another pillow.

"Oh, oh, oh--are you going to play now, will you practice now?" asked the brave little caterpillar, excited.

"You still here," said the cricket, looking at her through puffy eyes. He took a second to think, and then continued in a sleepy voice. "Well...sure I will practice, to be good at something you must always practice...but practicing takes energy...so first, I must sleep... soon I will get started and getting started is the hardestZZZZZZ..."

Then the brave little caterpillar was sure: the cricket would only play in his dreams. As she went away, she could hear him snore, and she wondered how such an earth-shaking rumble could come from such a small creature. And she wondered why such a small creature needed so much sleep. An insect's life was too short, she thought, to sleep away.

ജ

The brave little caterpillar continued her journey along the stream until she found herself in front of a strange little hut made out of mud, dung, and stone. Strange florescent yellow and green weeds that shook feverishly every time there was a noise surrounded the hut. Smoke rose from the chimney and there was such a loud racket inside--rasping, pounding, clinging, and clanging--that she thought there could have very well been a war.

Soon enough a strange little beetle wearing a pilot's hat and a pair of brown cowboy boots came hobbling out. In his grip was a beaker filled with a bubbling blue fluid.

"Hello there," said the beetle with a broad smile, happy to have a visitor.

"Hello," said the brave little caterpillar.

"So I take it you like my hut?" asked the beetle. "I made it myself."

"Well," said the brave little caterpillar, finding the hut disproportional, awkward, and crooked. "I don't know what to say..."

"At a loss for words," laughed the beetle, as if it were to be expected. "Say nothing then. Nothing. Nothing at all. Just admire. It's a marvel. A real marvel."

And he sighed and looked at his hut with admiration.

"Well," said the brave little caterpillar.
"Ahshhshhshh!" interrupted the beetle putting a silencing finger to her lips. "Don't struggle with the words..."

"But..."

"Ahbutbut!" said the beetle, pushing his finger against her lips. "Just admire. That's what it's there for. Simply admire."

The brave little caterpillar didn't know what to think.

"I'm an architect, you see."

"You are," questioned the brave little caterpillar.

"Yup! An architect. A painter. A poet. A pilot. A drummer. A designer. A doctor."

Once upon a time in a forest far away...

"Sheesh!" said the brave little caterpillar. "All those?!"

"And a sculptor," added the beetle.

And the brave little caterpillar thought a lifetime was hardly enough time to master one trade let alone six.

"Do you want to see a painting?" asked the beetle. "I started it yesterday and finished it today--I'm that good!"

And before the brave little caterpillar could answer, the beetle scurried into his hut, dropping, accidentally, his beaker at the doorway, where a new breed of weed, thick and purple and covered with sticky pink fuzz, immediately began to grow. When the beetle stepped out of his hut, the weed grabbed him and screamed, "HOW COULD YOU," and a fight immediately ensued, of which the beetle was soon victorious.

Gathering himself, the beetle, with his veiled painting, limped over to the brave little caterpillar and said, "You can create'em"--he heaved a deep breath and let it out slowly--"but I'll be damned if you can control'em!" And he took in another deep breath. Fighting for his life against that which he had created had drained him. Once he was back to normal beetle breaths, he wiped the sweat off his brow and added, "Well I just thank my lucky beetle-bum I didn't make 'em too strong." The beetle was thoughtful for a moment, and then he turned to the brave little caterpillar and asked, "Are you ready?"

She didn't answer but just stared at him with feigned interest.

The beetle took in a deep breath, unveiled his painting, and shouted, "Taaadum!"

She stared at the careless hodgepodge of colors on the canvas and thought she could have easily done better with a blindfold on. She didn't know what to say.   "It's...it's..."

"Ahtut-tut-tut-tut!" he interrupted, putting a silencing finger by her lips. "No need for words, no need for words. Simply admire."

"But..."

"Ahbutbut!" he interrupted and pushed his finger roughly against her lips. "Just admire. Just admire. Words alone could never do it justice."

And he stared at his painting as if it were the most beautiful painting in the world. "Do you want to hear a poem?"

"Well..."

"I wrote it as I painted this," he said with a confident smile. "I'm that good!"

And he cleared his throat, looked at her, then the sky, took a deep breath, closed his eyes, and, as a tear began to slip down his cheek, he recited, "Little Bunny Lolly, Little Bunny Lolly, why do you dance"--he opened his eyes and paused for dramatic effect--"in such a folly." And his head fell, as if he had just recited the most important poem in existence, as if the words deserved serious dissection and contemplation. The brave little caterpillar waited and wondered if that was the poem.

There was a complete silence; then, looking up to spy her expression, the beetle added, "It's symbolic." And he closed his eyes and began to cry. "Just can't bring myself to say it without crying."

The brave little caterpillar took a step back and stared at the beetle with curiosity. She didn't see how those words were in any way symbolic. "I don't..."

"Ahhbutbutbut!" interrupted the beetle with a finger to her lips, his head still in a slump, his eyes now closed.

"I don't..."

"Ahhbutbutbut!"

"Well..."

"Ahhbutbut...words alone could never do it justice."

"There is no equal," muffled the brave little caterpillar, and she was soon on her way. Now she followed a trail so thick and tangled that she had to climb over or crawl under weeds and twigs and boulders the entire way up.

ᔥ

The trail forced its way up through the mountain and by dusk of the very same day she had finally reached the Temple of Fleas. The temple was sublime and a flame of joy began to burn in her heart. She grabbed her hat, put it to her heart, let out a deep sigh of relief, and then admired the enclosed temple with her mouth slightly open. Though the temple was only half the size of the Silk Palace, it glowed a beautiful yellow under a molting red sun and was far more beautiful and breathtaking than anything she had ever seen.

She admired and could hardly believe her eyes. Made entirely out of white marble and gold, a gigantic black marble wall enclosed it and surrounding the wall was a moat filled with thick black molasses from which issued a thick dream-like mist which floated along the wall and poured over the ground. On a drawbridge, leading to a large arched gateway, sat a tiny flea wearing a thick gray robe. He sat with his legs crossed and he had his eyes closed and he seemed to be involved in some sort of a chant. Behind the flea, above the arched gate, was a white sign with gold writing. The sign read:

ENTER A FLEA. LEAVE A BUTTERFLY.

"Strange," thought the brave little caterpillar. "I didn't know fleas could become butterflies."

Her face grew bright with promise and she took a step forward, but as soon as she approached the drawbridge, the flea, without opening his eyes, raised an open hand to her and, in a deep and powerful voice, said, "Please go away."

Bewildered, she took a step back and rubbed her eyes. It was hard to believe that such a small thing could have such an intimidating voice.

The flea lowered his hand and went back to his meditations.

Cautiously, the brave little caterpillar tried to sneak around him, but she was soon met by the same response:

"Please go away."

The flea went back to his meditations; and she let out a deep sigh of annoyance and stared at him and tried to make out the words he was

The Butterfly

mumbling.

When she approached to listen, she noticed that he was repeating nothing more than "butterfly". She wondered if that was the secret to becoming a butterfly: to sit with your legs crossed and mumble "butterfly" over and over again until something exquisitely divine happened. And so, convinced a little meditating wouldn't hurt, she sat in front of the flea, crossed her legs, and began to meditate, mumbling, "butterfly" over and over again.

The flea opened a suspicious eye, shot her a suspicious look, and then went back to his meditations.

Shortly afterward, a bullfrog came hopping by. He hopped over the brave little caterpillar and landed right in front of the flea. But they didn't notice him. They were too involved in their mantra. The bullfrog tried to pass, but as the flea had done with the brave little caterpillar, he lifted an open hand and, without opening his eyes, said, "Please go away."

The bullfrog studied the flea with bully eyes and he let out a great big bully laugh, and, in an incredibly high-pitched voice, said, "Step aside puny plea! I have no beep with you. My beep's with the butterply. Or so he calls himselp. Takes all my gold, my wealth, my lipe and still I'm no butterply."

"Or so he calls himself," repeated the brave little caterpillar in a whisper, wondering why this bullfrog would question the authenticity of the butterfly. "Takes all my gold, my wealth, my life and still I'm no butterfly," she continued, and then she thought the bullfrog was just plain ridiculous for he was making the butterfly out to be a pretender. Or, as her teacher would say: a Great Thief. And the Silk Palace had known three Great Thieves, and they had all been properly exiled for having tried to sell things they couldn't possibly sell: a better life in the afterlife at half the price of a grain of rice. And this, her teacher would say, was just plain absurd. He had warned her well about the Great Thieves. He had taught her, he had cared for her, and he had given her strength, in the end, he had given her character, which scared off most Great Thieves, as they were always on the prowl for the characterless. And then a frightful thought entered her mind, "What if this butterfly was one of the exiles?" And then the thought left just as quickly as it had entered. She couldn't believe such a thing. Such a thing would undermine her journey.

The bullfrog took a step forward.

Once upon a time in a forest far away...

"Please go away," exclaimed the flea, his eyes still closed, not even remotely phased by the bullfrog's presence.

The brave little caterpillar felt scared for the flea and she could feel herself beginning to tremble.

Annoyed by the flea's refusal to respect his size, blubber, and wart infested skin, the bullfrog heaved a deep breath until he was three times his former size and, trying his best to make his voice seem a little more intimidating, said, "Get out op the way plea--or I'll squish you like a BEE!"

The flea opened one eye, judged the bullfrog, and, lifting an open hand, replied, "Please go away."
"Please, please, please go away!" yelled the bullfrog. "Do you have to make this hard for me!" He paused, waited for an answer and, receiving none, continued, "PINE! You pleas always have to learn the hard way!" He lifted a hand to the moonlight and said, "With this hand I'll send you to the MOON!" He lowered his hand and then, in the same fashion, lifted the other hand and said, "With this hand I'll bend you like a SPOON!" He smashed his hands together and then raised a leg like a sumo wrestler. "With this leg I'll kick you through the GATE!" He smashed his foot against the ground, raised his other leg, and said, " And with this leg I'll squash you like a GRAPE!" He smashed his foot on the ground, and, with a loud and piercing war cry, he charged the flea with all his might. But as soon as he was in reach, the flea, with but a finger, poked the bullfrog in the belly and sent him soaring through the air, turning head over heels. He smashed into a tree and all he could see were gold and silver tadpoles swimming around his head as a whole pile of leaves fell over him and buried him completely.   But no sooner had the leaves fallen than he was pushing his way out. Deeply humiliated, he shouted, "NOW YOU'VE DONE IT!"

And he charged.

And again he found himself thrown against the tree and buried under a huge pile of leaves.

"Pine," said the bullfrog, brushing himself clean of dust and leaves. "You win. I know when I've been beaten. Quite a pinger you got there. But I think there's one thing you've overlooked. And that thing is..." And he took in a deep breath of air. "I can swallow you in one GULP!" And he flung his incredibly long pink tongue at the flea.

And all the brave little caterpillar saw was a pink blur whiz by

The Butterfly

her.

But as soon as the tongue was in reach, fast as lightening, the flea raised an open hand, grabbed the moist pink flesh, wrapped it around his hand, twirled the bullfrog around his head, and with a quick burst of energy, flung him way over the trees across the forest and into oblivion.

And all the brave little caterpillar saw was a green blur scream by her.

The flea went back to his meditations.

The brave little caterpillar stared in mute amazement. She couldn't believe that such strength could come from such a tiny creature. She went up to the flea and, stumbling over her words, asked, "How-can-well-how do I enter? I mean is there... maybe...possibly a way?"

The flea opened an eye, scanned her from top to toe, and said, "A riddle. You must answer a riddle."

"Fine then," said the brave little caterpillar strongly. "I'm not scared of riddles."

The flea opened an eye, cleared his throat, and said, "Be wise caterpillar and go. For if you fail...you will die." And his words seemed to echo through the Forest.

"Oh," said the brave little caterpillar in shock.

With a sudden feeling of defeat, she sat down in front of the flea, who had quickly gone back to his meditations. She thought it over. Death scared her as death scared most caterpillars; but death didn't scare her nearly as much as not trying or going home a failure. And although she wasn't very good at riddles, she gathered up all her courage and said, "I'll do it."

And the flea opened an eye, judged her as serious, slowly rose to his feet, and led her across the mist-covered drawbridge.

ॐ

She was just about to go through the main gateway when the flea pulled her back and said in his deep voice, "Wrong." And he shook his head.

"Wrong," she repeated.

"Wrong," he said and pointed to a dark and deep pit lined with sticky fly tape. One more step and she would have thoughtlessly fallen and joined the countless corpses stuck to its caramel-like bottom, where bees, ants, and wasps had sadly met their doom.

"Creepers!" exclaimed the brave little caterpillar, staring at the corpses, now trembling at the knees.

"This way please."

The flea tugged at her shirt and led her away.

They hugged the marble wall until they reached a few overgrown strands of grass, which the flea pushed out of the way to reveal a huge opening in the wall.

"That's the way!" exclaimed the brave little caterpillar, looking back at the gate.

The flea stumbled through the opening and waited patiently for the brave little caterpillar. But she was frozen in place, still staring back at the drawbridge, thinking about the deception.

After a long while the flea stuck his hand through the opening, grabbed her arm, and, with the strength of a storm, pulled her through, and she went from silent thinker to screaming blur.

ॐ

Nothing could have prepared her for what she found within the confines of the marble walls: thousands upon thousands of similar-looking fleas, each wearing a dull gray robe, each sitting cross-legged with their eyes closed, and, as she had found the gatekeeper, each chanting "butterfly" over and over again in quick succession.

She looked at them and thought she could have easily mistaken them for dull gray stones. "Creepers," she mumbled to herself, and, for some reason or another, one she couldn't explain, she felt a queer emptiness surge through her body and settle in her stomach.

They weaved their way through the chanting fleas and stopped before a silk white curtain atop a golden stage adorned with the most exquisite jewels. The curtain revealed the silhouette of a butterfly smoking a water pipe. He blew out butterflies and they slowly rose into the air and, like a mysterious dream, disintegrated into the night.

The brave little caterpillar, upon sight of this mystical silhouette, did as the flea did and bowed low and respectfully. Then she stood upright and waited, and, as she waited, she stared at the silhouette. The sight of this silhouette warmed her heart and brightened her soul and soon enough the emptiness was gone.

There was a long moment of silence.

"So," said the silhouette, breaking the silence. "You want to be a butterfly?"

"Oh yes!" exclaimed the brave little caterpillar, shivering with excitement; hardly able to fathom the fact that she was in the Temple of Fleas.

"And you want me to make you a butterfly?"

"Oh please!"

"And so sure are you that I can do this that you are willing to chance your life? You are willing to answer the riddle of riddles? The most ancient of them all?"

She was silent.

"Speak up!" boomed the silhouette. "Are you, or are you not, willing to chance your life?"

He waited.

She shifted nervously. She felt the coldness of fear and her stomach turned, her breathing stopped, her eyes shifted everywhere, and her mind struggled and struggled and concluded she wasn't very good at riddles.

"Well!" boomed the silhouette.

She closed her eyes tightly and shifted nervously. Now the fear had overwhelmed her, and her thoughts struggled through her mind like an exhausted dog swimming in an endless sea. She turned to the chanting fleas, not knowing why, and there, amongst the closed-eyed chanters, was a young flea, looking up at her with a smile. She narrowed her gaze on him and he quickly closed his eyes and went back to his meditating. She turned back to the curtain.

"Well!" boomed the silhouette, waiting.

Stiff as a drowned dog, she scrunched her lips and searched for her courage: her mind began to rumble and bubble and tumble; and through all of this rumbling and bubbling and tumbling came a realization: she had come too far to give up now. And so, with renewed strength and energy, her eyes sprang open, she heaved a deep breath, she put her hands on her hips, and, with the certainty of a priest, said, "Yes! Yes I am."

"About time!" boomed the voice. He drew his pipe to his lips, inhaled a long and hearty smoke-filled breath, and puffed out one gigantic butterfly. Then he demanded:

"The scroll!"

A red turbaned flea, wearing a gold medallion and carrying a scroll three times his size, went tumbling by the brave little caterpillar and behind the curtain whereupon he handed over the scroll. The flea bowed three times, to which the silhouette gestured arrogantly and said, "Yes, yes--be gone then."

When the flea was gone, the silhouette untied and then unrolled the scroll. He inhaled his water pipe, blew out a butterfly, cleared his throat, and proceeded to read the ancient riddle. "I never was," said the silhouette. He paused, inhaled from his pipe, blew out a few more butterflies, mini butterflies, and then continued. "But will always be..."

"Em--always will be--that's a tough one," said the brave little caterpillar with a discerning hand under her chin. "Always will be?

The Butterfly

Always will be? It can be many things. Oh what, oh what, could it be...that which always will be?"

"I'm not finished!" yelled the silhouette.

"Oh..."

There was a short silence. He inhaled from his pipe, blew out a butterfly, and continued with the tone of a king. "No one ever saw me...no one can ever know me...and yet..."

"And yet," she repeated, attentively.

"I am the confidence of all!"

And all at once the fleas were silent, patiently awaiting her answer.

"Are you finished?" asked the brave little caterpillar, uncertain.

"I am!"

The brave little caterpillar thought a long while. Nothing came to mind and the fear of failure wasn't making things any easier. She paced around in nervous circles, staring at the ground, biting her nails. Fear had now completely replaced her excitement for being there and no matter how hard she tried no answer came.

"Well!" boomed the silhouette.

"Oh dear," said the brave little caterpillar, looking up quickly and then back down.

"May as well give up," said the silhouette. "Only fleas get it."

"Oh dear..."

And the silhouette released another butterfly from his lips. "Just give up--only fleas get it."

"Oh dear..."

The fleas awaited patiently and the young one, not wanting to sacrifice another soul to the horrendous Pit of a Ha-Ha-Hee-Hees, the horrible pit in which lived the great tickle beast who tortured its victims with feathers and laughs and really bad jokes, mumbled the answer silently, hoping to save the brave little caterpillar.

But the brave little caterpillar didn't take any notice. "I am the confidence of all," she repeated. "I am the confidence of all...I am the confidence...the confidence..."

"Come now," said the silhouette. "Today!"--and he let out a little laugh--"Not tomorrow!"

And at that very moment there came a shout from the ocean of fleas. "Tomorrow!" yelled one flea, with a laugh he couldn't stop. For he hadn't laughed in years and now laughter had found the better of him.

The brave little caterpillar turned to the flea and wondered what it was he found so funny.

"Guards!" yelled the silhouette in a panic, not wanting the others to catch the laugh, knowing there was nothing more contagious than laughter--especially amongst those who hadn't laughed in years, those who had forced and hidden their sense of humor under a leaden blanket of chants and prayers and serious gazes.

Two guards came out like two fierce hounds, and they grabbed the laughing flea and dragged him away. The flea laughed the whole while they dragged him to the pit where they threw him in and he was subsequently tickled to death. And the fleas subconsciously associated laughing with death. Which was a good thing, for the butterfly had told them over and over again that there was no greater sin than laughter, for laughter revealed too much of our imperfections and vulnerabilities, and a flea with imperfections and vulnerabilities could never become a butterfly.

There was a short silence, and then the silhouette boomed:

"Only those who have earned the medallion of super omnipotent butterflyness are permitted to laugh! Only then is laughter an act of divine, sublime, intertwined perfection!"

"Oh heavens," mumbled the brave little caterpillar, and she looked up to the curtain where the silhouette nursed his water pipe. She panicked and shook and began to walk backward, and, in her hysteria, she tripped over her legs and fell over the young flea. The flea, looking down at her, stopped his chanting, looked to see if any other fleas were watching, and, not finding any, whispered, "Tomorrow."

And she gave the flea a queer look and stood up slowly.

"Today!" boomed the silhouette.

"Tomorrow," answered the brave little caterpillar in a whisper.

"What?" questioned the silhouette, and all four arms fall to his side in defeat.

Observing the mingled surprise and disappointment in his voice, she turned to the young flea, and he smiled, nodded slightly, and then went back to his chanting.

"I am the confidence of all," repeated the brave little caterpillar as she sneakily edged backward, trying to get as close to the young flea as possible. "I am the confidence of all...the confidence of all..."

She edged closer and closer.

The Butterfly

As soon as she was in distance, she feigned a fall, turned to the flea, and quickly whispered, "Tomorrow? Is the answer tomorrow?"

He nodded reassuringly.

"Today!" boomed the silhouette.

She stood upright, turned toward the curtain, charged toward it, stopped right in front of it, put her hands on her hips, and, in a sure and strong voice, as if the answer were actually her own, said:

"Tomorrow--the answer is tomorrow."

There was a sudden commotion amongst the fleas.

"Silence!" yelled the silhouette, with a celestial wave of his hand.

All the fleas fell silent.

"You are wise and worthy...I suppose," said the silhouette, and his gaze pierced the curtain and found the flea who had helped her.

The young flea put his head down.

The silhouette continued:

"I will see you soon."

And With a loud bang and a huge cloud of smoke, the silhouette was gone.

The fleas went back to their chanting, and the brave little caterpillar was soon led away.

The two guards led the brave little caterpillar to a changing room and prepared her for her meeting with the butterfly. They enrobed her in a dull gray cloak, and she felt like a dull gray stone. Then they tried to take her blue hat, but she bickered like water thrown into a cauldron of heated oil and wouldn't have anything to do with it. She hoped to explain her reasons to the butterfly, and she was sure he would understand.
"Forgiveness, understanding, and the need to help, are the truest virtues of any real butterfly," her teacher would always say. Though, she thought, if he really wanted her to get rid of the hat, she would. But at least she would try to make him understand why her hat was so dear to her.

There was nothing wrong with trying.

And so, the guards, with a great sigh of disappointment, escorted her outside, to a courtyard soaked in moonlight and covered in yellow and red rose petals, where, on a jeweled throne, perched high up on a sunflower, sat the butterfly with his arms crossed.

"What is the meaning of that?!" boomed the butterfly.

"Your Greatness?" questioned the brave little caterpillar, recognizing the voice.

"That hat!" said the butterfly, now pointing at her hat. "What is the meaning of that!"
"I,I,I," stammered the brave little caterpillar, taken aback by his rather aggressive tone.

"I nothing!" interrupted the butterfly. "There is no I!"
"I..."

"Never mind!" yelled the butterfly, in a menacing voice.
"Understand this caterpillar: here there are no grades. No differences. No names. No thoughts. No hats. And especially NO 'I'! "

"Oh..."

"Especially if you want to be a butterfly!" continued the butterfly. "You will have to surrender all and everything"--he paused, crossed his arms, and then continued--"now tell me...where do I find your all and everything?"

The Butterfly

"All and everything? But Your Greatness...I have nothing."

"What?!"

"Nothing," said the brave little caterpillar. "Just my hat."

And she pointed to her hat.

The butterfly closed his eyes and said, "You must have something." He opened his eyes and gazed at her from top to toe. "We all have something, especially caterpillars. Caterpillars are notorious glitter chasers..."

"No Your Greatness--not this 'No-I.' This 'No-I' left with nothing and acquired nothing..."

"Nothing?!"

"Nothing..."

"I don't believe it."

"Believe it."

"Just you?!"

"And my hat."

She took off her hat and hugged it close to her heart.

"Can't be!" said the butterfly with a shriek. "No glitter? Come now, all caterpillars have glitter, I know this for a fact, you must have something, anything."

"Sorry, Your Greatness...nothing."

"No jewels?"

"No jewels."

"No gold?"

"No gold."

"NOTHING!?" boomed the butterfly.

"Nope, Your Supreme Stubbornness, nothing."

"Just that!" he yelled and pointed at her hat. "A tattered, sorry-looking, blue hat!"

"Yes," she said, tugging down on her hat. "My teacher gave it..."

"I don't care!" shrieked the butterfly.

And the butterfly gestured toward the two guards and they scurried away, leaving them alone to ponder the blue hat. There was a long silence before the butterfly finally spoke. "I'm sorry caterpillar...there is no room for you here. Not now, anyway."

"But Your Royal Butterflyness," said the brave little caterpillar, nearly fainting at his words. "I don't understand...what do you...I mean how can it be?"

"It's not for you to understand."

Once upon a time in a forest far away...

"Your Greatness--oh heavens please--what do you mean, I mean, well, what do you mean?"

The brave little caterpillar felt her insides turn and churn and burn.

"Go now!" said the butterfly, shaking his head, as if greatly disappointed in her. "Collect some glitter, some gold, something, anything, anything but hats, then come back."

"No. Please no--just listen..."

"I'm not asking!" interrupted the butterfly. "Be off then!"
"But I answered your riddle!" interrupted the brave little caterpillar, on the verge of tears, looking up at the butterfly.

"That's why I'm not closing the doors on you," said the butterfly.

"Then, then, then why didn't I just stay in the Silk Palace? It would have been easier. It would have come to the same."

"Because, caterpillar, I can make you real," answered the butterfly with a crooked smile. "And you know that. So why don't you just go find some glitter and come back when you're ready. And when you are, you will see, I will teach you how to beg like a true disciple."

"Beg? What are you talking about?" she questioned, suddenly looking at him with a piercing gaze. "Beg? Beg for what?"

And she thought about her teacher who had taught her all the signs of the Great Thieves; thieves who fed on the lives of lost souls. And they did this by first making them feel inadequate for being everything the Forest willed them to be; then, by promising them things they couldn't possibly promise: a better life in the afterlife at the price of their current life.

"Didn't they teach you anything in the Silk Palace?" asked the butterfly, highly offended by her lack of respect. "You never question your superiors! Understand?!"

"I was taught well," said the butterfly, thinking of her teacher who had taught her to question everything and anything--whether in print, verse, or lecture--that didn't seem right to her. "Teach me how to beg properly, that doesn't seem right to me."

"Silly worm!" interrupted the butterfly, steadily losing his cool. "How else does one become a butterfly?"

"Not by begging."

"Only by begging! Listen here, and listen well, if you ever want to become a butterfly, I mean a real butterfly you will accept my way and

116

The Butterfly

do exactly as I say...you will do as everyone else, you will sit like everyone else, cross your legs, close your eyes, and beg the Butterfly Diva for forgiveness and once forgiven you..."

"Forgiveness!" interrupted the brave little caterpillar. Now she knew he was a Great Thief. Her teacher had taught her that only a Great Thief would try to make her feel inadequate for things that were beyond her control. "Forgiveness for what?"

The butterfly immediately fell into a drum of laughter, and it was a while before he calmed down. "For what, the worm asks," and then his face became altogether serious and he beamed and pointed at her and said, "For being imperfect, of course."

"Imperfect?"

"Flawed! Flawed! Flawed!" he yelled. "Flawed with all those despicable wants and desires..."

"Wants and desires," she said, steadily feeling reason slip away. "But we all have flaws...we all have wants...we all have desires..."

"And that is exactly why only the select few can ever make Supreme Super Galactic Butterflyness."

"But isn't the desire not to have desire a..."

"Silence!" demanded the butterfly, not wanting to think or answer any more questions. He was the butterfly and that was all that mattered. The brave little caterpillar put her head down in mingled anger and despair. She didn't understand why she had to be forgiven for something she had no control over; nor had even been responsible for in the first place. She began to tremble; she knew that something about his words, his way, his glare, his grin just didn't make sense; and this feeling was overwhelming her, upsetting her, making her think. And things, powerful things, things from some remote region of her mind awakened. Things from her past. Things that came from long forgotten talks with her teacher--a teacher who had taught her to question everything and anything that didn't seem right regardless of who spoke. And, to be sure, begging for forgiveness for something she couldn't change, for being exactly what the Forest had intended her to be just didn't seem right. Yes, she did, she needed an explanation before she could accept such an idea, before she would beg for forgiveness for being, as her teacher would often say, "Beautifully flawed and chock-full of gorgeous contradictions." And so she looked up at him and said:

"Forgiven--explain--why should I be forgiven?"

117

Once upon a time in a forest far away...

"And if you are forgiven," said the butterfly, not paying attention to her," if you have begged your entire life without ever wanting or loving anything more than Supreme Omnipotent Butterflyness." He paused, looked down at her, and grinned a horrible grin. "Not only will you be saved from certain hell, which, I assure you, you will go to, but in the afterlife you will be made a butterfly."

"In the afterlife," she repeated with a painful shriek, now looking up at the butterfly fervently. That was the last word she needed to hear; and the word "afterlife" hammered in her mind like a jackhammer of despair pounding on her soul. Now she knew: he was a Great Thief. "In the afterlife," she mumbled to herself. "In the afterlife?" She fell silent and merely nodded angrily. She couldn't believe she had journeyed all this way for a Great Thief. She felt foolish and betrayed and tears started to slip down her puffy pink cheeks. Then with one quick brush of her hand, she wiped them away and said:

"No Your Falseness! I don't accept that! The afterlife?! The afterlife?! Why not this life?!"

"Stop with the questions! That is a command!"

And the brave little caterpillar, eyes glistening like sea-wet stones, spoke as calm as the sea before a storm. "Who are you? Really? Who are you? Not a butterfly. Definitely not a butterfly. See a butterfly can answer questions...a butterfly can answer questions. You look like one, you do, you really do. I'll give you that. Yes, you sure look like one, but you're not, you're not a butterfly."

She paused, thought, and then continued:

"My teacher always said a real butterfly helps, not hurts, and notice here the word is 'helps' not 'hurts.' And when you tell me everything that is wrong with me, when you point your finger at me and call me imperfect and ask me to change things I cannot change...when you try to steal my life promising me a better one in the afterlife...you hurt me, you hurt me Your Vilanry, not help me. You steal the one and only life I can be sure of, asking me to beg and hope for another."

"Silence! " yelled the butterfly, having never before been challenged or talked back to in such a disrespectful way. The lack of fear in her voice scared him most.

"No!" yelled the brave little caterpillar. "Waste this life begging for another--that's insolence!" She thought about her teacher and how he had taught her that her life was a gift and that to waste it begging for

118

The Butterfly

another was to insult and laugh at the one who had given her that gift.

"Insolence! Insolence!" boomed the butterfly, now standing up and pointing down at the brave little caterpillar, not knowing what to say or do next, as he had never been challenged before. "I demand obedience!"

"Demand?" questioned the brave little caterpillar who had never thought or spoken so much in her life. "A real butterfly doesn't demand anything!" She yelled and pointed back up at him.

"What do you know about being a butterfly?" questioned the butterfly.

"Enough to know you're not!"

She withdrew her hand and stared at her finger in disbelief. Things just didn't make sense anymore. This wasn't why she was here. And yet, here she was again, for the billionth time in her life, angry and out of control. And still things continued to stir within her. She had traveled so far; and yet her journey had been for nothing. She couldn't believe she had come all this way only to tell the butterfly he was not a butterfly.

"I'm not a butterfly?" questioned the butterfly, pointing to his multicolored wings, and he fluttered them a bit, as if to mock the idea.

"No, you're not," continued the brave little caterpillar. Her lips were drawn and sealed in a frown, her eyes were bright and angry, and her face glowed like a coal from the restraint of another outburst.

The butterfly let out a loud laugh. "Then what, pray tell, am I, if not a butterfly?"

"A destroyer of lives!" yelled the brave little caterpillar, who had never been very good at restraining herself once brought to the point of anger.

"How dare you!" boomed the butterfly.

"No, how dare you!" yelled the brave little caterpillar, steadily growing angrier and angrier. "Turning fleas into...into...into gravestones. Emotionless, loveless gravestones, laughing at and losing the one and only life they can be sure of by, by, by...begging for ANOTHER!"

"Silence!"

"Forgiven!" continued the brave little caterpillar, whose eyes burned with the fires of eternity--fires started long ago by a teacher who had cared enough to put them there. "If those fleas will ever need to be forgiven it will be in the afterlife!" And she paused to collect her thoughts. She thought about her teacher's words. And then she tried to calm herself. "And they will have to be forgiven because of you, because they believed in you. And as punishment they will be turned into stones. And why? For having forsaken this life begging for another--is there any other insult?"

"Silence!"

Then she had a flashback. She remembered how one of her sisters had once been given a birthday present which she had never opened because she was too busy telling her parents what she wanted for her next birthday. "Given a gift," the brave little caterpillar said, "and without even looking at it, without even admiring or enjoying it, without even opening it--begging and hoping for another--Ha! If I were the Great Butterfly Diva, I would never give such an insect another gift, let alone make them a butterfly...which you're not!"

"Silence!" yelled the butterfly, thinking hard for something else to say.

"Duped!" bellowed the brave little caterpillar, her voice crackling with pain and disappointment. "I come all this way for you; and you would have me laugh at my gift by doing nothing with it! Shame on you." And she put her head down and stared at the ground. "A real butterfly wouldn't lie. A real butterfly would help fleas become the best fleas they can be...instead you make them feel unworthy and flawed for being what nature had intended them to be and, and, and you make them beg for something nature had not..."

There was a moment of complete silence. Then the brave little caterpillar, having collected herself, looked up to the butterfly and, in a soft and curious voice, asked, "Are you really a butterfly?"
"Of course!" said the butterfly, after a moment's hesitation, fidgeting under the strain of her fearless gaze.

"Can you smile then?" asked the brave little caterpillar, with defeat quivering through her voice.

"Smile?" questioned the butterfly.

"Yes, smile," repeated the brave little caterpillar. "Simply smile."

"Really, I don't see what smiling has to do with being a butterfly."

"Just smile," she said, her voice crackling. "Just smile."

And the butterfly, with a little shrug of his shoulders, smiled a miserable smile. "Really," he said,"I don't see what smiling has to do with being a butterfly."

"Tell me," said the brave little caterpillar. "Can you fly?"

The Butterfly

"What?" asked the butterfly.

"Fly," repeated the brave little caterpillar, her voice rising again. "Can you fly? You have wings...you must be able to fly."

And the butterfly was suddenly overcome by an incredible sense of shame and panic. "Flying," said the butterfly. "Oh...flying..."

"Yes--fly," said the brave little caterpillar.

"Yes, well, flying," he said, paused, searched his mind for a suitable answer, that answer he knew all too well but had now forgotten. Then after a moment, having found it, he cleared his throat and answered, "Well, as you know, flying is for the birds."

And he sat on his throne, crossed his arms, and looked at her and grinned, as if he had stated something she should have known all along.

Rage immediately flared within the brave little caterpillar.

"Fraud!" she yelled and ran to the flower, leaving reason behind. She wiggled the green stem viciously and tried her very best to make the butterfly fall.

The butterfly staggered all over the flower and held on to his throne. "What are you doing?! What are you doing?!" She continued to shake the flower and the butterfly lost his grip and balance, and then he fell; as he fell, his wings separated and landed beside him. He was no more than a withered old caterpillar enrobed in a perfectly-designed butterfly suit.

All at once she felt a pain in her heart. She put a hand over her mouth and shook her head disbelievingly. It was as if the world had begun to shovel a thick suffocating black earth over her. She couldn't breathe. She ran up to him and pinned him to the ground and began to sob. There were no more real butterflies. Her life had been a cosmic joke. She would go home a failure. All had been in vain.

Then, without another word, she sprang off the Great Thief, dashed out of the courtyard, weaved her way through the chanting stones, and leaped through the opening in the wall.

§

The brave little caterpillar ran and ran and ran and didn't stop until she
reached the river's edge. In the duskiness of night she crawled up a
mighty oak tree and crawled across a thick branch where at the very tip
she sat solemnly and dangled her legs over the slick black silvery surface
of the water. She stared at the moon reflected in the water, and its luminous beauty stung her heart. All she wanted now was to become one with
the vast indifference above her, below her, around her, within her. All she
wanted to do was close her eyes, lift her arms, and just let herself fall.

She closed her eyes and wished she had never left the Silk
Palace.

Nothing had been as she had expected.

Dark clouds rolled across the sky and it soon began to rain.
Raindrops pounded over the brave little caterpillar's head, but she didn't
care to find shelter. The rain pattered over the Forest and sounded so
beautiful that all the animals and insects stopped all their singing and
humming and buzzing and chirping just to listen. From the mysterious
black abyss above came the rain, and the rain trickled down the branches
and leaves, and the rain fell over her hat where it collected in a pool, and
the pool slowly leaked down her back and face, down her soaked shirt,
down her arms and legs and into the river. She opened her eyes and tears
merged with the raindrops and then dripped off her chin. They fell silently and brilliantly; then they became one with the river.

She wanted to fall.

So she closed her eyes and prepared to jump in. But no sooner
had she closed her eyes than a voice startled her.

"You give up too easily," said the voice.

"Go away!"

She yelled and turned and saw something appear from the blackness as if it were made from it. Two yellow eyes beamed like lanterns out
of a thick green cloak. Try as she did, she couldn't tell who or what it was
under the cloak. She imagined an insect. Judging by the size, she thought
it could have been a praying mantis. And even though she thought it

The Butterfly

might have been a praying mantis, she had no fear. Not even a little. There was nothing a praying mantis could do to her that despair had not already done.

Unconcerned and annoyed, the brave little caterpillar turned back to the river, and the mysterious stranger said, "You know, if we all gave up that easily, there would be no more real butterflies..."

"There are no more!" she yelled, and she let out a laugh full of pain, and her laugh soon faded into sobs and cries.

The mysterious stranger put his hand on her shoulder and said, "It can't be that bad..."

"Ahh! Can you just leave me alone! Just leave me alone! I mean who are you?!"

There was a short silence, then the mysterious stranger, ignoring her, spoke as if speaking to some heavenly ghost beside her. "Yes, I agree, she must have been infected somewhere down the way."

"Who are you talking to? Are you crazy or what? Just go! Leave me alone!"

"Yes," he continued, still ignoring her. " I'm sure of it: the Prince Disease. The symptoms are quite clear."

"Sheesh--you are so annoying!"

"A hard thing to cure," continued the mysterious stranger. "The Prince Disease, that is."

And the brave little caterpillar turned to face him. "A million bugs get smashed everyday," she said and waited.

"Yes," queried the mysterious stranger.

"Why can't you be one of them!" she yelled and turned back toward the water, and then she added, "I don't have the Prince Disease! Sheeeesh you're annoying!"

"Caterpillar," said the mysterious stranger in a soft voice. "Only one infected with the Prince Disease would do what you're about to do." And she was silent and thoughtful. She turned to him and wanted to say something; but, without warning, her lips began to tremble and she began to sob, and her tears fell and mixed with the rain and river. Her eyes narrowed and her lips drew over her mouth and she sobbed like she had never sobbed before. And he comforted her and squeezed her shoulders and he tried his very best to calm her.

When her tears subsided, she asked in a quivering voice, "Who are you?"

"Do you think you're the only one who has ever been disappoint-ed?" he asked.

"No," she said with a sniffle, trying her best to regain her compo-sure. "Who are you?"

"Do you think you are the only one who has ever been sad?"

"No," she said and put down her head. "Who are..."

"The only one who has ever suffered?" he interrupted.

"No!" she yelled and turned to face him. "No! No! No!"

"See that lotus over there" he said and pointed toward the water where a lotus floated gently. "To get where it is"--he paused, shook his head, and sighed--"it suffered."

"A flower?" questioned the brave little caterpillar.

"Sure," said the mysterious stranger. "Surprising, I know, but true. Born in the muddy lurks of the river, its journey, believe it or not, is an impossible one. Not all make it, you see. Some give up too easily--not knowing how close they actually came."

"A flower," mumbled the brave little caterpillar, skeptically, now looking at the flower.

"Sure," continued the mysterious stranger. "Hard to believe, I know, but true. Very true. An impossible dream, the dream of a lotus. Impossible even! Strange as it may seem, they begin at the very very bot-tom of rivers and lakes--in mud and darkness."

"In mud and darkness," repeated the brave little caterpillar.

"Not much light makes it to the bottom of rivers, you know. A spec, a beam, a spot at most. And the flower--the lotus--has to push against the weight of the river, through pondweed, murkiness, and dark-ness following but a tiny spot of light that might, by chance, penetrate that incredible blackness."

"A flower?"

"Not all make it, you see. Some don't even try. Some have even forgotten there is a light to follow. And some, as I said, give up too soon, not realizing the light becomes stronger and stronger as one rises higher and higher."

The mysterious stranger paused, thought a short while, took in a deep breath, and then continued.

"But for those who persevere...for those who squirm, push, and struggle to the surface, for those who find that light and never lose sight of that light, no matter how weak or thin it may be, their rewards...their

The Butterfly

rewards are boundless--they see things they would have never otherwise seen."

"A flower?"

The brave little caterpillar questioned and stared at the lotus before her with a newfound respect.

"That flower has seen plenty," said the mysterious stranger, pointing to the flower with pride. "Bet you three moons and a galaxy it could tell you more about rivers than any book ever will."

And the brave little caterpillar thought he was right.

"The point is," continued the mysterious stranger, "flowers suffer too."

"So what," said the brave little caterpillar.

"So do fleas, trees, and honeybees."

"So what! What does that have to do with me?! Really! I'm no flower, no flea, and I'm certainly no honeybee. I'm me!"

The mysterious stranger shook his head in grave disappointment and continued. "And here you are about to tell all the flowers and fleas and all the honeybees in the Forest that you're better than them. You know, if that's not evidence of the Prince Disease"--and he sighed--"I don't know what is."

"Stop saying that!" exclaimed the brave little caterpillar. "What do you know about me? Huh! Huh! What do you know about me! Nothing! You come here all mysterious and creepy like and tell me I've got the Prince Disease--I mean who are you...what do you want...leave me alone!"

There was short silence, and then the mysterious stranger said, "Jump caterpillar...and tell the whole Forest and every creature in it, with an absoluteness you can never take back, that you're better than them, that you're too good to be sad. That you're too good to suffer...and let me tell you something, cause I have a little secret to share with you..."

He paused to make sure she was paying attention. She looked up at him and asked, "What?"

He waited.

"What?"

Still he waited.

"Whhhaaaat?!"

And just when he thought she could take no more, he whispered in her ear:

Once upon a time in a forest far away...

"We all suffer."

Then he stood upright and continued, "Sometimes joy, sometimes pain, but, yes, it's a fact, rich or poor, green or yellow, black or red, insect or plant, flea or bee, flower or tree--we all suffer--all of us."

"There's no hope!" cried the brave little caterpillar, and she began to sob, like a lost and tired soul, waiting for one gentle word, one loving look, one thin light to pierce the darkness.

"So you're not a butterfly!" howled the mysterious stranger, throwing his arms in the air, almost revealing his identity, but then quickly throwing them back down to cover his face. "You're not a butterfly, big deal! Boo! Hoo! Hoo! I cry for you!"

"What?" said the brave little caterpillar, turning, surprised by the sudden change in his tone and delivery.

"Why should I pity you?" asked the mysterious stranger. "Why? Tell me! Why? Look at you! You've traveled so far--so far!--within and without--and you've seen and learned more than any other caterpillar"-- and he paused to reflect--"well most caterpillars, anyhow."

"Most?" questioned the brave little caterpillar, staring deep into the mysterious stranger's yellow eyes.

"Well," said the mysterious stranger. "There were these five caterpillars, but you don't want to know."

"No, no--tell me. Please tell me," said the brave little caterpillar with haste.

"Well," said the mysterious stranger. "There were these five caterpillars who, not so long ago, set off for the Temple of Fleas, like you did..."

"Okay," interrupted the brave little caterpillar, suspiciously. She wondered how he could know such things about her. "Now what is this? Do you know me? Do I know you? How did you know--I mean who have you been talking to?"

"Do you want to know what happened or not?"

"Yes..."

And she was silent and attentive.

"Well then, where was I--blablabla--five caterpillars leave the Silk Palace--oh yes, so one caterpillar, at the very offset of the journey, was caught by a devilish little boy...the boy put him in a cage I heard..."

"I saw him!" wailed the brave little caterpillar.

"Yes, and then, then, then...what happened?--blablabla--boring,

126

The Butterfly

make a long story short--ah yes, and before they crossed the river, two fell in love and, well, they returned to the Silk Palace--everyone saw it coming...except them, of course..."

"I know them!"

"And another--and this is sad--thought he could find happiness upon the leaves of a Venus flytrap."

"They're tricky!"

"Yes, they are," he agreed. "And the other caterpillar, the last of the brave five, well he, yes, I believe he made it to the Temple...

"He did!"

"He did. But! But I believe, if I remember the story correctly, I believe he was gravely disappointed by what he found...and he left in haste, and, if what they say is true, I believe, like you, he came here and had a long chat with a..."

"What?"

Lost in thought, he didn't answer.

"What?"

Still he didn't answer.

"Whhhaaat?!"

"Oh--ah-with a flower--he had a long chat with a flower."

"A flower?"

"Yes, I believe it was a..."

"What?"

No answer.

"What?"

Still no answer.

"Whhhhaaaat?!"

"Oh--ah--a lotus--I believe it was a lotus."

"Really?!"

And she stared at the mysterious stranger with curiosity.

He put his head down and then continued in a soft voice. "And the lotus pointed out that he had things to fix. He had things to fix in his heart...he had to fix things within his heart before he could be focused enough to actually taste clearly and figure out his food plant, lest everything he tried would taste the same."

"Food plant?" questioned the brave little caterpillar, and she thought of the ant.

"Yes caterpillar," said the mysterious stranger. "A caterpillar must find that special plant that compliments the kind of butterfly he or she has the potential to be. But like an angry dragonfly who cannot fly, a caterpillar cannot taste properly until all that bitterness and anger"--and he put a hand on her heart--"is gone! No room for art...in the bitter heart. An ant taught me that."

And a tear rolled down her cheek.

He wiped her tear off her chin and continued. "Only when you come to terms with the way things are, when you stop blaming and accept--and I don't pretend to know your situation--but once you've cleared that heart, you'll search for your food plant and because you're clean-hearted, well, you'll be focused, and because you'll be focused you'll be able to taste clearly, and because you'll taste--well I bet you three moons and a universe--you'll find it. You'll find you're food plant."

There was a long thoughtful silence, and the brave little caterpillar stared at the lotus flower with admiration. "And what of the caterpillar?" asked the brave little caterpillar.

"Oh yes, the caterpillar," answered the mysterious stranger, standing behind her, watching and listening to the rain patter over the water. His cloak was heavy and drenched, though this didn't seem to bother him.

"Did he make it?"

"Oh yes, yes, I believe he did--I believe he smiles often."

"No--that's not what I mean--is he a butterfly--did he find his food plant?"

"Yes, I do believe he did."

"And now?"

"Now," said the mysterious stranger with a laugh. "Well now, I hear, yes, I hear he's a little lonely. Waiting, I hear, for another butterfly."

"Really?!"

"Sure..."

"Really?!"

"Sure."

"Really-really?!"

"Yes caterpillar, really. Though, I hear he's a little discouraged. A little sad."

"Sad?" questioned the brave little caterpillar.

"Yes," answered the mysterious stranger. "Sad because his only hope in a friend has an awful, awful, most awful disease."

And she swiftly turned to him.

The Butterfly

But the mysterious stranger had already begun to walk away, and soon he vanished into the blackness from which he came. In the distance, over the soft patter of rain, she could hear a soft flutter of wings.

§

The brave little caterpillar sat up the entire night watching the moonlight shimmer through the rain and over the water. She thought about home and all those who had never believed in her. And she felt the bitterness in her heart. And then, without warning, she began to cry and sob, and she cried and sobbed until she could cry and sob no more.

Empty, she finally brought herself to accept the way things had been, and she thought that, maybe, just maybe, they had been so for a particular reason. That had they been otherwise, maybe, just maybe, she would have never met her second great teacher: the Forest. And then she began to cry again, only this time they were tears of happiness--happy for having had two great teachers in her life. Most caterpillars, she knew, weren't so lucky.

Then, her heart empty of the bitterness that consumed her, she pulled her soaked hat over her eyes and said, "Thank you."

The rain stopped.

And there, in the mist of morning, for the first time in a long time, overwhelmed by a profound feeling of peace and contentment, she smiled. And it was her lost smile of youth. Suddenly she realized how lucky she had been: she had met a cat, a boy, a mantis, a mouse, a turtle, a tree, a bee, a flea and so many more she would have never met had she stayed at home. Then she thought:

"What was comfort and security in face of such a journey?"

Butterfly or not, she had had a butterfly's journey.

With her newfound smile, she descended the tree and set off to find her food plant. It would be difficult, she was sure, but being difficult was never an excuse for not trying.

❧

By the end of the day the brave little caterpillar felt like an overblown balloon. She had never eaten so much in her life. She sat on a half eaten leaf and held her belly gently and every now and then she let out a painful moan. She had eaten so much, and yet she hadn't found her food plant. And even though she hadn't found anything that quite satisfied her soul, she knew that through the process of elimination she would eventually find it.

She could hardly budge as she caressed her belly and stared at the clouds roll across the darkening sky. She didn't wonder where they came from, why they were there, or where they were going; rather, she watched them and hoped they were enjoying their journey. She smiled up at them and they seemed to smile down at her.

Now the moon had risen and the Forest was flooded in a pleasant silvery light. And there, by chance, she happened to catch glimpse of a web glowing in the night. And webs, I assure you, are more dazzling, captivating, hypnotizing, alluring than any flower you can imagine, especially when that web is adorned with little iridescent beads of rain that sparkle like little magic diamonds in the dark.

Which mine was.

And so, captivated by my web, which happened to be stretched across two gorgeous yellow dandelions, she sprang off the leaf and, with her hands still holding her bulging belly, as if holding a bag of precious antiques, she staggered toward my web and said:

"Booooooooteeeefulll..."

When she reached the base of the dandelion she stopped to soak in the web's magnificence: its charm, its elegance, its splendor, its silkiness, its symmetry. Her eyes widened in awe and her little delicate hands took hold of the fuzzy green stem; and she began to climb against the weight of her stomach. Once on top she narrowed her eyes on the masterpiece before her. She smiled. She tilted her head left and then right. She admired some more. And then suddenly she heaved a deep breath, sprinted across the fluffy golden bed, dove straight into the crisp night air, screamed, "Booooteeefulll!" as loud as she could, and landed flat into my trap.

And now it has been a few weeks since I released her; and still I have not heard from her; still I don't know if she has made it or not. I'm guessing she did. For with a smile like that you go far in life. With her heart so open, mind so clear, soul so free, I'm sure as sure can be, she found her food plant.

Solomon's Song

ॐ

In the morning dark the young porcupine made his way through the thick, overgrown path and halted only when his eyes met the oldest sycamore tree in the Forest. All around the sycamore were little green buds and trees growing strong and free. Close by, the porcupine could hear the caterpillars and their strange beeping and booping machines cleaning yet another lake. He was thankful for their abilities and for their unfaltering commitment to the Forest.

Such efforts focused on preservation and cleaning came as no real surprise. For the most part, all stories read and told in the Forest carried with them a strong message of equality, compassion, and community, a sense of oneness with all things; and so, it was difficult for this porcupine to imagine the caterpillars doing anything else other than Forest building with their time and technology; he found it even more difficult to believe the stories about a time when caterpillars were actually the Forest's supreme enemy; a time when all their effort was focused on war, profit, and land acquisition; a time when they had actually reduced the entire Forest to a desert of weeds, ruin, and rubble. Those, he thought, must have been some pretty dark times--strange times, senseless times, Stone Age times.

The sycamore saw the young porcupine walking cheerlessly toward him. "Oh no," he said in his deep, elderly tree voice, "What's the matter now?"

Tears in his eyes, the porcupine stared at the wise old tree and sighed heavily.

"Why is it so hard to convince my parents that I can do anything I put my head to?" He shook his head, and he could hear the fledglings playing in the leaves of the young trees. They shouted and giggled and laughed, and yet they were nowhere to be seen.

The porcupine, standing in front of the sycamore, continued: "Why is it so hard to convince them I can do it; that I, too, can build like a beaver, like a bee...like a featherless chicken! Why is it so difficult?"

Once upon a time in a forest far away...

Suddenly, all the chirping and laughing ceased for dawn. All the birds and fledglings and trees gifted their eyes with the arrival of the sun. The porcupine inhaled the clean, cool, golden air and let out another sigh full of despair. "It feels," he said, "as if my whole life will be a battle between being who I am and who my parents want me to be!" He gasped desperately. "Why is the hardest thing in the world just to be?"

At that moment the fledglings recommenced their cacophony. The porcupine continued: "My parents are barring me from my rightful path. That's what they are doing. They are condemning me to a passionless, soulless, superficial existence. I just won't invest a single second in the superficial...I won't!"

The sycamore said, "It's not easy being a porcupine, is it?"

"Not if you want to build things!" the youngster was quick to answer. "Ahhh! There is no more tormenting thought than having to live a life I wasn't destined to live. I wish I had been born a bee. Bees have it so easy, man!"

The tree smiled, then chortled. Bees were some of the hardest workers in the Forest. But he understood what the porcupine meant. Bees built things, and he wanted to build things. Had he been born a bee he would have been allowed to pursue the life of a builder. "Bees have it easy," the wise, old tree added. Then he corrected, "But not if they want to sing like a songbird." He remembered a familiar story. After a pause, he asked, "Did I ever tell you the story..."

All at once the fledglings went quiet and there was silence in the Forest. It seemed as though the entire Forest hushed for the story to come. Then, like big plump apples, the fledglings fell from the trees one thud at a time. One by one they stood, regained balance, and toddled clumsily to the porcupine. Then they made a story-circle around the tree. "I must remember," whispered the tree to the porcupine, "to say the 'S' word a little softer next time."

The tree cleared his throat. "Now...where was I?"

A fledgling answered, "Something about a story..."

"Yeah, a story," said another.

And there was great excitement among the fledglings at the mere mention of the word.

"Ah, yes," the tree said softly. "Did I ever tell you about the dove that saved my life with a song?"

Everyone sighed. It was a story they had heard many times in many different versions.

Solomon's Song

"How the dove, the ant, and the butterfly saved the entire Forest from the caterpillars," the porcupine answered. "Yes, you've told us that story many times."

"I see," the tree smiled, then paused to consider another story. "Well, did I ever tell you the other story? The one about how that particular dove came to sing. How that dove discovered his voice?"

"All doves sing," the porcupine said flatly.

"All doves sing," the fledglings repeated in unison.

"It's a fact," another fledgling added.

"Yeah, a fact," commented another.

"Not so," said the sycamore. "There was a time when doves couldn't sing, a time when doves actually believed in limits and boundaries..."

Solomon waited for his friend on a jagged cliff overlooking the ocean, trying his best to sing an ode to the beauty and grandeur that was the sun climbing and stretching over the horizon. The elders had already been up for some time now and were reciting poetry and telling stories on the beach, as these were the natural and expected pursuits of most sensible doves.

Doves, unlike most birds, believed they weren't born with any special ability or capacity to sing and left singing to the songbirds. They were rigorously taught in school that they had a natural talent to see stories and poetry in all manifestations of life, and to relate those impressions in tiny bursts of measured sentences they called the Koo or sometimes the Hi-Koo.

But Solomon never believed in such limits, ideas, or expectations. He believed his mind was vast, boundless, and capable of learning anything any other bird could learn, even a songbird. "What one bird can do another can too!" he would tell himself every morning as he flew to his cliff of solitude. He didn't believe songbirds were born with a song inside them. He believed they, too, had to learn how to sing as a dove learned how to recite poetry. Singing was a learned talent, and if he couldn't sing it was because there was no one to teach him how. Something he hoped to one day remedy.

Solomon believed and told himself every day that learning how to sing was simply a matter of practice and finding the right teacher, a teacher that would guide him in his practice to direct his effort in proper pursuits. And so, this morning, regardless of popular opinion, Solomon sang self-consciously thereby challenging the idea that he would never sing because he had been born a dove.

"Come on, Solomon!" said a voice from above, interrupting Solomon's practice. It was his friend Hannah. She carried a mango and glided above him a moment, then landed beside him with a huge smile and mango chunks all over her face. "Oh, Solomon," she said. "Why do you do this to yourself? You know as well as I do...doves weren't meant to sing."

Solomon's Song

"I don't know that!" he said firmly, tired of doves telling him what he could do or couldn't do. "I've been taught that and I've been told that. But I don't know that for sure."

"You're either born with a song in your heart or you're not," she said, biting into her juicy mango. She continued with a beak full. "And you, Solomon, were not. Had you been born to sing you would have been born a--"

"Nightingale! Yes, yes, I know."

Solomon picked up a stone and tossed it over the cliff, his soul as restless as the wind.

Hannah ate her breakfast, making a mess of her face.

A reflective silence fell over them. Then a voice startled them. "Solomon!"

They turned to face Solomon's father, clad in a resplendent purple gown. "Enough lounging," he said, "Come join the family on the beach."

"Yes, Father," Solomon answered obediently, and his father was gone. His heart seemed to stop right there and then. His breathing became heavy and laboured as he thought about the predictable routine his life had become. He was a devout dove, a reasonable dove, and, on this day, he was a miserable dove.

After a long silence, Hannah said, "Don't be sad, Solomon. It's such a beautiful day."

Overwhelmed by a feeling of powerlessness, Solomon's eyes filled with tears and he was silent as the ocean.

Hannah closed her eyes, felt the warmth of the sun and said, "It is so tranquil..."

"Not my heart!" Solomon stammered, his eyes blazing like fire.

"What is it, Solomon?" Hannah asked, opening her eyes, her voice full of concern. She took a small bite of her mango.

Solomon watched the mango juice drip off his friend's chin. He took in a deep breath and held it. "I don't know," he said with a strange heaviness. "I don't understand. I don't understand why everything I do feels so wrong, and yet to everyone else what I do appears so right." He reflected on his unhappiness and added, "I cannot sleep, and yet I dream. And it is precisely because I dream that I cannot sleep!"

"You're not making any sense!"

Solomon turned to her. "Am I not!?" He stood and found it difficult to control himself. With great energy and rising excitement he spoke and made wild, exaggerated gestures: "I want excitement! I want adventure! I want to sing! I want to sing my soul to the great beyond!"

Hannah had no idea what he was talking about.

He ran up to her, held her by the wings and with deep conviction said, "I want to meet new birds and see new places. Hannah, I want to sing like a songbird and be free like a swallow!" Then his heart sank with his head. "I want to escape this prison." He let go of his friend and sat with a great sigh.

Perfectly content with the dove way of life, Hannah put a wing around her downhearted friend and saw the impossible burning bright in his eyes. "Doves cannot sing, Solomon. You know this. Stop doing this to yourself. Why torment yourself with the impossible?"

"Because you're wrong!" Solomon answered, looking straight at her. "You're all wrong. Nightingales aren't born singing. It's a myth, a great lie. They must learn how to sing as we must learn how to Hi-Koo. It's a skill, Hannah. A skill! Lessons to practice, techniques to develop, methods that lead to freedom. Everything in life is a matter of learning. Okay, granted...maybe they have advantages in terms of support and expectations...but...they have no more inborn advantages than I have...I can try...Hannah, I can try and anything I do not know I can learn. I know I can. I really do."

Hannah wore a skeptical expression. "But who will teach you?" she asked plainly. "Solomon, there are no more songbirds. There are no more robins, no more nightingales because we are practical birds. Because we would not fly to the edge of the world and perish foolishly in pursuit of some fabled land of milk and honey. Only we remain because we do not believe in such foolish dreams. We are practical and reasonable birds..."

Solomon stared at the horizon. He picked up a stone and threw it over the cliff. Then he narrowed his gaze and declared, "Chichikaka is real."

"How do you know?"

"My heart tells me so..."

Hannah laughed. "Your heart!" And she repeated the word over and over again, clutching her side. Then, sensing the pain she was causing him, she went quiet and took a quick bite of her mango. "Foolish Solomon," she said, "Don't you remember what we learned in school? If you cannot see it, it does not exist! Follow your heart and you are doomed to fall off the edge of the world like all the other songbirds."

Solomon considered what he had been taught in school. He hadn't agreed with it then, he didn't agree with it now. He believed in mysteries, and he believed some things couldn't be rationalized or understood and these things he called the imponderable. There was much more to life than what could be seen, smelled, tasted, or rationalized. He thought for a moment as a strong wind ruffled the trees behind him. Then he saw a leaf torn from the safety and security of its branch. He watched the leaf twirl in the air until it vanished. Then he said with intensity:

"I do not see the wind, and yet I feel it. I cannot smell the wind, and yet I ride it. I cannot taste the wind, and yet I watch this imponderable force take leaves on great, wild, unexpected adventures. To places unknown and unimagined. I do not see the wind, Hannah, and yet every time it whispers…it whispers the existence of Chichikaka."

Hannah wiped orange chunks from her cheeks, then put a wing up in the air to feel this imponderable. Sensing only the cool ocean breeze, she said, "You will fall into oblivion if you trust your heart."

"Perhaps," Solomon answered plainly. "But I'd rather fall into oblivion than merely exist in the ordinary. Every single day doing the exact same thing. Every day the same. Every night the same. Every dove the same. What makes my father so different from your father? A name? Other than a name they could change lives and not feel the slightest difference. What makes them special? What makes them unique?"

"Well," Hannah laughed, "at least I know I'm special, right?"

She nudged Solomon but he did not answer.

Solomon looked at her severely.

"Right?" she said and smiled.

Still he didn't answer.

"Right, Solomon…?"

Solomon looked to the ocean.

"Right, Solomon…? I'm special…right…?"

Hannah's grip weakened and the mango fell with a thud. "Solomon, I'm special right…?"

Despair choked her voice.

Solomon's silence oppressed her.

Now she could no longer speak and a tear ran down her cheek.

Solomon turned to her and said, "What makes you so special?"

"Solomon!" she exclaimed in disbelief.

"I mean," he continued in a whisper, "what makes you so different from the rest?"

"Solomon!"

Once upon a time in a forest far away...

Now, without even realizing the crime, Solomon released all of his pent up frustrations on the one dove he loved the most, the one and only dove who deserved his anger the least. Everything he despised about himself he unleashed on this dove who had always been there for him. He continued, and every word was an assault on her innocent, unsuspecting heart:

"Like everyone else you're scared. Scared of what you really can be. Too scared of the adventure your life really should be. So you just find any excuse that will suit your decision to do absolutely nothing about your dreams. Talk and talk about a dream but never really do anything..." A sudden realization silenced him. He was only talking about himself. Now staring at a tear dripping off his friend's chin, he knew his mistake. But it was too late.

"You're the one who talks and does nothing!" she yelled, deeply hurt by his insensitivity. She wiped her eyes. Then she tried desperately to continue, but her throat was full of pain and her thoughts became a raging storm. She gasped with every attempt to speak and soon gave up. Without looking back, she took to the sky in a terrible rush. Solomon sighed and regretted his cowardice.

That same day Solomon avoided the beach and just watched the sky. Now the moon poured its silver over the water. In the distance, dark thunderheads gathered. Wearied and defeated by his thoughts, Solomon rose with difficulty and turned to the island's only mountain: one side was a prison and the other side a cave. He saw the orange warmth of a flickering flame illuminating the yawning mouth of the cave, and he took to the sky.

≈

Solomon paced in front of the cave for a long while before he finally decided to enter. When he did, the hermit dove, sitting cross-legged with his back toward Solomon, said:

"Yes, young Solomon."

"How did you know it was me?" Solomon asked.

Meditating on the candlelight, the hermit answered without turning. "You told the wind. The wind told the flame. The flame told me."

Solomon moved closer and observed the candle. The flame flickered with his every movement. "But how did you know it was me?"

The hermit let out a little laugh. "Solomon, young Solomon...who else comes to see me?"

There was a moment of silence, then the hermit said:

"Still here I see."

"Still here," Solomon repeated with a heavy heart.

The hermit stared contemplatively at the flame. "I see," he said with no emotion.

Solomon explained, "If I go, I will disappoint my family. It's not always easy you know..."

"I know," agreed the hermit. "It is not always easy. The universe of excuses is infinite and as you grow, so too will that universe. Soon, not only will you be finding excuses for why you didn't follow your dreams, but you will be finding reasons for why others do. You will become a Sour Heart. A jealous little dove searching desperately for the perfect excuse for your own cowardice while searching ever more desperately for the reasons why others were successful and you weren't. And you will find every reason and excuse you will need." He watched the flame and then added, "All you need is courage, Solomon."

"I have courage," Solomon said in a soft voice. "It's just I don't want to disappoint..." He couldn't finish the sentence and he sagged like a sad and humiliated bird.

The hermit peered into the flame as though reading something. "Not all of us were meant to follow the flock. That is important for you to understand. It is important for you to understand that those who do not follow the flock, those who take chances and do things differently often

143

bring new ideas and sensibilities to the elders...You have something inside you, Solomon, something that will one day be of great value to the entire flock. All you need is the courage to follow the path that is yours to follow."

The hermit closed his eyes and waited for a response. When none came, he opened his eyes, gazed into the flame and witnessed a vision. He said, "In my visions I have seen you singing, singing loud and proud, a song, a beautiful and special song, a song with great meaning...with powerful and touching words...words that will bring to the Forest a whole new sensibility."

Solomon's eyes widened. "Me! You saw these things...me...singing?"

"I saw these things in you," the hermit answered softly.

"But doves don't sing!"

"You don't believe that, do you?"

"Not at all!"

"You believe you can do anything, don't you?

"I do!" Solomon threw his wings to the air, now filled with the divine light of endless possibility. "We all can. It's our teachers, our school, our entire system that anchors us and convinces us of the opposite. The mind is huge...able to hold more skill and knowledge than an ocean can hold water! Why do they limit us so! I can and will learn how to..." Then dark reality settled in and his heart sank with his wings. "But my father would never permit..."

"Your only true obligation," the hermit said, "is to your heart. Be good to yourself so that you may be good to others."

"I've heard that so many times!" Solomon exclaimed. "It no longer has any meaning."

"Of course it does," the hermit responded, and he thought of all the meaningful ideas and proverbs doves memorized and mumbled without really understanding them or learning from them. "It's a simple and old truth, yet not so simple to put to practice, is it?"

Solomon shook his head.

The hermit turned a bit and gazed at Solomon's shadow cast upon the cave wall. "Yes," he continued with a grin, "we doves love to repeat poems and precepts but love even more to ignore their meanings, as if simply regurgitating an old truth is enough." The hermit studied Solomon's shadow and could see Solomon's head was down, his body slouched. "Your father is fearful for you, isn't he?"

144

Solomon's shadow nodded.

"There was a time," the hermit continued, "when his heart spoke to him. But he didn't have the courage to listen and was scared of all the things that could have gone wrong had he listened. So now he transfers those fears on to you. He wants you to follow the flock, doesn't he?"

The shadow nodded.

"Safer, isn't it?"

Again, the shadow nodded solemnly.

"But you want to sing?"

Solomon exploded, "More than anything in the whole world!"

The hermit rose and faced him. "Then," the hermit said, "there is no going around it. You will need courage, a whole mountain of courage. You will have to take lots of chances and be willing to make loads of mistakes, but you will need the strength of mind to keep on going despite those mistakes, learning from those mistakes and learning from all the teachers that will compose your one great teacher..."

"My one great teacher..." Solomon repeated.

"Your journey, Solomon," the hermit said. "Stay here and you will grow very little. The ocean that is your mind will turn into a stagnant pond, and there is a good chance you will lose all sense of your true authentic self. For we are all caught up in our own inner labyrinth, all of us searching for the core, for our essence, for our true selves, trying our best not to get lost in all the twists and turns put into us by others..."

"Others..." Solomon gazed at the hermit.

"When we are young," the hermit said, "it is easier. The labyrinth is small; the path is clear. Others have had less time to add their twists and turns and..."

"Dead ends!" Solomon interrupted.

"Take charge now," the hermit said strongly, "before the walls narrow in on you, before the labyrinth grows...before clarity is obscured and your path is lost. The labyrinth just gets harder and harder to beat."

A strong wind caused the candle to flicker, then nearly extinguish. Solomon's head fell once again and he said, "My father is scared for me..."

"That is his right," the hermit said plainly. "Just as it is your right to champion your labyrinth. Don't let his fear prevent you from reaching your essence. The only thing you need is the courage to listen to your heart. Being true to yourself is your only real obligation..."

"Being true to myself is my only real obligation," Solomon

repeated, but wasn't entirely convinced. Something about this idea just didn't feel right, and yet he couldn't name or define that feeling. But he would accept it as a temporary truth. Until his great teacher showed him otherwise.

The hermit turned and moved back to the candle. "The labor of your life must be spent pursuing what is in you to pursue." He sat down and crossed his legs. "Heed the dictates of your heart, or else your heart will stop speaking to you, and when that happens you will lose courage's big sister."

"Big sister?" Solomon questioned.

"Lady luck," the hermit answered. "Courage and luck walk hand in hand. It's really quite simple, you see. Luck, unlike excuses, is limited. There is only so much to go around. So like any lady, luck only sticks around where she is needed and appreciated. Take lots of risks, need lots of luck, luck will stick with you. Take no risks, need no luck, and luck will abandon you."

Solomon smiled at this and understood the need to feel needed. A long, reflective silence followed. The wind outside had subsided and now Solomon felt inspired to do what he had never done before.

"Go out there and embrace your great teacher," the hermit said, closing his eyes. "For if you stay here you will forever walk this life, lost in a labyrinth created by others."

With those last words, Solomon turned to face the moon, ready to cross an ocean.

Solomon sat on the beach gazing at the ocean, listening to the surf, convincing himself to go where no dove had ever gone before. He repeated to himself, "I believe I can and so I can. I believe I can and so I can." And with a great surge of confidence he took to the sky and flew toward Chichikaka. Then, all of a sudden, a horrible doubt crept over him like a dark cloud and he muttered, "What if I fall off the edge of the world? That wouldn't be good...that wouldn't be good at all!"

He quickly veered and found his safe spot on the beach. The sky rumbled and Solomon attempted the journey several times. And every time it was the same thing. He began with great confidence and returned to the beach with self-doubt. Finally, he decided he would return home and try again on the morrow.

"I am a coward," he told himself as he began to walk home, wilted like a lonesome, unappreciated rose. Dark clouds marched across the sky and covered the moon every now and then. In a moment the glowing disc all but vanished. The wind howled and pelted Solomon with little bits of sand and debris. The wind gathered up strength and bullied Solomon to the ground. When Solomon stood, rain fell like rocks and he soon realized he was in no ordinary storm. He balanced himself and looked to the sky. After a fearful silence, he yelled, "Monsoon!"

Just as he said the fateful word the sky rumbled and far off lightning flashed and illuminated the island in a silvery blue. The island quivered with a deep, roaring thunder. Trees shook, swayed, trembled and screamed. Solomon was thrown to the ground. He rose with difficulty and made a sudden dash for home. A thunderbolt blasted a tree, splitting it in two. One half almost crushed Solomon. Panting and his heart racing, he realized his only hope was to fly home. As soon as he flapped his wings he found himself caught in a wind current and was pulled out to sea.

Under a cloudless blue sky, Solomon awoke to the soft, tranquil hush of the sea. He stared at the sky curiously and wondered if he was in heaven. But when he glanced around he quickly realized he was floating on a log in the middle of the ocean. On one side he could barely make out his island; on the other side all he saw was the horizon.

For a long while he debated what to do. He didn't know whether to fly into the unknown or just go back home. He stood and balanced himself, glancing to one side, then to the other, trying to make up his mind. On one side, safety and security. On the other, danger and possibility.

Solomon gazed toward Chichikaka and an inexpressible feeling filled his heart. He turned around, sat on the log, dipped his feet in the cool water, and stared at his island.

It wasn't long before a school of dolphins swished by Solomon. They squeaked and whistled and jumped and twirled in the air. Solomon admired their purplish backs and fins as they cut through the water with incredible speed. He watched them and wished they could cut through his cowardice. That way he might find the courage to do what was in his heart to do.

"Takka Oloka?" a dolphin stuck his head out of the water.

"What?" Solomon asked, looking down at the dolphin. He had never heard such a greeting before.

The dolphin squeaked. "That's 'You Okay?' in Chichikiki."

Solomon was puzzled. "What's Chichikiki?"

"That's the old language of Chichikaka," the dolphin answered. "Sorry, guess I was showing off."

Solomon stood and turned to the horizon. Then he turned back to the dolphin, balancing himself on the log. "Then it exists!" he exclaimed.

"What do you mean?" the dolphin asked, and threw Solomon a confused look.

"Chichikaka," Solomon said, "Land of milk and honey...of...of...adventure and excitement...it exists!"

"Toka doya!" the dolphin confirmed with a smile. "I'm from Chichikaka waters." Then, as if seeing Solomon for the first time, he said, "Wowya! A white dove! A white dove! I have never before seen a white dove. Look at you...look at you!" The dolphin circled the log and admired Solomon. "You're all...all...all..."

"White," Solomon said.

The dolphin squeaked and laughed. "Yeah! You're all white. I've seen colorful doves before but never in my life have I seen a white dove. How special... No! No! No! Not special. I can do better than that. Wait...wait...wait...it's coming...I feel it... Magnificent! Absolutely magnificent! You're a true vision. A truly magnificent vision..." And the

Solomon's Song

dolphin admired Solomon intensely.

"Thank you," Solomon said, being his usual polite self. "But I'm really quite ordinary."

The dolphin squeaked hysterically. "No, no, no-humble pie. You are great...no...not great...I can do better than that...wait...wait...wait...it's coming...I can feel the mind, she's working, working, working...wait...something's happening...I can feel it..."

"Magnificent," Solomon helped.

"That's the word!" the dolphin agreed. "And that's what you are! Absolutely magnificent."

Solomon thought this dolphin was great for his self-confidence and wished he knew more creatures that thought he was magnificent-absolutely magnificent. Then, thinking about white doves and colorful doves, he became curious as to why he had never heard of a colorful dove. "Do colorful doves sing?"

"Heavens no!" the dolphin exclaimed. "Whoever heard of a singing dove? They tumble and they do all kinds of crazy acrobatics in the air...but they do not sing. Only songbirds sing."

"They tumble..." Solomon repeated, and found the idea interesting. He wondered if he could tumble in the air. He thought that it would be fun to learn and that such a skill would make flight so much more amusing.

"Yes," the dolphin said. "Fruit doves tumble. And when they are not tumbling they're going on and on about their conspiracy theories. They're fun to watch, not to listen to. They tend to be downers with their belief of some great evil that's going to poison all the air and choke all the birds out of the sky. They're a little fruity, if you know what I mean. But never mind fruit doves...what do white doves do?"

"Well," Solomon said, and considered the question. "I guess most of us spend the day reciting poetry and telling stories on the beach."

"Sounds great!" the dolphin beamed.

Solomon muttered in despair, "Not if all you want to do is sing like a songbird..."

"Sounds like a dream," the dolphin observed, reflecting on a dream he once had. He didn't remember the details, or even what the dream was about, but he did remember that he did in fact have a dream. "Now what was that dream I had when I actually believed I could do anything...?"

"A dream," Solomon said, "I will one day make a reality!"

149

Once upon a time in a forest far away...

"Wowya!" the dolphin exclaimed. "What determination! What admirable determination! What resolve...my friend, one day they will tell stories about you. They will! And they'll call it...they'll call it...wait...it's coming...the mind, she's working...they'll call it, The Humble White Dove That Could Because He Had The Courage To Move Mountains And Cross Oceans Regardless Of The Weather Or Danger..." The dolphin lost his breath.

"Kind of long," Solomon reflected, then added, "How about The Dove That Could."

"Please!" the dolphin laughed. "Too simple and short. Remember...we dolphins like long and complicated things. But in any case you will be a story...wait...not a story...not a story....wait...wait...ahhh! Yes! An Epic! An absolute Epic...and they'll call it, The Most Humble White Dove That Could Because He Had The Absolute Courage To Move Mountains And Cross Terrible Oceans Filled With Great White Sharks And Humongous Black And White Killer Whales..." And again the dolphin lost his breath.

Not too far away the dolphins sprang out of the water and twirled and squeaked happily as they waited for their conversant companion. One impatient dolphin whistled and called out to his friend to hurry up. At this the dolphin told them to come quick and witness the great Epic. Curious, they swam toward Solomon, circled him, admired him for a slight moment, and, not too impressed, the impatient dolphin said, "Wowya! Now lets go!" And the dolphins swam away.

"See!" the dolphin said to Solomon. "You're such an Epic!"

"No...really I'm not..."

"Ahhh...you're such a humble Epic!"

Now Solomon stood and faced Chichikaka and watched the dolphins swim away. "Is Chichikaka far?"

"Oh, yes!" the dolphin said. "Way too far! Even for an Epic such as yourself. Your small wings, epical as they may be, would never carry you that far."

"It's that far?"

"It's that far," confirmed the dolphin, nodding sincerely. "Oh well, I suppose you could float there...but that wouldn't be very epical, now would it? So I would leave that out when recounting the tale...no one really wants to hear about a dove that floated safely across an ocean...or maybe that works...I don't know..." He glanced at his friends, who were now leaving him behind. "Well," the dolphin squeaked, "It was nice to

150

know you, but now this fin has a school to catch!" And with one final squeak he was gone.

The idea of floating across an ocean exasperated Solomon. He slouched and sat on the log and splashed his feet in the water. Hope emptied from his very being and drained into the ocean. Filled with a dreadful mix of pain and despair and a horrible feeling of failure, he stared at the dolphin's fin and repeated, "This fin...this fin...this fin..." He didn't want to float on a log across an ocean. It could take forever, and he didn't have forever. Then, a sudden realization; his eyes widened with hope and he yelled, "This fin!" And he vaulted off the log in a terrible rush.

Laughing and enjoying the uncertainty of his journey, Solomon followed the dolphins to Chichikaka, taking a break every now and then on a slippery fin, which proved to be one of the most exciting and epical moments of his young life. He leaped and twirled and even plunged under water with the dolphins, and the dolphins would later admit that they had never witnessed a dove, or any bird for that matter, having so much fun participating in activities they thought only dolphins would enjoy.

Now speeding toward Chichikaka, Solomon held a fin tightly and was delighted. He was open to the world and the world was open to him. He was on his journey in search of a teacher who would teach him how to sing, and he felt as though nothing could stop him. Not even an ocean.

The dolphin was right: Chichikaka was a great distance away. Without help he would have never succeeded. But luck was with Solomon and dream-saving opportunities seemed to present themselves when he least expected them, when he needed them most. Solomon walked the beach and took in the new sights and smells. He said, "Thank you," without really knowing who or what he was thanking.

Solomon walked up and down the beach taking in everything except the beached killer whale right behind him. The whale was a thousand times bigger than the white dove and was entangled in a thick net dripping with slimy green seaweed, which made him look like a gigantic rock covered in moss.

The air was crisp and clean, the water warm and blue, and in the distance Solomon could see a colony of puffins lounging on a bed of rocks, enjoying the sun, enjoying the day, enjoying life. Solomon stopped in his tracks and could hardly believe he was on Chichikaka. He was taken by the grandeur and the novelty of everything. He felt remarkably alive. Much more alive than on his island where everything was known and predictable. He closed his eyes and attempted a song to capture the moment, the feeling; soon his singing melted into a soft, steady, self-conscious hum.

As he hummed his grand ode to Chichikaka he backed up slowly and gracefully, not conscious of where his feet were leading him. He tumbled over a crab and fell onto the whale. The crab cursed something vile in a strange sea language and went to attack Solomon with his deadly claws. But at the very instant the crab went to snap at Solomon's wing, the whale opened her gigantic eyes. The crab let out a scream of terror, turned around and scurried back into the water.

With his back to the whale, Solomon raised his chin heroically and stood strong. He pounded his chest with his wing and said, "That's right! I may be small but I have a BIG heart!"

"Help..." the whale said faintly.

Solomon glanced from side to side. "Who said that?"

"Here...behind you..."

Solomon turned to face the whale. He narrowed his gaze and considered something deeply. Then he said, "Now since when do giant rocks talk?" He examined and circled the whale; finally he concluded, "You're not a rock!"

"Quite perceptive..." the whale said softly, trying to conserve her energy.

Amazed by the enormity of the whale, Solomon continued to circle and admire her. Then he seemed to consider another thought very deeply. "Is it me?" he questioned, "or aren't you supposed to be somewhere else?" He went up to the whale and looked her right in the eyes. "Don't you think it's a little unordinary for a whale to be sun tanning like this?" He paused, then shrugged his wings. "But who wants to be ordinary! Carry on! Carry on! Don't let me get in your way..." And Solomon gave her a hearty pat on the back and smiled a knowing smile.

"Please," the whale gasped. "Please help..."

"Would love to," Solomon said and held his wings up to where the whale could see them. "But with your immense body and my tiny wings, I'm afraid it would take all day for me to rub you down...and I haven't got all day. You see, I've got a teacher..."

"No...net...take off..." she interrupted.

Solomon narrowed his gaze on the whale, then on the net, the whale, the net... "Oh dear, oh me," he said, "You're trapped...aren't you?"

"Quite...perceptive..."

Solomon gasped in terror. But he knew what to do. He began gnawing at the cord, pausing every now and then to make a comment about nets, about how he had heard about the carelessness and indifference and waste of the featherless chickens; about how featherless chickens used these giant nets to catch more fish than they needed; about how they used nets to empty the ocean of all its life; and finally, how they sometimes lost their nets and, not wanting to waste their time, didn't bother searching for them and left them adrift. Those lost nets would continue trapping until they became so heavy with the bones of unsuspecting creatures they would sink to the bottom of the ocean. The currents would eventually empty the nets of the bones and those lost nets would float back to the surface to trap again.

When Solomon had finished gnawing a good part of the net, he attempted to pull it off. But it was no use. The net was too heavy and by his hundredth try he was exhausted.

"No use," the whale said, and bowed before her sombre fate.

Solomon's head sank with his heart. Then a faraway laugh caught

153

his attention and he remembered the puffins. An idea presented itself at the last moment and he would not laugh and insult the one who had given him the idea by doing nothing with it. Solomon stood with new energy. The whale said, "There is no hope..."

"This dove," Solomon said proudly, "doesn't give-up that easy!" And Solomon made for the puffins.

After much heated debate Solomon returned in low spirits. He said that he could not convince any puffin to help him and that huge black and white whales terrified them. "I'm sorry," he said dejectedly and kicked the ground. "They called you a killer."

But still Solomon refused to give up. "I will try to roll you in..." "It's useless..."

"I may be small," Solomon said and made his way behind the whale. "But I have a big heart." And he began to push with all his might.

As the day wore on, the puffins stopped what they were doing and watched Solomon in mute amazement. Stubborn as gravity, the young white dove refused to accept defeat, refused to let this whale perish needlessly, refused to embrace a cowardly attitude of indifference. He pushed the whale, he pulled the whale, and he bumped the whale. By now the sun had already begun to make its descent and darkness was on the approach. Solomon took in a deep hearty breath; he knew this would be his last attempt as there was not a single drop of strength left in him. He took ten long paces back and stared at the whale's glistening black body. Then with a scream that challenged the indifference around him, he charged with wings firm and outstretched. He slammed into the whale's immoveable bulk and rebounded back to where he started, moaning, groaning, and saying, "Whale...I'm sorry...I'm so, so sorry..."

At that very moment, a black bird with a white patch for an eye and an orange bill towered over Solomon and said, "Don't give up that easy..." He offered his wing and lifted the fallen dove to his feet.

"Only you," Solomon said and stared at the spectators.

"Well," the puffin said, "One is better than none..."

Solomon nodded.

The puffin pointed to Solomon. "And two is better than one..."

Again, Solomon nodded his agreement.

Together they pushed and pushed the whale and fed off each other's energy. Then, one by one, the puffins, inspired by action, left their place of comfort and indifference and joined the duo, adding to their invisible pool of energy so that the pool filled exponentially until they

154

Solomon's Song

were all drawing strength and determination from a divine source that could only be tapped with a key of compassion and cooperation. In no time, the team had pulled off the net and rolled the whale into the water. Sometimes, the white dove reflected, what is impossible for one is a cinch for many.

The whale flip-flopped into the great blue, then turned to face Solomon. She didn't know how to thank this dove who refused to give up on her, who refused to turn his back on a fellow creature in need. "Dove," she said, and the words came from the bottom of her heart, "I am your whale."

Solomon was too weak to respond or say anything.

The whale turned and disappeared into the darkness. And there was great rejoicing among the puffins who loved to party and surf and who seized any opportunity to enjoy life.

One puffin yelled, "Party!"

Another answered, "For the whale!"

And then they all shouted:

"For the whale!"

Solomon found a quiet place by a rock and closed his eyes. When he woke up the next morning, the puffins were still dancing and singing and surfing. Then, one by one, they collapsed from fun exhaustion and fell into the deep and tranquil sleep common to those who collapse from fun exhaustion. Solomon stood and walked passed the snoring puffins toward a grassy plain. He attempted to sing what he was feeling inside; but then, feeling a little insecure about his voice, his song quickly turned into a hum.

&

As Solomon managed his way through the overgrown lush grass, he noticed something very peculiar: a slender, white bird with long, lanky legs and a long, curved neck. The bird jumped up and down, high and mighty, as though he were actually trying to touch the sky.

Always enthusiastic and curious, Solomon stood in front of the florican and observed him carefully. His head went up when the florican went up, and his head went down when the florican floated down. After a moment he asked, "What, may I ask, are you doing?"

The florican jumped up with all his might. "Jumping," he answered simply.

"Yes," Solomon said, following the bird's ascent, "I can see that. But why, may I ask, are you jumping?"

"To beat yesterday's record," said the florican, floating down.

"Record?" Solomon questioned.

"Going up," the florican said, "Yesterday I jumped three hundred and sixty-eight times. Today I must beat that record even if only by one."

"Wowya!" Solomon said, remembering the dolphin.

"And every day I hope to jump a little higher..."

Impressed, Solomon asked, "Can I jump with you?"

"As you please," answered the florican, reaching for the sky.

And Solomon began to jump with the florican. He admired the florican's ability to jump so high and with such grace, elegance, and perfect technique. "You jump so high!" Solomon said with a pleasant smile as the florican soared way above him.

"It's good to admire," the florican commented, but don't admire me too much or else you'll prevent yourself from jumping just as high. Don't think I'm special. Just know that I've worked very hard to get where I am."

"Oh," Solomon said, "I could never jump as high as you."

The florican bent, paused, then launched himself into the air. "You shouldn't say such things..." Floating down he indicated his head with his wing and said, "You'll only limit yourself in here." And he began to expound on the nature of the mind, about how everything we say, hear, or read has a very real effect on the way we carry our lives; about how

156

negative thoughts and words eat away at our sense of personal power; and about how one could achieve anything if one truly believed. For the florican, it was all about being positive. Finally, he concluded:

"Instead of saying, 'I'll never jump that high,' say, 'I am a good jumper and every day I get a little bit better.' This way you have small, daily goals that are realistic and attainable. Small goals will move you closer to your one big goal, and as the days accumulate, so to will your skill. You see, every day you practice is like depositing in the Experience Bank. Every day you miss practice is like a mini withdrawal. A little bit every day, and soon you will see that you can be all you ever wanted to be."

"Maybe," Solomon said thoughtfully. "I could say, 'I think I can and so I can.' That's something a teacher once taught me."

"Yes," the florican smiled. "That would be just fine. Just be positive, work hard, and everything will work out. Do your best and let the Forest take care of the rest. That's something an ant once taught me. So much did I enjoy his company that I spared his life."

"That's what I'll do," Solomon confirmed. "I'll do my best and let the Forest take care of the rest."

The florican smiled his approval and felt appreciated because Solomon really listened to him, unlike the other birds who only listened to hear their names. "I used to improve a nanometer every day," the florican continued, wanting to share the secrets his great teacher had taught him. "But improvement is exponential, and now I am at a level where I improve a millimeter a day. One millimeter every day, there is no other way. Soon I will be improving one centimeter every day..."

"And soon," Solomon said, "you'll be saying, 'One centimeter every day, there is no other way.'"

"Soon, indeed!" the florican said delightedly. "Soon I will touch heaven! And today I am one millimetre closer."

"Wowya!" Solomon said, "What it would be to touch heaven! And today you're one millimeter closer!"

The florican shouted proudly, "I am!"

Solomon confirmed, "You are!"

"I am!"

"You are!"

"I am! I am!"

"You are! You are!"

They both laughed. And then Solomon said, "Oh I am so very

glad to have met an inspirational bird such as yourself. A bird with a dream and the courage to do something to realize that dream. I enormously admire you. You are an inspiration...an absolute inspiration."

Inspired by the florican, Solomon continued to jump well into the afternoon. But since singing was his dream and not jumping he thought it would be better if he got on his way. "Well," Solomon said politely, now standing still, "It was nice jumping with you, but now I must say good-bye as I have a teacher to find." And Solomon made his way toward the Forest.

But before he entered the thick brush, the florican yelled, "Till we jump again!"

And Solomon turned to face him. He smiled and answered, "Till we jump again!"

The florican jumped straight into the sky and Solomon was simply amazed. Today this florican would be one centimeter closer to heaven.

Humming a soft tune and desperately hoping to encounter a songbird, Solomon entered the Forest and soon spied a strange looking edifice between two oak trees. For a long time Solomon inspected the bower and its many treasures, wondering who had engineered such a simple, yet alluring, leafy, thatched structure. He touched the leaves here and there and found the bower as enticing as a riddle. He thought it resembled a collection of some sort-it seemed to be a hodgepodge of artifacts found around the island. He observed the bower and noticed feathers, seashells, brightly colored stones, and even a perfectly crafted spider web. Coming closer, Solomon saw a feather that resembled his own, only this feather was pink and green and yellow. He reached for the feather and, in the sunlight, inspected it carefully and curiously.

"What is this!" a shiny blue bird bellowed, and swooped down in front of his creation. "What is this! What is this! No, no, no! Inbadooba! Inbadooba!"

Startled and somewhat confused, Solomon questioned, "Inbadooba?"

The bird wailed as though it were the end of the world. "How could you be so utterly inconsiderate?" He snatched the feather from Solomon's grip. "I'll never find the perfect spot…never…how could you be so inbadooba!" He tried desperately to find a perfect spot for the feather. Then noticing Solomon's perplexed expression he asked, "Why do you look like that?"

Solomon tilted his head. "Inbadooba…what does it mean?"

"Don't you speak the native tongue?" the bowerbird asked, and he put down the feather by his majestic structure.

Solomon shook his head. "I'm afraid I'm not from these parts."

Suddenly the bowerbird's eyes widened as he realized he was face to face with a white dove. He gasped his excitement and said, "A white dove!" He circled Solomon and admired him. "You are a treasure…a real treasure.…"

Once upon a time in a forest far away...

Solomon, who loved to learn new things, asked, "What does it mean...inbadooba?"

The bowerbird thought a moment. "Hard to say," he said, staring at Solomon and his creation thoughtfully. "Could mean many things...usually all negative...but mostly it is a word to describe the uninspired, the rushed, those who run around in perpetual meaningless circles not knowing what they want, not knowing where to invest their energy, not knowing how to approach things, or, in my case, place things, because they haven't taken the time to understand who they are. To know where you must invest your energy you must first know who you are." He paused, considered a few birds he had once known, then continued. "Usually the inbadooba don't take the time to get to know themselves. So their lives are everywhere and nowhere at the same time. They jump from one thing to the next searching for a quick fix of momentary happiness because being a stranger to themselves makes them unhappy." Now the bowerbird's head fell with mingled sadness and disappointment. "Seems to me like we're becoming a Forest of inbadoobas...seems like the whole Forest is going the way of the caterpillar and all they care about is glitter. Strangers to their families, strangers to their friends, strangers to themselves...and all they really know is glitter..."

Solomon tilted his head and seemed a little lost. "Glitter?"

"Never mind that," the bowerbird said and approached Solomon, admiring his white plumage with wide eyes. "I sure could use a few. If, that is, you don't mind."

"A few?" Solomon questioned, and he followed the bowerbird's sharp gaze. "Oh no! Oh no! Do you have any idea how much that would hurt?"

The bowerbird gazed at Solomon pleadingly. "One," he said, "All I need is..." He glanced at his creation, calculated, then said, "Two! All I need is two feathers."

"Two feathers!" Solomon bellowed, and then laughed at the request.

"Just a prick," said the bowerbird. "That is all you will feel. Such a little price for such a big cause."

Solomon shook his head rigorously. "What big cause?"

"Perfection," the bowerbird answered with a most serious and severe gaze. "My perfection. I've been working my whole life on this..." He indicated the bower. "And always...always...I knew there was something missing. An exotic and faraway touch."

160

Solomon's Song

Solomon shook his head. "Cannot comply..."

The bowerbird fell on his knees and begged. "Please, noble sir! Do not deny me perfection, lest I will be forced to cross an ocean to find another white dove. Oh please, noble sir! Show compassion for perfection..."

Solomon thought the bowerbird was certainly exaggerating the importance of his white feathers to an already impressive structure. When Solomon still didn't respond, the bowerbird stood and turned to his creation and threw his wings to the air, shouting, "Worthless! Worthless! Should be destroyed now that I know what it could have been."

Interrupting, Solomon said, "My feathers would make the difference?"

"Entirely!" the bowerbird turned to face him. "Your feathers would make the difference...noble sir..."

Solomon hesitated a long moment. "Well...I wouldn't want to be the one to deprive you of perfection."

The bowerbid beamed with gratitude. He bowed and said, "You, sir, are a real gent."

"Now," Solomon said, "be quick about it."

"But first," the bowerbird said, scanning and inspecting Solomon's plumage, "I must choose..."

The bowerbird prodded, felt, ruffled, rotated and judged Solomon's feathers one by one. He even moved Solomon to different spots of shade and sunlight to see how a particular feather caught and reflected light. And this went on for quite some time and only ceased when Solomon demanded that the bowerbird pick and pluck. But when the bowerbird did choose his perfect feathers it was Solomon who made the task impossible. Every time the bowerbird went to pluck, Solomon would scream and squirm and recoil five paces back.

"It won't hurt," said the bowerbird.

"I know it will," answered Solomon. "I know it will hurt."

The bowerbird tried several more times and each time it was the same. A scream, a squirm, and then five terrified paces back.

Solomon apologized. "I'm sorry. I want to help you but I can't. I can't because..."

At that moment the bowerbird plucked the two feathers and held them in front of Solomon.

"Because it will hurt too much," continued Solomon now peering at his own two feathers. "And really, I'm not so sure I could do without

Once upon a time in a forest far away...

two of my choicest feathers. I'm sure you understand. Besides you
already have two feathers that look just like mine."

The bowerbird smiled a victorious smile. "They are yours!"

"They are mine!" Solomon said, "Wowya!"

And the bowerbird searched intently for the perfect place for the
feathers. "Now," he mumbled over and over again as he inspected his creation, "Where to put...where to put..."

Day slipped into night and night into day. Still the bowerbird
searched for the perfect place. Solomon's excitement and attention waned,
and when night was on them again, he said to the bowerbird, "Does it
usually take this long?"

The bowerbird responded without taking his eyes off a possible
arrangement he was considering, calculating, evaluating. "Time is not an
issue," he said, tilting his head to examine the bower at a different angle.
"Only excellence." He tilted his head in the other direction. "Whenever
time is an issue, I stop. Or else...inbadooba...and I'm stuck with something really quite average." Now he stood on his head and examined his
bower upside down, considering every possibility. "Later is always better
than sooner when excellence is at stake." He ran a few hundred paces
back to examine the bower at a distance and yelled, "Time is never an
issue when creating." He ran back to the bower and took one of the feathers back into his wing and the other he left in the spider web. "This one
needs another place," he said. "But it's just not coming to me...and I
know it's better to sleep on it rather than force it."

"Good idea," Solomon said and yawned. He made a bed of leaves
and was soon fast asleep. After several more failed attempts the bowerbird joined the snoring white dove who, surprisingly, would burst into
dreamy songs every now and then.

"Wonder if he knows that he sings in his sleep," said the bowerbird to himself. "Peculiar for a dove to be singing in his sleep..." The
bowerbird yawned. Under a blanket of stars he fell sound asleep.

"That's it!" the bowerbird yelled with a start and rose in the full glare of
the morning sun.

"What! What!" Solomon awoke in confusion.

"I saw it in a dream!"

And the bowerbird placed the feather at the very top of his bower.

"There," he said proudly. "Perfection!"

162

Solomon's Song

Solomon admired his bower and knew he now had to be on his way. So he said good-bye and the bowerbird bowed before him and said: "I bow before you, majestic white dove, and thank you humbly for your marvellous contribution to my perfection."

Solomon bowed in return. "And I thank you humbly, majestic blue bird, for your marvelous contribution to my growth."

The bowerbird looked up and saw a flock of fruit doves tumbling and laughing in the clear blue sky. When he looked down again, Solomon was gone. In the distance he could hear a soft, steady, melodious humming.

Inspired by the dedication of the bowerbird, Solomon sauntered through the fragrant Forest when suddenly he heard something ruffle in the trees. He glanced around and soon spotted a stocky, thin green bird with patches of red, blue, and yellow. The manikin pirouetted from lower to lower branch, until finally he was on the ground. He pranced and shuffled toward Solomon. Then he twirled, froze like a statue, and shut his eyes.

"You like!" the manikin said, opening his eyes with a start.

Startled, Solomon answered, "I do…but it looks tiring."

The manikin laughed. "My friend, you never tire of the things you love. In fact, doing what you love only empowers you to do more. I do believe it was Plato who said that…or Nietzsche…anyhow, doesn't matter. They probably both said the exact same thing in entirely different ways. There is nothing new under the sun except everything." He shuffled a few feet back, twirled, froze, and closed his eyes. Opening his eyes, he added, "It's always one idea hooked onto the tail of another, tweaked and polished to suit the time." And then he did another dance and beamed at Solomon.

Solomon clapped loudly. "Well done! Well done! I enormously admire you! I may not know much about Plato or Nietzsche but I do know a magnificent dance when I see one."

"Ohhhh!" the manikin charged Solomon and hugged the white dove strongly. "Thank you! Thank you! I needed that. I needed that so much." Then he pulled away in a shuffle and explained:

"I've been working on this dance for years. It takes time, you know…the best dance begins with the best moves. And the best moves are those that most appeal to you. And what most appeals to you is only discovered through a long and tedious process of elimination. Of trying every move and seeing which one does well with you and which one you'd never do again. I watch other birds and try everything I see at least once. If it suits me, I assimilate it; if it doesn't, I toss it. At the very least I know a little bit more about myself and what I will not be doing. It takes time, lots of time, but when you are doing what you love time is never wasted."

Solomon's Song

Solomon, remembering the bowerbird, said, "Time doesn't matter, only excellence."

"Yes," the manikin agreed. "I must remember that one. Nothing is ever lost when your life is your work of art. Because, in the end, there is no one perfect dance-only what's perfect for you and what suits your soul. But to be able to judge what's perfect for you, you must first know yourself." He stopped to do a little dance. He froze and closed his eyes. He added, "Time is only wasted when you do not know yourself." He opened his eyes and concluded, "Self-knowledge is key to genuine art."

Solomon repeated thoughtfully, "Self-knowledge is key to genuine art."

"Yes!" the manikin said. "And I do believe it was Plato...or was it Nietzsche...who said, 'Time doesn't matter, only perfection.'"

The manikin broke into a graceful dance, which pleased and impressed Solomon immensely.

Clapping wildly, Solomon commented, "Simple yet elegant. Again!"

This encouraged the manikin to do another dance, this time longer, wilder, much more acrobatic.

When he finished, Solomon clapped joyously and said, "Wild yet peaceful. Again!"

The manikin opened his eyes, took a deep breath, and did another dance.

"Strong yet gentle. Again!"

The manikin broke into another dance.

"Happy yet sad. Again!"

"What are you doing?" the manikin panted, trying to catch his breath.

Solomon smiled. "Empowering you!"

"I'm so empowered," the manikin heaved a deep breath, "I could drop."

And the manikin collapsed and fell into a deep empowering sleep.

Solomon watched and admired the sleeping manikin. The manikin really knew who he was and this showed in his every movement and gesture.

Now Solomon knew that he would achieve his greatest potential by enhancing his ability to focus; and the only way he could achieve this was through self-knowledge. Self-awareness, he had learned from several

Once upon a time in a forest far away...

birds, would enable him to direct all his energy clearly and properly.

It wasn't long before Solomon came upon a flock of fruit doves, evaluating and teaching each other new tumbling skills in a small clearing in the Forest. He approached them slowly, admiring. They looked just like him except they were bright and colorful: yellow, pink, orange, red, and some even had hints of green.

One fruit dove took to the sky and in an instant was gone. But the doves continued to watch the sky patiently. Then, the dove suddenly returned in full tumble. He made his way back toward them and screamed his joy as he twirled, flipped and twisted in the air. He then landed directly in front of Solomon and, without noticing the white dove, turned his back on him and bowed to the rest of the flock.

The flock applauded, and only when they noticed Solomon was there total silence. The fruit dove who had just experienced a breakthrough turned to faced Solomon. He gasped and said, "Wonchoochoo!"

Solomon turned around to see who the fruit dove was talking about. Not finding any other dove, he turned back to the flock and said, "Won-Who? Who?"

At this the fruit doves kneeled before him and bowed. They rose in a flash. Two fruit doves ran into the brush and for a little while all that could be heard was the clatter and pounding of heavy construction. They emerged from the brush carrying a thatched throne made out of twisted braches, leaves, and ivy with four prongs sticking out of the sides. One fruit dove indicated respectfully to the throne and said, "Your Highness."

"Your Highness," Solomon said, amused. "I think you have me confused with some other dove."

"You are the one..."

A fruit dove named Saya said and stepped forward. She explained that there was no mistake, that they had been waiting for a white dove from another land for quite some time, and that if he would follow her to their kingdom she would show him the truth of her words. And so Solomon reluctantly took his place on the throne and was carried off to the kingdom of the fruit doves.

Once upon a time in a forest far away...

When Solomon reached the kingdom, the sun was already saying goodnight to the Forest. In crimson pools of evening light he could see thousands upon thousands of fruit doves living in homes carved into the mountain. In the sky he saw schools of doves, black against the sky, practicing and perfecting their art. And just below him he observed a mother trying her best to give her feisty fledgling a bath in a steady flowing, limpid stream. The fledgling cried and sobbed that he didn't want to take a bath, and Solomon remembered what it was like to be a fledgling, when his two greatest enemies were baths and sleep. Each robbed him of time, time for life and living. And now he felt like a fledgling once again. Every moment he saw and learned something new. His mind was fresh and awake like a sleepless river to the sea.

The fruit doves carried him to the palace cave whereupon Solomon rose from the throne and Saya beckoned him to follow her. She led him to a special room in the palace and pointed to a series of pictures painted on the stone wall.

"What does it mean?" Solomon asked, gazing at a picture of tiny yellow birds falling from the sky, holding their necks, as if choking on poison.

Saya moved behind him and began to relate the prophecy. "Birds," she said, and pointed to the picture, "will escape from their poisonous island and fall in a distant land."

Solomon moved to a picture of a white dove looking upon a mountain of tiny, yellow, lifeless bodies.

"A white dove," Saya said, and moved behind Solomon as he unflinchingly stared at the painting, "will heed the call of the Great Fall...he will leave his island to seek the source of this atrocity before his own island suffers a similar fate."

Now Solomon suspected he was not this fabled Wonchoochoo. He had not left his island because of any atrocity or Great Fall.

Solomon moved to the next painting of the white dove being carried across the ocean by a gigantic black fish. Dolphins, he thought, were not gigantic black fish. Now he knew for sure: he was not Wonchoochoo. But he didn't saying anything. Birds that believed in prophecies, he had learned, were fairly unreasonable and, at times, illogical.

Saya moved with him. "A gigantic fish will carry him to Chichikaka."

They moved to a picture of a massive palace.

"The white dove will learn many things," she said thoughtfully.

168

Solomon's Song

"The Forest will open his eyes and soul to the Great Evil."

"What evil?" Solomon asked, moving closer to the picture, inspecting the details of the palace.

Saya sighed and shook her head. "We are not sure. We've never seen such a palace. We don't even think it exists and believe there may be a few inaccuracies in the prophecy. I mean we're not unreasonable birds. We realize nothing is perfect, not even prophecies..." She paused and stared at the painting intently. There was no such palace on Chichikaka, and, if there was, it was either invisible or extremely well hidden. Then she thought about something her uncle had once told her. "The greatest evil," her uncle had said, "was the evil that convinced the Forest it did not exist."

"There is no such evil," Solomon said softly.

"We suspect," Saya responded, "the evil of the baboons."

Solomon turned to face her. "The baboons?"

"Yes," she confirmed. "They are like the featherless chickens. They capture birds and lock them up solely for entertainment purposes. They are wasteful and greedy and their egos know no bounds..."

Solomon made a face of disgust, and Saya nodded gravely.

Now he moved to a picture of two arrows indicating two possible outcomes of the future. "What does it mean?" he asked, touching the cold wall. His gaze followed one arrow that pointed to a painting of chaos, hunger and death; then the other which indicated a painting of joy, abundance, and celebration.

"Well," she said, moving closer to Solomon. "That is up to Wonchoochoo. That is up to you."

Solomon turned to her.

She peered at the arrows for a moment. Then she continued, "If the white dove becomes lonely and returns home without defeating the Great Evil..." She indicated the painting of chaos. Solomon gulped in despair. And Saya continued, "But if he overcomes his loneliness and completes his journey..." She indicated the painting of celebration.

Solomon moved up to the painting of chaos, then celebration. "But how does he do it?"

"The wall doesn't say...but we were told by our ancestors he will open the beats of the entire Forest with a song..."

"A song!" Solomon took two steps back and turned to Saya.

"Yes, yes," she said. "I know. Doves can't sing. Another inaccuracy. Nothing is perfect. Not even prophecies."

Once upon a time in a forest far away...

A thousand and one thoughts assailed Solomon at once and he ran back to the first few paintings and re-examined them carefully. Now he wondered if he really was this fabled Wonchoochoo.

Solomon lived with the fruits doves for several months playing the role of savior, and he often felt like an imposter. He knew now, more than ever that he was not Wonchoochoo; or at least, if he was, he would never learn how to sing bombarded with such suffocating luxury, comfort, and security. His mind was falling asleep and was beginning to stagnate and putrefy like a motionless pond. He needed to move on. And though he appreciated all the fruit doves had done for him, how they taught him to twist and twirl and tumble while soaring through the sky, he knew that he could very well get used to being served upon wing and toe, and that if he didn't leave as soon as possible he would forget why he had left his island in the first place. He was afraid he would never find his teacher. He was afraid he'd never learn how to sing. He was afraid his heart would stop talking to him.

Now he sat by the stream wearing a crown that reflect the stars above and he wore a purple and gold embroidered robe that resembled his father's. He gazed at the stars and didn't even notice Saya land behind him. She sat beside him, observed his despair, and said:

"I understand..."

Solomon turned to her without saying anything. Then he returned his gaze to the stars and thought he was tired of living the same day over and over again. Most doves enjoyed routines, he understood, but he was not like most doves. He gazed at one star intently and said, "What I have come here to learn,"he turned to her, "I have learned."

"I understand," she whispered, looking straight into him. "What you have left home to learn...you have not."

Solomon nodded and returned his gaze to his star. He realized his friend understood him; understood that he did not leave one routine to simply jump into another. His heart was tugging at his soul, reminding him it was time to go. He had everything here-perfumes, jewels, robes, distractions, and enough food to feed the entire Forest ten times over-and yet his spirit felt so poor. He couldn't understand why that was or why he, like no other dove, craved that which no material possession could satisfy. Adventure. Discovery. Learning. The endless possibilities and the great uncertainties of his journey.

Solomon's Song

"Where will you go?" Saya asked after a silence.

Solomon reflected, then answered, "I'm not sure yet."

"You shall be guided," Saya said with deep respect for the Forest.

"I hope so," he said and smiled. Then he stood and took off his robe. He folded the robe, placed his crown on top of it, and handed it over to his friend. "I'm sorry," he apologized, "I didn't turn out to be who you thought I was."

Saya smiled delicately. "That remains to be seen..."

And Solomon embraced her and thanked her for her kindness and said that he hoped to one day return the favor. He then turned toward the Forest and followed a path lit by a pale blue moon.

Solomon walked up the path and, not paying attention to where he was walking, stumbled over a buzzard in a three-piece business suit. The buzzard woke up and was at first upset; but then his eyes grew wide with delight and he quickly smiled at the sight of the white dove. There was something terribly suspicious about his smile. It was as authentic as a fish with feathers.

"A white dove," the buzzard said in mock amazement. "Now what brings a white dove to these parts?"

Solomon felt the buzzard looking at him strangely, as if he wondered how he might make a profit off a white dove. He had learnt much about the cleverness and untrustworthiness of buzzards back home. He remembered that buzzards were extremely charismatic and polite and that they used these qualities to befriend other birds only to lower their guards and later rob them of their wealth and resources. To know this buzzard's true intentions, Solomon knew he had to look beneath the smile and the honey-coated compliments and keep himself a stranger. He knew he couldn't say anything about his life or journey without making himself vulnerable to this polite and urbane scavenger in a red and blue business suit. The buzzard's only motivation in life was gain-gain at any cost.

"Nothing much," Solomon said, not really answering the buzzard's question. "I'm just out for a little stroll." He detected a cruelty without conscience in the buzzard's eyes.

"Oh come now!" the buzzard smiled. "Aren't you a far way off?"

"Yes," Solomon answered curtly. "But I like long walks."

"I see," the buzzard said. "Oh well, guess I just thought you were on some kind of a pilgrimage."

"Nope," Solomon said and crossed his wings stubbornly. "Not me. I'm not on any kind of journey to find any kind of teacher. I'm just taking a walk..."

"I see..."

But the buzzard was better at mining for information than Solomon was at concealing it. Within a few minutes they were exchanging small talk and the buzzard had Solomon exactly where he wanted him. The buzzard started a small fire and eventually Solomon was telling

172

him about his entire life from egg to Chichikaka. He told him about his dream and how he was patiently searching for a teacher. The buzzard listened and smiled and never told Solomon anything about his own life. He poured water into a kettle and placed the kettle over the fire and agreed with everything Solomon had to say. Buzzards knew one thing: if you wanted a bird to fully open up to you, you never disagreed on any point or issue.

And so they sat down in front of the fire and the buzzard began to prepare tea. As he listened to all of Solomon's thoughts and ideas, he thought he really didn't care for a single opinion the white dove had on dreams, or hermits, or following your heart. He just kept saying, "How very interesting!" And Solomon kept on talking.

"Is there much glitter to be made in singing?" the buzzard finally asked.

Solomon threw him a perplexed expression. "Glitter?"

"Oh!" the buzzard corrected himself, and laughed at his question. "Of course there is! Why else would a bird travel so far and spend so much time looking for a teacher. There's got to be tons of glitter involved." He broke into another laugh and then became serious all at once. "I'm afraid," he said, "You will not find a songbird on Chichikaka. You will not find your teacher here."

"I won't?" Solomon exclaimed in great distress.

The buzzard continued, "I don't understand it myself, but it has been a long while since I heard a song in the Forest."

Solomon realized that the buzzard was right. He had not heard a single song since he first set foot on Chichikaka. He despaired to know the reason.

The buzzard, adding coconut milk and ground vanilla to the kettle, offered an explanation. "Could be the air from the other side of the river. It's a different place on the other side of the river. Not green and fragrant like here. Dark and grey. A desert of rubble and dirt, and that's no exaggeration. Most of the trees are either cut down or sick with the air. It's such strange air...pretty and colorful, but strange nevertheless...but there's a lot of glitter in cutting trees, so it's all okay."

"Pretty and colorful?" Solomon said, and thought all air was invisible.

"Purplish green," the buzzard said and sprinkled some cinnamon and cardamom in the tea. "It's really hard to breathe down there and the songbirds, I heard, were the first to fall." He fell silent and then added

173

with a start, "Great air for business! Bad air for breathing. Well, you know what they say, 'one bird's disaster is another bird's opportunity!'"

Solomon made a face of disgust, as if he had just bitten into a rotten mango. He narrowed his eyes on the buzzard, who poured tea into small bamboo cups. The buzzard had a strange look in his eyes, as if he would sell his own mother for profit.

Laughing to himself, the buzzard concentrated on pouring the tea and continued:

"Anyhow, birds will get used to anything. And soon they won't even remember a time when the air was free or clean."

"Free?" Solomon questioned.

"Sure," the buzzard said, handing Solomon a steaming cup of tea. "One bird's disaster is another bird's opportunity."

Solomon didn't know much about poisoned air but he felt that those responsible for poisoning the air should also be responsible for cleaning it.

The buzzard sniffed his tea and relished the vanilla. "That is why I am on this side of the river. I'm trying to figure a way of bottling air over here in order to sell it over there. Believe me! The lack of supply is there. The demand is there. It's just good business. Pay up, or perish-business as usual!"

Solomon didn't know much about supply and demand or business as usual, but he felt that those responsible for this most unnatural demand for clean air should also be responsible for cleaning the air and supplying all creatures with free air. Dividing and selling air was just as absurd as dividing and selling water. What a ridiculous place the other side of the Forest sounded like to Solomon. Concerned, he blew on his tea and asked, "Shouldn't air be free?"

The buzzard gasped at the thought and nearly spilled his tea, which he had not touched yet. "My word, did you say free?"

Deeply concerned, Solomon continued, "Aren't all creatures entitled to free air? Isn't air a gift to all? I mean...wouldn't selling bottled air sound just as ridiculous as selling bottled water? I may not be from here, but the other side of the river sounds like a really, really crazy place."

"Birds can get used to anything," the buzzard said strongly. "As long as no one keeps the memory alive, they won't even remember a time when air was free."

"Yes, but aren't we all entitled to-?"

"Entitled!" the buzzard interrupted fervidly. "My word, entitled!

174

Solomon's Song

Well, it shows you are not from Chichikaka. That word was pulled out of all the stories and songs a long, long time ago. Little bird, no one remembers that word. The word doesn't even come to mind when thinking of air and water. In any case, you can be sure that only a hatchling believes that birds are entitled to anything. Everything has a price. Everything! And anything can be sold. Remember that and you will do well on Chichikaka."

"Then I shall pray with all my heart that I never grow up, that I always think like a hatchling, and that air and water shall forever be free on my island."

"You're talking like a hatchling," the buzzard said, and felt very mature with his thoughts and opinions about life and living.

Solomon took a sip of tea and suddenly had a thought. "What if one day there is no more clean air? Not even for you to sell. How would that be?"

"You have some imagination, Hatchling!" the buzzard sniggered. "In any case, that would never happen. Those are the thoughts of a malprogresso. And no one listens to malprogressos."

"Malprogresso?" Solomon questioned, having never heard of the word.

Now the buzzard seemed bothered by the thought of not having air to sell, business to conduct. He loosened his tie and continued with emotion, "And such thoughts would distract me from good, clean business. You want to do good business you got to think positive! You have to be positive. And so, that is not a 'what if' I choose to entertain."

"Choose or not choose, it could happen," Solomon said flatly. He took another sip of his tea and savoured the cinnamon. "What if the air poisoned all creatures and there was no one to conduct business with anymore? How would that be?"

The buzzard lost control. "What if the sun became stronger?!" he exploded and spilled tea over his grey wings. "What if icebergs melted?! What if there were no more trees?! What if all the canaries from Chichikaka dropped dead from the sky?! My goodness, Hatchling, we could 'what if' all day if wanted to and it would get us nowhere. Business is all about being an optimist, not a malprogresso."

"Does bottled air suggest you've gotten somewhere?" Solomon asked plainly. "And where? A better place? Not a better place, if you ask me. Give me a choice between a place in time where I have to buy bottled air and water or a place in time where air and water are free, and

175

regardless of anything else, I know exactly which place I'm choosing. Or maybe I'm just thinking like a hatchling." There was a thoughtful silence and Solomon had another 'what if' but he knew the buzzard wasn't willing to entertain any more 'what ifs'. "Well suppose," Solomon said carefully, breaking the silence, "Suppose creatures revolt and refuse to pay for bottled air? Suppose that. How would that be? "

"Won't happen," the buzzard said confidently. "All these crazy malprogresso ideas have been taken out of the stories and songs long, long ago. And I guarantee it! I guarantee it, little bird! As long as the invisible hand of business guides the storytellers and the singers, there will be no such revolt. Pay up or perish-business as usual. The caterpillar way!"

"Caterpillar?" Solomon questioned.

Suddenly the buzzard realized he was challenging his companion and that his companion would soon put his guard up. Perhaps Solomon would even stop drinking his tea. So the buzzard said, "You're right; come to think of it, air and water should be free. After all, these are things all birds are entitled to."

"Exactly!" Solomon said, and was at first perplexed by the sudden change in heart and then pleased the buzzard agreed with him. But before he could say anything else, a great wave of heat crashed over him. He felt woozy; his eyelids grew heavy; his head boiled as if in a cooking pot.

The buzzard winked and smiled his business-as-usual smile.

For a second Solomon had no idea where and who he was. A dark mist clouded his vision.

The buzzard's smile grew and he fixed his red and blue tie and cleared his throat.

Solomon dropped his bamboo cup and its contents spilled and sizzled in the fire. He rose on shaky legs and stumbled two paces back and watched in horror as the buzzard threw the contents of his cup into the fire.

As the buzzard laughed his business-as-usual laugh, Solomon lost all awareness of his senses and collapsed. Slowly his eyes shut and all went black.

᪥

Soft and curious whispers broke into Solomon's dreams as he awoke
slowly. He held his head and moaned. He was alarmed by a circle of
beady, black bird eyes peering down at him. Still drowsy and feeble, he
attempted to rise but stumbled to his side and ended up flat on his back.
Three hummingbirds hovered above him and helped him sit up.

Holding his pounding head in his wings, Solomon groaned and
asked, "Where am I?" He glanced around and saw that he was in a cave
filled with birds of every sort and size. At the mouth of the cave he saw
sunlight pouring through an iron bar door guarded by two heavily armed
baboons in oversized armor.

"I'm afraid..." said the green hummingbird.

"You belong..." said the yellow hummingbird.

"To the baboons!" finished the blue hummingbird.

"Belong!" Solomon said in a voice full of shock. He looked to the
birds, who encircled him. "What does it mean?"

A chubby bluebird answered, "It means you were sold to the
baboons and are now the king's property."

A proud and elegant cardinal added, "It means you are at the
king's service."

"What service?" Solomon asked with a deeply confused expression, unable to believe what was happening to him. Yesterday he was a
king, now he was a king's servant.

The cardinal continued, "Every evening the king chooses one of
us to entertain him..."

"And entertain you must!" interjected the robin. "If you fail, dinner you will become."

Solomon gulped at the thought of being the king's dinner and
stared at the birds with wide, disbelieving eyes. They nodded solemnly
and now he had a deeper understanding of the evil he was up against.
These baboons were far worse than Saya had described.

"Yes, but do something they love," said the bluebird, "And you'll
get a nice big baboon award." And the bluebird indicated a lyrebird who
was polishing up all his trophies and awards. He was the only bird in the
prison with baboon awards.

Once upon a time in a forest far away...

Solomon asked the obvious question. "What do they like?"

The bluebird had no answer. "Not sure," he said. "But they sure love the lyrebird. He's figured out something about baboons and won't tell a single solitary soul." The bluebird shook his head at the lyrebird, then continued. "But there is a plus side to his selfishness... I don't think you should ever have to worry about entertaining the king. Chances are you won't have to. The king is fond of that bird and hardly chooses any other."

Solomon observed the lyrebird praising his awards for a while and wondered what was so great about some shiny platinum baboon trophy awarded by-and if Saya was indeed correct-the great evil of the Forest. He didn't see why the lyrebird, with his long, elegant, trailing tail, should be so happy and arrogant.

Now the birds left Solomon to his thoughts and went to work on their routines. He glanced around the prison observantly and saw no escape except for a small tunnel in the back wall. He jumped to his feet, dashed to the tunnel and felt a cool breeze. He saw that he could easily fit through this passageway and make his escape to the outdoors; and he was curious to know why no other bird had done so before. Then the bluebird stepped up from behind and told him that the tunnel was a deathtrap, that some beast lived inside and that every night they could hear the terrible screams and agonies of some poor unsuspecting creature being tortured and eaten alive. Solomon recoiled at the thought and then sighed in defeat. He thanked the bluebird for the warning and turned his back against the wall. Slowly he let himself sag down, down, down; and all day he watched the prison without once realizing he was surrounded by songbirds.

At night, just as the bluebird had said, the screams filled the air and-except for the lyrebird, who was too busy with his awards to be concerned with the suffering of another-all the prisoners made a half circle around the tunnel and made a long, thoughtful prayer. When the screams intensified and distracted the lyrebird's thoughts, he sighed in annoyance, plugged his ears and went back to his trophies and plaques and everything else that made him feel superior to others.

Solomon studied all the prisoners in the torchlight. And as they walked back to their places, he saw them for the first time. He was amazed by what he was seeing: bluebirds and cardinals playing cards; kookaburras and kiwis building cairns, parrots talking and mocking canaries, and a group of hummingbirds dressed in el mariachi gear passionately practicing their instruments. And as he scanned all the birds, he suddenly had a realization that filled his heart with intense hope. He realized he was surrounded by songbirds, and he knew this prison was exactly where he wanted to be. He closed his eyes and silently thanked his great teacher for his encounter with the buzzard.

The next day Solomon went from songbird to songbird asking if they would teach him how to sing. But from songbird to songbird it was the same: he was met with laughter, then a strange, disbelieving stare, and finally they told him to be realistic, that doves weren't meant to sing, and that if he had been meant to sing he would have been born a nightingale.

By evening there were only two songbirds left for him to approach: a nightingale and a lyrebird. So Solomon approached the lyrebird politely and asked if he would be his teacher. But the lyrebird's reaction was the same, though far more excessive and demeaning. The lyrebird laughed at Solomon, pointed and said, "A dove! A dove...sing!" And the whole prison exploded with laughter; the only one who did not laugh was the nightingale. But the poor, humiliated dove was too busy being ridiculed to notice the nightingale's concern and compassion.

Their ridicule emptied Solomon of all hope and confidence; he didn't even bother with his last hope. He merely found a dusty, lonesome corner and sat with his head slumped and his whole body sagging. He sighed and sobbed silently.

After a while, a kind voice startled him. "Cheer up," said the voice, "It's not your fault they're Stone Age thinkers."

Solomon gazed up in disbelief. Was this nightingale really being friendly? Or was he going to be the victim of another joke?

"Enough!" Solomon said with pain and defeat caught in his throat, "I can't take any more...I know! I know! Doves weren't meant to sing...had I been born to sing I would have been born a nightingale!"

"I'm not here to ridicule you, dove," the nightingale said, "Nor am I here to propagate old lies and limitations. If you want to sing, you can. It's all up to you. All you need is patience and determination..."

Interrupting, Solomon said, "And a teacher! But no one will show me..."

"Ahh, they're just scared and insecure," the nightingale said, "Don't be defeated by their insults, which only betray their own inner fears. Remember, they're all competing for the king's attention and awards. If anything, feel sad for them. The invisible hand of the king secretly composes all their songs. They've forgotten themselves, or why they even sing in the first place. Instead of singing for the Forest-which endowed them with their gifts and talents-they sing for the king, who silences them with awards. Only in their last days will they realize the absurdity of this. But in their last days, it will be too late. One day they'll wake up and realize they wasted all their talents on the king when it was the Forest that needed them most."

The nightingale paused and realized he was digressing. He turned to the lyrebird. The lyrebird practiced a song that glorified the baboon way of life. The nightingale sighed and turned to Solomon. "Don't burden your mind with the opinions of a lost lyrebird. He's more conceited than a peacock and is just afraid you'll one day sing better than him."

Solomon was surprised. "He is!"

The nightingale nodded. "That's why he won't help." Then he gestured to all the songbirds and added, "That's why none of them will help."

Solomon said, "They're afraid..."

There was a moment of silence.

Solomon could hardly believe the songbirds were afraid of his potential. And the nightingale, not wanting to dwell on the insecurities of songbirds, broke the silence.

"So you want to sing?" he asked.

Solomon jumped to his feet, his eyes on fire. "More than anything in the world!"

The nightingale smiled at the dove's enthusiasm and excitement-his need to be the best dove he could be. "I will teach you," he said.

Now Solomon's soul was on fire.

The nightingale said, "But there is one condition."

"Anything!"

"You are not to quit until you are better than me."

"Promise! Oh, yes. I promise."

At this the nightingale smiled for he needed to be the best teacher he could be.

Solomon had been learning from the nightingale for nearly a week now, and he could see that it would be some time before he found his voice. Regardless of the laughs and whispers, he spent entire mornings warming up his vocals by repeating silly tongue twisters and humming different tunes that strengthened his control and stamina. Then he would take a small break and start up again in the afternoon.

Regardless of the rumors and comments, his afternoons were spent learning how to sing a sequence of songs that gradually increased in difficulty; and he found that as the songs progressed, so too did his breathing and his technique. He listened to his teacher sing, emulated him as best he could, and soon came to realize that singing was as much a hearing art as it was a vocal art.

And regardless of how many birds chided him and laughed at his efforts, Solomon stayed with his lessons well into the night; he even attempted to emulate the songs of other songbirds. Solomon practiced and practiced as he knew one day he would experience a breakthrough. Not overnight. Not in a week. Eventually. Eventually, was good enough.

"Day by day," he told himself, "There is no other way." Solomon closed his eyes and was proud of how hard he had worked all day. Soon, he thought, he would touch his heaven.

A month passed and Solomon, a dedicated and focused student, could now sing several difficult songs from beginning to end without receding into a self-conscious hum or losing his breath or control. And even though he could sing, he was grateful that the king had never called upon him. Being forgotten and unknown had its advantages. He had all his time to practice and not worry about pleasing some baboon or ending up on some baboon buffet table, which he was very much against. He was quite satisfied that the lyrebird was the king's favorite.

Every evening the baboons would march the lyrebird from the mountain prison down to the courtyard where he would sing his songs. And those songs would rise up to the prison where Solomon, though he had practiced all day and was to a degree exhausted, would do his best to emulate them.

One evening the nightingale interrupted Solomon as he stood by the mouth of the moonlit prison and said, "You've been emulating him too much." Solomon went quiet. "Granted, it is good and healthy to emulate. That is how all songbirds learn, even the best of them. I won't deny that. My goodness, anyone who does not emulate has no understanding of songbirds or what it takes to sing." He paused for a moment, and he thought about how hard songbirds had to work to find their voices. "I, too, emulated my favorite songbird in my village and only stopped when I realized I was losing my own voice."

"You were?" Solomon listened carefully.

"Yes, Solomon," the nightingale said. "When I was young, like every other bird, I modeled my very favourite singer. And when I was ready, when I had acquired much skill, technique, and understanding through emulation, I knew I had to search within." He considered his words then said, "That is to say, I knew I had to search in here..."He indicated his heart with his wing. "To find my voice. Now, though I may sound extremely similar to other nightingales, I am me because of my voice, because of what I choose to sing about."

They fell silent and listened to the lyrebird's song. The nightingale sighed and continued, "He can mimic every bird in the Forest and he can sing very nicely. But his songs say nothing. His songs mean nothing. All they do is praise baboons and please the king's ears. "

Solomon was perplexed. "But what more can a song aspire to?"

"Much, much more," was the nightingale's quick and serious reply. "Solomon, never underestimate the power of song and its ability to touch and inspire souls. Never underestimate a song's ability to move creatures to great feats of action. That is why,"he said, covered his beak for a moment, and shook his head, "it is so important for baboons to have such a stranglehold on songbirds. That is why they've created a system in which the songbird puts on his own muzzle without even realizing it. You see, Baboons control songs through an incredible and very precise reward system they modeled from the featherless chickens." The nightingale went quiet and searched his mind for a way to help Solomon understand what he meant. In a moment he said, "Let me tell you a story..."

And Solomon leaned forward and waited with interest.

The nightingale began. "Once upon a time in a Forest far, far away..."

"Wow!" Solomon commented. "What a great beginning."

"You like it," the nightingale said proudly.

"I sure do!"

"Then it's yours," laughed the nightingale, and he went on to tell the story of a songbird who had once heard about the tyranny of the baboons, how they caged and robbed other creatures of resources and land to appease their insatiable and most unnatural appetite for nuts and bananas. He described how this songbird, with great courage and compassion, composed a song to expose the tyranny of the baboons to the entire

Solomon's Song

Forest, to let all creatures know that they weren't powerless, that they could make a difference, and that it was their indifference or even their cowardice that permitted baboons to treat the Forest the way they did. Then he described how the baboons were quick to catch this songbird, and how, unable to muzzle him with awards or bananas, they threw him in a prison and forgot him so that he could no longer sing his song.

"But," Solomon interrupted, staring at the nightingale with new-found respect, "Why didn't they just serve you for dinner?"

"They wanted to," the nightingale answered, not realizing Solomon had just figured out who the story was about. "But not a single baboon would do the deed. They all felt this songbird had some help from above, that he was some kind of a messenger, and that whoever let the axe fall would forever bring a terrible curse upon their family."

A silence followed. Then the nightingale added, "I wish they had, though. I miss home so very much."

Solomon said, "Well, it is my luck that you are here."

And the nightingale couldn't help but smile. "The point is, Solomon, you mustn't sing for reward or praise. You mustn't let the king control you like this. You must sing whatever is in your heart to sing. Sing what your heart tells you to sing, even if that song will get you into trouble. Listen to your heart and be true to your art..."

"Listen to my heart and be true to my art," Solomon repeated pensively.

"And never..."

"Never..."

"Turn your back on the Forest."

At that moment the lyrebird began another song and the baboons went coocoo-bananas. They clapped and hollered and then went silent to listen to their way of life being praised and glorified. Solomon inspected the lyrics carefully and was appalled to discover the lyrebird was singing a song about greed and ego, about vanity and acquisition, a song that very much pleased baboon ears.

Shaking his head, the nightingale said, "In five years he'll be for-gotten. Yes, he has understood the baboon reward system very well. Yes, he can sing exactly what they want and need to hear to go on with their destructive lives. But no, his songs will not be remembered. They won't be remembered because we don't care to remember songbirds who sing for the king." He paused and sighed. Then he added, "But we remember, with great and intense pride, songbirds who sing for those who live under the king."

The lyrebird finished his song and there was bewildering
applause. Soon he was back in prison polishing and admiring another trophy. Solomon stared at him and lost all respect. How, he wondered, could
a bird with such a powerful gift turn his back on the Forest? He then
swore that he would never go the route of the lyrebird and that he would
always sing what was in his heart to sing regardless the consequences.

The time came when the king tired of the lyrebird and the lyrebird was
subsequently forgotten.

Two guards stormed into the prison and surveyed the birds and,
seeing him for the first time, chose Solomon. Under an incandescent
moon, they marched him down to the courtyard and placed him in a gold-
en cage surrounded by banquet tables covered in nuts and bananas. The
baboons ate the bananas without enjoying them and watched Solomon
with interest. The king ordered the white dove to sing, and Solomon
responded by clearing his throat and beginning a song he had learned listening to the lyrebird.

"Not impressed!" the king stammered and fixed his crown. "I
have another bird that sings that exact same song. And I'm tired of it!
Have you any original songs?"

Realizing he had no song of his own, and staring at all the
baboons in fear, he shook his head.

"Not impressed!" the king exclaimed, throwing a banana at the
cage. He had bananas in abundance and so he felt at ease in his waste.
"What else can you do?" He asked and fixed his crimson robe.

Solomon thought about the question. "I suppose," he said, "I
could Hi-koo."

The king devoured a banana, then tossed a peanut in his mouth.
"Hi-koo! What is this! Never heard of it!"

"A hi-koo," Solomon explained uneasily, "is a mini impression of
life or nature. A testament to all that is simple and beautiful in the Forest.
We white doves hi-koo all day and in the evenings we tell stories. It's
what we're all supposed to do as doves, but I always dreamed--"

"I don't care about your dreams!" the king interrupted. "Let's hear
it!"

And Solomon, fearing for his life, did what he thought he would
never do. He dictated mini impressions glorifying the baboon way of life;

Solomon's Song

he dictated testaments to all things that perpetuated excess and greed; and he found himself surrounded by wild applause. The baboons prized the novelty of these little poems and that night Solomon automatically became the king's new favorite. When he was escorted back to prison, he had a lump in his throat and felt a great shame for the trophy under his wing. He smashed the trophy against the floor and considered himself a coward.

From the dark tunnel in the prison wall came the cries and agonies of some poor creature caught by some unimaginable beast. The birds gathered around the opening and made faces of compassion for the victim. But they were all secretly happy that they were safe and secure. When the gasps and screams subsided, Solomon went back to his corner and despaired over all the broken plaques and shattered trophies he had piled up into a little mountain of cowardice. Every night he told himself he would show courage. And every night he disappointed himself.

The nightingale pushed aside a few broken trophies and sat beside Solomon. "I wonder," he said, "if they actually think trophies make their oppression more bearable?" He went silent for a moment then he said, "I sure miss home."

Solomon looked at the tunnel in the wall. "Me too."

The tunnel was his only hope for escape. And yet the beast made escape impossible. He wondered what kind of a beast dwelt in the tunnel and all kinds of horrible images came to mind.

The nightingale asked, "Did I ever tell you I met a caterpillar?"

Solomon, snatched from his imaginings, looked to his teacher in surprise. "They exist? Mythical fuzzy worms that turn into creatures of unparalleled splendor and beauty!"

"Yes," the nightingale said. "They sure do. And I ashamedly almost ate her..."

Solomon recoiled in disbelief.

"But I didn't," the nightingale reflected. "I didn't because she had this smile that outright flattened me. My goodness, I could spend days describing her smile and the power of smiles..."

"Please don't," Solomon said with a friendly grin.

The nightingale thought about the caterpillar. "Her name," he said, "was Akiru; and she told me this incredible story about what had happened to all the caterpillars."

185

Once upon a time in a forest far away...

Solomon waited silently.

After a moment, the nightingale continued, "They aren't extinct as we all suspected. You see, they have a Silk Palace where they all hide. Now they live in total isolation from the rest of the Forest, and somehow they have forgotten the fundamentals of caterpillar existence. They have even forgotten how to become real butterflies. So instead of becoming real, they work for the leaders of the palace and are given glitter with which, if they work long enough, they can buy a caterpillar suit at the end of their lives. Everything is artificial and plastic in the Silk Palace. And to keep all caterpillars in their stations, the leaders pump caterpillars with fear about the outside world so they won't venture out to discover the way things used to be."

"Soon the memory of the way things used to be will be lost," Solomon said, thinking about the buzzard.

The nightingale went on, "It's just work, work, work for the caterpillar and at the end of their lives a butterfly suit. A far different life than they used to lead...now they are a spiritually poor lot, completely lost and out of touch with reality. They have completely forgotten their potential of becoming real. They have completely forgotten about their food plants. And Akiru, amazingly, had the courage to leave the palace to find her food plant."

Solomon didn't know what a food plant was and when he voiced his ignorance, his teacher told him that it was a very special plant, a plant that was different for all caterpillars and that this plant helped caterpillars change into butterflies. Solomon was amazed at this idea of one specific plant helping a caterpillar change into something so majestic and beautiful. He found it so strange that a creature with such potential would give everything up for glitter and a butterfly suit. He spent the whole night contemplating butterflies and the palace whose highly sophisticated system of mass control and mass amnesia could erase from an entire population the memory of something so simple and yet so magical.

Patient as a bee, Solomon continued to practice his lessons day in and day out.

Then one day, without realizing the change, a breakthrough occurred.

All the birds, except those jealous of his achievement, surrounded him and admired him as he sang a song about his journey, his lessons,

186

Solomon's Song

and how grateful he was to the Forest for having shown him the way. The song came from the heart and his voice was like heaven and all his courage, hard work, and determination had finally paid off. He sang with passion, and he sang with warmth, and his song was not forced or false, but was pure and honest and seemed to radiate from the depth of his soul. Music was no longer a dream but a reality.

Eyes closed, he lost himself in his song and was so deep in flow and concentration that he didn't notice his audience and was taken aback when he opened his eyes to find birds staring at him in stunned silence. He surveyed the birds and their eyes said it all. Some gasped in disbelief, while others were puzzled, perplexed, awestruck. He could see that they could not believe a white dove could sing, and sing so beautifully. He even wondered where that song had come from, and slowly he put a wing over his heart and breathed slowly. From now on music would be his other self. He could release his soul at any given moment without strain or effort. Then, all at once, the entire prison boomed with applause.

Only a few birds refused to clap. But those birds didn't bother Solomon. Those birds, the nightingale had once said, were zeros. And a zero, the nightingale had explained, was a bird who dreamed about doing great things but never did anything except spend a lot of time searching for every reason for why other birds could realize their dreams and why they couldn't.

But Solomon was proud of himself, and he knew his accomplishment. He had proven to himself that he was capable of the impossible and that he could learn anything he wanted to, as long as he invested all his energy and focus wisely and was willing to make as many mistakes as it took to reach a breakthrough.

The nightingale walked passed all the zeros, and the zeros had already begun their whispers and rumors and were feeding off each other's negativity. He ignored them and smiled. He then stood proud in front of his pupil and said, "You have fulfilled your promise."

And Solomon was in shock; he knew he had passed a point where learning would be easier and growth would be exponential. A great surge of pride filled Solomon's chest as he respectfully bowed before the one who had freed his heart.

The next day Solomon inspected the narrow tunnel and waited for the screams; he waited for the beast to be fed and thought that a fed beast would be far easier to outrun than a hungry beast. All he knew was that he missed home; he missed his family; he missed Hannah. And now he couldn't get the sight of Hannah's despairing face out of his mind. How could he be so foolish! How could he speak so coldly and harshly! He needed to make things right again.

The hummingbirds observed Solomon carefully, and they knew his plans. In the evening they hovered above him as he stared longingly at the tunnel.

"Don't even think about it," said the blue hummingbird.

"That is not escape," said the green hummingbird.

"That is certain doom," said the yellow hummingbird.

The screams began and the birds gathered around the tunnel and made small prayers. They made faces of empathy, but were each glad and grateful that they were in a safe and secure place, even though that place was a prison.

When the prison was quiet again, and the screams had receded, Solomon embraced his teacher and thanked him for being so patient and apologized for winning so many trophies. To which the nightingale replied that being a good teacher was the easy part and that being a good example was the difficult part. Solomon smiled, said he had been a great example, and then said good-bye with tears in his eyes. The birds wished him good luck, and, as he entered the tunnel, they shook their heads solemnly but admired his bravery.

ॐ

Feeling his way through the dark tunnel, Solomon moved toward the moonlit exit. Ahead, he could see a room glowing and flickering with torchlight. He supposed the beast lived in the room and that he would have to make a spectacular dash for the exit or suffer the same fate as the others. The sobs and cries began and Solomon froze with terror. Then he took a deep breath and took smaller and more careful steps. As he approached the room, the cries grew louder and his heart pounded faster. His legs shook like reeds in the wind and it was a while before he calmed himself enough to make a dash for the exit.

Solomon gulped heavily. Now he could only hear the pounding of his heart in his head. He peeked in the room and recoiled at the mere sight of a humongous and grotesque looking shadow against the wall; he could hardly fathom the beast that cast it. He closed his eyes and gathered his courage. He bent down and prepared to make a dash for freedom. In an instant he exploded toward the exit; but as he sprinted by the room he happened to catch a quick glance of the monster. The vision stunned him. He stood before the exit, bewildered. He had a rather difficult time accepting what he had just seen. Surely his mind was playing tricks on him.

Slowly, he crept backward and peeked into the room. Then and there he saw with great shock and surprise a tiny red ant sobbing and crying through a mini bullhorn. Solomon studied the ant carefully, and the ant continued his theatrical performance, not realizing he was being observed and evaluated.

Solomon approached the ant and stood behind him. The ant squirmed and flip-flopped over the ground as if he were being tortured or eaten alive. The ant was so into his role as victim that he didn't notice the white dove towering over him.

Solomon smiled and thought the ant could win an award for his performance; then he finally confronted him. "Overactor!" Solomon said.

The ant jumped back in terror, then dropped to his knees and begged for his life. The dove quickly assured him that he had no intention of making a meal out of him. So the ant introduced himself carefully and sat on a stone under the warmth of the flickering torch. Shaking his head,

Solomon could hardly believe a mere ant could keep dozens of birds imprisoned with a bullhorn. The combined power of illusions and fear baffled him. But this red ant intrigued and amazed him. So he sat down in front of him, crossed his legs, and asked him what he was doing living in a cave so far from his family and friends.

Goro became very uneasy at the question. "Don't judge me," he said, betraying signs of insecurity. "Not all hermits are crazy."

"I'm not judging you," Solomon answered sincerely.

Goro inspected Solomon's expressions for a moment; then he explained, "Buddy, I've been living in exile for years now. It's not that I don't like fellow ants-it's not that at all. It's just that sometimes you must find a quiet place to deepen your understanding of an issue. A place of solitude with no distractions so you can think single-pointedly on whatever it is you want to understand."

"And what is it you want to understand?" Solomon asked.

The ant sighed heavily. "Ants. I want to understand what is happening to ants. Everything is changing so fast! So fast that it's as if we ants don't even have time to think anymore. It's like we're living on accelerated time or something and we don't even have time to determine whether we're moving in the right direction." He sighed and stared deep into his thoughts. He continued slowly and meditatively, "That's why I'm here, I guess. I came here to think...to just think...it's almost like not being able to think is somehow part of the caterpillar plan...somehow done on purpose...to keep us distracted from all the crime and destruction going on in the rest of the Forest."

The ant's voice died away. When he spoke again, it was with sadness and concern. "Buddy, don't misunderstand me," he said. "I have no problems with fellow ants. In fact, I love them. Maybe I love them too much. Perhaps that is my problem." He paused and a great love for ants shone in his eyes. After a reflection he added, "I just love them way too much to blindly accept what is happening. Ants are going the way of the caterpillar and it's awful; so awful that it almost feels like the beginning of the end."

Solomon was curious so he asked, "What, may I ask, is the way of the caterpillar?"

Without hesitation, Goro answered, "To live poor so that you may die rich. To think about yourself only and forget everything else. That is the way of the caterpillar."

With a perplexed expression, Solomon repeated, "To live poor so

Solomon's Song

that you may die rich. It's a strange idea, don't you think?"

Goro placed his bullhorn on the ground. He looked into Solomon's confused eyes. "Look," he said plainly, "There is nothing wrong with the caterpillar way of life in moderation. In moderation the glitter system is perhaps one of the better systems of control any species has ever come up with. But in excess...in excess it is quite the opposite. In excess it is quite possibly the worst system that has ever existed." He paused, laughed sadly, then went back to his first thought. "But in moderation the glitter system is magical. It's a fantastic, fantastic system of directing communal focus and energy."

At this Solomon immediately thought about the florican and the manikin and how they, in their own way, had conveyed a similar idea. They had taught him the value and importance of knowing where to direct his personal focus and energy. If he had wasted all his focus and energy on negativity in the prison he would have never learned how to sing. Now he wondered if this could also be true of an entire palace, an entire species. Could an entire species keep itself from reaching a higher and better place by merely misdirecting focus and energy? Could reaching a higher and better place simply be a matter of directing communal energy in places that added to one's standard of living?

"It's a great system," Goro went on, "to get really, really good and positive things done...but...but...the whole system depends on the leaders. See, buddy, that's the thing! When the leaders are focused on community and Forest, building really beautiful things can happen." He laughed angrily. "But therein lies the problem," he said harshly. "The leaders of the ants and the caterpillars only care for war, domination, and acquisition. More, more, more, until, and you will see, there is no more, not even for them."

"Just like the baboons!" Solomon interrupted.

"Worse I think," Goro said confidently. "Even worse than the featherless chickens! Worse because the leaders of the Silk Palace use incredible tools and techniques to get everyone's focus on all the wrong things. When caterpillars are all thinking war, the magic glitter turns sinister and is used to create awful, awful weapons. Weapons you could not even imagine. Not unless, of course, you were focused on hurting, destroying and dominating. And how proud they are of their weapons! It's sick. It's repulsive. It's absurd. They can murder in great, thoughtless quantities, and yet half the Silk Palace can barely eat or afford clean air. And then their tools of mass deception actually convince the population that they live in a place far, far superior to any other place in the Forest. And the hunger of half the palace is kept secret." He thought a moment, then nodded as if he were one of the nameless leaders of the Silk Palace. "Guess they would have to do that for great changes would occur. Which would be good for many, bad for a few."

Solomon hissed with disgust and imagined a spiritually empty palace focused on war, acquisition, and domination. Did focusing on war and domination really use up that much magic? Did focusing on war and domination really prevent a species from reaching a higher place of existence? After considering these questions he thought the caterpillars were a fiercely confused species. He said, "Sounds like they live in the Stone Age."

Goro laughed genuinely and then became serious. "They do live in the Stone Age, buddy! Even if they can make plastic flowers and flashing lights, they are a spiritually poor, poor lot. And now they're using their tools of mass deception to reduce the entire Forest to their inferior level of existence. I mean, if you think about it, the only thing really progressive about the Silk Palace is their tyranny..."

"Tyrants like the baboons!" Solomon interrupted, thinking about the baboons and how they trapped and imprisoned birds for their entertainment.

"Oh no, buddy, far worse," the red ant said with a great seriousness in his eyes. "Far, far more sophisticated. Far worse and sophisticated because of their unbelievable system of invisible control. The baboons control through force and violence. Their tyranny is out in the open, and therefore, vulnerable. But the caterpillars control your dreams, your thoughts, your opinions... No, buddy, their tyranny is far more oppressive and destructive because it's invisible. Invisible and untouchable. Hard to destroy what you cannot see."

At this, Solomon thought about Saya. She had once told him that the greatest evil that ever existed was the evil that convinced the Forest it did not exist. "Invisible and untouchable," Solomon repeated. "How is it possible?"

"Look buddy," Goro said evenly, "I have been thinking on this for a long, long time. Believe me, it is very possible." The ant stopped to gaze at his shadow cast over Solomon's white plumage. Then he began to explain what he had come to realize in solitude. "Time is your true wealth," he said. "Time for family. Time for friends. Time for community. Time to think. But the leaders of the Silk Palace don't want you to think.

Solomon's Song

This is why they do all they can to own your time, to own all your focus and energy, to use your focus and energy to keep their select group in power. Keeping themselves in power is something they can only do if all our focus and energy is on war, greed, and acquisition. Take all that energy and direct it on harnessing the sun's energy, on food farms, on free medicine, on a better and improved glitter system and I guarantee you, you'll see some new inventions. Inventions you could not even imagine."

Solomon tried to imagine such inventions and stopped when nothing came to mind. He thought such inventions might be impossible and that to come up with such things would take quite a great deal of focus and energy.

Then Goro smiled and repeated, "Liberating inventions you couldn't even imagine." He laughed as he watched Solomon struggle to imagine such inventions. "Not unless," he said, "you were focused on peace and equality and Forest building. Oh, then you would see these things. And how scared they are of equality! It's sick. It's repulsive. It's absurd. And, buddy, the leaders will do whatever they can to keep caterpillars from real growth." He fell silent, then added, "And now they have to force the Forest to go their way, and think their way, so that these inventions do not spring up in places they do not control. The whole Forest has the potential to move to a much, much better place. But the leaders won't give up their power for that place. "

The ant went quiet, lost in thought.

"There's a lot to think about," Solomon said, and was now glad he did not live on Chichikaka or in the Silk Palace. He was beginning to sense that this island was a far more complicated place than he had realized. Things were so much simpler back home, even if doves were a little limited in their thinking.

Goro went on, "Time for family and friends to empower us. But the leaders don't want this. They don't want you to have any time to strengthen yourself from within. Because the stronger you are on the inside the less you need on the outside. The less you need on the outside, the fewer things you need to buy. The fewer things you need to buy, the less glitter you need to make. The less glitter you need, the less time they own. They want us running around like featherless chickens, each of us trying to be better than one another in very insignificant and superficial ways. They want to rob the Forest of its sacredness and make you only think in terms of glitter and their idea of progress. They want all to bow to the glitter God."

193

Once upon a time in a forest far away...

The ant paused to reflect on glitter, and Solomon shuddered at the thought of doves bowing down to some glitter God. He then repeated what he understood: "When caterpillars bow down to the glitter God, the leaders end up owning all their time."

"And," Goro was quick to add, "If you don't bow, they've got ways to make you bow."

"They've got ways...?"

"Oh yeah, buddy," Goro laughed. "They've got many ways. But their main way is fear. Fear is very, very powerful, you know."

"I know," Solomon answered, and glanced at the ant's bullhorn.

The ant sighed for the caterpillars. "They make everything that should be free in a truly progressed society only accessible to a select few." He went silent, his head fell; then he exploded, "Buddy, it's crazy! Water! Air! Education! Medicine! Things that should liberate the soul are used to oppress the soul. Ahhh...theirs is not a healthy community, not in the least. And you can actually see the sickness in their eyes, you see it in their smiles, you see it in their egos. Their souls are sick and exhausted. Sick and exhausted by their own greed, excess, and indifference; their indifference to all the crimes that their leaders and stations commit in the Forest to satisfy such a palace of greed."

The ant let out another heavy sigh for the caterpillars. "But what can a caterpillar really do?" he laughed scornfully. "They cannot revolt against the invisible. And if they live in the Silk Palace they have no other choice but to embrace the game excessively. Fear. Fear. Fear. Scared to get sick. Scared to get hurt. Scared to breathe. Scared of the outside. Scared of the inside. Scared everyday life. For the caterpillar life is misery, death is relief, and that is just sad. Buddy, if they get sick and don't have enough glitter to pay for medicine, they are left to die because glitter is worth more in the Silk Palace than life. Most of the time they don't have enough glitter anyway because they don't make a lot; to make a lot of glitter you need an education. But you can only get an education if you have a lot of glitter. But they keep education so expensive, expensive and inaccessible, so that they can make glitter-poor caterpillars fight their wars and do all their dirty work. The dirty work necessary for a palace of greed, and a caterpillar can get a 'free' education if he joins their war machine. So instead of paying for your education in glitter you pay in blood. You pay in blood because you're afraid to get sick. You pay in things that will haunt your mind for the rest of your life and curse your soul for the rest of eternity."

194

Solomon's Song

"I'm glad," Solomon interrupted, utterly disgusted with the Silk Palace, "it's not like that on my island."

"Oh, buddy," Goro said, "Hate to break it to you. If it isn't there yet, it will come soon. Caterpillars are the masters of exporting their way of life, and if not through force, then under the guise of aid. And if you don't need aid, if you do not need their air and water and food they'll make sure you eventually do. The caterpillars must make everyone in the Forest go their way. Because there can be no other way for caterpillars to compare themselves to. Eventually, dissatisfied with the way things are in the Silk Palace, caterpillars will seek another way, another system, a better and more compassionate and spiritually progressed system. But what will they find if everyone is just as sick as they are? Who will they compare themselves to? The sick will compare themselves to the really, really sick and feel a whole lot better about their system. An ulcer comparing itself to a tumor, they will be convinced of their superiority. They won't think anything needs to be changed. You can be sure of this: if doves offer free medicine or education, that system will be destroyed because it must be destroyed."

Solomon laughed. "Doves will never go the way of the caterpillars. That's just crazy, paranoid talk."

Goro saw he was in denial. He simply added, "If everyone is sick, then no one is. If everyone is a glitter slave, then no one is. That is why there can be no other way of life in the Forest. The discontented caterpillars should not have another option in front of their eyes."

There was a moment of silence. Solomon thought about the ant's words. He repeated, "If everyone is a glitter slave, then no one is."

Goro nodded and continued, "See, ants have adopted bits and parts of their system but not everything. Not the crazy things. For now we are still moderate and we still offer free education and medicine and you can be sure the leaders of the Silk Palace are already working on ways to make us totally caterpillaristic. I mean, they cannot have ants giving free education and medicine while caterpillars die in their wars to obtain the very same education that's so expensive and inaccessible. Ants cannot give free medicine while they let caterpillars, who cannot pay for medicine, die.

"Goodness, if caterpillars one day compared themselves to ants they might all want to become ants! Or make the Silk Palace's system resemble the ant system. So the leaders of the Silk Palace must do what they always do. Get to ant leaders and use the leaders to destroy their own system. And the leaders must find ways to make their free system fail. They must corrupt the ant system from inside. From inside is how it's done so no accusing fingers are ever pointed back at the Silk Palace. Then caterpillars come in as great saviours..."

Solomon studied the ant and found he looked pale and worn down with worry and thought. The weight of all he had been contemplating in solitude was riding heavy on his spirit.

The ant reflected on the Silk Palace and laughed sardonically. "The leaders of the Silk Palace poison the water and air making their plastic flowers. Then caterpillars who can't afford to buy clean water and air get sick and have to buy cures they cannot afford. So they put themselves and their young in debt. Because they are in debt they cannot go to school, and since they cannot go to school they go to war and destroy any species living a way of life that stands in direct comparison to their own. Silk Palace oppression, unlike the baboons, is all about mind tyranny and economic impossibility."

Solomon thought about all this. Then, deeply concerned for his community, he shook his head and said, "It will never happen to doves."

The ant replied, "Buddy, don't be so sure."

"I am sure," Solomon said firmly. "Because if I wasn't sure I wouldn't even want to return home! To do what? Bow down to some heartless glitter God?" He shook his head gravely, then stammered, "It will never happen, and I am sure."

"Well, buddy," Goro said, "Watch your leaders and protect your stories."

Puzzled, Solomon repeated, "Watch our leaders and protect our stories?"

"Yes, buddy," Goro confirmed. "Protect your stories and watch your leaders. Watch your leaders very, very carefully. And always remember the caterpillar way is not the baboon way. They are far more civil in their tyranny and will resort to force only as a last resort. Their assaults on other communities and cultures are invisible and almost undetectable." He reflected for a moment on the caterpillar way of domination, and then explained, "Caterpillars take over by corrupting and owning leaders, by promising leaders great riches to betray their own. With community leaders in their pocket, they get tight control of opinions, desires, dreams and laws, the whole while remaining invisible. They push their way without the community even knowing it, because they push their way through their leaders. Make no mistake, dove, they succeed by controlling leaders

Solomon's Song

and stories."

"They succeed by controlling leaders and stories," Solomon repeated to himself, but had a hard time making the connection.

For a moment Goro looked at his own shadow; then he observed Solomon's worried face. He continued on caterpillar tyranny. "Leaders, controlled by caterpillars, will somehow make sure all stories told impart deep, underlying caterpillaristic messages. Through constant repetition of the same idea, expressed in many different ways, your young will read about the glitter God, be made to bow to the glitter God, and will not value the sacredness of all things, nor the merits and sensibility of free education, medicine, water, and air; there will even come a time when their minds won't be able to conceive of such things as possible. And so, Solomon, an entire culture, an entire way of life will be defeated without anyone knowing there was even a war being waged. An invisible war; a scramble to own and corrupt leaders. The caterpillar way."

Then the ant continued about stories, speaking about their ability to influence an entire generation, and Solomon remembered all the stories that had marked him: stories of courage, stories of friendship, stories of communities working together. He then wondered if he would have even had the courage to leave his island had he been filled with stories of glitter, greed, and the endless pursuit of more. Would he have even wanted to? Perhaps if there had been the promise of making much more glitter abroad than at home. It was, he thought, a strange outlook on life and dreams. Then, suddenly, he began to feel a great sadness and a profound pity for caterpillars, whose dreams and lives were controlled by glitter; how those who controlled glitter used all their focus and energy for all the wrong things. Then the ant described how the caterpillars had corrupted and purchased ant leaders, and how caterpillars took over ant words, songs, and images until soon an entire way of life had been slowly washed away; the ant way had been replaced by the caterpillar way and only a few ant leaders benefited.

"Goro!" Solomon exclaimed, utterly sickened by the caterpillars, "That would be horrible! That would be awful. We are made up of stories, aren't we? Those that unite us, those that build us, those that inspire us, those that drive us... Why, if caterpillars owned dove stories they'd own doves."

Goro nodded slowly. "That's what it amounts to, buddy. A whole generation growing up with the wrong story in them. And if caterpillars own your stories you can be sure most will be about greed and excess and the uselessness of the Forest; very few will be about cooperation, community, and the sacredness of all things." He looked Solomon long in the eye. Then he added, "It's a really simple idea, buddy. The more greedy you are the more glitter you need. The more glitter you need the more they own your time. The more they own your time the easier it is to keep the cycle going; the easier it is to keep your mind off the Forest and what's really going on."

The ant paused for a moment as he considered his thoughts. Then he began to describe another type of story. He spoke passionately about reports and how caterpillars were taught to believe everything they read or heard in a report. He went on to say that this was a very clever way for the minority to control the majority, saying that the reports were essential to their control and that the reports were tools that served several purposes. They kept the masses silent in the belief that they were information rich, convincing caterpillars that all they would ever need to know about the Forest could be found in a report. They served to provide caterpillars with a lot of distraction, a lot of meaningless stories that would keep their minds off change or revolt while leaving out stories that had any true significance to the Forest, the Silk Palace, or the quality of their lives.

He said reports prevented caterpillars from investigating matters and issues further by providing the illusion that another caterpillar was going to do the investigating for them. And all this was basically done to keep the majority ignorant of Silk Palace crimes in the rest of Forest.

Then Goro described how the reports were being used to install a great fear in the masses, that fear of death and poverty was the quickest way to enslave the soul. He talked about how there were so many more sunsets in the Forest than storms, and yet the reports only focused on the storms. The reason, according to the ant, was simple. Fear not only enslaved and weakened one's spirit, but also pushed one to great acts of consumption. Which was good for a few. Not so good for many.

Goro then finished his tirade by saying the reports were the invisible tyrant's greatest weapon-the weapon that kept them invisible.

"The reports," the ant said, shaking his head with concern, "are weapons of mass deception. If you want to bring change to the Silk Palace, you must first go after the reports. You must first find a way to make the reports work for the majority and not the minority." He paused and laughed at the fact that so many caterpillars trusted the reports. Then he continued, "Remember, buddy, like everything else, tyrants adapt, molt, and evolve..." He considered his thoughts carefully. "Yes, tyrants certainly do adapt to times...to the point where today's tyrant's greatest success is..."

"Invisibility," Solomon answered.

"T=D+D+D!" Goro exclaimed. "That's the new formula. Memorize it. Take it back home. It may just save your island."

"T=D+D+D?" Solomon questioned, and threw the ant a confused look. "What does it mean?"

"Total Tyranny equals Debt plus Dependency plus Distraction."

Solomon memorized the formula to take back home and teach his community what he had learnt about the new tyrant. He knew awareness would be half the battle, should the caterpillars attempt to corrupt dove leaders, change dove stories, and get all doves to bow down to some glitter God. And at that very moment Solomon felt the pangs of separation and missed home. And though he appreciated the truth and wisdom of the ant's words, his mind was beginning to tire of invisible tyrants, caterpillars and the Silk Palace. So he stood and simply said, "I must go now."

"Solomon," Goro said, and searched the dove's face closely, "I humbly ask that you please do not tell anyone about my weapon of mass deception." And he held up his bullhorn. "Though I may not look appetizing to you, other birds may think otherwise."

"I understand," Solomon said, and was amazed at what one tiny red ant could do with fear, and he was even more amazed at the power of fear to drain the spirit of its senses: sense of confidence, sense of worth, and sense of power. But then, thinking he wouldn't mind company and conversation on his journey back home, Solomon had an idea. "Say," he said, "Would you like to return home with me? There is so much you could teach my community."

"No, thank you," Goro answered politely. "My place is here for the time being. You see, buddy, I have a lot to think about. I have to think single-pointedly on the word, 'malprogresso.'"

Though he had heard the word before, Solomon still didn't know what malprogresso meant. When he voiced his ignorance, Goro explained that the word was a weapon used against those who chose to investigate matters of the Forest for themselves without permission from caterpillar leaders. A word-weapon used to conjure up negative images and feelings toward any caterpillar who would dare criticize the Silk Palace. He said that to be described or called a malprogresso in the reports was enough to undermine your criticisms. When Solomon laughed at the idea of one word being so powerful, Goro said:

"Buddy, make no mistake. Malprogresso is the label the leaders have come up with to get caterpillars to mistrust and go against those who criticize their system. And the leaders have built the word up carefully and precisely. They have built the word up in their reports and they use the word against those who would dare threaten their profits.

"And the reports have made the word so strong that they can keep a caterpillar scared and silent even if he has something really, really important to say. The reports can call a caterpillar a malprogresso without having to prove his guilt or innocence. And once the reports say he is, he is! And once labelled a malprogresso his life in the Silk Palace could conceivably be ruined. Yes, indeed, once you're called a malprogresso the majority instantly assumes you're against progress even if you're not.

"Nope. They won't listen to you because they think you're against caterpillars as a whole and not just caterpillar crimes against the Forest. It's a clever weapon. They've got the entire population scared of being called the word, and fear of being called the word keeps so many quiet and indifferent-exactly how they need caterpillars to be in order to continue their crimes."

The ant paused and gazed off in the distance for a moment.

Solomon had never heard of such a powerful word, but was now fundamentally tired of dissecting the Silk Palace.

"It's genius," Goro continued, "Make up a word, use the reports to attach all the negative images you can possibly attach to the word, then get an entire population scared of being called the word. That, buddy, is mind tyranny at its best. That, buddy, is the way to make an idea or species or system untouchable."

Solomon nodded and repeated what he understood. "Create a word," he said, "that no one wants to be called; then call whoever criticizes the system that word."

"And," Goro added, "Poof! Magic. No one listens to what the malprogresso has to say."

"Pretty powerful word," Solomon commented as he slowly turned to leave. Now his mind was genuinely exhausted from contemplating the creation of weapon-words, the evolution of tyranny, the oppression of caterpillars, and the Silk Palace. He just wanted to go home and forget these crazy caterpillars. They were Chichikaka's problem, not his own.

Solomon's Song

So he said good-bye to the ant and moved toward the tunnel. And as the white dove walked out of the room, the ant grabbed the bullhorn and made horrible, excruciating noises that carried far into the prison where the birds prayed and sobbed for Solomon and wished he had listened to them. Solomon walked toward the moonlight and freedom, feeling a profound pity for any creature that lived in the Silk Palace.

Solomon leaped out of the mouth of the tunnel and admired the full moon with a free and relieved heart. He breathed the fresh air and turned toward the beach. But before he could take to the sky, the island grew pitch black as thick, billowy blue clouds covered the moon. When the sky cleared, the light returned, and much to Solomon's horror the baboons stood before him. He was surrounded. The king yelled, "Not impressed! Not impressed in the least!" And they marched Solomon back to the courtyard and locked him in the cage.

The baboons took their seats and attacked their nuts and bananas. The king told Solomon that he was tired of music and poems and that if he didn't entertain them with something new they would quickly make a dove casserole out of him.

Solomon couldn't understand how anyone could tire of music or poetry. But the king looked genuinely bored and unhappy, alive but somehow dead inside. Solomon supposed he had too much, too easily and without any effort. He was suffering as much-though on a very different level-as those with too little. One suffered in the mind, he thought, while the other suffered in the belly. One needed to constantly feel alive while the other needed to constantly stay alive.

"Well!" the king bellowed, snatching Solomon from his thoughts. "What will it be?"

Hesitating, Solomon said, "I will recount a story..."

"Recount it then!" the king stammered, and swallowed an entire banana without chewing or savouring it.

The award-giver dangled a little bronze baboon trophy in front of the cage to remind Solomon what kind of story it had to be if he wanted to achieve any sort of acclaim or baboon prestige. But Solomon was altogether tired of glorifying a way of life so detrimental and destructive to the Forest. This time he would take his chances. "If it is destiny that I shall be a dove casserole," he mumbled to himself, staring at the king with a smile, "then let it be. I am tired of these apes..." And so he decided to forfeit his trophy and tell his story. Sitting before the king and his subjects, he suddenly realized the invisible control and power award-givers actually possessed. He took a deep breath, thought about the ant, and began his story:

"Once upon a time in a Forest far away there lived a rabbit..."

At this there was a general sigh of disappointment and it was obvious the baboons didn't want to hear a story about some silly, random rabbit.

"There was a porcupine," Solomon said softy. He was met by the same response. He stared at the baboons and already knew he had to change the main character if they were to even listen. The character, he thought, he would tailor to his audience's needs. This he could do. So long as the DNA of his story remained true and honest to his heart. And so he closed his eyes and corrected, "Once upon a time in a Forest far, far away there lived a baboon."

And the audience clapped their approval.

One baboon yelled, "I love baboon stories!"

"Me too!"

"Me three!"

"Me four!"

"Get on with it!" the king ordered, raising a hand to silence the audience.

The award-giver wiggled the trophy and smiled a knowing smile. Ignoring him, Solomon went on with his story. "Now this baboon was no ordinary baboon. No sir. No sir, indeed. This baboon was a very special baboon. And do you want to know what made this baboon so special?"

The baboons stopped everything and leaned in toward Solomon. Solomon waited patiently.

"What?"

"What?"

"What?"

Solomon smiled," This baboon was so special because...because...

"Because?"

"Because?"

"Because?"

Solomon answered, "Because this baboon understood things other baboons didn't understand..."

Now each baboon searched within themselves for the things they believed they understood more than any other baboon. One baboon, not finding much, asked, "What sort of things?"

Solomon thought a moment; then he answered, "This baboon had foresight. This baboon had insight. This baboon had hindsight. This slightly more sophisticated, slightly more intelligent, slightly more evolved baboon, unlike any other baboon, understood...the power of birds."

Each baboon nodded inwardly and mumbled that they had always understood the power of birds. One baboon, not so sure about the power of birds, questioned, "There is power in birds?"

"There is great power in all creatures," Solomon answered, and the award-giver shook his head and began to put away the trophy. As far as he was concerned, only baboons had power, and he refused to award any story that suggested otherwise. But at this point Solomon didn't really care for baboon trophies or awards. As far as he was concerned trophies were for lyrebirds and peacocks.

And, in the end, all his trophies ever did was sit in some corner, collect dust, and remind him that he had allowed his poems, ideas, and messages to be guided by the invisible hand of the award-giver. By fear, want, desire, recognition, ego. He wondered what it would be like to act with no real end in mind. To act freely, speak freely, say something a little dangerous, but very honestly. In any case, he didn't need another trophy to remind him of his past mistakes and cowardice.

A baboon exclaimed, "There is power in all creatures!"

"Yes, of course there is," a baboon answered as if stating the obvious.

Another said, "I have always understood that!"

"Me too."

"Me three!"

"Me four!"

"Yes, there is great power in all creatures," Solomon continued, "but the birds are special, and this one baboon, this slightly more intelligent baboon knew that one day the birds would save the Forest from total desertification."

"The Forest will become a dessert!"

"Not a dessert!! A desert!"

"The Forest will become a desert!" the baboon corrected and immediately thought about his belly and where he would get all his nuts and bananas. He never once considered all the other creatures that would suffer from the desertification of the Forest, which might have had something to do with the stories and songs he was used to.

"Not a plant," Solomon said, "Not a tree. Not a banana will

remain. All will be lost."

Some baboons gasped at this, while others straightened their backs and whispered they had known about the desertification of the Forest for a long time now, and that it was pretty much common knowledge.

Solomon continued, "See, a certain bird was destined to sing a song that would spread a message of change throughout the Forest, but...well...the baboons were on a campaign of owning every bird for their own selfish pleasure...and...and...they had sadly caught and imprisoned that bird." Then Solomon digressed to describe the loneliness of each and every bird they had imprisoned and how each bird had family and friends who missed them dearly.

"Birds feel lonely?!"

"Birds feel pain?!"

"Birds have friends?!"

The award-giver was red in the face.

A few baboons sobbed quietly.

The king's eyes began to water.

Now the award-giver fumed and his face glowed with rage. He approached the cage and attempted to prevent Solomon from continuing his story. But the king was touched and curious and, feeling a little more alive, a little more stimulated, like he was learning something new about things he never really cared about before, he demanded that the award-giver hush up and sit down. Then he politely asked Solomon to please go on.

Solomon smiled at the award-giver and cleared his throat. "But as luck would have it the baboons caught a dove, a white dove, and this white dove would remind the baboons about what they already knew."

"Hey, you're a white dove!"

"You are!"

"He is!"

"I know!"

"Could be him!"

"Could be..."

Solomon said, "You must understand this white dove was a messenger of the Forest. He was sent to remind the baboons about the power of birds and how one bird would one day save the Forest. The plants...the trees..."

"The bananas!"

Once upon a time in a forest far away...

"The nuts!"

"Our bellies!"

As Solomon described the message, baboon eyes widened. They could easily imagine life without trees, but never ever without nuts and bananas. They stared at Solomon with new respect, and they silently wondered if he was this fabled messenger.

Solomon smiled at their bewildered expressions and continued, "But only one slightly more intelligent, slightly more sophisticated baboon would answer the messenger's call to action. This call to free all the birds."

Now each baboon thought he or she was that slightly more intelligent, slightly more sophisticated baboon.

Solomon stared at the king, then the other baboons. "And...well...I don't really need to finish the story. You all pretty much know what's going to happen next, don't you? I don't really need to go into the details, do I? This slightly more intelligent baboon is going to free the birds; then the chosen bird will get to sing the song of the Forest; and the Forest will be saved. The plants. The trees..."

"The bananas!"

"The nuts!"

"Our bellies!"

An uncontrolled cheer came from the audience. Everyone was rejoicing except for the award-giver. The king, baffled by the idea of freeing the birds, seemed slightly confused.

When the baboons settled down and hushed up, Solomon said, "After freeing the birds this courageous, slightly more intelligent baboon began to educate other baboons on heroism and sophistication. He spent the entire day convincing and explaining to others the inherent wrong in trapping and imprisoning birds. Then he taught them about the importance of sustainable harvesting and the great insult of waste. He taught them about respecting the interconnectedness of all things and how they were not owners of the Forest but mere caretakers of the Forest; that they were keeping the Forest strong and healthy so that future baboons could also enjoy the gifts they were at present taking for granted."

The baboons began to chew their bananas slowly, enjoying and appreciating for the first time, every mouthful. One said:
"Gosh, all you really need is one banana and few nuts. Enjoyment is the same."

"You know, you're kinda right."

206

Solomon's Song

The award-giver could not believe his ears.
On baboon laughed and said:
"So he freed the birds!"
Another baboon, a little incensed, retorted challengingly:
"So SHE freed the birds!"
"He!"
"She!"
"He!"
"I'm not finished," Solomon interrupted. "The birds were freed and the Forest was saved; but who do you think was the real hero of the story? The bird who freed the Forest? Or the baboon who freed the bird?"

Each and every baboon fell into deep thought. Solomon stared into their calculating eyes. Then the slightly more intelligent baboon of the group said, "The baboon!" And they all repeated in unison, "The baboon!"

The award-giver hollered, "This is an outrage!" And he approached Solomon's cage and snarled, "I'll see to it you never tell another story!"

Solomon beamed at him with confidence. "I won't have to."

Then several guards marched Solomon back to his cave where his friends were sobbing and crying, already conducting his funeral.

That very night a very strange thing happened. One by one the baboons woke up to free the birds. But one after the other they fought and wrestled with one another and knocked each other unconscious in a desperate attempt to be the only hero of Solomon's story. When finally only one baboon was left standing, she unlocked and opened the prison door and woke up all the birds. She told them to be quick about their escape as they had very little time. As the birds flew over a pile of unconscious baboons, they screamed, "Thank you, Solomon!" And quickly made way for home.

When all the birds were free, the slightly more intelligent, slightly more sophisticated baboon paced in front of the prison thinking of some clever words to lecture fellow baboons on the inherent evil of wasting the gifts of the Forest.

The nightingale walked by the baboons. He turned to Solomon with a smirk and asked, "A song?"

"A story," Solomon corrected.

Once upon a time in a forest far away...

The nightingale gazed at the pile of unconscious baboons and marvelled at the effect of one story could have on an entire kingdom. He simply said, "Nice." Then Solomon tried to imagine a thousand and one stories and songs all spreading and repeating messages guided and controlled by Silk Palace award-givers. Suddenly, he understood in one evening what had taken the ant an entire lifetime to understand. But he knew that it had been the ant who had opened his eyes to this truth about stories.

Under a sky slowly waking with dawn, Solomon and his teacher embraced one more time and said their good-byes. Then, just as Solomon was about to take to the sky, he heard a familiar voice amplified by a mini bullhorn.

"Buddy!" Goro said, "I've changed my mind."

Solomon whirled around and smiled at the sight of the tiny red ant.

Goro questioned, "I can do that, can't I? Change my mind?"

Solomon laughed tenderly. "Of course you can."

"Great," the ant said. "I'm tired of being alone. It gets lonesome being alone, you know what I mean?" And he watched the nightingale fly toward his home, black against the rising sun. After a moment, he sighed and said, "Sure wish I could fly."

"Buddy," Solomon said, "You can do anything you want!"

Goro pointed to Solomon's wings. "Buddy, I don't have any wings!"

Solomon knelt before the ant. "Buddy," he said, "when you have a buddy with wings, you don't need wings."

Goro shook his head, laughing softly, amused. He climbed Solomon's back and together they dove into the liquid gold sky.

ఴ

All morning they tumbled through the sky as Solomon sang an ode to the day and Goro tried, without success, to follow along. The ant went quiet when he spotted a fuzzy pink caterpillar sitting on a branch hanging over the river. The caterpillar held a blue cap in her hands. She regarded the cap for a moment and then tossed it into the river. Solomon, at Goro's abrupt silence, followed the ant's gaze and soon spied the caterpillar. They both whispered, "Akiru," and Solomon swooped downward and landed a few inches behind her.

Goro climbed down and stood for a moment, observing, disbelieving. She turned to them and smiled; then she turned back to the river and watched her cap being carried away.

The ant inched up to her. "You're Akiru, aren't you? You're that brave little caterpillar who left the Silk Palace…"
Akiru turned to them and flashed a smile like a star. "I am that caterpillar," she answered kindly.

"You sure have a pretty smile," Solomon commented, taken by her smile's authenticity.

"Yes," Goro added, "You sure do."

"So I've been told," Akiru said. "I accept your compliment and I thank you for it."

Goro sat beside her and let his legs dangle over the water, staring at his reflection. He had heard so much about this caterpillar and now he could hardly believe he was sitting beside her.

Solomon stood behind the ant and the caterpillar. "What, may I ask, are you doing here?"

She tilted her head back to see the dove. "Still searching for my food plant." She gazed back at the river. "It takes a long time, and I must be patient…but…but the river hopes I find my plant soon."

"The river?" Goro questioned.

Akiru sighed as she spotted a florescent purple chemical spill in the water. "Yes," she said, "I'm afraid the river is suffering and the water is dying and only those who take the time to listen can hear her cries." Slowly, she pointed to the chemical spill and a few dead fish floated on the river's surface. Then she laughed cynically at the caterpillars' idea of

209

progress and slowly her eyes began to water.

Solomon said, "Tell us more..."

Akiru wiped her tears. Clearing her throat, she explained:

"It's no secret. The caterpillars, in their excess, have become Creatures of Mass Destruction. They come from the Forest, they live in the Forest, but they actually believe they are superior to and separate from the Forest. With this idea of superiority comes the strange belief that the Forest owes them everything, when really it is they who..."

"...owe the Forest everything," Goro finished.

Akiru glanced at the ant. "These CMDs are killing the Forest and they don't even know it. They don't know it because of the reports. The reports..."

"...make them feel information rich, when really they are information poor," Goro said.

"Yes," Akiru agreed, "That is true. That's what I wanted to say. See, the leaders keep caterpillars information poor by making them feel information rich, and they won't let them know the truth about what is really happening to the Forest because such truths would interfere with their profits. Say anything against their idea of progress and they'll just call you a..."

"Malprogresso!" Goro exclaimed. "They'll call you a malprogresso and no one will listen to anything you have to say."

The caterpillar smiled at the ant and knew he had been doing some deep thinking. "Yes, ant. You are right. The slow death of the Forest is kept out of the reports and caterpillars are taught from a very early age to only care and trust what they read in the reports. Yes, it is true...since they do not know about caterpillar crimes and destruction or where their idea of progress is leading them, they do nothing to stop the abuse."

"Because they feel information rich," Solomon repeated. "The leaders silence an entire palace by making the information poor feel information rich."

Goro added, "And every other creature in the Forest suffers because of their ignorance. And they will not change until the entire Forest beats down the palace gate and demands for them to change. Then they'll wonder why everyone is so upset and the reports will blame everyone else for the great anger and not those truly responsible."

"Their leaders," Goro said.

"Their crimes," Solomn said.

"Yes," Akiru agreed, "the reports will convince them the Forest is to blame, and because the reports say this is so, they will believe it so and nothing will change. They will call everyone else in the Forest third-class malprogressos when they are responsible for reducing the Forest to third-class status, so they can hoard all gifts of the Forest. So they can have more than they need. So they can waste. They are such strange, lost creatures and like little children they will always say it is someone else's fault and that it is never their fault."

"The moon is made of cheese because Daddy told me so," Goro laughed out loud; then all at once he became serious and spoke slowly and solemnly. "The moon is made of cheese because the reports told me so."

"Yes, it is true," Akiru said. "If the palace is to change, the reports must first change."

Solomon shook his head and began to despise the reports and how they kept caterpillars in the dark, the whole while making them feel enlightened. Then Goro saw with horror another chemical spill, this time florescent green, floating down the river, patiently making its way to the sea.

Akiru regarded the spill, sighed, then said, "When the river is dead, it will poison the sea. When the sea is dead, it will poison the ocean. And when the ocean is dead, it will poison the sky." She stared at the sky and saw thick green and purple clouds in the distance. She thought about the awful poison pouring down from these thick clouds of waste; then in her mind's eye she saw the poison melting away all the color of the Forest. And she saw an entire Silk Palace sick and starving while their leaders lived in great abundance. She felt disgusted at the thought and continued, "And when the sky is filled with the ocean's poison, it will poison the entire Forest. And the poison of the caterpillars will return to them and destroy them."

"All because," the ant said, "they could not see or appreciate all the riches they had already been blessed with...and for free!"

"They are destroying the soul of the Forest," Akiru said, and observed more dead fish rising to the surface of the river. "Soon all will be grey, and not a creature will smile for a lack of green."

"They will reduce their lives to glitter," Goro said pensively, staring at the silver fish floating at the surface, reflecting the harsh sun. He thought about the ant and how they foolishly embraced a new divinity, a divinity that had the tendency to bring out the worst in ants. "They will forget the important things," he sighed heavily. "They will lose love and compassion and friendship because these things get in the way of glitter collecting. Then they are all going to have to pay glitter just to have a fellow ant listen to them. When the best one to listen to your problems is a friend or a loved one. They will lose love and friendship because these things cannot be reduced to glitter. They will lose these things because these riches cannot be bought, only earned, earned through giving another ant one's time, time which they will only see in terms of glitter."

Solomon thought about his friend Hannah. He thought about all the days she had wasted listening to his ambitions and his dreams. She had always been patient with him, kind in every intention, thought, word, never jealous of his other friends, never envious, spiteful, or rude, and always, always forgiving. Suddenly, he realized how she had shared with him her most valuable resource, and he felt ashamed for the way he had treated her. His dream had blinded him. Wanting to sing so bad, he had hardened his heart to everything that had ever been beautiful in his life. He had been such a fool; he shook his head at his own ignorance, and he was racked with guilt and regret. He needed to undo what he had done.

With a deep sigh, Goro continued, "But ants have gone the way of the caterpillar." He turned to Akiru. "They do not 'give' their time anymore, they 'sell' it. They have become so time-glitter conscious that they can hardly undertake an activity if there is no promise of glitter in the end. There are many other pursuits than the pursuit of glitter. And now ants, maybe not as bad as the caterpillars, but getting there, are living glitter-rich but spiritually poor lives; and only because things that build and fortify the spirit cannot be bought or sold or bartered, only earned, earned through purists that do not quite earn glitter, things like teaching, compassion, caring for community, things that are cleverly undervalued by those who control the glitter system.

"Now an ant who teaches, an ant who is in charge of our young and our futures makes less than a third of what an ant who cuts up and destroys the Forest makes. It's crazy! A teacher makes less than one who is responsible for the slow destruction of our future. It wasn't always this way. Ants once valued teaching more than any other pursuit. And good teachers built strong, empathic, reasonable ants. But those who control the glitter system don't want strong, empathic, reasonable ants. They want passive, insecure consumers. They want robots that ignore the pain and suffering of others..."

Solomon had a thought. He thought that the glitter system was, to a degree, like the baboon award system, and that caterpillars could control and direct thoughts and aspirations by undervaluing pursuits that fortified the spirit and by overvaluing pursuits that weakened the spirit. It was a thought. Something he would have to explore and give his time to and think single-pointedly on. But now, all he wanted to do was go home. And he missed home so very much.

Akiru considered the ant's thoughts on love and friendship. She had never seen things the way the ant saw them, and she saw the wisdom in his words. Her mind was begging to open up to new perspectives, and she began to understand things she had never quite understood before, but somehow always knew deep in her heart. "Caterpillars will feel alone and isolated," she said pensively, "even though surrounded by thousands like themselves. But the game will blind them to others and they will become sick inside, sick because of their self-imposed isolation and their excess and their inability to share equally all the gifts of the Forest."

"But that's what the leaders want," Goro said rapidly, "Friends, family, community-these things fortify us, these things build us on the inside. They fortify and build your spirit. And the stronger you are on the inside the less you need on the outside, the less you consume, the less you embrace their game, and the less time they can steal from you. The less focus and energy they can direct on their destruction and wars and greed. So all is done to isolate, weaken, and empty caterpillars. For this is a tried and tested formula to turn sharp-minded, compassionate butterflies into thoughtless, greedy little caterpillars in butterfly suits."

Solomon was impressed by this little ant and the truths he had uncovered about caterpillars.

Akiru gazed sadly at a silver fish struggling for life, trying its best to submerge itself, but always floating back to the surface. She said, "I never thought about that before..."

"Sure!" Goro said, "Look at their reports. My goodness! There are a million billion kabillion more sunsets than storms in life and yet all they ever report are the storms. So many great and beautiful things happen in the day and all they ever report is the darkness. Why? Why is that? Fear. Fear eats at your spirit like a termite on a tree. Imagine for a second they did the reverse. Imagine the change. Imagine the change in spirit and attitude toward life. If they would report all the good that happened every day in the Forest...well...that's crazy...it would never happen, as the leaders of the Silk Palace know very well how hard it is to control an empowered soul on the verge of true butterfliness...would never happen..."

Once upon a time in a forest far away...

Now Solomon felt mingled disgust and pity for the caterpillars. Again he wondered if he would have even left his island had he been so time-glitter conscious. Perhaps. Perhaps if following his dream entailed glitter, more glitter than, say, staying at home. "Poor caterpillars," he thought. "The potential to be butterflies thrown away because being a real butterfly doesn't yield glitter."

Thinking about the reports, Goro continued, "And when they're not reporting a storm their reporting distracting stories about glitter and greed." He fell silent a moment, then said, "The reports are controlled by the stations, the stations are controlled by the few, and it wouldn't be so bad if the few actually cared about the many. Great things happen with great leaders. Awful things happen with awful leaders."

He fell silent again. Then he turned to Solomon. "Buddy, those reports just make you want to hide under a rock and collect useless junk for the rest of your life. You may not understand now...but you'd have to live in the Silk Palace to really understand what I'm talking about. Live two minutes in their spiritually poor palace and you'll see... You'll end up scared of everything. Even life! So scared that you'll end up living only for retirement and a better butterfly suit than your neighbor. And you'll never smile again, or if you do, it will only be for the promise of glitter. You really have to live there to understand how bad it is."

Solomon found it hard to believe that caterpillars would so blindly trust something so obviously crippling to their spirits. And he saw how such reports, how such tools could be beneficial to those who wanted to make sure everyone's focus and energy was directed in the pursuits that would forever keep them in power. Then Solomon thought that the day they could put a storyteller in every home was a day caterpillars would have something to really worry about. Then, he thought, the control would be absolute.

Akiru tilted her head back and looked into Solomon's eyes. "The Silk Palace must change," she said firmly. She then turned to Goro. "They must not be permitted to destroy and poison the Forest with such impunity. And if they do not change, the Forest must force change upon them; and the Forest you can be sure has her ways."

Akiru paused and thought about the mysteries of the Forest and the mystery of necessary coincidences.
Goro and Solomon waited patiently for more.

"Right now," Akiru said, "The Forest is preparing a few for the special task of change. Each will be endowed with special powers of

214

communication, and each will use their gifts to bring about a special awareness and a new sensibility to the Silk Palace. And change, my friends, will not be a matter of right or wrong, but of life or death." She paused and gazed at all the death floating on the river. The she added, "Right or wrong can be debated. But death, my friends, is final."

Solomon was silent and still, listening intently. Then Akiru began to tell her story. She described her journey and her lessons. She talked about leaving the Silk Palace and how she always felt she had special guidance and the sort of luck only truth seekers had. She then spoke of her lessons, lessons of love, lessons of kindness, lessons of patience, and lessons of anger.

"Anger," she said, "anchors one from within and must be dealt with and subdued in all instances but one." She paused to reflect on anger and its uses to bring about change and justice. "The only anger that is ever justified is anger born of compassion; anger born of the inability to accept the unnecessary suffering of others; anger born from the inability to accept the unnecessary destruction of that which breathes life into our very souls. This anger you shall never have to apologize for."

The caterpillar paused to look carefully at the dove and the ant. She could see that they, too, were on their own journeys and how meeting them was somehow a necessary coincidence. "For the longest time," she continued softly, "becoming a butterfly was my only purpose. But now my journey has broadened my mind. It has taught me that becoming a butterfly is only the beginning. A new purpose has emerged within me, a purpose born of the realization that the Forest needs help; that if I do not help, no one else will; that if I turn my back on the Forest, everyone else will; that I must exchange my own safety and happiness for the safety and happiness of others."

Amazed at how similar he thought to this fuzzy pink caterpillar, Goro inched closer to Akiru and said, "I like how you think, caterpillar."

And Solomon stared at the caterpillar, wondering if learning how to sing was only the beginning. But then his heart felt lonely, and his heart told him he needed to return home and show all doves what he had learned. He wanted to show all doves what they were capable of. And, to a certain degree, he felt that the Silk Palace was a problem for this island and not his own.

After a long silence, Akiru said, "I am here for a reason. We all are. I am afraid it is the game that makes us forget about our purpose and our duty to others and the Forest. The game replaces the 'we' with the 'I' and I can think of no greater tragedy."

Feeling as lonely as a dove lost at sea, Solomon looked in the general direction of his island and wondered what Hannah was doing.

Akiru peered at the water a long time. "Yes," she said, raising her voice slightly. "I must discover my food plant and finish what I have set out to do. Once I am a butterfly I must not let my ego take over. I must use my blessings for the betterment of Forest or else maybe in another life the Forest will not waste those blessings on me." She glanced at the water and the fish were gone and were now floating and decaying in the sea, contaminating and poisoning other fish.

Goro inched a little bit closer and said, "I like how you think, caterpillar."

"My ego," Akiru said with a hint of worry, "will be my final test. What will happen when I do become a butterfly? What will happen when I do have power? Will I turn my back on the Forest and return to the Silk Palace and make lots of glitter? Or will I be true to the Forest?" She paused to listen to the steady hum of the river, and was happy it was still moving for she knew, like the mind, a stagnant river putrefied.

"The only thing that scares me is ego," she went on, "Ego, my friends, can rationalize anything. It can convince one of anything it wants...that it is your right to have abundantly more than anyone else, that it is your right to flaunt and waste and insult the Forest because you worked so hard to be who you are, denying all the invisible help and guidance and necessary coincidences you were exposed to." She sighed and her tone became sombre. "I hope I do not fail myself. I hope I do not fail the Forest."

Goro put a comforting hand on her shoulder. He said, "You won't fail."

Akiru put her hand over his. "I hope you are right."

Solomon had hard time understanding her worries. They almost seemed ridiculous. But, then again, he came from an island where community and selflessness was commonplace, and he had no idea what it was like to have grown up in a palace where ego was everything and glitter was the measure of one's worth.

But now he was deeply tired of thinking of the Silk Palace and reports and ego and glitter. The whole thing, he thought, was really none of his business. And so, thinking of home, he said goodbye and was not at all surprised when the ant decided he was going to stay with the caterpillar. They wished the white dove a safe and pleasant journey, and

Solomon's Song

Solomon vanished into the clear blue sky.

When night fell, Solomon had reached the beach and was watching a swollen sea brimming with millions of winking star diamonds. A strong wind began and the puffins, admiring the enormous waves, hobbled toward the water. The puffins swam into the heaving sea and waited for their wave.

"Ahhh!" a puffin hollered as he rode a monstrous wave into shore and crashed into Solomon. He stood wearily and, focusing on the white dove, exclaimed, "Solomon!" And he hugged him and told the dove how happy he was to see him. Then, noticing a change in him, he said, "Hey, you've changed! It's like...it's like...you've ridden your dream wave!"

"I have," Solomon said miserably.

"Then why so glum?"

"I fear I may not...make it home."

The puffin scoffed at the idea. "You got here didn't you?"

"I did."

"Then you'll get back. Have a little faith, brother."

"It's far..."

The puffin shook his head at Solomon's negativity. "Well, if you start off so negative, I'm not betting on you. If you start off so negative, I agree, you probably won't make it. It takes up way too much energy and focus to think so negatively, makes you feel useless, brother. Energy and focus is limited, brother. Don't waste it on negativity. You'll feel too scared and weak to accomplish anything."

The puffin fell silent.

Solomon thought that birds on Chichikaka had quite a deep understanding of energy and focus, as if it were one of the island's greatest resources, as if it were water or air or food. Now he began to understand why the leaders of the Silk Palace would want to use the reports to direct caterpillar energy and focus into black holes of negativity. If the leaders wanted to, Solomon thought, they could conceivably give the invisible message that the only safe thing to do in life was to work, consume, and collect.

"What I think," the puffin said, "we are going to need is a lot of positive energy to counter all that negativity." He indicated Solomon's head. "And if I'm correct...the only way to counter such terrible, terrible negativity is...is..."

"Oh no!" Solomon interrupted and tried to cover the puffin's bill. But it was too late.

"PARTY!"

And the puffins in the water responded in unison, "PARTY!"

And the puffins rode into shore on magnificent silver waves and broke into wild dancing fits and frenzies. Solomon tried to hide and say that he didn't want to dance, that he needed some rest for his long journey home. But the puffins weren't listening. They refused his every excuse, telling him that some activities exhausted one with positive energy; that some activities weren't as draining as he thought; that those activities that made him forget all his problems would exhaust him physically but empower him mentally. They told him that such positive activities would help him rejuvenate and achieve the kind of peaceful and restorative sleep he would need for such a long journey home. They told him that those who did not take the time to dance in life did not succeed as easily as those who did. They told him that those who did not dance did not grow.

And so, with no sense of time or time passing, Solomon danced with the puffins and forgot all his worries. When his legs began to shake and he could take no more, he found an area and fell asleep under a blanket of stars where his soul would quickly abandoned its limits and travel though time and space so easily that when he would wake up he would think of his strange, boundless journey as a mere dream. Reason and what he had been taught in school would not let him think otherwise.

When he awoke the next day, night was already beginning to fall and he thought he had never slept so much in his life. But he felt like he could swallow the ocean as easily as fly across it. So he walked by a few puffins who were still dancing and smiled. One by one they collapsed of positive exhaustion and began to snore. Slowly they abandoned their bodily prisons. For a moment Solomon even thought he could see a few puffin spirits dancing in front of the moon. He shook his head and thought these puffins even partied in their sleep. In an instant they vanished. He then gave Chichikaka, the Forest, and the puffins one last look and dove straight into the liquid silver sky.

Panting and exhausted, searching for land or anything to rest on, Solomon began to sink into the dark abyss below. He struggled without success to stay up, but with no land in sight, he lost all hope and soon dropped into the ocean with a small splash.

Solomon trembled in the cold water and swam toward his island, warmed only by the thought of his friends and family. He thought of Hannah and he wanted to tell her all about his journey, about all that he had learned, felt, and experienced. He wanted to tell her about the birds and the baboons and the ant and the caterpillar. He wanted to tell her about the Silk Palace and the reports and how they would have to keep a very close eye on their leaders to make sure they were working in the best interests of doves and not caterpillars. Caterpillars, he remembered, conquered a species by first corrupting and conquering their leaders and then their stories.

Now he knew, more than ever, he needed to reach home. Doves needed to learn and be warned about the Silk Palace. How he dreaded the vision of doves embracing a way of life that reduced them to unknowing slaves, bound by limitless and seemingly unbreakable shackles. He loathed the vision of doves bowing down to some glitter God. And the thought of caterpillars taking a caterpillar armada to his island made him laugh, then tear, then swim faster, much faster, much, much faster.

Suddenly, Solomon saw a white fin cut the water in front of him. He forgot all his worries to embrace new ones. He froze, and he prayed; he prayed that the great white beast would somehow miss him.
Time stood still, very still, and he was conscious of every passing second. All Solomon could see was the fin bright in the moonlight. When the fin lowered, Solomon sighed with relief and believed the shark was gone. He thanked his luck, and he hoped luck would stay with him for the rest of his life.

But just as he began to swim again he felt something swish under him. He froze in the black ocean, paralyzed by some nameless fear. He narrowed his gaze on the dark watery surface. Everything was calm. There was nothing but stars and darkness, infinite darkness. He thought he was only imagining things, that his mind was playing tricks on him. He thought that maybe the fin belonged to one of his dolphin friends and that he was just worrying for nothing. "Just a dolphin," he said and felt a little bit better about his situation, though not entirely convinced. "Yeah, probably just a dolphin." And at that very moment he saw a cloud of white emerging from the depths below. In an instant he gasped in terror as the deathly jaws of a great white shark chomped down on his tail feathers and he scampered backwards and yelled:

Solomon's Song

"Not a dolphin! Not a dolphin! Definitely not a dolphin!"

His heart skipped three beats and then beat faster than light. He leapt backward and barely escaped those long, razor sharp teeth. Then the shark was gone, and all was moonlight and silence. His heart pounded in the water, so loudly he thought all the fish in the ocean could hear it. Solomon searched the water and turned round and round frantically, not sure from which side the shark would attack next.

His heart continued to pound the ocean. After a long moment, the shark blasted out of the darkness and was on him again, leaping, snapping, chomping. Solomon screamed in terror and evaded every assault. In another moment the shark was down, down, down in the deep, hiding, plotting, preparing.

Empty. Weak. Exhausted. There was no more strength in Solomon and he knew the shark would have him on his next attack. But even though he knew and felt this, he refused to bow down to the inevitable force before him. Not without a fight, he thought, would this shark have his dinner. And so he closed his eyes and waited, calming his heart, sensing and focusing on the slightest ripple or movement. When he opened his eyes he saw the calm water bulging in front of him.

The shark blasted out of the water with a roar and fell on Solomon almost knocking him unconscious. Solomon pushed, kicked, and scratched for dear life. Twice he jumped straight out of the shark's mouth and twice the shark broke a tooth trying to snap his slimy jaws on the poor dove. Solomon flew a few feet, fell in the water, and the shark gave chase. Solomon did this several times until his wings gave up and the shark smiled and knew he had his dinner. The shark charged and just as he was about to close his jaws on the poor seemingly helpless dove, Solomon's eyes widened, he forgot his fatigue, and he willed his wings to obey. He leaped off the shark's nose and, with newfound strength and vigor, flew straight up into the sky.

Solomon rocketed toward the moon.

The shark simply waited below, and he smiled a horrible shark smile when he saw the dove's energy waning.

Solomon flew up, up, up. Then he said, "Oh, oh!" as his wings became stubbornly disobedient and failed him. He began to fall down, down, down. He looked at the shark directly below him. The shark smiled a smile of victory and opened his ghastly jaws. And there, plummeting to his certain death, Solomon felt strange. For some reason or another he wasn't worried or panicked. He sighed resignedly and thought about home, his family, and his friends.

How lucky he had been to have had such great doves in his life. Then he thought of Hannah and wished he had been given the opportunity to apologize. He loved her and was only sorry that he had not told her so years ago. "I will tell you," he said, as if speaking to her, "when you, too, are free."

As he fell blissfully, feeling as though he were on the brink of total freedom, he thought about how happy he was and how content he was with the life he had lived. He had done what he had set out to do, what he had dreamed of doing, and that was everything. He looked down at the shark's terrible teeth and laughed out loud.

Now of course the shark, hearing his laughter, and being particularly scared of death himself, felt terribly insecure at this dove's fearlessness. And so he thought that maybe the dove didn't quite understand the gravity of the situation. So he responded with a great, exaggerated shark roar and widened his horrible mouth exposing more razor sharp teeth.

Death came to all, Solomon thought. And he knew that he had felt, experienced and accomplished in his short life what most doves would never feel, experience or accomplish in an entire lifetime. He closed his eyes and felt ready to start all over again.

Solomon fell in the water and wondered what had happened to the shark. With weary eyes he searched the water and saw that the shark was being thrown into the air, tossed around the ocean as if he were nothing more than a toy ball. His eyes now closed, now opened. He struggled to remain conscious. One moment he opened his eyes and saw the shark soaring through the air, the next he opened his eyes and saw the shark crashing into the water. The last thing Solomon saw before he fainted of exhaustion was the shark exploding out of the water and disappearing far into the distance.

When Solomon opened his eyes, he thought he was in heaven. He lay on his back and stared at the black sky and felt a cool breeze. He thought it was awfully cold in heaven. He saw the stars moving real fast and every now and then he would hear the crash of a wave and be covered with ocean spray, which he found kind of strange for heaven. But when he rose, he quickly discovered that he was not in heaven at all; he was riding on the back of a killer whale.

Solomon approached the whale's head and asked in a weak, quiv-

Solomon's Song

ering voice, "What happened?"

"I told you," the whale answered softly, "I am your whale."

Solomon watched the sky and thought about his journey. Slowly his strength began to return and his spirit began to glow with the memories of all the new friends he had made.

Smiling blissfully he thought about the hermit and felt he now had a thing or two to add to his ideas on others and obligations. The hermit had once told him that realizing his dream was his only obligation; but Solomon's experiences no longer allowed him to believe this, although his ego really, really wanted him to. He felt that this truth was only a half-truth and that realizing one's dream was only half the obligation. The other half, he was sure, had something to do with others.

Yes, he agreed, we had a personal obligation to realize our dreams; but once realized, we had the other half of the obligation, the communal obligation, the obligation to share our lessons and insights and light with community; to help others champion their inner labyrinth and realize their own dreams. He wanted to tell the hermit that he needed to come out of his cave and be with others because if there was one thing Solomon knew for sure it was that others made him rich. And the things that make doves rich, Solomon reflected and inhaled the crisp, fresh air, were free.

After a while the whale asked Solomon what was so important on his island. He asked him what would impel (compel?) him to cross a dark and dangerous ocean all by himself. When Solomon answered, his friend Hannah, the whale laughed a beautiful laugh and said, "You must truly miss her."

"Words alone," Solomon answered, now sitting cross-legged on the whale's crown, "could not express how much I miss her." And as they approached his home, he gazed at the silhouette of his island longingly.

"She must be special."

"Special!" Solomon exclaimed, and his heart continued, "She is the most special dove in the whole world. Of course, if you saw her you would think she was just an ordinary dove, a dove like any other dove. But that would only be because you'd be looking with your eyes and not your heart. But if you would learn to look with your heart, you would see...oh my whale! If you could only see her smile, hear her laugh, watch her eat a mango, you would know how special she is."

Solomon lost himself in his thoughts for a moment, remembering his dear friend. Now he just wanted to embrace her and tell her what a fool he had been. He laughed at his own blindness and was thankful for his new eyes, thankful for his second chance, knowing others weren't so lucky.

"My whale!" Solomon said, "spend an hour with my Hannah and you will see how special she is. How she looks at you and sees you for who you are and not who she wants you to be. How she listens to you and really hears your words, all your words and not just her own name. Yes, my whale, she is a dove like every other dove, yet unique among all other doves. There is no dove like her in the whole world. There is no friend like her..."

The whale said, "Sounds like you're very lucky to have a friend like her."

Solomon beamed at the fading stars and knew his luck. The poverty of words could not describe his feelings, and all at once lyrics came surging from the inner depths of his soul. So quickly they came he didn't permit himself the time to think. Without warning, he closed his eyes and opened his heart. Then he began a song that soon brought tears of joy to the whale's eyes. The whale listened to Solomon's song and thought of all her friends, past and present, and felt good inside, really good. And, as she transported this special little dove into dawn, the little dove transported her back into time. Soon she remembered an old friend she had long ago lost touch with but was now determined to revisit. She would probably have to cross a dark and dangerous ocean, but her friend was worth it.

&

The sycamore ended the story there, and in the eyes of the porcupine he could see a white dove riding on the head of a killer whale, singing a beautiful ode to friendship. In other eyes he could see the story had already been taken much further and he could see Solomon was already embracing his friend or teaching the hermit the importance and value of being with others. The fledglings sprang up and ran wildly in all directions, each singing their own version of Solomon's song.

"My head," the porcupine jumped up and hugged the tree, "is spinning with hope. Why, if a dove can learn how to sing like a nightingale, a porcupine can learn how to build like a beaver!"

"There you go!" the sycamore smiled, and the porcupine made a dash for the river, determined to find a teacher.

Not too far away a fledgling yelled, "PARTY!"

Another fledgling answered, "PARTY!"

Then the entire Forest resounded with the word. Soon there was much celebration and jubilation for no particular reason.

Once upon a time in
a forest far away...

‹›

The elderly dove sat cross-legged on the beach meditating by a small campfire, listening to the surf with his eyes closed. Behind him, he could hear mothers calling out for their young, saying it was time for bed and not time for hiding or playing silly games like hide-and-seek. Suddenly, a soft voice startled him from his meditations. "Uncle Solomon," the voice came from behind, and a young bunny approached as Solomon opened his eyes.

"Could you please tell us a story?" said a doe, following close behind the bunny.

"A story?" replied the elderly dove. He turned to face a few dozen children staring at him with the cries of their mothers echoing behind them. "Aren't you supposed to be in bed?"

"Ahh!" exclaimed a fruit dove. "Who wants to sleep?"

A raccoon added, "Yeah, sleeping is for kids! And we ain't kids!"

All the children of the Forest sighed at the idea of sleeping when there was so much life to be lived.

Solomon laughed. "Your mothers will be upset with me if I-"

"No they won't."

"Not at all."

"Please, please!"

"Are you sure?" Solomon said. He remembered what it was like to be young, when life was his friend and sleep his foe; then he remembered how their roles had reversed for a time in his life, and all he ever wanted to do was sleep and forget that he was alive. He pondered this for a moment, but the impatience of youth wouldn't allow him to think too much.

"Uncle Solomon! Pleeeeaseeee stay here!" the bunny exploded with impatience. "Stay in the now."

A bear added, "Ohhh! Please! Please! Please, tell us a story."

A porcupine pleaded, "Pretty pleeeeeeaseeeee, with sugar and honey and cinnamon and, and, and sugar and honey and vanilla and, and, and sugar and honey and…and…and…" A hamster whispered in the porcupine's ear. "Oh yeah...and blueberries on it!"

"Blueberries!" Solomon laughed a hearty laugh and smiled. "Now how can I say no to a pretty please with blueberries on it?"

The children of the Forest shook their heads.

"Don't think you can."

"Nope, you can't!"

"Pretty please with blueberries on it is ten times stronger than pretty please with raspberries on it."

"Yup."

"Yup."

Solomon lifted his wing to silence them. "Sure," he said, "I will tell you a story."

At that, a fluffy owl whistled loudly. Before Solomon knew it, he was surrounded by a hundred more children: doves, cranes, manikins, nightingales, robins, bluebirds, cardinals, hummingbirds, dragonflies, beetles, turtles, and a few honeybees. He stared at the children and lost himself in a memory. But, as usual, the impatience of youth would not allow him to forget himself or them.

"Uncle Solomon!"

"Oh!" said Solomon with a start, gazing at all the children surrounding him, illuminated by the warmth of the fire. "Ahem... well...which story shall I...how about the story of Akiru, the brave little caterpillar who left the Silk Palace to find her food plant?"

"Too slow!"

"Yeah, too slow."

"We want action!"

All together, the children exclaimed, "Action!"

"Action," Solomon repeated thoughtfully. "Now which story would that be?"

"The one," said the bunny, "when you and your friends save the entire Forest..." the bunny finished with an evil, eerie voice, "...from the caterpillars."

At the word 'caterpillars' all faces became pale and terrified and many gasped with fright.

"Oh, that one," Solomon said and considered a moment. Then he concluded, "I think that story is a bit too long for this evening. In fact, a really good storyteller could keep it going all night."

The bunny quickly retorted, "But a really, really, really good storyteller wouldn't need all night."

Once upon a time in a forest far away...

Solomon smiled, then laughed out loud. "You may be right," he said and breathed in the fresh air. "Well then...where to begin?"

A porcupine yelled, "At the beginning! Uncle Solomon, don't be silly, everyone knows that."

"I suppose you're right," Solomon said softly. "The beginning is always a good place to start."

"That's why it's called the beginning," the porcupine said, crossing his arms, feeling pretty smart.

Solomon put a meditative wing to his head. "But what to start with..." He stared at the children of the Forest and watched the fire shadows caressing their faces softly. A long silence followed as all the children searched their minds for the best way to begin the story. Then a turtle suggested, "How about...Once upon a time...?"

"Brilliant!" Solomon said firmly. "Absolutely brilliant!"

The turtle raised his shy chin with pride. "Hear that! Brilliant! Absolutely brilliant!"

Solomon cleared his throat and waited for silence. When everyone was quiet and paying attention, he began:

"Once upon a time in a Forest far, far away..."

❧

Doves crowded the beach in droves and recited their poetry, waiting for the light that would soon dissolve the greyness and bring clarity back to their world. When the sun peeked over the horizon, a profound silence came over the congregation as they witnessed, with great respect, the sun rising over the ocean. Slowly, their spirits filled with divine and imponderable warmth. Every day it was the same, and yet every day it was different: a splash of orange, a wash of red, an explosion of yellow and, suddenly, an island of color. But on this morning the darkness would return much sooner than expected.

"Mummy look!" a squab said, and pointed toward and immense black monster speeding across the sky.

Hannah, the squab's mother, lifted her baby and ran toward the water only to stop short. She narrowed her gaze on the great darkness approaching rapidly. Everyone gazed up and whispered worriedly. At first she thought she was staring up at a dark cloud. But now she knew differently. Scores of little yellow birds were blocking the sun as they flocked madly toward them. As far as the eye could see, canaries rushed forward in some great panic.

Never in her life had Hannah seen so many birds. Their panicky cries were deafening as they charged forward. It seemed as though they were trying to escape something terrible and unforgiving. Her stomach felt weak and her mind was suddenly empty. She didn't know what to do or think.

When the cloud stormed overhead, she saw that the canaries were coughing and choking and calling out inaudible warnings to the doves below. Amazed, the doves smiled hugely and happily, and they pointed and shouted greetings. Then, when the dark shadow was completely over them, the tiny birds slowed and weakened.

The squab turned to his mother. "Mummy, where do they come from?"

"I don't know," Hannah answered, looking up into the darkness, thinking about her long lost friend who had claimed to have visited a faraway island tyrannized by caterpillars. Everyone scoffed at him; he was laughed at and imprisoned as a radical.

232

Once upon a time in a forest far away...

Suddenly, a canary fell and landed with a heavy thud. The bird shook violently and coughed up green muck. The poor little canary was dead.

The doves stared at the canary in horror.

"Mummy...what happened?"

"I don't know," Hannah answered thoughtfully; then she thought about her friend and the prophecy he had brought home from Chichikaka. He had said birds would fall from the sky in great numbers. He had said this and the leaders went red and called him a malprogresso. They instantly accused him of being against progress. At this, her friend, Solomon, went wild with accusations. He accused dove leaders of being corrupted by the caterpillars, and he warned all doves to keep a strong and critical eye on their stories. Dove leaders laughed him off, said there was no such thing as Chichikaka or caterpillars, and they immediately had Solomon put in prison for attempting to corrupt the dove way of life. She hadn't seen or heard of him since. But she knew he was up in the mountains, in some forsaken cave where all prisoners were kept.

Hannah ran with her squab in her wing and quickly found cover under a rock as doves stared at her strangely, as if she was overreacting.

And that's when it happened.

One by one, all at once, the canaries dropped like a hail of stones, and the doves scattered helter-skelter for cover. The light soon returned. The shadow was gone, and the sun shimmered over a beach completely carpeted with bloated yellow bodies.

The squab looked up at Hannah with tears in his eyes. "Mummy," he said with a shaking voice, "They all died...just like that..."

Gazing at the beach in horror, Hannah embraced her child and held him tighter than she ever had and tried not to show her fear. Now she remembered the entire prophecy, and she knew this was only the beginning.

233

☙

"Chichikaka is real!" Hannah spoke firmly to the elders as the sun began to set over a forbidding beach fouled by a great big mountain of death. She pointed to the yellow mountain and said, "What more proof do you need! Where did they all come from? Explain. Do explain. Where? Where did they all come from if not Chichikaka? Where did they come from, if Solomon wasn't...wasn't..." A sudden realization came over her, and her eyes widened.

At the mention of his name, the elders looked to the ground in shame.

Hannah nodded knowingly. "That's it, isn't it? You won't admit your mistake. He was right and you were wrong. He made it to Chichikaka and he learned how to sing and you called him a malprogresso. You said he was possessed. You called him crazy and locked him up and now you won't admit your mistake." She went quiet for a moment. Then she said, "He must be freed!"

They all lifted their heads and regarded each other with obvious expressions of worry. One of the elders said, "The dangerous one remains in his cell until we investigate the matter further."

Hannah laughed absurdly. "Investigate the matter further!" She indicated the mountain of death. Then, with the passion and determination only a mother understands, she said, "Elders, with all due respect, I have a family. I have young ones. One day they will have young ones, and you want to investigate the matter further? You remember his song, don't you? Don't you?"

Again, their heads fell.

Hannah stared at them. "Elders, if you're waiting for a sign all you need do is...is..." She gazed down at her squab, then threw them a searing look and lost momentary control. "OPEN YOUR EYES!"

All doves within earshot froze in disbelief. No one had ever spoken to the elders in this manner. They waited for a response or reaction, but the elders had no response or reaction, only despicable silence. A strange aura of regret radiated from them.

Ashamedly, they despaired over the sudden mess they were in and how secret circumstances prevented them from acting in the best interests of doves or truly investigating the matter further. Then one elder raised his eyes and tried to tell her a grey lie, saying that nothing was wrong, that these things were a part of nature, and that these things happened all the time.

When he finished his weak attempt to dilute the truth and hide the facts, Hannah held her squab and took two disgusted steps back. No matter what she said it would not matter. She now lived in a meritocracy. Doves would only listen to those with the right certificates, and only the elders had the certificates. She had no voice and felt useless. She pointed at them and opened her beak but no words came out. Finally, she collected her thoughts and said, "Solomon was right!" And she took another two steps back. "You were bought by caterpillars! That's it, isn't it? That's why our stories and poems are becoming greedier and greedier! That's why there is so much discontent among doves. Oh, my goodness, he was right..."

"Don't be foolish! Caterpillars don't exist," one elder shot back.

"Mummy...what's happening?"

She continued to back away. "He warned us to watch our leaders...and that's when you locked him up!" She went to continue, but no words came out. Tears trickled down her cheeks as she grabbed her little one and vaulted straight into the thick black sky.

Under a dark, cloudy sky, Hannah soared toward the mountain and landed on a rocky cliff. In front of the prison, a guard looked up and saw Hannah approaching him.

She faced him strongly and said, "I am not asking."

"Hannah," he sighed disappointedly, "I'm under strict orders not to let you through."

She stared at the ground and thought of her little one. She sighed heavily. Then she raised her gaze and, pronouncing every syllable, repeated, "With all due respect to the uniform, I am not asking."

"My orders..."

Hannah said firmly, "I don't care about your orders. I don't care about these new laws and these new technicalities. I don't care about the elders! They put us in this mess. Those we trusted put us here and now they want to tell us everything is all right." She shook her head and let her words sink into the guard. Then her voice softened and she said, "You heard about what happened today..."

He hung his head.

After a short silence, Hannah let out a little laugh. "They are debating whether there is a problem. You understand...our future is not debatable."

He nodded solemnly; then he thought about his own young ones.

She continued, "You have heard Solomon speak of the Silk Palace, of the caterpillars and how they conquer other communities by corrupting their leaders..."

The guard looked up at her. "You don't think..."

"I'm not willing to wager," she answered rapidly. "And if I must wager, well, I'd rather believe in Solomon and be wrong than believe in the elders and be wrong."

The guard sighed again and thought about this. If Solomon was wrong, and everything was done to prevent the slow death of the Forest, then the worst that would happen is their island would become a little greener, a little cleaner. But if the elders were wrong, and nothing was done to prevent the slow death of the Forest, their very existence was at stake. Suddenly, the issue was no longer grey. The guard sighed deeply

Once upon a time in a forest far away...

and shook his head. "Well," he said, "I'm thinking it's time for my break..." And he walked away, dropping his keys with a loud clang.

"Solomon," Hannah called out as she opened the creaky prison door. She stepped inside the dank and miserable torch-lit cave. Then she approached a dark shadow hidden in the far corner. "Solomon," she whispered, "It's me...Hannah..."

"Go away!" a harsh voice came from the shadows.

"No," she answered, "I will not go away." She approached him slowly and saw that he was scrunched up in a ball, covered in dust, holding his legs, cursing. She sighed heavily. It was difficult to see her old friend like this. "Everything you said, Solomon, is happening. Everything we didn't listen to is coming true..." She kneeled down in front of him and went to touch his wing, but he shoved her away.

"Let it happen!" His eyes were filled with anger, not the kind that impelled one to pursue justice, but the kind that ate one up inside. "What do I care?"

"Oh, Solomon," she took his wing, almost forcefully. "Do care. Do, do, do care... Care, care, care, and never stop caring."

Solomon pulled his wing away. "They locked me up! And forgot me..."

She took his wing again. "Oh dear friend, I know they did. They were wrong, and whether they want to accept it or not, they need you...they need you now more than ever."

"I hate them!" he bellowed, and tried to pull his wing away, but his friend held on tightly.

Hannah shook her head and refused to let go. "You don't hate them, Solomon."

"I do!"

"No," she continued, "You hate what they've done to you, not them. And there is a difference."

"They left me here to rot!" he cried, and now tears spilled from his eyes.

She hugged him and said, "They didn't know any better, Solomon. Please don't let their mistake defeat you. Don't let their mistakes change you on the inside-destroy all that goodness and love that burned so fiercely for the flock. Now, more than ever, I need the real

Once upon a time in a forest far away...

Solomon, the caring Solomon, the Solomon who sobbed at the mere mention of an injustice, even if that injustice occurred a long time ago in a land far, far away. Oh, friend, I am here begging for that Solomon. I need that Solomon. My family needs that Solomon..."

She released him and rose slowly.

Silently, Solomon stared up at her, tears flowing down his cheeks like a river of anguish.

Hannah took in a deep breath. "If the Solomon who feels and cares is no more," she said gently, "then the Solomon I know and love is no more." She then turned and made her way toward the outside.

At the entrance, she paused. She turned to him one last time and said, "I'm leaving the door open. It's open for the Solomon I used to know. The Solomon who cared about others. The one who used to always say that the pain of one is the pain of all. But I ask that you please leave the indifferent Solomon in this cave. Leave him here to dry up and turn to stone. There is no room for him in a world that needs love, difference, and action." And with those words she was gone.

Tears continued to stream down Solomon's cheeks, and he scrunched his wings with uncontrollable emotion and slammed the wall. Suddenly, he gasped and sobbed violently. Deep in his heart, he knew she was right.

As soon as Solomon stepped outside he heard the shouts. A group of guards rushed toward him screaming that the lunatic was escaping. Solomon heaved a deep breath and let out a heavy sigh. "I do not despise you...I despise what you are doing to me." Then he took to the sky and flew toward the beach. The guards gave chase and only turned back when he flew out over the water. They were sure he was crazy enough to lead them across an entire ocean. He was.

"My whale!" Solomon shouted, scanning the ocean, calling for his old friend the killer whale. But he had only succeeded in attracting a great white shark. "Not you again," he said, gazing at the shark who waited for the dove to plop into the ocean. "My whale! My whale!" he continued in a panic and began to sink unwillingly. Gradually, his wings grew tired. He gazed down at the shark and the shark smiled up at him. "I hate sharks!" he said, and plopped into the ocean. In an instant the shark was on him, and Solomon ran on the water trying to fly away. The shark lunged at the dove with its jaws wide open. When Solomon looked back he screamed, for the teeth were about to chomp down on him. But the mouth did not have time to close. Before the shark knew what was happening, a killer whale battered the beast here and there, and Solomon was grateful and singing a song about how splendid it was to have a killer whale as a friend.

"It's been a while," said the whale.

Solomon lay on the whale's back and rested. "It's a long, sad story," he said, and went quiet. Then he chose to accept what had happened to him. To accept and not dwell. To focus on what he had to do, on what he could change, and he absolutely refused to waste a single drop of his energy on what he could not change. "What's important," he continued, "is that I'm back."

"Glad to hear it!" the killer whale said joyfully. "Where to, captain?"

"Chichikaka..."

"Ohhh," the killer whale said gravely. "Can't do it. Can't approach that island anymore. Anything that does never returns."

Solomon was confused. "I don't understand."

The killer whale replied, "It's not hard to understand. The water surrounding the island is dead, and dead water no longer sustains life. Don't kid yourself, Solomon, Chichikaka is not what it used to be. Strange things happen there. Last I heard the island was shrouded in a thick, perpetual grey fog. There is no night or day, and all that is left is rubble. Not the same place you left years ago."

Solomon shook his head sadly. "That is precisely why I must return. I must put an end to the Silk Palace before this darkness reaches home." He patted the whale gently. "How far can you take me?"

The killer whale took a moment to calculate. "Not far, Solomon. Not far at all. The dead water is spreading...spreading fast...I'm afraid one day the whole ocean will die and my babies--"

"Babies!" Solomon quickly interrupted.

"Twins!" the whale said, "And they know all about you and how you wouldn't turn your back on their mother."

Solomon said, "And now I won't turn my back on her again, and that is exactly why she must bring me as close to Chichikaka as she can."

"If you fall in the dead water," the whale said gravely, "you will perish."

Solomon stood and stared ahead. "I won't fall."

"But if..."

"If I fall," Solomon cut in, "I'm afraid we will all perish."

"It's worse than I thought," the whale said, and she thought about her twins and became terribly worried. "Solomon," she said, almost in a panic, "My babies...will they be...?"

"I won't fall," Solomon said.

"I hope and pray," the whale said. "I have lost too many friends already."

Solomon patted her back reassuringly. "I will do my best."

"And I will do mine!" the whale promised and accelerated.

"That's all I ask," Solomon said. "That's all I ask."

The whale thought of her young ones and sped toward the island like their lives depended on it. It did.

"This is as far as I go," the whale said apologetically, as they were still a great distance from Chichikaka. A strange bubble of grey enshrouded the island.

"It will have to do," Solomon said, and almost fainted when the acrid odour of sewage hit him like a plank across the face. He coughed and made a face of disgust and asked, "What's that smell?"

The whale answered, "That, Solomon, is the smell of dead water. It will worsen as you approach the island, and at times it will be unbearable."

Once upon a time in a forest far away...

"Horrible!" Solomon declared, with his wing over his beak, trying his best to hold his breath. Slowly, he felt the air weakening him, draining him of strength and spirit, and only now did he realize the importance of one of the Forest's great gifts. He thought of his island and cringed. He knew it was only a matter of time before this air became his air, the air he had always taken for granted.

And so, with a deep sense of urgency, he said good-bye to his friend and made way for the greyness.

The whale watched Solomon with worry. She sighed for the dove as she watched him weaken and descend toward the water. "You can't fall," she muttered. "You can't fall!"

But Solomon was indeed falling.

"No! No! No!" she shouted, and made a quick and irreversible decision. Thinking only of the future, she took a deep breath and thundered toward Solomon.

When Solomon was just about to touch the water a huge black and white tail broke the surface and batted him to safety. Unconscious, he soared over the water and landed on the skeleton-covered beach.

&

When Solomon woke up, he was shocked to see the whale wheezing on the beach. He cried out loud and struggled through the skulls and bones to help his friend. "My whale! My whale! No! Ahhh...pleeeaseee nooo..."

The whale opened her eyes and smiled. She was glad to hear his voice. She thought she might have killed him by whacking him so hard.

"Oh noooo..." Solomon gasped and tried desperately to push her back into the water.

"Not this time kid," she said softly. "Not this time..."

But Solomon refused to give up, and he pushed and pushed until he could push no more.

When he realized the certainty of her situation, he stood in front of her with his head down. "I'm sorry," he said. "I'm so sorry."

She smiled faintly. "That's three," she said and sighed with pain. "And...and if I can help from above...I'll make it four..."

"That's not fair!" Solomon half laughed, half sobbed. "How will I ever repay you?"

"My babies," she replied. "Make sure...make sure they always have a home."

Solomon put a wing over his heart. "I swear it!"

And the killer whale released her last breath and left the world peacefully. All her hope in one little dove, she had done her best to make sure the world she was leaving would eventually be a better place for her young ones.

Solomon staggered backward and held back tears. He wished it didn't have to be this way, and the grey atmosphere became greyer and thicker. Solomon felt his throat prickle a little, then a lot. Soon he was struggling for air. And though he took in great quantities of air, the quality was so poor that every ten deep breathes on Chichikaka was like one shallow breath on his island. "How did it come to this?" he asked himself, and then fainted from a lack of oxygen.

"Your water or your life!"

A porcupine loomed over Solomon.

Still a bit drowsy, Solomon opened his eyes. "My what? Or my what?"

With his quills at the ready, the porcupine demanded, "Your water or your life!"

Solomon stood slowly, and the porcupine took a cautious step backward.

"Watch it!" the porcupine warned. "My spikes are dipped in dead water!" And he indicated his back.

Solomon said, "But I haven't any water!"

The porcupine narrowed his gaze, "Soooo…you want to be like that!"

"Like what?"

"Like that!"

"Like what?"

"Like that!"

"Like what, that?! What do you mean? What are you talking about?"

The porcupine pointed an angry finger at Solomon. "Okay! Be like that!" And he took a threatening step forward.

"I haven't any water," Solomon pleaded and took a careful step back.

The porcupine wasn't listening anymore. He circled Solomon slowly and waited for just the right moment to attack. When he felt ready, he turned abruptly and exposed his deadly spear-like quills. With a wild war cry, he charged backward. Solomon leaped high, glided over the porcupine, and landed right behind him. The porcupine turned with a scream and charged again. But, unable to see where he was going, he stumbled and tripped over a rock while Solomon found it extremely difficult to hide his pleasure at the porcupine's clumsiness. Solomon glided over him and begged him to stop. But the porcupine wouldn't stop, even though he found himself on the ground more often than he would have liked, always cursing and admonishing himself for still not having mastered the art of charging backward.

Solomon had little difficulty evading the porcupine's every attack. But it happened that while backing up, the dove got his foot caught in a tangle of weeds and vine. He tried to yank his foot out desperately, but to no avail.

"Haaa!" the porcupine yelled. "Now where will you run to?" And he stomped his foot menacingly as he closed in on the dove.

Solomon tried to yank his foot free. "I don't have water!"

"Too late for that!" the porcupine rebuked, and turned to expose his weapons. But as soon as he attempted to launch himself at the trapped dove the ground held him back. "What the...?" He looked down and suddenly realized he was caught in something awful. "Aarghhh!" he howled in surprise as he felt himself stuck in a kind of mud. Upon further inspection he gasped dreadfully as he realized he was stuck in a deadly trap of quicksand. He struggled and struggled to free himself, and as he struggled he sank deeper and deeper. Then he cried and begged Solomon for help and apologized for being so crass, rude, and demanding.

Solomon freed his foot and debated whether or not he should help this porcupine. When the porcupine was waist deep in quicksand, Solomon couldn't take his cries anymore, and he decided that he couldn't let this helpless porcupine perish because of some slight misunderstanding. So he hovered above him and tried to pull him out. But the air was more than he could bear. He felt fatigued and weak and could hardly budge the poor panicky porcupine.

Now the porcupine was neck deep in quicksand with one arm extended to the heavens. But there was nothing Solomon could do. It was hopeless. He didn't have the strength or energy to pull this heavy porcupine out of his mess. So he sat down and his head sank sadly. Without looking at the porcupine, he said, "I'm sorry." His eyes gazed at the ground, at the rubble, the weeds and the vine. He stared at the vine, then the hand, the vine, then the hand. The porcupine sank and sank. Soon only his dark arm could be seen.

A realization struck Solomon. It was the porcupine's last hope. Without a second to lose, Solomon grabbed the longest and toughest vine. He jumped up in the air and hovered over the porcupine and placed the vine in the steadily failing hand. The hand gripped the vine and pulled, first weakly, then fiercely. Soon the other hand burst out and grabbed the vine. With a deep breath for life, the head quickly followed.

"I am the last porcupine," Terku said to Solomon as they sat on a boulder staring at the seemingly endless desert of dunes and rubble. "We wouldn't embrace the caterpillar way of life, so they found another way." He sighed sadly, then added, "We wouldn't give up our land and we even told them that the land wasn't ours to chop up and give away for short-term gain. Our elders told them that we had simply borrowed the land from generations yet to be born. We told them we were merely the caretakers and not the owners. That to destroy the land and the Forest was a crime against our children and future grandchildren."

Solomon was quiet as he listened to the porcupine, waiting for more. After a moment, the porcupine continued. "They laughed at us. They called us foolish and romantic and said there was no more room for our kind anymore, that our kind would soon be extinct. They said everything could be bought, and what couldn't be bought could be stolen through clever laws and treaties. But our leaders laughed at them and were firm. They swore there wasn't a porcupine among them that would betray the tribe or the Forest. And there wasn't."

Solomon waited for more, his eyes wide with interest. The porcupine stared at the emptiness all around him and shook his head. "Then they did to us what they do to those they cannot change. They declared war on us, but they had the skunks do all their dirty work. They gave skunks all the glitter and weapons and training they needed to eradicate the Forest of porcupines... Then...well, then the poor skunks were given clothing and blankets steeped in horrible diseases that only the caterpillars had cures for. They died horribly, and only a few survived, and those who survived formed a resistance against the caterpillars. Now the caterpillar's greatest enemy is the enemy they trained, armed...created...."

Solomon's head fell gravely. He couldn't believe what he was hearing. He even wondered how the general population of the Silk Palace would allow such a thing to happen. Then he remembered that they wouldn't know; their reports would keep them in the dark; their reports would keep caterpillars information poor by making them feel information rich. Solomon looked up at the porcupine and asked, "Well, why'd they kill the skunks?"

Once upon a time in a forest far away...

"The skunks wouldn't give up some land for one of their dams," Terku explained carefully, "The skunks got greedy cause that's what the caterpillar way does to you...and the skunks demanded lots more glitter and weapons. But caterpillars don't bargain! They exterminate! They exterminate because it's cheaper and faster. Then they wonder why the entire Forest hates them! They call the Forest savage, yet they are the only savages in the Forest."

Solomon listened to the porcupine, but didn't blame all the caterpillars. And he certainly did not share the same anger toward caterpillars as this porcupine did. In fact, he only blamed the leaders, the invisible caterpillars that no one heard about. They were the savages. And if the ordinary caterpillar was to be blamed for anything, it was solely for allowing the ignorance that inspired indifference to continue, for it was this indifference that permitted the leaders to act with such disregard and impunity toward the Forest.

Terku scrunched his fist into a ball. "Dams exist solely to rob the poor and gift the rich! I don't know how they convinced leaders all over the Forest to agree to dams...well...I guess I know how they did it; I guess I just can't believe they did! Dams stop the flow of the river and displace thousands upon thousands of villages. They destroy the land and cause uncontrollable floods and earthquakes...the imprisoned water putrefies and spreads all kinds of diseases. And this is all proven, proven even by their own experts; and yet they still build 'em. And why build a dam? 'Cause the one who controls the water controls the entire Forest."

"I can't believe it," Solomon said.

"Believe it," Terku retorted strongly. "I've been here a long while. I have seen it all! And I'm not bombarded by the lies of the Silk Palace. They reduced the entire Forest to a slave factory so that a few can live like kings in the Silk Palace. And notice I only said a few. More than half of their palace is filled with caterpillar slaves working for basics, distracted by puppet shows, always worried they're gonna fall sick or something. It's so berserko!"

There was a long silence between the two of them. Then, breaking the silence, Terku said, "Water is scarce and controlled and that is how caterpillar leaders control the inhabitants of the entire Forest. All the fresh water is funnelled to the Silk Palace and then sold back to the Forest at a price only the rich can afford." He laughed out loud, then screamed at the great joke being played on the entire Forest. "Everyone working just to buy a little water. It's so berserko I want to scream! It's so beserko that those who live outside the palace would kill for a mere drop of water."

"Yes," Solomon said firmly, "I know."

Terku sighed with shame. "I'm sorry about that."

"The leaders of the palace are to blame," Solomon responded, not blaming him for the acts of savagery the caterpillars had reduced him to.

"But tell that to a caterpillar and they'd think you were crazy."

Solomon agreed with a laugh. "Yes, their ignorance is absolute." And then he stopped laughing abruptly as their ignorance was no laughing matter.

"Growing up," Terku lamented, "surrounded by so much green and fresh water, I never would have guessed in a million years that things would have turned out like this." He sighed and another silence fell over them. "Sometimes," Terku said, breaking the silence, "I discover things caterpillars have done to the Forest and I just go...I go beserko inside and...and...and I just want to scream my very soul out 'cause I just can't believe anyone or anything would commit such crimes." He turned to Solomon and asked, "Ever get like that? So upset and confused all you wanna do is scream...scream so loud to wake yourself from the nightmare...only it ain't a nightmare and the more you scream the more you realize it ain't a nightmare, and the more you realize it ain't a nightmare the more you scream...and you're screaming and screaming for all the injustices that ever were, are, or will be. Ever get like that?"

Solomon shook his head and regarded the porcupine with concern. He had neither felt like that, nor had he even thought such emotion possible. "Never like that," he said. "Never like that...."

Tears blurred Terku's vision and he struggled to suppress his emotions. "Lose everything you love," he said, his voice steeped in despair. "Watch others lose everything they love..." He fell silent and hung his head. After a short silence, he said, "I'm the last of my kind."

Solomon didn't know what to say. He didn't know what it was like to be alone in the world, to be the last dove. But he knew he had to make sure he never found himself in such a situation. So Solomon asked, "Where is the Silk Palace?"

"I don't know," answered the porcupine. He looked up at the dove and his cheeks were wet. "I've been looking. I've been looking real hard 'cause there's something I gotta do. But I never found it. Never. And yesterday, I gave up."

Once upon a time in a forest far away...

Solomon remembered the brave little caterpillar who had left the palace to discover the old ways. She would know where the Silk Palace was, of that he was sure. He put his arm around the porcupine. "We must find a red ant and a pink caterpillar. They will lead us to the Silk Palace."

Terku didn't have time to react or ask any questions. A loud beeping and booping noise distracted them. The sounds grew louder and louder. Finally a platoon of butterfly robots emerged at the top of a dune. The robots were ten times the size of the dove, and inside the cockpit was a caterpillar in a black soldier's uniform.

Terku screamed, "CATERPILLAR!" Loud mechanical sounds drowned out his voice. He grabbed Solomon and yanked him from his spot just as a laser blasted the boulder they had been sitting on. The boulder exploded into bits and pieces and flew in all directions. All that was left when the smoke cleared was debris. Then they ran into the wild, thorny shrubbery as red, rapid-fire laser beams blasted all around them.

The robots gave chase, but they were too heavy and bulky, and soon the dove and the porcupine were out of range, quite some distance away. It wasn't long before they reached the edge of an area overgrown with hybrid weeds and grass. The porcupine looked at the jungle of weeds and listened to the eerie howls and rattles. He shook his head violently. "Not the jungle of failed caterpillar experiments," he said, "I swear it! Some horrible beast lives in there!"

Solomon listened intently for the sound of the butterfly robots, and the beeping sounds grew louder. "Do we have a choice?" he asked with panic in his voice.

Terku said stubbornly, "I'd rather deal with a caterpillar than whatever beast lives in there. Every night you can hear the agonies and screams of its victims. Terrible! Terrible!"

Solomon smiled and thought of a red ant he had met on his last journey. He remembered how this ant once used a mini bullhorn to scare possible threats away from his home. "I think," he said, "I know this so-called beast."

Suddenly, a laser blasted nearby and ended the discussion.

Unafraid and without a second to lose, Solomon ran into the jungle saying, "If I'm right, we have nothing to worry about!" And his voice faded into the darkness.

Terku considered his words a moment, slightly concerned. He said pensively, "You know...the beast?" A laser blast at his heel convinced him to trust the dove, and he leaped into the jungle, screaming

Once upon a time in a forest far away...

after Solomon:
   "You'd better be right!"

ɞ

"I was wrong!" Solomon whispered harshly when Terku finally caught up to him. Terku stepped behind him and took a few startled steps backward. He froze with fear and turned white as marble.

They both gaped at the unsightly mass of beige fur before them. The beast was a giant ball two times the size of a butterfly robot with long, massive, furry arms, short chubby legs, and a face that could not be discerned through soft, thick fur.

The beast took a step forward, and they took three steps back.

"What is it?" Terku asked in a trembling voice.

Uncertain, Solomon whispered, "A big…ball of…fur."

They took two more steps back, preparing to make a run for it.

"Slowly," Solomon cautioned. "We wouldn't want to upset the fur ball…."

At which the big ball of fur roared his sensitivity at being called a 'fur ball' and charged them with crushing blows, repeatedly screaming, "BAD GUY!"

They dodged the big ball of fur several times and the incensed beast continued his attacks without exhibiting any signs of tiring. The dove and the porcupine, however, were soon tired. When the beast pounded and shook the ground, Solomon fell semi-conscious and the panting porcupine quickly pulled him to his haunches. Then the beast screamed, "Bad guy!" and grabbed a boulder. He lifted the boulder over his head and held it over those who had so insensitively called him a 'fur ball' and was ready to crush them with one fatal throw.

Then a faithful voice, a voice Solomon immediately recognized, called out, "Furbul, no! Furbul, friend!"

The beast turned and looked down at a red ant speaking through a bullhorn. "Friend?" he questioned, then turned to Solomon and Terku and, remembering the insult, yelled, "Bad guy!"

"Friend!" Solomon shouted.

"Friend!" Terku pleaded.

"Fuuuuuurrrbul," the ant said, "Friend!"

"Bad guy!" Furbul responded, and was about to release the boulder.

251

"Friend!" Solomon yelled in a panic. "Friend! Friend!"

"Friend! Friend! Friend!" Terku exclaimed.

The ant tugged at Furbul's furry leg.

Furbul looked down at him.

"Friend," the ant said tenderly. "Furbul...friend..."

Repeating the word, Furbul placed the boulder on the ground. At which point the porcupine and the dove fainted with overwhelming relief.

When Solomon opened his eyes he saw a massive ball of fur towering over him. He gasped and jumped to his feet in a panic and attempted to run away. But Furbul caught him and hugged him and said lovingly, "Ahhhh...friend...."

Terku laughed as he sipped on a small container of water the ant had given him. "Looks like," he said to Solomon, "you have a new friend."

Engulfed in fur, Solomon couldn't answer.

Goro added, "Better friend than foe!"

"Agreed," laughed Terku.

"Agreed," said Solomon with difficulty.

Furbul yelled, "Friend!" and placed Solomon on the ground.

Terku gazed at the beast in wonder. "What is it?" he asked the ant.

Goro narrowed his gaze on the mass of fur and said, "Buddy, I really don't know. But I think he's just another failed caterpillar experiment left out here...or something like that. I call him Furbul but never call him-"

"Looks more like a fur ball!" Terku interrupted.

At the sound of the word, Furbul flew into a rage, attacking Terku and screaming, "Bad guy! Bad guy! Bad guy!" Terku evaded the beast for his dear life, and Goro pleaded with the incensed ball of fur and tried desperately to assuage his emotions. Finally, the beast sat down miserably and sobbed like an overgrown baby.

Panting and trying to catch his breath, Terku demanded, "What did I do?"

Goro was angry with the porcupine. "You called him a F-U-R-B-A-L-L is what you did!" He went up to his friend and told him that everything was going to be all right and that he wasn't at all what the porcupine had called him. Then he turned back to the porcupine and said, "How would like it if I called you spikey? Or pointy? Or..."

252

Solomon was altogether surprised. "You mean he understands?"

Goro said, "Buddy, just because he can't speak, doesn't mean he isn't intelligent or sensitive."

"Two words," the ant said in warning, after a silence. "You can't say F-U-R-B-A-L-L and you can't say M-A-M-A."

Terku said, "I S-E-E."

"You don't need to spell 'see,'" Goro said, "Only M-A-M-A and F-U-R-B-A double L."

Terku slipped, "So only fur ball and..."

Solomon tried to slap a wing against his mouth. But it was too late. Furbul went into a rage again and the ant tried to calm him down again. When finally Goro finally mitigated his friend's deeply offended pride and comforted him by singing a lullaby, Terku yelled, "That is one seriously unstable Furbul!"

Furbul giggled at the mention of his name.

"Oh!" Terku yelled, "I can call him Furbul but I can't call him..."

Solomon leaped on the porcupine and covered his mouth.

Eventually, Furbul was himself again: loving, joyful, and expressing great affection for his friends. He petted Solomon and he called him his friend. And with the other hand he petted Goro gently with his pinky, which was still three times the size of the ant. Sensing the porcupine was feeling left out, he went to pet him, but recoiled in great pain, then anger, thinking Terku had hurt him on purpose. The ant and the dove sighed, as the big ball of fur chased the porcupine around the clearing. But this time nothing would stop Furbul. As a last resort, Terku screamed, "MAMA!" and the big ball of fur froze in his tracks. He shook violently. The next moment he was on the ground sobbing for his mother.

Goro and Solomon threw Terku a searing look.

"What?" Terku responded, feeling a little self-conscious, a little bad for what had transpired and what he had to resort to. "What was I suppose to do? He was gonna smash me!"

They spent the rest of the day comforting the ball of fur. In the greyness they weren't sure if it was night or day, but they all felt tired. Goro and Solomon slept on a comfortable belly covered in fur, while Terku slept on the ground muttering and cursing under an angry breath. It was tough having quills.

The next morning they rode Furbul to the riverbed where Goro said he had last seen the brave little caterpillar. He explained that she had disappeared for quite some time, that he had been looking for her for several days now and that they probably wouldn't find her. When they reached the empty river, Goro climbed down his furry friend and threw his arms to the air. "See!" he exclaimed and twirled, "No caterpillar!" Then he walked toward a long twig and pointed to a chrysalis and made a face of disgust. "I don't know what it is! But when I got back, she was gone and this...this...probably some new caterpillar monster or weapon or trap or...well, she's gone! No more! Caput! Amen!" He put his head down and sighed.

Solomon sprang off Furbul and swooped toward Goro. He examined the chrysalis carefully. "It is a curiosity."

"It's gross," was Goro's immediate response, and he made exaggerated faces of revulsion.

Terku approached the twig slowly and examined the silky white substance.

Solomon went to touch it, but Terku held him back and said, "I think it's a bomb..."

Goro agreed, "Yeah, a bomb. That's exactly what it is."

Solomon began to say something to Terku, and when they weren't looking at the chrysalis, it moved a little bit. Goro jumped back a few feet, panicking and pointing. "It moved! It moved!"

They watched the chrysalis closely, but there was no movement. "I think," Terku said to the ant, "you need some clean air."

Solomon shrugged. "I didn't see anything either."

They went back to their discussion, and again the chrysalis moved.

Goro ran behind Solomon's leg and pointed at the chrysalis. "Monster!"

They narrowed their gaze on the chrysalis but nothing happened. Terku looked down at the ant and said, "I think you really need some clean air...you're seeing things."

Goro looked up to Solomon for support.

Once upon a time in a forest far away...

But Solomon simply shrugged and said, "Sorry, I didn't see anything either."

Then Terku and Solomon turned their backs on the chrysalis and
made way for Furbul, who sat on the ground making a cairn. Goro
walked backwards, refusing to take his eyes off the strange, gooey substance. He made faces and muttered that it was the most disgusting thing
he had ever seen. It moved again and he screamed and pointed and
yelled, "Monster! Monster! Monster!" They rushed to his side and
observed the chrysalis with keen eyes. And just when they were about to
admonish the ant for seeing things, the chrysalis jerked left, then right.
Goro gazed up at them. "Ah-ha! Now if you didn't see that, it is you who
needs the clean air!"

"No," Solomon said, keeping his eyes on the chrysalis, "I don't
need clean air, I saw that." He took a few steps forward and muttered,
"Could it be?"

In a sharp tone, Goro warned, "Get away from that thing!"

"Careful, Solomon..." Terku warned.

"Could it be?" he moved closer and closer, showing no signs of
fear, just curiosity.

"What are you doing?" Goro exclaimed.

"Careful, Solomon..."

Solomon peered down at the chrysalis and saw a shadow moving
inside.

Terku gestured for him to come back. "I would get away from
that thing if I were you."

Solomon turned to them. "I'm not sure. But I don't think it's what
you think it is."

"Oh, be sure," Goro said, "Be very sure!"

Suddenly the chrysalis jerked rapidly and the whole twig shook
violently. The chrysalis bulged and pushed and stretched in all directions.
Seeing this, Goro screamed as loud as he possibly could. Furbul jumped
up and screamed and didn't even know why he was screaming. Terku
soon followed, adding his own racket to the cacophony of fear and uncertainty. Only Solomon was still and calm, observing. Whatever was inside
the chrysalis broke out and there was immediate silence. They all stood in
muted awe. A beautiful pink and purple and yellow butterfly smiled at
them and stretched her wings.

Once upon a time in a forest far away...

Akiru searched the riverbed for a puddle as they watched her curiously. When she found a puddle, she examined her reflection in awe and disbelief. Approaching her slowly, Goro warned her not to drink the water as it was probably rainwater, and rain water was poisonous.

Solomon followed behind Goro. "You are so beautiful," he said to Akiru.

"Yes," Terku agreed, "You are beautiful."

Akiru turned to them. "Beautiful? My goodness, I'm gorgeous!" Then she turned back to the puddle and admired her reflection.

At this, Goro made a face. The Akiru he knew wouldn't say such a thing.

Swelling with pride, she continued, "I'm the most gorgeous thing I've ever seen." She examined herself from every angle. "I can't believe it's me..."

In a sarcastic tone, Goro said, "I'm having a hard time believing it myself."

She turned on the ant. "You're just jealous!" Then she turned back to the puddle, muttering that everyone would be jealous of her now because she was so beautiful.

Goro inched closer to her. "Akiru," he said gently, "Never forget why you're so beautiful..."

She swivelled and snapped, "Why? I'll tell you why! Because I worked hard. Because I put in the time and effort. That's why, ant." His name slipped her mind, though she did recognize him from somewhere. She also recognized Solomon and Furbul, but not Terku. She tried to place them, but gave up in a moment.

'That's partly why," Goro corrected, gazing at her with concern.

She laughed at this. "That's exactly why! And now it's only fair...yes, it's only fair that I get what's coming to me."

Solomon and Terku couldn't believe what they were hearing.

Goro moved closer. "And what's coming to you?"

"Glitter!" she answered quickly. "Glitter! Glitter! Glitter! Lots of it. And why not, I deserve it..."

Goro gazed at her sadly. "Don't you remember how much the Forest helped you?"

"Did it by myself!" she answered without a doubt.

Goro laughed a disbelieving laugh. "By yourself!" he exclaimed. "By yourself! Are you kidding me or what?" He turned red with anger. Terku shook his head and turned his back on her. He walked off toward Furbul. The mass of fur hummed a friendship tune as he built his fifth

256

cairn.

"You're just jealous," Akiru said, admiring her wings.

"Are you seeing okay?" Goro asked.

"Fine!" she snapped. "I am seeing fine." She turned to the puddle and wondered how much glitter she could make as a real butterfly in the Silk Palace.

"No," he corrected, and he indicated with his arms all the dunes, death, and destruction surrounding them. "I don't think you're seeing fine at all. In fact, I don't think you can see at all."

"I see fine, ant," she rebuked. "But I do thank you for your concern." Goro pointed at her. "No, you don't remember, and you don't see. You see and believe only what will permit you to turn your back on the Forest and feed your ego. But you can't see. You're blind...blind inside..."

"Oh, please!" Akiru chortled. "What's wrong with the Forest? Nothing is wrong with the Forest. "

Solomon gazed around and couldn't believe what she had just said. "Nothing is wrong with the Forest," he repeated softly. Then he gazed down at the ground. Wherever he looked he saw fish skeletons. Then he wondered when he had last seen night or day. This butterfly was truly blind, like the entire population of the Silk Palace.

Goro knew she was blind to everything else but herself and that more words would only be a waste of time and breath. But he continued, despite her ego. "What's wrong with you?" he asked with rising anger. "You actually think you succeeded by yourself." He paused and took a step closer. He gazed right into her eyes and continued. "Without the Forest you would have never succeeded...and now you're turning your back on the Forest, to endorse all those stations and leaders that destroyed what was once a great wealth for all."

"I don't believe in that kind of stuff anymore," she answered plainly. "That stuff is for children. Saving the Forest! Saving the trees! Saving the honeybees! Paah! Only young ones believe in that kind of stuff."

"Because they are not blind!" Goro replied. Red blazed in his cheeks. His darkening eyes narrowed on the butterfly. "But I guess your attitude is convenient...and you will do what they all do...conveniently turn your back on oppression and tyranny. So long as it is not in your face, it is not happening. Right, Akiru? Isn't that the caterpillar way?"

"You're just jealous," Akiru hissed. "Our walls cough glitter and wealth and ants can barely feed themselves... You're jealous of me. You're jealous 'cause I'll go back and they'll give me my own puppet show, my own report with my name on it, my own line of butterfly suits.

Goro shook his head sorrowfully. The caterpillars were entirely responsible for the poverty of ants. Silk Palace walls could only cough glitter because of their oppressive Forest policies. But he knew that she, for convenience sake, would never accept this or even consider investigating it. She had reports that would conveniently do that for her. He said, "Now you'll add to the psychological tyranny of those you once pretended to love. Make them want things they'll never really need, wanting the things you endorse while neglecting all the things they do need! And caterpillars will love and trust you, and you will do this to them...do to them what all the leaders do to them." He hung his head and swore this wasn't happening. Then he looked up at her with a start and said, "You're not Akiru! Akiru would never think like you. Akiru would never say the things you say. I don't know who you are, but I know who you aren't!"

"I'm sorry you still think like a child," she said, and turned her back on the Forest and took to the sky. Slowly she fluttered away and disappeared into the greyness.

After a long, oppressive silence, Goro said incredulously, "Defeated before we even had a chance. Without her, we will never make things right again. Caterpillars will only listen to a real butterfly...and the leaders will silence her with glitter." He clenched his fists and added, "Only a real butterfly can change caterpillars, and they will silence our only hope with glitter!"

Solomon stepped behind the ant and peered into the greyness. "So long as we do not give up on the Forest, the Forest will not give up on us."

Terku stepped behind Solomon. "Scream," he suggested kindly, then explained, "It will make you feel better."

Goro turned to him and regarded him strangely. Unsure, he let out a little scream and thought the porcupine was right. He did feel a little better. Then Solomon followed suit and felt the same. Furbul let out a little scream, and the fifth cairn went tumbling down. One after the other they screamed and screamed into the greyness until they broke out into fits of laughter and released all their negative energy. They laughed and laughed and begged each other to stop laughing for they didn't really know why they were laughing, only that they needed to laugh and that laughing almost seemed to prevent their spirits from breaking.

All of a sudden the island turned a silver-blue, and they all felt a little lighter, a little freer.

"Laugh," a mysterious apparition hidden under a cloak said, floating toward them. To each of them the apparition was different. To Solomon the stranger was exactly his size. To Goro he was the size of an ant. To Furbal he was big and round. And to Terku he had quills that poked through the cloak. And though he was completely different to each of them they all thought they were seeing the exact same thing.

They fell silent and slowly made a circle around the mysterious stranger. Solomon gazed at Terku and saw a strange silver cord attached to him. He followed the cord with his eyes and the cord lead down to the ground, which was covered and hidden by a heavy, blue mist. He then turned to Furbul and Goro and saw the same strange, silvery cord attached to their bodies and the mist enshrouded them. He quickly gazed at his back and saw the same cord keeping him connected to something he couldn't quite make out in the mist. But before he could consider the matter any further, the ant spoke.

"Who are you?" Goro asked, staring at the apparition in disbelief. The stranger answered, "I am different for each of you. I am whatever your minds will understand and respond to. I am the images you know, the sights and smells that speak to you, the language you respond to. I am luck and fortune to those connected to the spirit of all things, misfortune and indifference to the disconnected. For you, I am an omen, a sign, a helping hand."

"How can it be?" Solomon asked, trying his best to peer into the cloak.

The stranger looked at each one straight in the eye and all at the same time.

Suddenly, Terku's heart raced at an incredible speed at the mere thought of not being alone, of not being the last porcupine.

"I am here," the mysterious stranger continued, "to tell you that you must continue. I am here to tell you that the Forest and everything in it depends on you. That you will make it to the Silk Palace and that you must not doubt the power within each and every one of you. You have all

259

been brought together for a reason. Together you are magic and you can and will defeat the grey force. It will not happen overnight. But once change begins it will be exponential. First you must believe you can do it. You must believe and never doubt. There is no time for doubt."

Solomon asked, "But why has it come to this?"

Without hesitation, Terku answered angrily, "Glitter!"

The mysterious stranger shook his head under his cloak. "No," he said plainly, "Not glitter. Glitter was a gift of the light. Glitter is what I brought to the Forest so that great things could be accomplished. So that all of you could evolve to a higher level of existence. No, there is nothing evil about glitter. Glitter was meant to organize souls to work on incredible systems of energy, food, and shelter. If you think glitter is evil it is only because the grey force has succeeded at obscuring the real issue; it is because the grey force has succeeded at keeping your focus on glitter when all your focus should be on the way glitter is used."

Goro nodded slowly. He knew that the glitter system was possibly the best of all possible organizing systems, and that glitter only became evil in the wrong hands. Glitter, he was sure and always said, was like magic. It could bring things into being and it could prevent things from ever being. Caterpillar leaders were using glitter to bring about creations of mass distraction and destruction to make sure glitter wasn't used for the things it was intended. If glitter was in fact magic, then everything depended on the wizard. The grey force made one forget the wizard and blame the magic.

The mysterious stranger smiled at Goro as if he could read his thoughts. "Glitter," he continued, "was meant for the emancipation of all, not just a select few, not just the caterpillars." He paused and reflected on the constant battle between light and dark. "But this has happened many times before and it will happen many times after. And this time I have selected you five to meet and expel the grey force so that the balance between light and dark may once again tip toward the light."

Terku said, "I have never heard of a grey force..."

"Grey is the precursor to darkness," the mysterious stranger answered simply. "It is what is needed right before total darkness steps in and reigns through chaos, violence, and oppression. The grey force dilutes and clouds truth. Those born of the grey force are there to help everyone forget that there is such a thing as light and dark, good and evil, right and wrong. The grey does not ask that souls choose between light and dark. Rather, it makes you forget that there ever was a choice to be made. The balance tips toward darkness because of indifference and inaction. The more souls you turn grey, the easier evil becomes, the faster darkness settles in." He went quiet and allowed his words to be absorbed and understood. "The battle between light and dark," he went on, "has been waged many times before. A few times light has won. A few times dark has won. Now we are in the crucial time, the grey time, the time when the grey will do its best to empty all the Forest of value and meaning while my force..." the apparition indicated all of them, "will try to remind all about the sacredness of the Forest and the interconnectedness of all things."

A long, reflective silence followed. Each felt a great responsibility on their shoulders.

The mysterious stranger broke the tense silence. "Now my gift of glitter has brought the entire Forest to the brink of renaissance or apocalypse. Caterpillars have the technology and potential to create paradise for all. It is up to you to remind them of their abilities and their obligations. It is up to you to remind them that there is still time..."

"If we fail?" Terku asked softly.

The apparition said, "If you fail, there will be a total cleansing."

With an expression of worry, Solomon replied, "Total cleansing?"

The mysterious stranger nodded. "Not too far away, icebergs are already beginning to melt. The extra water will disrupt the fine balance between earth and water. The extra water will cause great instability. This instability will cause massive earthquakes, which, in turn, will cause tidal waves the size of mountains that will move faster than the speed of sound. The water will inundate the world and the filth of the caterpillars will be rapidly washed away. Then, some water will freeze up again and everything will start anew and the whole cycle will repeat itself." The mysterious stranger scanned their concerned eyes for a moment and continued. "And then I will see you in another two thousand years, and I will again tell you these words: 'Apocalypse or renaissance, it is up to you.'"

"Our choice," Terku repeated thoughtfully.

Concerned, Solomon said, "Alone we cannot succeed! Their reports and weapons are too strong. Their power, too great. Their technology, too advanced. Did you see those butterfly robots? I have never seen such things!"

Goro considered caterpillar power and technology. He thought they paled in comparison to mountain-sized tidal waves moving faster than the speed of sound. He wondered if anything could possibly survive such an onslaught of water; he wondered if there would be anything left of this world. He glanced around at the dunes, garbage and rubble, and he thought that perhaps it would just be easier to start all over again.

Pondering this, he wondered if the icebergs were a sort of reset button for the world; a button to be pushed when things grew out of hand; a way of repairing environmental damage before things became irreparable and the earth became permanently barren and uninhabitable. A self-contained planetary cleaning system.

The mysterious stranger nodded at Solomon, understanding his concern. "But imagine, dear Solomon, all that technology working for the Forest and not against it...all that technology for the emancipation of all and not just a few."

Solomon still doubted. "But alone-"

"Solomon," the mysterious stranger interrupted, "do your best, and let the Forest take care of the rest. There is no time for doubt." The mysterious stranger hovered above them and demanded, "Everyone wake up! You have a Forest to save."

Goro scrunched his face in confusion. "Wake up? What are you talking about?" He was shocked when he floated toward the sky, held only by his silver cord.

Solomon wore the same confused expression. "Wake up? What do you mean?"

"I am awake," Terku said, feeling completely awake.

The mysterious stranger uncovered his face slowly and they each saw their reflection. They gaped incredulously and couldn't believe what they thought they were seeing. Then all of a sudden the mysterious stranger disintegrated into an overpowering light source. When they woke up, they were amazed to discover that they had each had a very similar dream with only slight variations.

ॐ

With great excitement and a renewed sense of purpose, Terku led his friends across dunes and hills of waste, sewage, and broken up butterfly robots. Solomon, Goro and Furbul followed close behind. "Where are you taking us?" Solomon yelled out to the porcupine.

Continuing forward, Terku answered, "There's a place I know. Untouched by caterpillars. Last piece of Forest on Chichikaka. Last place you'll ever see green." The porcupine began to tire and stopped to rest at the base of a fairly large hill of junk. The air was getting to him and he was struggling for breath. Breathing heavily, Terku explained carefully, "Just over this hill of scrap you will find thousands of trees and flowers. And when you see it you'll know why we gotta do what we gotta do."

"Do the caterpillars know of it?" Solomon asked, wondering how such a place could exist in a place where profit ruled all.

"Sure do!" Teku answered with a smile. "Only there is nothing they can do about it. Rumour is a few concerned caterpillars beat the leaders of lumber stations at their own game. They started a station as well. Only instead of buying up the land and destroying it, they were buying up the land and conserving it. They handed out certificates to caterpillars, which described which tree they had helped save by donating glitter. And those certificates could be handed down to children and grandchildren. And then the idea caught on and more caterpillars started creating Forest-conserving stations and handing out certificates. These trees are now owned by some large-hearted caterpillars and there is nothing the leaders can do about it." After a moment he laughed. "I wish a lot more caterpillars would go on Forest-buying binges."

Solomon smiled. "Now that's magic!"

Goro shook his head sceptically. "I hardly believe it. I will have to see it with my own eyes."

"And your eyes will feast, little ant!" Terku bellowed with glee in his heart. Then he bolted up the hill, waving his arms and screaming his joy.

263

Once upon a time in a forest far away...

When they finally reached the top of the hill, they gazed down into the clearing and saw Terku walking in circles amid piles of lumber. As far as the eye could see were freshly cut trees and tree trunks. The porcupine's eyes were wet and lost, furious and confused. Nothing was left. Everything was gone.

Solomon dismounted Furbul and whispered, "Oh no..."

From above they could hear the porcupine muttering angrily.

Terku paced anxiously and bit his lower lip with mounting anger. He searched the land, benumbed and bewildered by the dark, oppressive emptiness. Slowly his confused faced tightened and despair filled every fibre of his being. Something pointy and prickly irritated his throat as his chest throbbed with care-stricken thoughts.

The ant peered down at the porcupine. "Poor, Terku...I told him it couldn't be."

Terku gazed around frantically. Suddenly, there came a deep flash of red into his eyes. Nothing was left; nothing was left because nothing was sacred anymore. He looked up to his friends as if to ask them to make the scene go away. But this was no nightmare.

After a tense moment, Terku went back to his pacing. "Why! Why! Why!" he muttered, pausing every now and then to close his eyes and attempt to make sense of what he was seeing and how he was feeling. He soon froze like a statue and gasped. He held his head in his hands and fell to his knees. "Why! Why! Why!" Then he let his hand pass over the naked surface of the ground and he fell completely silent. A tear slipped down his cheek and a lump grew in his throat. He held his throat and the lump became heavy and unbearable. Everything. Everything he had ever loved in his life was gone. In an instant his heart and soul snapped and he threw his head back and opened his mouth as pain and despair gushed out of him all at once. He screamed and screamed as loud as his tiny porcu-pine lungs would permit, and soon he was screaming and no sound was coming out. To deal with the madness the poor porcupine was reduced to madness.

Solomon and Goro and Furbul made their way to the voiceless porcupine who continued with his mouth wide open without making a single sound. They had never seen anyone so angry. Solomon put his wing around his friend and embraced him strongly while Goro embraced the porcupine's finger. Furbul lifted all three of them in his big furry hand and Terku closed his mouth, realizing he had completely lost his voice. Suddenly, they heard a loud beeping noise followed by thunderous caterpillar insults. There was an indecisive moment between them. Then Goro ordered Furbul to seek out the source of the commotion.

"Bad guy," Furbul whispered as he stood atop a dune. He watched a butterfly robot attempt to get close enough to the very last sycamore in order to zap it down with a blaster.

The robot approached the tree, and the tree hurled another insult at the caterpillar and attempted to smash the robot with a huge, leafy branch. After several attempts the tree managed to whack the robot to the ground and with a few other branches he tried to hold him down. But the robot was too strong and was soon on its feet, attempting to destroy the tree.

Terku tugged at Solomon, tried to say something in a hurry, but no words came out. He gave up and groaned that they should go down and help the tree. So Goro gave the order and they rode Furbul as he charged wildly toward the robot, screaming, "Baaaaaaaad guy!"

Before the caterpillar realized what was happening, he turned and gasped at the furry sight before him. In an instant the big ball of fur flattened him. The robot quickly stood and regained its composure. He fired at Furbul, but every time Furbul was hit he sustained no real injury other than being momentarily paralyzed by laughter. Realizing his blaster had no effect on the furry beast, the caterpillar aimed his blaster at Solomon.

Solomon gulped and knew there was little he could do.

But before the caterpillar could pull the trigger something wrapped around the robot's leg and pulled him screaming to the ground, pinning him tightly. In all the excitement, the caterpillar had forgotten about the tree.

Then, much to Solomon's surprise, a group of rebels came running from all over and surrounded the robot with their own blasters. The rebels were of all sizes and were all covered in black rags so that only the whites of their eyes could be seen. They approached the robot slowly and carefully, and the tree was wild with rage and could hardly think straight. Then the tree pounded the robot senselessly and, in his blind rage, attacked the rebels who desperately pleaded with the tree that they were there to help him.

The tree was hurt, mad, confused, scared, and when he went to strangle the leader of the rebels, all blasters were instantly aimed at him. Solomon screamed for the rebels to put down their weapons. They would have fired had Solomon not swooped down toward the tree singing a soothing song that immediately snatched the tree from its prison of anger. The tree let go of the rebel leader and the rebels lowered their weapons. Goro sighed with relief.

ॐ

The rebels led them to their camp and gave them food and water to share. The camp was full of rebels, all surrounding the prisoner, interrogating, taunting, and hurling insults of all degrees of hate. Gazing helplessly back at the rebels, the prisoner couldn't understand why they hated him so much when he truly believed that caterpillars were doing great and positive things for the Forest.

Terku took a sip of water and passed the flask to Solomon as they watched the rebels interrogate the prisoner. They were astonished, for when a few rebels removed their face coverings, they saw that the rebels were nothing more than children.

Goro savoured a drop of water and said, "Why, they're just children..."

"We are," the leader said, as he approached them, slowly taking off his desert mask. When his mask was in his hands, they saw he was a young, handsome raccoon.

The leader stood beside them and watched his subordinates, a bunny and a skunk, interrogate the prisoner while Terku inspected all the young animals, desperately searching for a porcupine.

Concerned, Solomon asked the leader, "Where are your parents?"

The rebel turned to him and thought about the question for a moment. Then he sighed and answered plainly, "Busy destroying our future, I suppose." And he turned back to the prisoner. "But I'm sure they'll leave us lots of glitter, as if glitter will mean anything once all the important things are destroyed." He shook his head gravely. "Our parents have fallen under the spell of the caterpillars, and they won't listen to reason unless reason comes with a big purse of glitter." He frowned and his eyes were profound and cheerless. "No, we cannot wait for our parents to do something about what is happening. It is up to us, entirely up to us. And what is worse is their inaction is the biggest part of the problem. They have failed us. They have failed us dearly. And if we don't do something about what they choose to turn their backs on, no one else will."

Goro inched closer to the raccoon. "I like how you think, buddy," he said, and he was genuinely happy that children were able to see what their parents couldn't. He was happy because now he knew things would

267

truly begin to change for the better. Or at least he hoped.

The raccoon took a few steps toward his retinue. He ordered, "Prepare the prisoner!" He turned back to Solomon, Terku, Furbul, and Goro. In a proud voice, he said, "We are the children of the Forest and we will not accept the unnecessary destruction of that which gives us life!"

❧

Senseless vengeance was thick in the air. The rebels surrounded the prisoner, who was now chained to a small stone, struggling wildly and helplessly. The rebels roared and pounded the hilts of their blasters on the rubble floor as their leader approached the prisoner with lethal intent. Though the raccoon could have simply squashed this caterpillar with his fingers, he held out a sword and wished to maximize this caterpillar's squirming and suffering. It was clear he intended on making an example of this caterpillar; that he was willing to go to any extreme to make this caterpillar pay for the crimes his leaders were responsible for. Never had Solomon seen such disgust in a child's eyes.

"No! Please no!" the prisoner pleaded as the rebels cheered their leader on.

The leader held the sword up and cried, "See how they squirm without their weapons and technology!"

The prisoner cried, "Please! Please! I have a family..."

"How many families have you caterpillars destroyed?" the leader shot back, and he took another step forward.

The caterpillar stopped his wild struggling and looked genuinely confused.

"You will be a message," the leader said in a tone of pure acid, "to those who would destroy our lives to conduct their business. If no one will do their dirty work, if their dirty work is no longer profitable, they will have no reason to invade and destroy our homes!"

The rebels hollered their anger and approved the dark act yet to be committed.

But before the raccoon could take another step forward, Solomon unexpectedly swooped down in front of him, held out a strong wing, and said, "No!"

Startled, the leader lowered the sword. "Out of my way, dove!"

"No..."

"What do you care about some caterpillar?" the leader demanded.

"Believe me, dove, he wouldn't do the same for you if it meant a slight loss of profit. So step aside!"

Solomon closed his eyes for a moment. Opening his eyes, he

269

repeated, "No..."

Goro, sitting on Furbul's crown, yelled through the bullhorn, "Solomon, he's right! Out of the way! Out of the way, Solomon! O-U-T O-F T-H-E W-A-Y!"

Terku, standing beside Furbul, nodded. He also believed this caterpillar deserved to serve as a message to caterpillar profiteers.

The prisoner yelled, "What have caterpillars ever done to you?"

At once the rebels laughed. It was a question they were all quite used to: caterpillar ignorance was common knowledge to all in the Forest except caterpillars.

When the raccoon spoke up, the rebels went silent. "It's always the same with you caterpillars, isn't it? Isn't it? Ignorant of all your crimes against the Forest but so quick...so, so quick to remember all those against the palace. That is precisely why I have prepared a little something so you do not go to your grave in the festering ignorance your leaders keep you in." He gazed to his side and indicated something to a group of bunnies and bear cubs. A little bunny responded by hopping over to him and placing a scroll in his hands. The raccoon unrolled the scroll and began, "Caterpillar Crimes Against the Forest...by the children of the Forest..." He went on to list over a hundred crimes that the prisoner had no clue about; and he genuinely believed this scroll was one great lie to justify their rebellion against caterpillars. For if these crimes were true, he could not accept living in a palace whose very foundation was built on the blood and suffering of so many children, families, and cultures. For if these crimes were true, he would not only be ashamed of his flag, but he would outright burn it. If these crimes were true he would join their cause.

When the raccoon finished reading, the prisoner had tears in his eyes and his face betrayed signs of cognitive turmoil; but his mind could not, or would not, accept these accusations. They were so contradictory to all he had ever learned in the palace and they just had to be lies. So he yelled in protest, "It's not true! It's not true! All of it, a lie!" But he himself was not sure. He needed, for his own peace of mind, to believe it was a great lie.

Goro thought about the Silk Palace. He whispered, "Everyone is ignorant, so no one is."

"I'm not going to argue with you!" the raccoon said firmly, and rolled up the scroll. "The brainwash is absolute and your ignorance is too thick." He scoffed loudly, then said, "I'm afraid, not even one of your lasers could penetrate your ignorance. But you asked, and I told you, and now you know why you must be made an example of."

The prisoner bellowed, "Those are nothing but lies! Please don't kill me!"

The leader ignored his words. "You caterpillars can call yourselves as superior and progressed as you want," he said flatly, "but with these truths I hold here..." he held up the scroll and continued with a great rush of emotion, "you will forever be remembered as the most savage! The most horrible! The most ruthless worms to have ever slimed across the Forest floor!"

The rebels screamed in chorus, "Death to the tyrant!"

The raccoon took a determined step forward and Solomon lifted his wing higher, shaking his head.

The rebel sighed at this stubborn dove. He turned to his rebels. "Is there anyone here who objects?" he asked, and was quickly met by the same response.

"Death to the tyrant!"

Solomon took a step forward and faced the raccoon. "I object. I object with all my heart." He paused, shook his head gravely, then continued slowly. "Son, I also care to make things right again...but not like this..."

Goro grabbed his bullhorn. "Solomon, out of the way!"

"Death to the tyrant!"

"Lay upon the criminal his crimes!"

Gazing into the raccoon's eyes, Solomon continued, "Do not do this, young one. Not like this. You do not meet savagery with savagery. Please...please...don't do this...for your cause...for the Forest...don't do this...don't become what you hate..."

Goro rolled his eyes. "Buddy, out of the way!"

Terku hung his head. Though he knew Solomon was right, he needed to see a caterpillar suffer for all the pain they had caused him. And though he understood the dove, he also understood the raccoon: a message had to be sent to those who would dare to do the Silk Palace's dirty work.

The prisoner stared at Solomon in disbelief.

Solomon continued. "If you do this, you are just as savage as they are. But if you were to open their eyes, open their hearts...they would change...I know it..."

The raccoon answered, "You dream!"

Once upon a time in a forest far away...

Goro echoed, "Yeah, buddy, you dream!"

Terku shook his head slowly, and Furbul didn't know what was going on, but he shifted nervously. Like a newborn he could sense all the negativity in the atmosphere.

"Death to the tyrant!"

"Lay upon the criminal his crimes!"

Solomon said, "We all belong to the same spirit, young one. We all have the same capacities to care and feel and despise injustice and do something about injustice so long as…as we are connected…and remember that the unnecessary pain and suffering of one is the pain and suffering of all." He gazed deep into the raccoon's gaze. Then he added, "And that's what we must do. We must reconnect caterpillars despite the system that disconnects them so effectively and absolutely…so long as we are tuned in with our essence we are tuned in with all…"

Solomon went quiet. He turned to the prisoner and felt sorry for him, and the prisoner listened to Solomon with hope. Then Solomon turned back to the leader. "Don't you see? If you, too, lived in the palace you'd be just like him, just as ignorant, just as oblivious, just as indifferent to all that takes place on the outside. You really would…no matter how strong you think your mind is. And you would be made so, so scared of the outside, that you just wouldn't care what went on to those you were programmed to fear; you, too, would happily close your eyes and ears to all the pain and suffering your indifference is responsible for." He paused to reflect on the dark intentions of the raccoon.

After a moment he said, "Go through with this crime, young one, and the reports are going to use this most savage act against you and your cause. And I promise you this: no one will want to know or care why you did it. They'll just hate you more for having done it. You'll give them more fear and anger for their reports to inject into caterpillars, and this will only serve to increase their hatred of the outside. Just one more wall raised against your cause."

For a moment the raccoon seemed confused. He turned to Goro, Furbul, and Terku. Then his eyes scanned his rebels. After some thought, he ground his teeth angrily. His eyes flashed vengeance, and he thundered, "The prisoner must pay!"

Solomon sighed heavily. "Don't do this. I beg you. Young one, please… Like it or not we need the caterpillars if we are ever to fix this mess. We need the Silk Palace to change the Silk Palace if we are ever to get things right again. Caterpillars will change caterpillars; I am sure of

272

it; but they will not be open to what we have to say if you do this..."

"You dream, dove!" the raccoon exclaimed. "Caterpillars will change caterpillars! They don't give a damn!"

"Don't kid yourself," Solomon said to the raccoon. "We need caterpillars. We need their technology and their abilities to make things right again. They just need someone to help them...help them reconnect...all they gotta do is reconnect... Please, young one, listen to reason. You must be given to understand that the way of the rebel is not to put on his oppressor's mask, but to open his heart."

The raccoon stared into the dove's eyes for a long, anxious moment. Then he looked up to the grey sky and wondered if he would ever see the light of day again. "You're wrong," he finally whispered and looked back into Solomon's eyes. Then he bellowed through clenched teeth, "You're wrong!" He pointed his sword at Solomon. "The only way is to teach these...these...creatures of mass destruction a lesson. Or else they keep coming back!"

Solomon shook his head severely. "I can't let you do this." And he took a small step forward.

The leader tilted his head toward his rebels. "Children of the Forest! Where today are the riches that were gifts to all?" He waited for an answer and continued when none came. "Gone! Where today is the river that gave life to all? Gone! Where today is hope? Gone! Vanished from the Forest before the greed and oppression of the caterpillars and the blindness of our parents. Shall we let ourselves be destroyed so easily? Shall we? Shall we, without an effort, give up whatever is left of the Forest in exchange for...for...glitter? I know the answer. And I know you know the answer. And I know you will join with me and say, 'Never!'"

Everyone shouted the word. Solomon took a deep breath, closed his eyes and prepared to die.

The prisoner cried, "No...please, no...I don't want to die!"

Goro warned Solomon, "Buddy, time to step away!"

But Solomon had lost his fear of death long ago, and he knew he couldn't turn his back on this poor prisoner, whose only real crime was ignorance. Change, he knew, would never come this way.

The raccoon continued with emotion. "What does this dove know of pain and suffering! He is just as ignorant as the caterpillar." He laughed absurdly, then his eyes went dark and he became altogether serious. He hated caterpillars with a burning, all-consuming rage, though his rage would have been more suitably directed to caterpillar stations and

273

leaders, not ordinary caterpillars. Ordinary caterpillars actually believed they were doing good things for the Forest. And so, without taking his eyes off Solomon, he called out to his rebels, "Brothers and sisters! They have destroyed entire civilizations. Murdered leaders who only wanted the best for their own. Murdered all those who stood in their way! And they called their crimes collateral damage." He gazed at the prisoner in disgust and said, "All those in favour of the death of this caterpillar say 'I!'"

The entire island shook with the word.

The prisoner sobbed, "I don't want to die! I don't want to die!"

"Move out of my way, dove!" the raccoon demanded, and he placed the point of the sword on Solomon's neck.

Solomon didn't move or answer. He waited stubbornly, wishing it didn't have to be this way.

"Move away!" the leader bellowed through clenched teeth. "Move away or I swear..."

Then, unexpectedly, Terku grabbed the sword, stepped in front of Solomon and placed the point at his neck.

Alarmed, Solomon opened his eyes and whispered, "What are you doing?"

Terku didn't respond. He merely watched the raccoon carefully and hoped for a change of heart.

The leader gulped. "What is this! Are you all mad? Can't you see what they've done?"

The very next moment Goro climbed up Terku in a rush. Panting and trying to catch his breath, he stood on the porcupine's chest, grabbed the sword and placed the point in front of him. "No wait," he corrected, and placed the point where he thought the penetration would hurt the least. After much consideration and indecision, he finally placed the point back in its original spot and said, "There!"

"They killed the Forest!" the leader shouted.

Goro closed his eyes and nodded. Opening his eyes, he said, "I know, buddy. It's not me you gotta convince...I'm on your side...but I cannot let you hurt my friend no matter how silly and melodramatic I may sound...just make it quick, okay..."

At which point Furbul heard a word he liked. "Friend!" the ball of fur repeated happily, standing in the distance, not fully comprehending the gravity of the situation.

Once upon a time in a forest far away...

The leader's arm trembled violently. "Let them be scared of coming here!" he said viciously "Let them be scared and let his tortured body be what scares them." He pointed the sword at the prisoner. "There will be no caterpillar business or development here. Not while I'm alive!"

Goro spoke through his bullhorn. "Buddy, I understand your point of view. But I'm still not moving."

The leader laughed sardonically. "Open their hearts," he said, and gave the prisoner a searing glance. "Open your eyes and look around you...they have no hearts!"

Goro said, "Heard, processed, and understood. But I'm still not moving..."

"Fine!" the leader said, and he prepared to do what needed to be done to get to the prisoner. "If that's the way it's going to-"

Goro interrupted, "Bad guy!"

Puzzled, the raccoon asked, "What guy?"

Goro repeated, "Bad guy!" He repeated the word several times in a great panic. Unlike Solomon, he was pretty scared of death.

The raccoon scrunched his face. "What? What are you saying? Bad guy? Why are you...?"

At that very instant Furbul charged the raccoon and grabbed him tightly. With one mighty thrust the big ball of fur screamed, "Bad guy!" and flung the raccoon way over a dune. The rebels stood in shock, not knowing what to do or how to react. Soon their leader came cursing over the dune. In an instant he pulled out a caterpillar blaster and fired at Furbul.

As always, Furbul laughed and giggled and became angry and frustrated, only because he wanted the tickling to stop. Realizing the lasers were useless against the big ball of fur, the raccoon pointed his blaster at Terku; but before he could pull the trigger, a platoon of butterfly robots emerged from behind him.

The robots stood menacingly behind the leader and all the rebels screamed and scattered for their lives. When the raccoon swivelled to see what was behind him, his hands shook uncontrollably and he dropped his blaster. Before the blaster hit the ground, a robot vaporized him without warning or remorse. Then the firing commenced. And Solomon, Goro, and Terku were already holding Furbul tightly as he thundered away. When Goro turned round to take one last look at the camp, his eyes became wet as he witnessed a great and unbelievable slaughter. All the children of the Forest were gone. No more. Vaporized. Collateral damage.

"Wait!" Goro said and tugged at Furbul to stop.

Furbul halted abruptly.

"What is it?" Solomon asked.

"We'll follow them back," Goro answered quickly.

Solomon could still hear the beeping of the robots behind them. "Too dangerous," he said.

"Without Akiru," Goro responded, "there is no other way."

Solomon sighed; he knew the ant was right.

Terku opened his mouth. When no words came out, he merely nodded his agreement. With their consent, Goro tugged at Furbul and directed him back toward the camp.

&

Following the platoon at a safe distance, they were led to a faraway dried-up river shrouded in a purple mist. They hid behind a dune and peeked over the top, observing the robots carefully. The robots stood in formation as a scout ventured into the purple void and tested the ground to make sure it wouldn't crack open and swallow them whole. A small gust of wind cleared the sky for a brief moment, and in the small window of time, they all saw the Silk Palace on the other side of the river. They gasped at its enormity and couldn't believe their eyes.

Goro whispered, "Did you see that!"

Solomon nodded. "It's gigantic..."

Terku's face wore an expression of disbelief.

And Furbul didn't know what to say or do, but seemed lost in a memory, as if he recognized the palace.

The mist grew thicker, and now the robots looked everywhere with an aura of great anxiety. They observed left, right, and straight ahead; and they repeated this cycle several times, seemingly uneasy about crossing the river.

After a moment, Solomon narrowed his gaze on them. He whispered, "What are they afraid of?"

"Their own monsters," Goro was quick to answer. "They created so many monsters to do their dirty work that they have to be extremely careful wherever they go. They are their own reason for their fear, for why they need all those weapons."

When the caterpillars finished scanning the river and were sure there were no monsters, they charged their laser blasters and their leader gave the order to cross the river. Each caterpillar watched a different side of the river nervously.

"So scared," Solomon observed. "What could make them so scared with those weapons?"

"I don't know," Goro whispered with concern. "But whatever they're scared of...I definitely don't want to meet up with it."

Terku nodded, tried to say something, then gave up.

Once upon a time in a forest far away...

They watched the caterpillars until they disappeared into the mist. When they vanished, they mounted Furbul and made their way down to the river.

"Slowly" Goro cautioned Furbul. "Not too fast, buddy. Not too fast...this is unstable ground...earthquake ground..." Furbul moved cautiously around skeletons and crevices and florescent pools of waste. A sudden burst of hot wind filled their lungs. Coughing desperately, their lungs burned with fire.

As they struggled for air and peered around the river, searching for monsters, they moved forward. But they could hardly see two feet ahead in any direction, and often Goro would command Furbul to halt for reasons of poor visibility. Only when they could see a few feet ahead, would the ant have his big, furry friend continue.

Suddenly, the ground grumbled.

"Halt!" Goro commanded.

Furbal came to a full stop.

Solomon asked, "What is it?"

Goro gazed at the ground. "Did you hear that?"

"I didn't hear anything," Solomon said plainly.

Terku shook his head in answer.

Goro turned to them, but still he seemed to be listening for something. Then he commanded, "Forward!" And he gave his friend a little tug and the big, furry legs trudged forward.

After a few steps, there was another soft grumble. Goro yelled, "Halt!" He turned to Solomon and Terku and asked, "Did you hear that?" Both Solomon and Terku shook their heads and shrugged.

Goro listened intently. Then he commanded, "Forward!"

In an instant there was another faint grumble, and Goro turned to Solomon and Terku. "That! Did you hear that?" he asked.

"It's nothing," Solomon answered. But before he could say another word the ground split open and in one faithful gulp swallowed them whole. Furbul cried out loud and quickly grabbed hold of the edge and hung on for dear life. With red lava bubbling and sizzling below, Solomon screamed, "Lift! Lift! Lift!" And Goro added, "Furbul, up! Up! Come on, Furbul!" And Terku gazed downward with overwhelming fear. As they screamed for Furbul to lift them all to safety, a loud, sonorous roar came from above and instantly silenced them.

278

Once upon a time in a forest far away...

Goro turned to Solomon. "What was that?"

"Are we sure we want to be up there!" Solomon said. "I mean, maybe we should hang out a bit-no pun intended." But then a burst of lava changed his mind.

Terku shook his head wildly and tugged at Solomon.

Solomon yelled, "Lift! Lift! Lift!"

Goro added, "Come on, Furbul!"

After many failed attempts, Furbul, let out a mighty roar and pulled himself over the edge. Slowly and weakly, they rolled off Furbul and rose with difficulty and brushed off the dust. They gazed disbelievingly at the glowing red crevice that separated the riverbed in two.

"Well," Goro commented, "there's no turning back now."

But before anyone could respond, the roar came again.

They swivelled frantically in all directions.

"What is that?" Goro demanded.

"Where is it coming from?" Solomon added, and could see nothing through the purple mist.

Terku shrugged, and a nervous moment of silence followed as each of them searched for the source of the great roar. When they didn't find anything, they mounted Furbul and started toward the Silk Palace. After a few cautious steps, Furbul bumped into something with a loud clang. He backed up and tried again, but as soon as he took a step forward he bumped into the same metal obstacle.

They peered deeply into the mist.

Goro said, "Must be junk or some…"

His voice faded as a draft cleared the mist and unveiled a round, thick monster clad head to toe in shiny blue armour. For a long moment they all stood paralyzed with fear, staring into the glowing green eyes under the helmet. The monster huffed and puffed and stomped the ground and there was brutality and fierceness in every movement.

Sensing danger, Furbul took a step backward.

The monster beat up dust; then faster than the eye could see, it lunged at Furbul and thrashed him to the ground. They flew off Furbul and soared in all directions. Goro rolled over the ground and fell down the crevice toward the bubbling lava. Without hesitation, Solomon jumped down after him and caught the screaming ant just before he fell into the river of fire. Goro's eyes widened. He was alive. He sighed heavily and was glad he had not been transformed to ash and smoke.

Once upon a time in a forest far away...

"Thank you, buddy," Goro said in a weak voice, exasperated.

Solomon flew upward. He smiled and answered, "You're welcome, buddy."

"Glad you have wings, buddy."

"Remember," Solomon said, "I have wings, you have wings. Way it goes with friends."

Remembering their time together a long time ago, Goro laughed weakly. "I remember, buddy. I remember..."

Solomon flew to the top only to find Furbul and the monster in a heated battle, throwing each other across the ground and hurling giant boulders at each other. Not too far away, Terku lay on the ground unconscious. Solomon and Goro immediately rushed to his aid.

Gently, Solomon held him up and Goro said, "Buddy...buddy...wake up, buddy..."

Slowly, Terku began to rouse.

Solomon sighed in relief.

And when Goro saw Terku was alright, he turned to the great battle and cheered for Furbul, who seemed to have a slight advantage in strength and speed. Goro yelled through his bullhorn, "Go Furbal! Yeah, Furbal! A left! A right! Yeah, Furbul! That's it! That's it! Give it to 'em!"

The two monsters grappled and roared like a great tempest. Furbul jerked suddenly and sent his foe straight to the ground. Goro laughed with joy at seeing his friend defeat the monster so easily. Then Furbul charged the groaning monster and jumped on top of it and they rolled over the ground. As they rolled wildly, the ground roared its displeasure and cracked open. Instantly the two monsters were devoured.

Goro looked on helplessly. His eyes grew wide with disbelief and he fell as silent as the rocky desert surrounding him. "Furbul..." he said in a shaking voice, and his eyes filled with tears. For a long moment he gazed ahead, hoping his friend would somehow reappear. Then a terrible certainty seized him and an awful sense of loss and grief filled his heart. He whispered, "Furbul..." But Furbul was gone.

బు

Following the edge of the river, they couldn't believe their eyes. The other side of the river was a decrepit camp brimming with species of every sort. From the edge of the river all the way to the walls of the Silk Palace there were little campfires surrounded by wasted and hungry eyes, the remnants of fallen cultures and civilizations. The camp was dirty, miserable, and lawless; the homes were scattered at random: holes in the ground, rubble caves, weed-thatched enclosures, huts made out of junk. And on days when the sky released its deadly acid, many homes washed away or melted under its torrential wrath, and many camp dwellers died of exposure, disease, hunger, and dehydration. Many died unnecessarily of want and need while, conversely, so many in the Silk Palace died of diseases born of excess and waste. These were strange times.

They walked through the camps and a great feeling of urgency filled them. Solomon closed his eyes for a moment. He hated not being able to help or change things right away. Terku and Goro gazed at a bone-faced rabbit in the distance. They watched her split a crumb of bread for her three children; she handed each of them an equal portion. One child split his portion in two and gave back half to his mother, and his mother shook her head and said she was full, that she had eaten earlier in the day. Then her empty stomach moaned deeply and betrayed her lie.

Goro sighed. "It's worse than I ever imagined."

Terku clenched his hands into two angry fists.

Solomon gasped at the scene. Then, without warning, a tear slipped down his cheek as he scanned over the hungry eyes sitting by little campfires just below the Silk Palace wall. The wall was covered in posters and billboards depicting every possible luxury these camp dwellers would never have or be able to provide for their children; in this way, prosperity was always there to remind them of their poverty; their inner suffering was intensified and the oppression was constant. Many even felt that the caterpillars were laughing at them with their billboards and advertisements; for they all knew one truth: caterpillars could not enjoy one fourth of their luxuries without covertly reducing the Forest to conditions of hunger and slavery.

281

Once upon a time in a forest far away...

Another tear slipped down Solomon's cheek. He went to wipe his inexpressible pain and profound anger away; but then he stopped himself and let his tear fall. He accepted and owned his anger, and he knew he was angry for a reason. He knew why he was angry and who he was angry with. And he knew he would turn this very negative emotion into something solid, positive and constructive. But what he absolutely refused to do was suppress it, hide from it, do nothing with it; he could no more stifle his anger than stifle laughter, for he knew anger existed for a reason. It was an emotion like any other emotion, important and necessary, there to send signals and raise warning flags. Not born of envy or jealousy, this anger, Solomon was certain, was a warning flag raised to let him know that something was wrong and that some things needed to be changed and changed soon.

At that moment a siren sounded. The gates of the Silk Palace opened. Before long the Silk Palace slaves gushed out like a river of despair. They slowly returned to their rag homes with the little water they had earned in the day. At that moment Solomon approached a crestfallen raccoon and asked him where he was coming from and what he was doing inside the Silk Palace. Completely resigned to his fate, the raccoon looked up at Solomon with dark, vacant eyes.

"We enter the Silk Palace every morning," the raccoon explained to Solomon, Terku, and Goro as they sat quietly in his tiny, weed-thatched tent. He spoke about his situation with a sort of resignation, and he refrained from becoming too emotional. He had no more energy for emotion and needed to conserve his energy for his family.

Solomon looked through the doorway and into the greyness. He asked, "How do you know when it's morning or night? Everything is so grey. How can anyone around here tell the difference between night and day?"

Goro nodded; he thought it was a good question.

"Their sirens and white lights tell us," the raccoon answered plainly. "Or else we wouldn't know. We rely on the caterpillars to define night and day. It's been that way for a long time now. And when the siren blows and the white lights blast open to light up the palace like the sun, we enter and are escorted to the rich part of the palace where we do our jobs and make six drops of water per hour. Today I made seventy two drops and that's hardly enough for one."

The raccoon looked over to his wife as she hushed their children to sleep. "But we put all our water together and share with the children so that they have the strength to make the butterfly suits." He sighed at the thought that his children could not be children. He wished he could have done more for them, somehow. "See, the men work in the palace," he continued, "and the women and children stay out here and make their suits…" He stopped suddenly, shook his head gravely, then said sadly, "I don't get it. I don't get it, 'cause they sell those suits for enough glitter to buy an entire lake and they pay us three drops per suit…I just don't get it…"

Goro, who had once meditated a long while on caterpillar ways, knew why they had to keep the Forest in a state of oppression. He explained, "If they paid you a lake, you wouldn't need water. If you didn't need water, you wouldn't make their suits. Slavery 101, buddy."

Solomon nodded, and knew the ant was speaking the truth.

"Give us just enough to keep us manufacturing," the raccoon said, and felt sick inside. "How did it come to this?" He looked at them imploringly, his face wracked with infinite suffering.

Again, Goro explained, "Racoons decided to play their game. Only caterpillars had a head start and were taking no prisoners." He shook his head and felt sorry for this father. "Believe me," he added, "I thought single-pointedly on their game for a long, long time."

"Oh," the raccoon said, "We all know that now. But now it is too late. We all blindly took part in the destruction of everything that was ever important to us and before we even realized what was going on we were slaving for all the things we once had for free. And when we tried to change things for the better, our very own leaders went against us. And when we tried to change our leaders, the caterpillars came in with their robots and suppressed our rebellion in the name of peace. Sometimes a rebellion is a good thing. It says something about the leaders, not those rebelling..." Another deep sigh. "And so with our leaders doing all the destruction we had no one to blame but ourselves. Our leaders betrayed their own kind and the caterpillars continued to amass our resources at a pittance. Now hundreds die every day of dehydration while we slave so a few caterpillars can live like kings."

Goro jumped in, "It's exactly what they did to ants. They cloud truth by making you think a product or a name is worth more than your resources. You're so cloudy in the mind you don't even know the difference between something that is useless and something that is priceless. So you give them lots of glitter for their worthless things so that they can buy back from you all your riches at a pittance. I must admit..." he gazed outside and sighed at the poverty, "it's an effective formula."

Solomon turned to the raccoon. "Only a few live like kings?" he asked, seemingly confused. He was under the impression all caterpillars lived like kings.

"Sure!" the raccoon said, and his wife quickly hushed him. His voice then tapered to a whisper. "In the beginning things were pretty fair for caterpillars. I mean, the Silk Palace was always a cold-hearted place, which would let you die if you didn't have the glitter for medicine. But the good thing was that if you worked for a station, that station took real good care of you. Medicine, benefits and all that good stuff. And that had a lot to do with the fact that stations were competing against each other..."

The raccoon went quiet and meditative; he looked at the ground and thought about stations and how they no longer cared about their workers; how workers now lived fragile, uncertain lives. He wondered how a worker could even be productive if he was always worried about job security. And the raccoon knew it hadn't always been this way. There was a time when stations made a caterpillar feel like they belonged to something bigger than they were. Now they were all temporary-permanent employees with little or no benefits. Replaceable like a light bulb.

Shaking his head slowly, the raccoon raised his chin. "Now the leaders of these stations have organized," he said softly, and felt a little sad for the common caterpillar. "Stations are working together and against the common worker. Now they got caterpillars competing with each other for work and most of the work goes to us because we'll work for water...and there is no more security or benefits for caterpillars because they don't need to give 'em...see, that's one benefit of uniting...and now the Silk Palace and the stations are both cold and ruthless beasts and that's why the majority of caterpillars live exactly like we do, only-and this is funny but sad-they don't know, and they don't know it 'cause they're lost in some strange idea that they're actually doing better than us. Them puppet shows and reports are really powerful, I tell ya. They keep the needlessly poor silent in a prison of fear and illusions."

"It's beserko," Goro said with a little laugh.

"It absolutely is," Solomon agreed.

Terku closed his eyes and nodded.

The raccoon continued, "But their way cannot last for very long. You cannot have the owners of stations making five hundred times more than the average worker and offer them no security, benefits or respite..." He paused, his eyes calculating. Then he said, "There are too many like us in the Silk Palace now, and when one day they wake up and realize what is happening to them there will be a great revolution. And when they change things maybe they'll try and help us out here." He paused for a moment, then continued with a glimmer of hope. "Maybe. Maybe, they'll think of us. I mean, having been through the same suffering and all."

Tapping his bullhorn unconsciously, Goro said, "Seems like you've been thinking quite a bit." He leaned toward the raccoon and said, "I'm glad you've been thinking, buddy. It's the first step..."

The raccoon nodded. "We all have," he answered strongly. "We all know what's going on, and we're all ready for change. I guess all we're really waiting for is a leader."

Suddenly, a sharp beeping noise followed by a loud cry interrupted him, and they gazed outside and saw a caterpillar in a butterfly robot pushing a wheelbarrow. The caterpillar yelled, "Bring out the dead! Bring out the dead!" Another robot followed close behind and handed out little white boxes bearing the red and blue butterfly flag. Then a few mothers brought out their dead children and placed them in the wheelbarrow. Terku hung his head and clenched his fists and couldn't believe his eyes.

Keeping his eye on the robots, Solomon asked, "What's in the box?"

The raccoon laughed. "Processed crumbs!" he answered in contempt, and his wife told him to hush. He lowered his tone and pointed to the robots. "They're what the palace calls 'aid' workers." He shook his head and laughed mockingly. "Don't get me wrong, those are some really good caterpillars at heart. They mean really, really well; but, in reality, all they're really doing is putting a little ointment on a massive tumour." He laughed again, then went quiet all at once. "Their hearts are in the right place, but their energy and focus isn't."

The raccoon let his head fall, and he seemed to be meditating on a stone. Solomon remembered how everyone he had once met on Chichikaka seemed to have had a keen understanding of energy and focus and the importance of guidance, direction, and leadership. He thought about the raccoon's words and concluded that some of the leaders of the Silk Palace were the real problem and that was probably why they were directing everyone's focus and energy away from them.

"You don't solve a problem by dealing with the symptom," the raccoon said, raising his head. "You solve a problem by dealing with the source. You focus your energy on curing the disease and, as the rich caterpillars say, 'ipso facto' you eliminate the symptoms. We are symptoms of a much bigger problem and if they really, really wanted to help, they'd change the policies of the Silk Palace; fix their leaders; fix it so we don't need those boxes of processed crumbs."

Again, the raccoon stared at the stone meditatively. After a moment, he raised his gaze and concluded:

"If all them 'aid' workers would just turn their attention to the leaders and the stations and demand change...well, I think this Forest would be a much, much better place. Instead, the leaders go out of their way to organize and fund these 'aid' missions, and they do so because they know these 'aid' missions get all the focus and attention off the real problem. They know these missions keep potential rebels busy and distracted with symptoms while oppressors hide behind a mask of some great and most divine benefactor."

286

Once upon a time in a forest far away...

There was a moment of silence, then the raccoon went on. "It's like they're laughing at us, you know. How are we supposed to be grateful? They steal the loaf and return a crumb all nicely packaged with their flag stamped all over the box." He sighed angrily. "And to add insult to injury they give us napkins!" His wife hushed him again and made an angry face; then she gestured to the children who were now sound asleep.

The raccoon pulled out an aid box and pulled out a napkin. He whispered harshly, "Now why does my family need a napkin for a crumb?" His eyes watered and he sighed. "Are they laughing at us or what?"

Goro thought a long moment. "I think," he said truthfully, "we should be thankful for their aid. We should. We should be thankful that some caterpillars still have their hearts in the right place. And I think...I think that we should pray that one day their energy and focus will be better directed; that one day caterpillar aid workers will choose to make a greater difference in the Forest by focusing on the inside rather than the outside, by dealing with the disease, as you put it, and not the symptom. But till that day, I do believe we should be thankful."

With another deep sigh, the raccoon nodded. "I know you're right...it's just...why the napkins...why the napkins?"

Solomon stared at the flag on the napkin. He shrugged and said, "Just another place to put their flag."

And Goro added, "Colonization 101."

❧

They took their talk outside. The raccoon led them out into the silence of what seemed to be night, and they began to inspect the sticky, silk walls of the Silk Palace. Behind them, wasted faces conspired together in low tones so that no one could hear their plans and turn them in for water.

Solomon inspected the wall carefully. He knew that the only way in was through the gates. "Is there a secret way in?" he asked and turned to the raccoon.

"Afraid not," the raccoon answered.

"Could we break through?" Goro asked.

"Impossible," the raccoon said, "You'd have to be a monster to break through that stuff." He touched the wall and had a difficult time pulling his hand away. "It's sticky like a web...and besides, it's extremely well guarded. You exert too much force and they'll be on you faster than a caterpillar on glitter."

Terku tried to say something to the raccoon. The raccoon narrowed his gaze on the porcupine's mouth and tried to make out his whispers. Soon the raccoon was nodding. He said, "Yes, I know where that is..." He kneeled on the ground, cleared away some rubble, and drew a map of the Silk Palace in the dirt. Then he showed the porcupine where the dam was.

Peering down at the dirt map, Terku muttered something else with difficulty. The raccoon struggled to make out his words; then he nodded and said, "Yeah, I know where that is, too..." Terku watched the ground carefully as the raccoon's finger zigzagged from the entrance of the Silk Palace through elaborate roads and avenues. Finally, Terku's eyes went wide when the fingers stopped at the museum. He then closed his eyes and memorized the path.

Solomon gazed at Goro and wondered why Terku wanted to know these things, to which
Goro shrugged and said, "Buddy, I haven't got a clue."

"How will it all end? Apocalypse or renaissance?" Goro asked Solomon and Terku as they sat on a boulder gazing in disbelief at a billboard bearing a picture of Akiru in a butterfly suit and the slogan:

"Be real, Buy more!"

Solomon threw a rock at the wall. The rock bounced back and flew over their heads. "We cannot know," he answered thoughtfully; then he lobbed another rock at the wall. The next moment the rock soared over their heads.

Goro thought about the young rebels. "Maybe the kid was right. Maybe the only thing to do is blow this place to smithereens."

"The kid was wrong," Solomon said, and then he indicated a few robots guarding the gates. "Look at those robots! Look at them...can you even begin to imagine the knowledge and abilities they possess? I'm afraid we need the caterpillars...we need the minds that came up with those weapons to focus on inventions that will make things better for us...for all of us..."

Solomon fell silent as he studied the robots carefully. Then he turned to Goro and said, "You know what I'm betting?" He paused and glanced at Terku. "I'm betting it's just a few greedy caterpillars keeping the palace so focused on war and greed. I'm betting the majority of caterpillars don't even know what's going on, really going on outside this place. That's what I'm betting."

"I won't bet against you," Goro said without hesitation. "I'm betting you're right."

Solomon added, "Awareness is everything, my friend. Ignorance, indifference, and distraction are our true enemies. That's what I've come to realize."

"Buddy," Goro said, "that's exactly why we need Akiru. Don't you see? Even if we get in, there is absolutely nothing we can say or do. Caterpillars won't listen to us! Are you kidding me! To them we're the enemy. They need one of their own to say what we are saying is true, or else the reports will dilute and deny all the truths we will bring to them."

Solomon sighed. "I haven't given up on her just yet."

"I have!" Goro exclaimed, now red with emotion. She had turned her back on her friends and the Forest, the only ones who had ever believed in her; and he didn't care to talk about her anymore.

Suddenly, Terku stood and began to mumble and whisper. They noticed that they could now make out his words and that slowly his voice was recovering and returning.

"What is he saying?" Goro asked Solomon.

"I don't know," Solomon said, but was genuinely glad to hear his friend speak again.

With his eyes closed, Terku had his arms outstretched. He whispered, "Oh restless ancestors...please...please help us find a way in. Please help us do what is in us to do. Please...we have not come all the way here to fail you now." He staggered left, then right, and it almost seemed as though some invisible force was guiding him. He turned round and walked toward the wall. "Please," he continued, "so that I may return our stolen treasures to our land...please..."

Goro observed, "His eyes...his eyes are closed."

Solomon added, "It's like he's being guided."

"I think he's peeking!" Goro said, observing Terku carefully.

But Terku wasn't peeking, and he was guided right into the wall. He opened his eyes and sighed angrily and banged the wall softly. At his despair, Goro mounted Solomon and they flew toward him.

"Terku," Solomon said, landing right behind the porcupine, "Don't worry...somehow...we'll get in...somehow, Terku." At which point Terku whispered harshly, "It's no use!" and he pounded the wall as hard as he possibly could.

The next instant they were surrounded by robots, staring down the barrels of chrome laser blasters.

Eyes so wide they seemed ready to explode, Solomon gulped and said, "This was not the 'somehow' I had in mind!"

၆၁

Above, fake stars and a moon presented a false picture of a clear night sky. The robots marched them through the decrepit streets of the Silk Palace, and Terku felt a tremendous grief for all the tired, poverty-stricken caterpillars that surrounded him. Solomon's heart almost stopped when he saw how many poor caterpillars there were in the Silk Palace. And a great feeling of sadness swept over all of them as the robots commanded and prodded them on.

Everywhere they looked they saw desolation below billboards of prosperity. Glow lights hung from poles and cast streets in orange monotone pools of light. Half-destroyed homes were rebuilt with garbage taken from the other side of the Silk Palace, where a select few lived in homes made of polished stone and marble. Sobs and hunger cries filled the air while Terku thought these caterpillars looked like they worked more hours than there were in a day, and that this still wasn't enough to make ends meet. He couldn't help but feel sorry for these caterpillars. They weren't any better off than those who lived outside the Silk Palace.

Shaking his head in disbelief, Goro stared at all the homeless families. Then he thought about the aid workers who left the Silk Palace every morning to help the outside. "Aid!" he scoffed, "How can they even pretend to be in a position to offer aid when they cannot even take care of their own?"

They walked by a billboard of Akiru, and Solomon read, "Be real, Buy more!" and then he laughed and repeated the slogan several times.

Goro questioned, "How could she? How could she?"

The robots ordered them to be quiet and move faster.

Ahead, they could see a crowd and they looked at one another in curiosity.

As they walked by the rowdy crowd they saw a caterpillar in rags reading passionately form a scroll. Behind them, a soldier mumbled something quickly in his communicator. Upon further inspection they saw that the one responsible for the crowd was none other than the caterpillar that Solomon had saved from the rebels.

Once upon a time in a forest far away...

One caterpillar in the crowd screamed at the caterpillar rebel, "Those are lies! Those are lies! How come we never heard of them on NCC!"

"Yeah," another caterpillar agreed. "If that were true, we would have heard about it on NCC!"

"Exactly," another caterpillar added. "What are you trying to tell us? That we're not the saviours of the Forest...that we're destroyers and tyrants...that the Silk Palace's most trusted source for truth is twisted and tweaked to keep us silent...?"

"That's crazy!"

"Preposterous!"

"Ignorant!"

And before the newborn rebel could retort or explain what he meant, an NCC stage on wheels honked and puffed by them. In an instant, everyone turned their attention to the puppet show. "NCC!" one caterpillar yelled in excitement and ran over to the stage. The others soon followed, and the caterpillar rebel hung his head, feeling as if his efforts were basically useless against such a giant.

Solomon, Terku and Goro walked by the puppet stage and peered at a well-groomed caterpillar puppet. The puppet politely introduced itself to the crowd and said, "In today's news, rebels were suppressed by caterpillar forces, but rumour is they're growing and getting stronger. I'm afraid we still have a lot more to fear before anything gets better. Experts don't know how, don't know where, don't know when, but they all agree it might just happen soon." Solomon inspected the puppet and wondered where the source of the voice was coming from. The puppet continued. "In other news, some malprogressos are saying the sky is falling and that we must reduce production, consumption, and waste. Unbiased experts with many degrees from the most prestigious schools agree there is nothing to worry about and that these variations in weather and atmosphere are really quite normal. Here at NCC, you can be sure, the environment is very important to us."

The puppet bowed out politely and there was much discussion among the crowd:

"What was it we were thinking about before?"

"I forgot..."

"Me too."

"Something about problems in the Forest...or was it...ahhh..."

"Ah, who cares? Doesn't really matter, our walls gush glitter, theirs don't. It's just jealousy...they all want to live in the Silk Palace."

292

Once upon a time in a forest far away...

"Yeah, I suppose you're right..."

Then a caterpillar hushed everyone down as a play sponsored by the Silk Palace museum began. Terku clenched his fists angrily when he realized the play was about a noble porcupine trying to defend his way of life in face of the 'civilised' caterpillars. Within seconds the robots were pushing them toward the prison.

"Don't touch!" a caterpillar in a striped black and white uniform warned Goro as he approached a green energy wall that imprisoned them. "It will paralyse you for hours. Believe me, I know." The cell was small and there was only one barred window and one tiny prisoner.

Heeding the warning, Goro backed away from the humming wall. Then he climbed up Terku and balanced himself atop the porcupine's highest quill. "Where are we?" he asked, gazing down at the prisoner.

"Caterpillar prison," the caterpillar answered plainly. He considered caterpillar prisons for a moment, then added, "From what I know, we got plenty of them in the palace. See, it's really rather ridiculous: instead of trying to fix things so we don't need prisons, they just keep on building more."

Solomon remembered the raccoon and what he had said about caterpillar aid workers. He commented, "Instead of curing the source of the problem, they cure the symptom..."

"Yup," the caterpillar said, "That seems to be the caterpillar way."

The small window brought in the sounds of a steadily growing crowd. After a short silence, Goro asked, "So, buddy, why are you here?"

The prisoner looked up to the ant. For a moment he seemed lost in his thoughts, mumbling curses. Before long he was shaking his head sadly. "I don't really know. All I wanted to do was create and implement a system where the elderly took care of the young...and I thought it was a pretty sensible idea until one morning I woke up...I woke up in here... It doesn't make any sense..." He fell silent and meditative, trying to understand why he had been imprisoned.

Goro climbed down Terku and approached the prisoner. "Tell me more," he said softly. "Tell me more..."

The prisoner looked to the ant, then the porcupine, then the dove. "Seemed like a good idea," he said with a sigh. "Way I see it, adults in their race for more have no more time for their own kids or parents...so I figured instead of putting them in separate, loveless institutions, we could maybe combine the two. You know, have the elderly teach the young. I don't know. It's just something I thought of like that. On the spur, as they say. A kind of intuition. I mean, the elderly have so much to teach and the

294

young have so much to learn. It doesn't make sense that we separate them. Does it? Not unless you want to teach caterpillars to be cold and heartless like the institutions that raise them."

Goro suggested, "To be frank, buddy, I don't think the caterpillar way has room for emotions. Emotions get in the way of profiteering. Emotions get in the way of greed and conquest."

The prisoner nodded gravely. "I think you may be right."

"Combining the elderly with young makes a lot of sense," Goro said, and sat beside the caterpillar. "It makes a lot of sense."

"Sure does," Solomon said, and he was genuinely surprised a caterpillar could think beyond glitter and gain. Now he felt that maybe things were already beginning to change.

The prisoner said, "They separate the young from the elderly and put them in institutions where caterpillars work from a motivation for glitter, not love; and, from what I know, love is what we're going to need if we're ever going to fix this mess." He looked to the small window and could hear the excitement of the crowd rising. Gradually, the coliseum was filling. With a sigh, he turned back to his inmates. "I don't understand this place. We undervalue the teacher and esteem the pirate, and then we wonder why the entire Forest despises us and wants to see us fall." He paused to mumble to himself. Then he said, "Teachers are ridiculed by their salaries while those who head stations responsible for massacring the Forest are rewarded like kings. And through this very clever reward system, they get all the young and emotionless wanting to work for these pirates; then we wonder why there is a shortage of teachers and classes are overcrowded. It wasn't always this way, you know. There was a time when teachers were revered more than pirates and teaching was the most respected profession. But that memory is lost...like so many other important memories."

Goro gazed at the green wall. "I don't think your leaders really care for education...otherwise you wouldn't be in here..."

Terku added, "They wiped out our entire species because our leaders would not undervalue education, because our ways would not change, because we laughed out loud when caterpillars demanded we divide up our sacred land and sell it for glitter. And now look at the land. Rubble and mud. No soil. No life."

"I'm sorry," the prisoner apologized to Terku. "I wish it didn't have to be that way."

Goro looked up at the porcupine and added, "But it has to be that way. Caterpillars can't have any competing ways of life around them, Terku. Already caterpillars look so unhappy here and I'm sure some are already looking for another way. The leaders here win by destroying the options before they are even sought."

The prisoner closed his eyes and thought about the ant's words for a long while. Outside the crowd was deafening. "Of course," the prisoner said with the fire of a new realization in his eyes, "I should have known. You see, the day before I found myself in here I had written the magistrate with a few ideas on how we could maybe solve the great teacher shortage. I told him we could get all the elderly out of retirement homes and into classrooms. I told him I thought the whole idea of retirement as bunk, as a lie. Retirement, I told him, was just an illusory finish line to silence the wise and get us collecting more." He closed his eyes and spoke thoughtfully. "Better have all you ever wanted before retirement...life ends with retirement, be scared of retirement...better have that butterfly suit before retirement...and why? Why...?"

The caterpillar went silent. Then he opened his eyes and answered, "Love. Could it be? Naaahhhh...maybe...well love...love is why we want the best butterfly suit. Isn't it?"

Solomon shrugged. "It's a theory."

Terku said, "Never really thought of it."

"Yes," Goro said, nodding. "I think I understand..."

"Sure!" the caterpillar said, "We want to be loved and appreciated." His eyes were bright with a new truth, and he began to understand something he had somehow overlooked before. He was thankful for these three inmates who somehow pulled the thoughts and realizations straight out of him by making him think and talk. "Love," he continued, "builds and fortifies us. The lack of love drives us to pursue whatever we think will bring us love. Isn't that right?"

"It's a theory."

"Never saw it that way."

"Yes," Goro said, and he could see where the prisoner was going with this.

The prisoner continued, "Do we want the best butterfly suit to be better than others? Or do we want the best butterfly suit to be loved and appreciated by others?"

Goro put a friendly arm around the prisoner. "Go on," he said. "I like where you're going with this."

Once upon a time in a forest far away...

"Well," the prisoner said, "from what I know, it seems like the leaders have systematically destroyed all that ever built genuine love in us; seems like they've found a clever way of emptying us of what we all seek and need. You could even say they turn us grey so that we no longer know the difference between what's true and what's false by making us too busy for...for the things that make us real." He closed his eyes for a moment and pondered how much caterpillars had sacrificed to gain material comforts. He even remembered one teacher who had once told him that there was a time when caterpillars could actually turn into real butterflies. But later he had read in the reports that this was just a myth, a lot of hocus-pocus.

Now Solomon stared at the prisoner. "The grey force," he whispered to himself and remembered his dream. He wondered if the Forest was speaking to him through this caterpillar. The Forest, he knew, worked in mysterious ways.

"Of course," the prisoner said, and sprang up to his feet, startling Goro. "That's why my idea is so dangerous." He walked toward the green energy wall, his face awash in its green glow. "Love is what the elderly would give children, and love and appreciation is what children would return to the elderly. And that's why they won't put the two together." He turned to his new friends. "Institutions don't love! They suck the very soul out of you. You're just a number. You're nothing. And then what happens...what happens when you're missing so much love?"

Mumbling rapidly, the prisoner struggled to answer his own question. "Ahhh...ahhh...what happens...what happens...?"

After some time, Solomon said, "Could be bad...I think..."

The prisoner said, "I'm sure it is! My goodness, I am starting to see things I never saw before."

Goro stood and declared, "Buddy, you're not alive until you're awake!" Then he gazed at the ground and whispered to himself, "And I'm not exactly sure what that means...but I'm sure I'll figure it out."

The prisoner met Goro's gaze. "Oh," he said, "I'm awake. I've never been so awake in my whole life. It's strange, isn't it? How a few strangers helped me see what was always in me to see."

Solomon lifted the prisoner in his wing. He said, "Nothing strange about necessary coincidences."

"Or the workings of the Forest," Terku added in a harsh whisper.

The caterpillar put a thoughtful finger to his chin. "My goodness," he whispered to himself. "It makes perfect sense. Inner power increases with age, but how to prevent this? How to prevent caterpillars from being strong on the inside so they buy more on the outside...rob them of love and fill them with fear...no...yes...no...well...why are the reports so negative...maybe...well, it's something I have to work out..."

Goro said, "Buddy, sounds like you're almost there."

"Make them scared of aging," the prisoner continued in a whisper. "Could it be? Could it be that simple! Naaahh..." He went quiet for a moment. Then his mind jumped to another thought. "Teachers and grandparents are the pillars of inner power...and...and...see...the leaders undervalue both with their reward system. Yet they overvalue the pirate? Why? Why is that? They freely allow the education system to fail so that pirates can come in and 'save' schools on the condition that they can put their pirate logos everywhere. Why? Why do they do this? We can afford weapons to destroy the entire Forest, yet our schools are failing and need to be bailed out by pirates...pirates who make the weapons...the pirates who need to keep the Forest in a state of slavery...nahhh...could it be? Couldn't be! Could it?"

A roar interrupted his thoughts. Terku looked up to the window and wondered what was going on outside. The prisoner looked up at Solomon and sighed miserably. "They are preparing to commit another crime in the Forest."

Concerned, Goro asked, "How do you know?"

"Outside," the prisoner answered, "They are preparing a great distraction."

Goro asked, "Will we be able to see this distraction?"

The prisoner gazed at him, shaking his head. Pity for his new friends glistened in his eyes. He said grimly, "You are the distraction." And they all gulped simultaneously.

298

ॐ

Solomon, Terku and Goro stood at the center of the coliseum as caterpillars booed them and continued to fill the stands. All around were the posters and billboards of Akiru in elaborate butterfly suits. When Akiru entered to take her seat high above everyone else, the crowd went silent. They admired her and wanted to be just like her while Goro made a face of absolute disgust and disappointment. After a moment, she sat around a few caterpillars that no one recognized or knew, but who owned several stations and who made all the decisions in the Silk Palace. Their strength was invisibility.

One caterpillar admired Akiru and thought he, too, would one day own such an elaborate suit and be loved and appreciated by all. But at the moment he had too much debt and needed to work more hours than there were in a day simply to make ends meet. Otherwise he feared he would end up like those poor, homeless caterpillars he had read so much about in the reports. What he had not read in the reports, however, was that more than half of the Silk Palace was poor and in need of help, and that those numbers were increasing daily as the Silk Palace stations became more and more indifferent to those caterpillars who willingly sacrificed their lives to them. He had read about symptoms not sources. Sources were protected and hidden. Sources could afford advertisements.

Akiru stood, and all gasped in awe. Then the crowd clapped and roared their love and admiration for her.

"Look at her!" Goro exclaimed. "Why does she wear a suit? She's real? She doesn't need a suit." He watched the crowd and saw the respect everyone had for her, how they all envied her, and wanted to be just like her. "So full of herself. After all she has seen, after all she has experienced, after all she has learned...look at her! How can she inspire in others what she never embraced in the first place? Why won't she show them her real wings? Why won't she tell the truth?"

"Glitter," Solomon answered.

"Glitter," Terku repeated; then added scornfully, "The great silencer."

When her ego was satisfied, Akiru smiled and gestured for silence. When there was silence, she spoke into a microphone and said,

Once upon a time in a forest far away...

"Thank you. Thank you. Before the games begin, I just wanted you to know that I've been through a lot in my life, a lot of hardships..." Her head fell and her tone became low and sad.

"Yes!" Goro waited eagerly. Now he felt a surge of hope. He felt she might actually be honest with those who would clearly cross an ocean for her.

Akiru continued, "I've struggled quite a bit and learned many lessons..."

"Yes!" Goro said and took a step forward. "Yes! Yes!"

"Yes," Solomon said, "that's right...remember...please remember..."

"And this is what I know for sure..."

"Yes, yes!"

"Remember," Solomon whispered. "Please remember."

"You are..." she said thoughtfully, "What you buy!"

Everyone nodded and considered her wisdom carefully. And her wisdom validated the life they had recently grown accustomed to. So their minds did not challenge but embraced her words unquestioningly.

"It's true," said one caterpillar.

"She's right," said another.

"She's so honest."

"I will take that loan!"

"What's a little debt when comes to being real?"

Akiru waited for silence to return.

Goro turned to Solomon. He placed his bullhorn in front of his mouth and bellowed, "Have you given up on her now?"

Solomon didn't answer. He still couldn't believe her words.

Now everyone was quiet, waiting for her closing remarks. She beamed at them and said, "Be real!" and the entire coliseum automatically answered in unison, "Buy more!" The coliseum shook with the answer and Goro shuddered in horror. Then Akiru laughed falsely, giggled exaggeratedly, and blew kisses to everyone. "That's all," she said, and took her seat.

Solomon burst out, "That's not all!" And he took a furious step forward, much to everyone's surprise. A robot went to restrain him, but Solomon outmanoeuvred the slow and clunky machine and evaded every laser blast as he flew up to where Akiru was sitting.

Not intimidated in the least, Akiru asked the dove, "Who are you?"

The nameless leaders mumbled harshly in their communicators.

Once upon a time in a forest far away...

She leaned forward. "Do I know you?"

Solomon could hear the guards running up the stairs. "Don't you remember?" he asked, gazing deeply into her eyes. "Akiru, you're the one! You're the one. You're the only one with the power to make things right again."

"Make what right?"

Solomon pointed to the leaders. "You think they're responsible for your strength, your abilities. They had nothing to do with your success. They don't care about you. They just care to silence you with glitter...with your own ego...your own greed...Akiru, the Forest is dying, the Silk Palace is decaying...Akiru...listen to your heart..."

She stood slowly and all five leaders went to pull her back. She brushed their slimy hands off her and approached the white dove. "Who are you?"

The leaders pleaded with her to ignore him.

Ignoring them, she said, "We've met, haven't we? I recognize your voice."

"Yes," Solomon said, "But don't remember me, remember the Forest. Akiru, remember..."

"The Forest," she said, "But everything is fine. I read..."

"Forget what you read! Remember what you saw! Remember what you saw outside the Silk Palace."

"What I saw," she repeated slowly, "outside the palace."

"Apocalypse or renaissance...it's up to you..."

One leader stood to cover her ears, but she turned on him and pushed him back in his seat. Then she turned back to Solomon. "Apocalypse or renaissance? What are you saying, dove?"

"You are the key," he said with deep conviction. "You have more power than all the reports put together. Everyone loves and adores you. And you have these powers for a reason." Solomon could hear a platoon of soldiers rushing to Akiru's booth. He spoke with a deep sense of urgency. "You hold their very hearts and souls in the palms of your hands." He gestured to the entire coliseum. "Be true to those who trust you. Be true to yourself."

Below, Goro gazed up at Solomon and Akiru. He said, "I wonder what he's talking about?"

Terku shrugged; then he recoiled when he heard a roar coming from behind an ornate metal gate.

Once upon a time in a forest far away...

When the gate shook with violence, Goro turned to Terku. "Buddy," the ant said, "I think we're in trouble."

Terku nodded with concern. "What is it?"

Goro said, "I don't know. And I don't want to find out!"

Above, a few dozen caterpillars tackled Solomon and dragged him into an aisle. Despite Akiru's pleas to let him go, they pulled and pushed him back down.

Goro watched Solomon struggle as they dragged him down. "That's it!" he threw his hands to the air and gave up. "It's over!"

Terku studied the scene. He narrowed his eyes and said, "I haven't given up on Solomon just yet."

"Akiru!" Solomon shouted with difficulty. "What I am saying is true. And you don't even have to look as far as the Forest to see that I'm right! Just look at the palace to know what I'm saying is true! Half of those you say you love cannot even afford medicine or education...can't even send their kids to real schools...have to work two or three jobs without vacation... Is this what you want for those who would do anything for you? For those you profess to love? It doesn't have to be this way...the palace is ready for change..."

She turned to those who controlled her voice. "Is what he says true?"

The leaders scoffed and said that he was exaggerating, that he was a malprogresso, hoping the weapon-word would automatically bring all kinds of extremist images to her mind and thereby discredit his every word; for now they could see a strange stirring in Akiru's eyes.

Akiru turned back to Solomon, not knowing what to do.

They yanked Solomon roughly as he yelled in her general direction. "You're worth more than all the glitter in the world! Akiru, don't turn your back on the Forest." He didn't know what to say anymore, and wasn't sure if his words were even penetrating. When they dragged him into the courtyard, he exclaimed, "It's high time you take off that suit!"

The ornate gates shook violently. But Terku and Goro didn't notice as their eyes were glued to Akiru.

Akiru didn't know what to think. But she knew that malprogressos exaggerated everything. So she sat back down slowly and smiled a reassuring smile to the leaders, and they were glad the dove's words had not penetrated.

Goro said, "Now it's over!"

And Terku turned his attention to Solomon and whispered,

Once upon a time in a forest far away...

"Haven't given up just yet."

The guards dragged Solomon to his friends. But before they could bind his wings, he broke free from their hold and rocketed toward Akiru.

Akiru jumped to her feet and approached the railing. Below her, Solomon perched on a ledge where he would be momentarily safe from the guards. But this time he did not beg or speak. He merely looked up at her devotedly. He closed his eyes and opened his heart. He reached deep within for the magic he hoped would melt her heart's armour. A chain of events had brought him to this moment and nothing was coincidence.

There was a tense silence and the leaders stirred restlessly. When they demanded she sit back down, she turned abruptly and hushed them strongly. Turning back to the dove, she saw his beak beginning to open.

At that moment Solomon began a song, a song so beautiful and intense that the entire coliseum went silent. He sang and sang and forgot time and place as he poured out all his agonies, all his pain for the unnecessary injustices and inequalities he had witnessed firsthand in the Forest. And magic being stronger than weapons and armour, his song pierced her soul and took her on an incredible journey along the paths of memory. Her whole body tingled as if some ancient spirit was speaking directly to her, and everything she had conveniently forgotten came rushing back to her consciousness.

Without warning, Solomon's song struck her hard, battered her ego, and left her vulnerable to truths she had tried so hard to sweep under the carpet of her mind and forget. Her eyes glistened with tears and her lower lips quivered uncontrollably. Then a laser blast under the ledge silenced Solomon and, shot down by surprise, he plummeted to the ground where he was quickly subdued, his wings bound by a seemingly indestructible silk. Then he was quickly dragged to center.

But it was too late. Tears streaming down her cheeks, remembering all she had learned on her journey, Akiru gazed at the leaders, incensed, dismayed, disillusioned. She took a step back, and they told her she was being silly and emotional. Then, all of a sudden, she tore off her suit and the entire coliseum was instantly dumbfounded.

The leaders didn't know how to react, for they knew how much everyone loved and trusted her. It was for this precise reason they needed to own her voice; they needed to use her in order to seduce caterpillars into an empty life of greed and selfishness, for they knew she had the ability to do just the opposite.

Once upon a time in a forest far away...

Goro laughed with incredible delight. He lurched forward and threw his hands to the air. With one hand he held his bullhorn to his lips and said, "Ladies and gentlemen...The Butterfly!"

From the stands came a great commotion:

"Where did you get that suit?"

"I have never seen such a suit!"

"What brilliant colors!"

"Must be expensive!"

"Yeah, must be..."

"Hey, wait a minute. Was that dove singing? Doves don't sing, right?"

"Was there truth to his song?"

Akiru fluttered around the coliseum. She yelled out, "This is no suit! It is the real me!" Then she went on to explain how being a real butterfly was a possibility within each and every one of them so long as they could shut out all the distractions of the palace and have the courage to go out there and discover what would help them be real, which was unique for each one.

Slowly, the caterpillars began to reflect on their lives and what she was telling them. She went on about the palace and its system of invisible tyranny. And half the coliseum mumbled that the tyranny was real while the other half crossed their arms and stiffened uncomfortably and insecurely and said that such a system was impossible, that they were free and that no one had control of their opinions, desires, dreams.

But when she began to describe how more than half the palace was poor, living in conditions worse than the outside, no one questioned her. The poverty was in their eyes every day, and the gap between rich and poor was widening every second; and the reason was simple: stations were organized, caterpillars weren't; stations controlled the reports and had a voice, caterpillars read the reports and had a semblance of voice.

Suddenly, she began to call the leaders of stations pirates and assured them that the first step toward change would be to return the reports to caterpillars, to separate stations from reports. She then said that this was necessary for a very simple reason: pirates would never report their own plunder. And still, only half the coliseum agreed with her. The other half was certain that they did in fact have a voice and that a report would expose a pirate's wrongdoing, no matter how much that pirate paid per day in advertising.

Once upon a time in a forest far away...

And finally, when she went to tell them about another way of life, another way of thinking and being, one leader stood to silence her immediately. He merely pointed at her and yelled, "Malprogresso!" Then all the leaders stood and followed suit, yelling the same word in chorus. In an instant the coliseum shook with the word and all caterpillars were against her. Weapon-words were a form of magic in and of themselves.

Goro looked on helplessly as the coliseum booed Akiru and threw plates of food and cups of water at her. His head fell dejectedly. He knew the power of the word, and there was no hope. "That's it," he said in a drawl. "It's over."

"I'm sorry I failed, "Akiru said, standing next to her friends, listening to the monster roar behind the gate. The crowd was screaming for entertainment, and the leaders were beaming down at them. Slowly, the white lights of the coliseum began to dim.

Goro said, "There's not much you can do against a word like that."

She nodded. "I know."

Solomon searched the stands and noticed something promising; some spectators were not as excited as others; some were now looking down at him with confused and slowly changing eyes. "I haven't given up on caterpillars just yet," he said, and turned to Goro with a mysterious smile.

"I wonder," Terku whispered fearfully, "what's behind the gate?"

"If we're lucky," Solomon turned to him. "An ant with a bull-horn." Then he looked down to the ant with a friendly grin.

But Goro was too scared to respond to Solomon's little joke. His legs were shaking terribly and he cried, "I can't take it...I can't take it...buddy, I can't take it!"

There was the loud clang of a lock snapping open. A few seconds later the gate began to rise slowly, and the coliseum went quiet.

"It was nice knowing you," Solomon said softly.

Terku shook his head and put a hand on Solomon's wing. "And I, my friend, haven't given up on the Forest just yet."

"I have," Goro yelled. "It's over! It's over! I can't believe it ends this way!"

The rising gate began to reveal a massive, round monster clad in shiny red armour. Lights flashed everywhere, and the sound of a gong shook the air.

"Ahhhhh!" Goro yelled and hid behind Solomon's leg.

Terku asked out loud, "You think we can take it?"

"Take it?" Goro asked frantically. "It? It, as in that?" And he pointed at the monster. "Honestly...let me see..." He pressed the bullhorn to his lips and yelled, "Noooo! I do not think we can take it!"

The monster pounded its chest and the crowd went crazy with

excitement. Then it slammed one foot forward. The ground rocking under his feet, Goro screamed in terror and dashed behind Terku's leg. "I can't take it," he screamed as loud as he could. When the monster took another step forward, Goro lost his mind and, without warning, ran up to the monster and challenged, "Not without a fight!"

The monster didn't even notice him.

Regardless, Goro didn't wait another second. With all his strength, he held his bullhorn behind his head and with a war cry he thrust it against the armour. "Take that!"

Nothing.

Eyes wide with terror, Goro fell to his knees. "I give up! Okay, I give up! Please...fast! Make it fast..."

The monster stomped by him.

Not too far away there was an echo of someone or something yelling an indiscernible word or name.

Akiru said, "Did you hear that?"

Terku and Solomon listened for a moment. Then they both shook their heads.

Goro ran back with his bullhorn. "I didn't hear anything!"

Akiru said, "It sounded like...like..."

Now the monster faced them and let out a roar that sent them stumbling backward with mingled bad breath and fright.

Akiru heard it again. "Again!" she said, "Did you hear that?"

They shook their heads in reply, and never took their eyes off the monster.

"It sounded like..." she considered. "'Friend.'"

Goro's eyes went wide with hope. "What did you say?"

"'Friend,'" she answered, "I thought I heard..."

Goro didn't wait for her to finish. He grabbed his bullhorn and screamed for Furbul.

The monster stared at the ant rather perplexed, listening intently for the strange voice.

Now they all heard the faraway echo. It was the sound of a massive ball of fur searching desperately for his long lost friends. "Friend!" the word echoed through the Silk Palace. And Goro jumped for joy.

"Furbul!" Goro yelled gleefully.

"Friend!" came back, louder and stronger.

"Furbul!"

"Friend!"

Once upon a time in a forest far away...

"Furbul!"

"Friend!"

Suddenly, the sound of lasers blasting willy-nilly could be heard outside the coliseum. Then all went quiet.

"Furbul!"

But there was no answer.

After a moment, the monster roared its anger at being so rudely interrupted. It pounded its chest and raised its gigantic arms way above the prisoners, ready to smash. But before its hands could smash down on them, Furbul charged into the coliseum throwing butterfly robots in all directions.

For a long moment they gazed at their furry friend with over-whelming relief.

Each caterpillar inspected his neighbour's expression to make sure what they were seeing was true and not an illusion.

Instantly, Furbul recognized the threat. "Bad guy!" he shouted, and pointed at the monster.

"Bad boy!" the monster shot back.

"Bad guy!" Furbul retorted.

The crowd cheered at the sudden and most unexpected change of events. The excitement was unbearable, and they could hardly wait for the battle of the beasts that would shortly ensue.

"Bad boy!" the monster yelled and took a step toward Furbul.

"Bad guy!"

"Bad boy!"

All of a sudden, Furbul felt a strange stirring inside. He didn't know what to make of it. He didn't understand what was happening to him, but he did have a momentary recollection of the voice yelling at him. Searching for the voice in his mind's dusty box of memories, he froze in his tracks. He repeated slowly, "Bad boy?"

Goro didn't understand what was happening to Furbal. "What?" he asked, "What's the matter? Go! Attack! Bad guy! Bad guy, Furbul! Bad guy!"

But Furbul remained frozen with a strange tingling sensation. "Boy!" the monster yelled, and she threw off her armour and opened her arms lovingly.

Now Furbul was choking with emotion. With all his heart, he yelled, "Mama!" Then, tears soaking his fur, he ran into his mother's loving embrace, and mother and son were once again reunited after years

Once upon a time in a forest far away...

and years of separation.

Goro stood back astonished. "Wow! Who saw that coming?"

"Not me," Solomon said, shaking his head in disbelief.

"Not me," Terku echoed. "Not me..."

Wiping a tear, Akiru said, "I guess even monsters have parents."

The crowd booed their disappointment. They wanted blood, violence and gore. And so the leaders sent in a platoon of butterfly robots with laser blasters glowing red, ready to fire. The robots circled the monsters and the prisoners and waited for the order.

Akiru saw that they were hopelessly outnumbered. She said, "We're not out of this one just yet."

At which point the robots began their attack. But they stood no chance against mother and son. Their movements were quick and fierce as they giggled helplessly for the laser beams that blasted uselessly against their fur. Robots went flying in all directions and the crowd went wild with excitement. Goro smiled at his friend and thought he had never seen him fight so fiercely and strongly, and the leaders called in more robots.

Tired and needing help, Furbul stopped suddenly. He took a deep breath, then yelled, "Sissssssssssterrrrr!"

All went quiet.

Caterpillars gazed at each other, repeating the word with fear.

Suddenly, another round, furry monster clad in shiny blue armour came charging into the coliseum. She threw off her shiny blue armour and, much to Goro's amusement, the three balls of fur continued to pummel, batter, and beat the butterfly robots.

Everyone admired the strength of this monster family. They struck and giggled and showed no signs of tiring. The battle was unlike any the crowd had ever seen, and this time their technology was losing because the monsters were one, fighting as one, singular in thought, united in spirit, not motivated by glitter but life and family. In other words, the robots didn't stand a chance.

When the leaders saw they were losing, they called in the entire army, and Furbul's sister responded by yelling, "Cuzzzzzzzzzzzins!" And soon, two round, furry monsters came charging into the coliseum.

A terrible panic spread through the crowd.

In a heartbeat, the robots were on the fur balls. The monsters swung and crunched and battered metal. Caterpillars in the stands ran out of the coliseum screaming their terror of the monsters. The leaders were

309

Once upon a time in a forest far away...

already gone. Brothers and sisters and cousins tossed and spun robots around the coliseum as if they were playing with toys. And they were. When they were through with the army, all that remained was a smoking heap of twisted metal, wire, and broken glass.

Eyes wide with delight, Goro said, "It's great to have friends!" And he mounted Furbul with an explosive disbelieving laugh.

Akiru smiled and mounted Furbul's sister. "I agree," she said.

Already sitting atop Furbul's mother, Solomon nodded and smiled. Then he searched for Terku but couldn't find him. Sweeping his gaze across the chaos, he soon spied Terku running out of the coliseum, and he had a good idea as to where the porcupine was headed.

With great pleasure, Furbul and his family demolished the dams and returned to the Forest what belonged to the Forest. Water filled the empty rivers in no time. Life, freedom, and dignity returned to the outside and there was at first disbelief then great celebration everywhere. Then, not having found Terku, Solomon led his friends toward another place he suspected the porcupine might be.

࿂

When Solomon entered the caterpillar museum, he found Terku praying under the porcupine exhibit. His eyes were closed, but tears shone on his dark cheeks. After some time he stood proudly, clenched his fists, and, with one furious thrust, broke the window that separated him from his ancestor's peace. He placed the vases, pottery and sculptures in a box and walked out without saying a word. His ancestors would soon rest.

Solomon sighed and went to join him, but as he stepped outside he was startled by a faint cry for water. He inspected the museum carefully and saw a small, dark room he had somehow overlooked. He turned round and approached the room from where a soft sobbing came. Then he cautiously entered the special exhibits area where to his great surprise he found a cage. The sign above the cage door read:

The Last of the Porcupines
(Do not feed)

The moon glowed high above Solomon and his young audience. "And that, young ones, is how the story ends," Solomon said, and he finished his story with a pleasant smile. But the children didn't seem satisfied.

"No it's not," a young porcupine said after having considered the story.

"Yeah," a bunny added. "You didn't even tell us what happened with the caterpillars."

Solomon didn't seem sure. "I didn't?"

"Nope," a baby raccoon confirmed and crossed his arms.

"You said," a turtle spoke up, "you beat 'em and...but..."

"Did they change?" a young beaver asked, then looked down at the ground for he was quite shy.

"Oh!" Solomon said, "Oh yes! Yes, they did. But not all of them at once. Not overnight. That day when Akiru spoke, she only managed to open the eyes of five caterpillars in the thousands that heard her. But five was enough. Five was enough because change, well change is...is...exponential..."

The children struggled with the word, and each one tried to pronounce the word without success.

"What does expo...?"

"Netrial...?"

"Expossstrical?"

"What does it mean?"

Solomon laughed. "Exponential means to grow so, so fast it's too hard to keep up. It means that when Akiru changed five caterpillars, they each changed ten caterpillars; and then ten caterpillars each changed one hundred caterpillars. Ten became one hundred, one hundred became one thousand, one thousand became..."

"One billion!" a fledgling yelled.

"That's right," Solomon laughed heartily. "One billion caterpillars changed and grew within. And these changed caterpillars made extra sure no station did bad things in the Forest; these changed caterpillars made sure no station did bad things in the Forest to give caterpillars or the Silk Palace a bad name. Change came so fast that the leaders didn't even have time to figure out clever ways to undo what had been done or steal back all the water that had been given back to the Forest. And eventually, caterpillars reconnected to the sacred and spent all their time and energy on things that would help all and not just them." He thought for a moment about what had happened; then he concluded, "The Silk Palace changed the Silk Palace."

In the distance, mothers began to shout for their children.

"Oh-oh," they all said in chorus and then stood on shaky legs.

They surrounded Solomon and tried to hug him all at once. And as they hugged him, Solomon felt strong inside, really strong.

A few more shouts from angry mothers startled them and they wobbled off home. When they were gone, Solomon walked over to the water and watched the ocean. Soon, two little black and white heads peeked out of the water.

"Still telling stories about Mom, Uncle Solomon?" one of the whales asked.

Solomon smiled. "Just making sure we never forget..."

"Wanna see Goro?" the other whale asked with a start.

"Oh, I can't," Solomon said.

"Why not?"

"Yeah, why not?"

"Too far. Too old."

"Ahhh pahhhh-leeeeaaase!" one whale exclaimed.

"Ahhh pahhhh-leeeeaaase!" echoed the other. "Hop on! Tell us Mom stories on the way there, and before you know it you'll be with an old friend."

Solomon shook his head. He threw his head back gleefully and laughed at the stars, and the stars laughed back at him. With a deep breath of fresh air, he flew to the whale's crown and said, "Let's seenow...where do I begin...?"

313

Siberia

Prologue

In stories, it is love not treasure or power or revenge that inspires us. Even those who swear they will never love, that they do not believe in love, that they will never surrender their hearts to another are often the first to fall under love's spell. And for these lovers, the journey from first encounter to final separation is often beautiful and tragic.

In Siberia, wolves often tell the story of Gabriel, the arctic wolf--how he traveled from mountain to mountain searching for his treasure. How he nearly died several times searching for his treasure. And how, in the coldest and harshest of lands, he found a treasure greater than he had ever hoped for.

ॐ

A violent wind shrieked through the snowy desert of ice and rock as Gabriel toiled up the mountain path in search of his treasure.

"Today," he growled, "is a good day. Today I will find my treasure."

Long ago, Gabriel had left home. His family and friends had told him it was time to find a partner and have pups. It was time to do what every other responsible wolf did when they grew up. It was time to follow the way of the pack.

But Gabriel refused to listen to others, and he genuinely despised formulas. His grandmother had taught him to think differently, to question everything, to think outside the pack; for she too despised formulas, and she had passed down a lot of her thoughts and feelings to Gabriel. She used to say:

"No love, no passion. No passion, no heat. No heat, no life."

And Gabriel wanted passion. He wanted heat. He wanted life. And he most certainly did not want to be like the others: doing nice things for his partner because he had to. For such a life was a trap, and he had observed it countless times before--love turned routine, routine turned contract, contract turned cage.

"Passion gone, the heart turns to ice," his grandmother had once said. "But wolves would rather be trapped with a partner than free and alone."

Indeed, Gabriel was convinced wolves generally lived inauthentic lives to please others, and he did not wish to live a life of appearances. He wanted passion. He wanted life. He wanted what his grandparents had.

True love.

Or nothing at all.

To do things because of heart and not obligation.

And there was a difference.

And his grandmother had taught him the difference.

"Anything short of true love," his grandmother used to say, "is not worth your time. For it is love that makes us and everything in this world real; and it is usually the most passionate and intelligent of wolves who understand this and who, refusing anything less, are quite often the most alone. Don't be scared of being alone, my dear Gabriel. Be scared of settling for anything less than what you deserve."

Unfortunately for Gabriel he never met his true love and was often discouraged by the wolves he met back home. They were so different in mind and opinion. So superficial and scared that they would often settle for less than what they deserved.

And often he felt replaceable with those wolves he had met. It was not him that they really wanted to be with; it was the idea of him, the idea of not being alone. His partner could be with anyone so long as she was not alone. And this hardly made him feel special.

And Gabriel wanted to feel special. And he often wondered if there was anyone out there like him. Sometimes he even wondered if he even had a soul mate.

Sometimes he even doubted there was someone out there for him, and sometimes he wished his grandmother had not put the idea of true love into his head.

But every time he would doubt his grandmother would come to him in his dreams and reassure him. She would tell him that he and his true love were once one spirit, that they had been split into twin spirits, and that they had fallen to the planet where over continents and oceans a special star--their star--would reunite them.

She told him that this star would make sure they met, but only when they were both ready. She explained that perhaps he had not met his true love because he had not lived and experienced enough to truly appreciate her; that she had not met him because she had not lived enough to truly appreciate him. And she told him to be patient, that timing was everything, and that their star knew best.

But time wore on and Gabriel never met his true love. Finally, he decided he didn't have a soul mate, and he pushed the idea straight out of his head, leaving his heart open for a new passion, one which had come to him in his dreams.

One night Gabriel had dreamt of a big black wooden treasure box hidden way up in the frozen mountains of Siberia. Not having found true love, and unable to settle for anything less, he said good-bye to the familiar and began on a new adventure.

છ૩

The wind bit through Gabriel's thick white fur like teeth, and he lifted himself over a snowy ledge and found a small ice cave. He entered cautiously and felt that today would be his lucky day. Today he would find his treasure. It was the cave he had seen in his most recent dream, and the thought of success filled his sad blue eyes with hope. But by the day's end he had found nothing and was exhausted. Defeated, he lowered his muzzle and made way for his cave one heavy paw at a time.

&

When Gabriel reached his dark cave, he collapsed with a heavy sigh.

Every day for the last ten years, he had been convinced he would find his treasure, and every day, he had been wrong.

Now Gabriel was older, alone, and discouraged. Now he lived a life dominated by cold and solitude, and the only thing that kept him alive was the thought that somewhere out there, somewhere in the snowy desert that had become his life, was his treasure.

As Gabriel watched the moon rise, he listened to the wind cry and felt a great pain in the pit of his stomach. Then, without understanding why, he threw his head back and howled at the heavens.

He choked up and his eyes watered. But he shed no tears. Instead he shook his head and cleared his throat. "Breathe," he said. "Breathe."

After some time he quieted his anxious heart. He could feel the cold of night settling in and biting through his fur. With glassy eyes, he looked up to the stars and remembered his grandmother. Then he remembered to pray.

Ever since he could remember, he had prayed right before bed to thank the Great Mystery for all his blessings.

"Pray for your dreams, Gabriel," his grandmother used to say. "Prayer can overcome enemies, conquer death, grant wisdom, and answer your heart's biggest dream. Never underestimate the power of prayer because prayer draws on the Great Mystery of the universe and that Mystery wants to help you."

He remembered his grandmother's gentle voice and felt warm inside.

"Don't try to understand what you cannot, Gabriel," she had said. "There is magic in this world. There really is. And those who try to understand and explain magic find that the magic in their lives soon disappears."

She had paused then and looked into his little blue eyes. "Love is pure faith in another soul. And you must have the utmost faith in the Great Mystery, as it will one day lead you to her."

"To whom?" Gabriel asked.

She laughed at him. "Why, your true love, of course."

"My true love?"

"You are connected to something glorious, radiant, and spectacular, something beyond understanding. And it is this glorious magic that sophisticated wolves will try to rob you of by trying to simplify the universe with their proofs and formulas."

She shook her head at the thought. "Believe in your star. Believe in love. It's the only reason we're here, though if you asked me to prove it, I probably couldn't."

Although Gabriel did not believe in the names and divisions other animals created for the Great Mystery, he believed strongly in the power of prayer. The Great Mystery had always existed and always would no matter where one lived or what kind of animal one was. The name changed to suit the time, place, and species. But the Mystery always remained the same.

Gabriel knew that if his prayer came from the deepest place in his heart, the consciousness of the world would hear him and work to answer his prayers.

So he closed his eyes and thanked the Great Mystery for all his blessings. Then, on the verge of tears, he got up and walked out of his cave.

The wind howled violently around him, and he looked to the brilliant moon and prayed that he should find his treasure. And he prayed like he had never prayed before. A prayer from the deepest and purest place in his heart.

෮

Gabriel roused to the smell of wolves, and his ears pricked up as he heard movement outside his cave. Suddenly, a twig snapped. When he looked up, he saw Viktor and his pack entering his cave.

Viktor was the leader of the gray wolves. He had gray and black fur, and his fierce red eyes glowed like embers. Untouched by compassion or scruples, he was a frightening wolf to meet, and many years ago, he and Gabriel had clashed.

Viktor had asked Gabriel to join the pack, but Gabriel-- needing and cherishing his time--wanted to be alone.

Gabriel had refused to belong to any pack. Bound by others, he felt he would never find his treasure. He felt drawn by his treasure and never allowed anything to enter his mind or life that would distract him from it.

Deeply insulted, Viktor had attacked Gabriel and nearly killed him, releasing him only because Gabriel had offered him half of his treasure if he should ever find it.

And so Viktor spared Gabriel on the slight chance that he might in fact find a treasure buried in the mountains.

Viktor approached menacingly. "What do we have here? It's the loner--the treasure hunter." He scowled at Gabriel as his wolves sniffed around the cave, searching for a scent.

Gabriel felt weak and ashamed. His tail fell, and he lowered his gaze to the ground. "What do you want?"

"What do I want?" Viktor said. He approached Gabriel and growled. "My portion of the treasure, of course. Or have you already forgotten?"

Unable to meet his gaze, Gabriel shook his head and felt like he shrank ten times in height and width. "I have not forgotten," he replied. "I have not found it yet."

Viktor smiled. "What a surprise! Do not worry, Treasure Hunter. I'm not here for some fabled treasure. I'm here for Vasilia--

324

a deserter."

Suddenly, Lavinia cut in. "Obsession!" she corrected. "You mean obsession." The poor wolf loved Viktor even though he did not love her back.

Surprised, Gabriel looked up for a moment. "Deserter?" he asked. He knew desertion was punishable by death in Viktor's pack. Then his eyes met Viktor's for a moment, and his head fell again, and now he became fifty times smaller inside with fear and shame.

Lavinia approached Viktor. "You want to kill her because you cannot have her! You want to kill her because you cannot force her to bow down to you--"

Viktor whirled around. "Quiet!" he commanded.

Lavinia held Viktor's gaze for a long moment. Then she turned to the others, and they stared at her pityingly. They all knew how much she loved Viktor and how much she despised the deserter for having what she wanted more than anything else in the world. With a heavy sigh, she lowered her gaze and quit the cave.

Viktor looked to his wolves.

One after another they shook their heads.

No one could pick up the deserter's scent.

"She's not here," Viktor said. He looked around the empty cave and added, "What respectable wolf would live in such squalor?"

Gabriel didn't respond. He didn't really care about his cave. It was merely a place for him to rest after a long day of treasure hunting.

Laughing, Viktor turned, gave a quick order, and led his wolves outside to continue their hunt.

Gabriel kept his muzzle down until Viktor was gone, and he was now a hundred times smaller than the wolf he had been.

8003

Gabriel and Vasilia met in the snowy mountains of their shared dreams, and did so every night, knowing they would forget everything when they woke up. It was their special place in eternity.

"We haven't met yet," Gabriel said.

"I don't think we're ready."

"When?"

"Soon..."

"I wish it could be now. I feel so alone."

"Our star knows best," she said.

He pulled her closer. "I don't want to wake up."

"Me neither."

၈၃

Alone and lonely, Gabriel gazed at the wide desolate landscape
before him. He breathed the morning air and walked toward the
mountains, preparing himself for another long search. "Today," he
said, "I will find my--"

Suddenly, a soft cry startled him. His ears perked up in
attention; he turned and narrowed his gaze.

The cry came again.

And again.

Then whimpering.

Curious, he followed the sound to Avalanche Valley.

＆

Gabriel soon spotted a wolf with her paw caught in the steel jaws of a hunter's trap. He inched toward her as she groaned and begged for help.

"Quiet," he cautioned. "You should be quiet."

He peered at her and thought he had never seen anyone so beautiful in his life. She looked unlike any wolf he had ever seen with her soft, beige fur, her strong muzzle, and her eyes green like emeralds. When she looked up at him, he melted.

His heart leaped. He stopped breathing. The world froze. He felt a great emotion surge within him, and his heart instantly understood what his mind could not.

He was in the presence of his true love.

Her heart recognized the same thing as she momentarily forgot her pain. Both hearts understood their lives would never be the same again.

They stared at each other as if in a trance.

Silenced by magic.

Suddenly, pain fired up her leg and jolted her back to reality. "I'm going to die," she whimpered, for she had lost a lot of blood and felt faint. "I'm going to die! Please don't leave me...please..."

Gabriel looked to the mountains behind her and said, "Quiet. You must be quiet. Don't you realize where we are?"

She followed his eyes to the giant mountains and observed the snowcaps. She nodded her understanding.

Gabriel approached her and inspected the steel jaws. After several hours of struggling with the trap, he freed her paw and carried her back to his cave.

଼

"My name is Vasilia," she said to Gabriel. "What's…what's your…?"

"Gabriel," he said. "My name is Gabriel." He placed her gently on the rocky ground of his cave.

"Gabriel," she repeated and smiled. "What a beautiful name…"

But before she could complete the sentence, her eyes closed, and she fell asleep. Weak and exhausted, she slept for several days while Gabriel watched over her and nursed her back to health.

In the weeks that followed, Gabriel and Vasilia became very close. They were like two souls that had traveled through a hundred universes together, had been separated for but a brief moment in time and were now catching up with each other. So much...

To say.

To hear.

To understand.

They spent entire nights talking about everything and anything, describing to each other in great detail the events and sights they had missed in each other's absence.

Vasilia told him about Viktor's pack. How they had slaughtered her pack when she was very young, and how he had kidnapped her and forced her into a life of violence and cruelty, fighting and hurting other wolves for territory.

She spoke about how she could no longer bear the injustices, and how, without any idea of where she was going or where she'd end up, she had deserted in the middle of the night.

Gabriel listened without missing a word, and his intense blue eyes shone with awe. And he respected and admired her for her strength and courage.

He did not judge her or feel upset about what he could not change. He understood she had a life before him, that until they were ready for each other, they were doing the best they could without each other. Each experience reaffirming their deep longing for each other.

Still, Gabriel could not understand how some wolves could be so cruel.

Vasilia quickly assured him that cruelty was instinctive to all wolves. More so, she argued, than compassion.

But Gabriel disagreed completely and told her so. And it was clear that she came from an entirely different pack with a whole other set of values and stories.

For Gabriel believed the soul was like a garden. In the soil of the garden existed every possible seed: weeds and orchids. He thought the garden of the soul was nurtured and pruned by the pack. That they would nip weeds and encourage flowers by the stories they told, the values they revered, and the actions they rewarded.

Cruelty and compassion began as seeds. Where they ended up, depended on the gardeners.

That's why Gabriel's grandmother always warned him to watch what stories he permitted into his mind and heart. Stories were responsible for germination like water and light. When a new leader wanted to change the pack, the first thing he did was reward and encourage the stories that suited his end.

"A story is more than a story," his grandmother used to say. "You want to know where a pack will be in the future, observe the stories they are
listening to now."

Vasilia thought about this a long while. She thought there was truth to his grandmother's theory. Perhaps, she reflected, this was why Viktor rewarded those stories that encouraged greed and cruelty while he discouraged stories that perpetuated generosity and compassion.

As the days progressed, Gabriel told Vasilia stories about his youth, living with his pack and parents, his long talks with his grandmother, and his dreams and how they continually guided him to his treasure.

He spoke about leaving home for his treasure and his many travels and encounters, and her beautiful green eyes widened with fear and delight. She admired the look in his eyes when he spoke about his treasure, and she respected him for his strength and courage.

One night, Gabriel told her the story about how his grandparents met.

"My grandparents met by a river," he said. "They too were from separate packs with very different ideas on life. But that didn't stop them. There was something unexplainable, something invisible that drew their hearts together. And so, they loved despite their differences and knew they'd be together forever."

Vasilia listened quietly.

"They were like the sun and moon. Perfect. Beautiful together. Bringing light and happiness wherever they went, and they were always together. Wherever she went, he went. Whatever she felt, he felt. And nothing could come between them. Not even death."

"Not even death," Vasilia repeated, amazed. She turned, giving him her back, and he knew what to do. Scratching her back, he continued:

"When he fell sick, she did all she could to bring him back to health. But one evening--the suffering too intense--he let go. We tried to pull her away, but she wouldn't leave him. She howled with anguish, a howl that sent such waves of despair through the entire pack that we decided to leave her with him overnight. When we returned, she was dead. No wound. No reason. No explanation. She merely let go of her body to follow him into the Great Mystery."

Gabriel broke off, remembering. He stopped scratching and a faraway look passed over his face.

Vasilia had heard stories of how some birds were inseparable as partners, and that if one died, so did the other. But she had always regarded such stories as myth. Now she wondered if the same could be true of wolves.

She turned to face him. She looked deep into his eyes and saw how much he loved his grandparents. Their love had inspired him, and their story was a big part of who he had become, and was still becoming.

Finally, she broke the silence. "Do you think your soul can let go of its body like that?"

"I think so," Gabriel said with a nod. "If it really wants to."

She smiled at the thought. "It's nice to love like that." She took a deep breath and turned again to give him her back.

That night Gabriel and Vasilia forgot about the world and all their problems. They exchanged confidences until morning, and the whole while he scratched her back, and she was in heaven.

ಌ

Days passed, and, neglecting food and sleep, Gabriel and Vasilia became weak with talking. The energy of their relationship was hard if not impossible to maintain, and they both needed time to rest and recuperate.

And so, having worn down their immune systems to such a degree that they both caught the flu, the Great Mystery forced rest upon them.

Coughing miserably, Gabriel turned to Vasilia and watched her sleep in the moonlight. He still had so much he wanted to tell her.

He smiled at her and wished he could be with her forever, and he thanked his star for guiding him to her. He didn't question or doubt his happiness; for he knew the only way to truly thank the Great Mystery for a gift was to enjoy it.

"Thank you," he said, staring through the mouth of his cave. "Thank you." The moon shone like a giant pearl in the sky, and the world seemed perfect.

To Gabriel's surprise, the next morning they woke up forehead to forehead.

For as long as he could remember he didn't like sleeping close to others, and when he did sleep next to anyone, he had a terrible sleep and felt extremely irritated the next day.

Not this time.

This time he felt at ease.

As if he had been sleeping next to her forever.

When he opened his eyes, he found her looking straight at him, admiring him in the deep golden light that poured in through the entrance. After a moment, she moved closer to him and smiled. She touched his muzzle with her nose and said, "I love you."

He couldn't believe his ears. His heart pounded, and for an instant he remembered what it was like to be young and alive. At last he replied, "I love you."

And for the first time in his life…

He meant it.

But he was scared.

He could see that they shared a deep and pure bond, a bond that existed and grew on its own, with no effort from either of them. And this bond was so powerful that it frightened him, though he knew his fear was perfectly natural.

"Soul mates," his grandmother had once said, "experience such a deeply powerful love when they first meet that it often overwhelms and frightens them; they sometimes doubt their feelings and run away from each other. It's important to embrace and accept those powerful feelings and not be scared. Or else you risk being separated from the one who will support you, strengthen you, and fulfill you."

He admired her for a long while. Then a realization seized him and a light of infinite bliss came into his eyes. He knew and had no doubt that he would spend the rest of his life with her.

He knew that he loved her beyond everything, and he wanted to voice the million words racing through his mind but knew the futility for the poverty of words could never do justice to his feelings.

Tears of joy came to her eyes and streamed down her face.

Tears of joy came to his eyes, and he held them in.

Breathe, he thought, *breathe...must maintain control...*

After a few deep breaths, he regained control of his emotions.

She inched closer to him, and they embraced.

Holding each other tight in their love, the heart of each held infinite warmth and compassion for the heart of the other. And that night, in their dreams, they met at their special place.

෪

*Gabriel and Vasilia held each other where time and place ceased to
exist.*

"I'm so happy!" Gabriel said.

"Me too," Vasilia said. "I feel like I can fly."

"You can..."

*She laughed. "Why do you suppose we don't remember this
place when we wake up?" She looked into his eyes and felt she
had known him for a million years and would know him for a million more.*

"Don't know."

"How long do you suppose we've been together?"

"A long time, I imagine. An eternity, even."

Vasilia smiled. "Eternity is pretty long."

"Yes," Gabriel said. "I suppose it is."

"Ever wonder what this is all about?"

*"You shouldn't try to understand what cannot be under-
stood."*

*"I do...all the time...I feel as though we are one and the
same. Think we were birds in another life?"*

"Could have been."

"Ever suppose things, Gabriel?"

"Like what?"

"Like, suppose we were the creator of all things."

"Us...the Creator? The Great Mystery?"

*"Yeah, suppose that. Suppose we split up just to find each
other again, to become One again."*

Gabriel went quiet and thoughtful.

After a moment Vasilia continued:

*"Suppose we created time and place. Suppose time is noth-
ing more than the opportunity to learn the language of the heart,
nothing more than the opportunity to learn about love. Suppose*

337

that. Suppose we are the creators of the world and everything in it. And suppose, just suppose we create the maze, the traps and the obstacles to each other--"

"*I don't see why we would do all that. Why wouldn't we just stay together? You know, just stay put?"*

"*Ahh, Gabriel, you're no fun!"*

"*But why would we do all that if we could just be together?"*

She thought a moment. "Eternity can get kind of boring...don't you think?"

※

For a few days, Gabriel and Vasilia did nothing but sleep.

"We have to do something about this place," Vasilia said as she awakened.

"What?" he asked through a yawn. "What's wrong with it?"

"Functional," she said. She looked around. "A place to sleep,

perhaps. But not a home."

Gabriel examined his cave but did not understand.

Vasilia went on. "It's nice to

pursue a dream, Gabriel. But if you only think about your treasure, you will lose your life. Don't you care about how you live?"

"How I live?" It had never occurred to him.

"Never mind," she sighed.

He shook his head and left to search for his treasure.

It was dark and the wind was screeching and howling when Gabriel returned from yet another failed treasure hunt. Though now, for some reason or another, he wasn't really bothered by his bad luck. His mind was always on Vasilia. She had taken over his life in a way he had never expected.

When he entered his cave, he smelled a sweet perfume and could not place the fragrance. He looked around puzzled, wondering if he was in the right den. Ivy covered the walls; purple and yellow petals covered the floor; a soft fire burned in the middle of the cave.

Vasilia lay by the fire sleeping.

He admired her lovingly.

Sensing him, she looked up.

When their eyes met, she took in a deep breath and smiled. She released her breath slowly. "You're back," she said. "I missed you."

The words were jewels to Gabriel. "I missed you, too," he said in a whisper. The sound of her voice sent shivers through his body, and he thought her voice was more soothing than the rays of the sun.

She smiled and went back to sleep.

Inside, he felt like he never wanted to leave her again. Inside, he was at peace, secure, comfortable. "I missed you, too," he repeated softly. Then he looked around and admired his surroundings. Now he understood the difference between a cave and a home.

ॐ

It wasn't long before Vasilia let doubt creep into her mind as she always did when good things came to her.

Throughout her life, she had built tests, walls, and gauntlets against those who tried to get close to her. Now a master of self-protection, she panicked and could not believe someone had passed the tests, climbed the walls,
beaten the gauntlets; she could not believe love had found its way to her.

Gabriel seemed too good to be true. Scared and insecure, she demanded proof.

She needed proof. And proof was the only thing he could not give her.

"I don't understand!" she cried and stood up. She regarded him a moment, and then walked toward the entrance where the wind blew softly, and the moon shone bright behind a
curtain of snowflakes.

Gabriel looked up to her. "What don't you understand?"

"I've never felt like this before," she said, gazing at the moon. "And I don't understand why I feel like this now. I'm not sure this is really happening...I mean, is it? And how do I know for sure. How do I know, Gabriel, that this is true, that this is love?"

"Don't," he replied, "Don't try to understand." He inched closer and stood beside her, staring at the fat snowflakes falling gently to the ground.

"But I need to." She turned to him.

He held her gaze strongly. "Just have faith," he said. "Just believe."

She turned back to the silver night. "Is it how we look at each other?" she asked. "Is it how we live together?"

"Please, don't. It's not so simple, not so straightforward. It's not as important for you to understand as it is for you to believe.

Believe in our love; believe you are worthy of love. And have faith."

"Faith?" She laughed at the idea.

"Yes, faith," he said. "Faith is so much stronger than proof."

She stared at him, wanting to believe. "I think," she said, "it is how we are together." She needed to know why.

Gabriel sighed. "Could be," he said. "But don't you see? Our love is far greater than the sum of you and me and what we do for each other or how we are together. Why do you need to break it down?"

He paused for a moment and thought back to his youth, about his talks with his grandmother. "What is proof of love?" he asked. "How can anyone prove love?"

Vasilia didn't know. She shrugged.

Gabriel continued. "Maybe the nature of love is that as soon as you try to prove it, it vanishes. What you see and what your mind records and analyzes is not proof. So why pickle our love like those humans in white coats?"

She smiled. "I'm not."

"They would place the entire universe in sample jars if they could. And all those jars would not come close to what the universe is."

She laughed. "I'm not trying to pickle our love, Gabriel!"

"You can't explain the unexplainable," Gabriel went on, echoing his grandmother. "If your heart could speak and record data and truths, then maybe we would be closer to understanding. But until we understand how to observe with the heart...we will never understand things like love."

She was silent and thoughtful.

Gabriel sighed. He turned, walked to the back of the cave, and stood in the shadows, shivering in the cold. He could not prove his love to her. And he knew it.

She continued to peer at the night. Snowflakes fell faster and heavier, and they glowed and reflected silver in the moonlight. For a long moment there was silence.

Vasilia stood hypnotized by the majestic flecks of silver

falling from the sky. She had never witnessed such fleeting and inexpressible beauty. An attempt to put her feelings to words would be to miss the moment and thereby forfeit beauty.

A snowflake fell on her nose and melted faster than words could describe it. She closed her eyes, took in a deep breath, and felt a tug of despair in her heart. One day the Great Mystery would separate them.

"If you want," Gabriel continued without looking at her, "you can try to figure out the whys and the hows of us. But I'd rather accept that I don't know why...why..."

He went silent.

"Why?" She opened her eyes and turned to him. "Finish. Why..."

"I don't know why my heart wants to leap out of my chest every time I see you! Why I feel so alive when I am near you, and why this vast desert of rock and snow has suddenly transformed into something so beautiful and promising."

She walked to him and moved so that she faced him.

Gabriel lowered his gaze. "You can try to figure out the whys and the hows of us," he said. "But I'd rather accept that I don't know."

She laughed and nudged his nose with her own so that he would look up. Gazing into his eyes, she licked his nose lovingly and decided she would accept the magic of their love without needing to prove it. "Faith," she said, "is so much stronger than proof."

കൗ

Gabriel forgot about his treasure for weeks and stayed in the comfort of his home.

"Have you forgotten your treasure?" Vasilia asked him one day.

"No," he said. "It's this place..." He smiled blissfully and took in a deep breath.

"What's the matter?"

"I never want to leave! I feel so good here with you. My soul is at peace."

She laughed, for she felt exactly the same way.

"You aren't looking for your treasure anymore."

"I am comfortable."

"You must continue to search, Gabriel. I feel as though we've been through this many times before."

He didn't respond.

After a moment, she continued, "You'll get used to us. You'll adapt to me. You'll forget how you felt without me. Then you'll blame me for not
finding your treasure."

"No, I won't."

"But you will regret. And maybe we'll be happy, but you'll always wonder if you would have found your treasure had you continued searching. Being in love, Gabriel, does not mean forgetting who you are."

ಐ

Months passed, and as she had predicted, Gabriel eventually started blaming her for his idleness. "If we hadn't met," he said one morning. "I would have found my treasure!"

It seemed like all they ever did was watch the stars or hide from the cold in his cave.

He felt as though he had lost his passion for life. His heart had never been so at peace before, so comfortable. He didn't even know how to motivate himself. Even his dreams about his treasure had died. And he felt sure this was because he stopped being true to himself.

Tears sprang to Vasilia's eyes. "No," she said, shaking her head in disbelief. "Why are you saying those things? I have always supported you. You chose to stay home."

Gabriel shook his head. "I'm more responsible when I'm alone," he said. "I have lost my desire, my restless heart. I don't understand what has happened to me! I used to work so hard. My dreams used to speak to me!"

Now he despised what she had done to his cave for the same reason he once loved--comfort. And now he remembered why he had kept his cave in such squalor. He didn't want to be at home. He wanted to be out there searching for his treasure. His cave used to be a place to rest, nothing more. She had changed him, and he resented her for it.

"I never stopped you!"

"The most passionate and intelligent wolves are often the most alone."

"You want to be alone? Is that it?"

"Sometimes…"

Vasilia couldn't believe her ears. "Don't blame me for your choices," she cried. She couldn't believe what he was saying. Somehow, she knew this would happen. She felt it inside and

couldn't explain why.
"I'm stronger when I'm alone," he said.
"Then maybe I should leave!"
"Maybe!"
"Gabriel!"
Her muzzle fell.
Her throat tightened.
Impossible sorrow filled her eyes.
He lowered his gaze, and his heart cautioned his mind that he was not thinking rationally. That he was being impulsive and inconsiderate to the one wolf who meant the world to him. But Gabriel's mind, stubborn and emotional, ignored his heart.
She swallowed, spun away from him, and started out the cave. She stopped at the entrance. She turned and looked at him gravely. She waited for a word, any word.
None came.
He stared at the ground, motionless.
His silence was like a million teeth biting into her heart.
Her eyes paled with misery and heartbreak, and her mouth trembled. She turned abruptly and, stepping into a freezing blizzard, never looked back again.
Gabriel stood for a long while, frozen like a glacier. He felt the cold Siberian desert, deep and unforgiving, penetrating his bones. Finally, he whispered, "I'm stronger alone." He repeated this over and over again and tried to make himself believe it.
But he remained unconvinced. His heart rebelled and shouted that he was a fool, and he shrank within and was a hundred times smaller than the wolf he had been. And the desert took hold of him and did not let go.

ॐ

In the days that followed, Gabriel was furious with himself, and he could feel his strength deteriorating. He knew he had made a grave mistake, and as he slogged against the wind and searched the mountains for his treasure, all he thought of was Vasilia. Every tree, every rock, every star brought back a memory of her.

He had ruined something so fragile and precious because he had been upset with himself. He could blame no one else for his idleness. And yet, he had blamed her, the closest one in his life, the one who had always supported him and encouraged him. What a fool he had been!

"How could I say those things?" he asked himself, completely forgetting about his treasure, wandering about the snowy desert, cursing himself for being so inconsiderate.

And then one day, as he went through the motions of searching for his treasure, he stumbled upon a wild purple and yellow flower growing amidst a vast expanse of black and gray rock.

At first he laughed at the flower. Then, all at once, he went silent. The desert closed in on him, and tears came to his eyes. "Breathe," he said to himself. "Breathe!" He closed his eyes and struggled to regain himself.

When he opened his eyes again, he stared at the flower, and he gazed at it the entire day. At last, racked with guilt and grief, he resolved to find his Vasilia and undo what he had done.

৪৩

It snowed hard, and Gabriel thought about Vasilia every second of every minute of every hour of every day since she had left.

His heart felt as heavy as stone, and he hadn't slept for days. He was inconsolable. He searched everywhere: the mountains and valleys, the rivers and streams, the caves and crevices. But Vasilia was nowhere to be found.

One night, unable to sleep, he rose and went outside his cave. He looked up to the moon, closed his eyes, and prayed to see his beautiful Vasilia again.

The next morning, Gabriel roused to the sound of movement outside his cave. Grief-stricken, his ears pricked up, he lifted his muzzle, and he watched the entrance carefully.

A short silence passed.

Suddenly, Lavinia emerged.

"Go away!" he growled.

Ignoring him, she moved inside.

"What do you want?" Gabriel asked.

She inched closer and gazed into his troubled eyes. She
gave no answer but stared at him profoundly.

"What do you want?" he
repeated.

"To help you," she replied.

Gabriel laughed. "You? Help me?"

She stared at him a long while. "He has her," she said.

For a moment, Gabriel heard nothing. His breathing ceased.
He didn't hear right. It couldn't be true.

"Where is she?" he cried. "Is she okay?"

Lavinia shook her head solemnly. "You know what happens
to deserters."

Horrified, Gabriel's fur stood up. He gasped. "When?"

"Tonight. Moonrise."

"Why are you telling me this?"

Lavinia thought for a long moment. "Because, when I spoke
to her, her first words were for you. Will you ever forgive her for
keeping you from your treasure? Not once did she express fear for
the death to come. All she spoke of was you."

Now Gabriel took deep breaths, controlling his emotions.

After a moment, Lavinia continued:

"Most of us search our whole lives for what you two have.
You don't know how lucky you are to have found her, Gabriel. In

this cold, unforgiving desert of doubt and deceit, you have truly found your treasure."

Gabriel felt a tug, as though a chord had been tied to his heart. His eyes widened. He whispered, "What? What did you say?"

She didn't answer. She merely stared at him and envied him silently.

He staggered backward.

"My...treasure..."

His eyes watered.

"My treasure..."

He felt faint.

"My treasure..."

His eyes drowned in unshed tears.

"My treasure..."

He could not believe he had not realized what his heart had always known. Now he understood. His dreams had stopped because he had found his treasure, not because he wasn't true to himself anymore.

Lavinia sighed heavily. "You still have time, Gabriel," she said softly. "Most of us aren't so lucky." Without another word, she turned and made her way out.

Gabriel lowered his head, stared at the ground, and felt very alone. A tear slipped down his face, and he pawed it away, taking several hard, deep breaths.

ॐ

The moon bright and full, Gabriel raced up the path leading to the ice cliff where Viktor executed all deserters. His tail and ears were up and his senses were so sharp that his entire body quivered as he ran.

When he reached the cliff, he saw that Viktor's gang had already turned on Vasilia. She was bloody and beaten, lying on the snowy ground motionless, groaning, barely alive, unable to keep her swollen eyes open.

Viktor commanded his wolves to move away from her. He wished to be the one to throw her down the cliff. His jaws closed over the back of her neck, and he dragged her toward the edge.

Gabriel's whole body went ridged. The fur on his back stood on end, and he felt strength rising from within. "Viktor!" he roared.

Viktor froze. He instantly recognized the voice, though he felt sure he was mistaken.

The voice thundered again. "Viktor!"

Stunned, the wolves turned to Gabriel. But he was not at all the wolf they remembered. He seemed bigger, stronger, and fiercer.

Vasilia roused slowly. Every inch of her battered body ached. She squinted and could barely make out Gabriel through her puffy eyes.

"Viktor!" Gabriel yelled again, his eyes fierce and focused. Inside blazed the thought of losing Vasilia forever.

Viktor turned.

Gabriel barked, "Let her go!"

Viktor's eyes widened with disbelief as Gabriel approached him.

Slowly, he released her. "So," he growled, "this is what she leaves me for. A treasure hunter! I should have known."

Siberia

"Get away from her!" Gabriel demanded, took a step closer, and grew ten times taller and wider with his love.

Viktor gave him a long look, and his muzzle slowly creased with a wide, menacing smile. "Does your memory fail you?" he asked.

"Get away from her!" Gabriel took another step closer and grew fifty times taller and wider with his love.

"This time I will not spare you!" Viktor bellowed.

"I said," Gabriel replied through his teeth, "get away from her!" And he took one final step closer, growled, and grew one hundred times taller and wider with his love.

"No," Vasilia groaned in despair and felt a great fear for Gabriel. But she could not see what the others saw, that Gabriel was a hundred times the wolf he had been because of their love. Nothing could stop him from being with her. Not even Viktor.

A look of worry filled Viktor's eyes. He swallowed. He looked to the other wolves and saw their fear as they stared at one another, unable to understand why they were so frightened of one wolf.

There was no explanation.

They only knew that this was not the same Gabriel they remembered.

This was a giant.

One by one, they backed away and grew ten times smaller with every step.

Viktor growled with hatred. A moment later, he lunged with bloody claws and razor sharp teeth. Gabriel moved at lightning speed and met him in the air. Claws crossed and teeth shone in the moonlight.

They grappled, growled, and cursed each other.

They slammed against boulders and rolled over the ground and moved closer and closer to the edge of the cliff.

Soon it seemed as though Viktor had the advantage as he held onto Gabriel's back and tried to bring him down.

Gabriel jerked left and right
trying to fling him off.

Jay Singh

All in vain.

But then, suddenly, Gabriel looked to Vasilia. Their eyes met. His heart thundered. He gathered his strength, bent his legs low, and with a fierce turn, he thrust Viktor over the ledge.

But Viktor did not fall.

His desperate paws caught a branch, and he held on for his life, begging for mercy. "Gabriel," he begged. "Gabriel, please! I spared you once!"

It was true.

Gabriel knew it.

So he inched toward the edge and pulled Viktor up.

When Viktor regained his strength, he looked up and saw Gabriel carrying Vasilia on his back. He watched them until they disappeared, and he burned with hate and jealousy. If he could not have her, no one else would!

A brutal wind shrieked, and Gabriel carried Vasilia through Avalanche Valley. "Just a little bit more," he said. "We're almost home. It's all over now. We'll rest and I'll take care of you and before you know it you'll be as good as--"

A thunderous shout interrupted him.

"Vasilia!"

Gabriel went pale. "No," he said. "Oh…no…"

In the distance, Viktor stood atop a snowy mountain ledge and yelled in despair, "Vasilia!"

The name echoed through the mountains, and Gabriel began to race for cover. Suddenly, the ground shook under his paws, and the terrible roaring began to fill his ears. He ran faster and faster, but to no avail; for, when he looked back, a churning mass of snow was on him.

⅋

The snow settled, and a white blanket covered the land and sparkled in the moonlight. After a long silence, a paw broke through the snow, and, an instant later, Gabriel pulled himself out of the snow, gasping and calling out for Vasilia. No sooner was he free than he began searching for her.

It was long while before Gabriel found Vasilia and pulled her out of the snow.

Vasilia lay still on the ground and Gabriel tried to wake her up. He lifted his muzzle and looked to the heavens for help. "Please," he growled. "Please..." But that was all he could manage. "Please..."

She struggled to open her eyes. "Gabriel," she smiled weakly. "You're alive...you're okay..."

"I'm alive!" he laughed out loud. "I'm okay!"

He was so happy he could scream. But his happiness was short lived. To his horror, her eyes began to shut again.

"No!" he pawed at her desperately. "Please don't. Not now..."

Her eyes shut.

His muzzle began to quiver. "Vasilia...Vasilia....please no..."

Her eyes blinked open for a second.

She smiled, and he looked into her eyes and saw that life was fading.

Then, slowly, her eyes closed.

Forever.

Tears began down his face and he wept a lifetime of stored tears, unable to grasp the truth of what was happening. He wouldn't see her again. He wouldn't laugh with her again. He wouldn't hear her again. And once again...

Nights bitter and long.

Alone and lonely.

Cold and empty.

Again...

The desert.

Jay Singh

The horrible desert!

And now he knew more than ever he could not go on without her. He felt instantly condemned to a solitary life he could no longer assume after having known the magic of their love. And now he knew with a terrible
certainty that it was better to have never known how great his life could be with her than to have known and have to continue on without her.

For a long while Gabriel sat in front of her in silence, frozen tears dangling in tiny icicles from his muzzle. He breathed slowly and heavily, and his heart refused to believe what his eyes were seeing. Then, from the very depths of his soul, he threw his head back and broke the suffocating silence.

The howl shook the night and quickly rose to the stars and moon and seemed to fill the whole world with sorrow. Impossible pain and anger coalesced and echoed through the land and sounded like a million wolves howling at once.

Creatures from all across the land heard his call. One by one, they came from the white desert and mountains and surrounded him. This was a howl they would never forget. A howl they would later call the howl of ultimate despair.

When anguish finally squeezed Gabriel's howl to a whisper, he didn't notice he was surrounded by foxes and rabbits, wolves and deer, bears and birds, mice and moles--all the creatures of the land.

All he saw was her.

All he felt was the desert.

His breathing slowed, his heart slowed.

Gently, he curled up beside her and put his forehead next to hers. His eyelids grew heavy and fell slowly until they were closed. He had found the greatest treasure in the universe. And nothing could separate him from that treasure. Not even death.

Olivia Garcia La Funk
Poor Little Church Mouse

៙

Not so long ago in a small, rundown church in the heart of New York City there lived a fuzzy brown mouse named Olivia Garcia La Funk. Well, to be fair, calling Olivia a mouse might be a little bit of an understatement. Yes, she was cute. And cuddly. And yes, she could dance every dance in the history of dances. But she was more. So much more. You see, Olivia was...an angel. Well, maybe not exactly an angel. But something very close. For Olivia had been blessed with all the power of an angel in a diamond that she wore around her tiny little neck. A diamond she called the Radiance.

You see, a long, long time ago the beautiful angel Ashrualla was sent to earth to protect the poor and oppressed from evil. But the shadow aggies--invisible demons who love nothing more than to terrorize and torment people--used a dark spell to trap her inside a majestic blue diamond. These demons then used all the power embodied in this diamond against the very ones Ashrualla had vowed to protect. But all this was long ago. Long before one humble little church mouse had stolen the diamond from them and--through stealth, cunning, and ingenuity--kept it hidden from them for centuries. Now, for the last few centuries, kept young and strong by the power of the Radiance, Olivia does with the Radiance what had always been intended.

Yes, indeed, I am sure there are many of you who will doubt me, many of you who will raise a skeptical eyebrow and say I am exaggerating, say that a mouse couldn't do the things I have herein chronicled: that a mouse couldn't bring down entire gangs, or help the police capture crooks, or find a way to redistribute stolen money to the poor. I am sure there are those of you who would even say that a mouse would stand no chance fighting against evil in a dark and dangerous world of drugs, thieves, and gang warfare. That a mouse couldn't be a fierce and most dedicated soldier of the light. But I assure you, every word of it is true. True as the sun, moon, and stars. And this, dear reader, is but one of the many volumes that relate the three hundred and some years of this little angel's life. And it begins, like most of her stories, with a prayer.

ॐ

"Dear God," the young boy began, kneeling before the stone Madonna in the quiet, empty church, "I know I have asked for many things in the last few years: bikes, toys…better marks in math… But this time it's different. This time I am not here for me. I'm here for my sister, Jenna."

The boy's voice was low and sad. Olivia couldn't really hear him as she listened to a reggaeton jam on her old transistor radio and pattered and drummed out an accompanying tune with her fingers and tail on a collection of tin cups. After a moment the boy continued:

"Jenna has been working on her music for her whole life now, but has yet to have a lucky break."

The boy paused, collecting his thoughts. Then he explained:

"When mum returned to you, Jenna was the only one left who could take care of me. Which she did. She didn't send me away like other big sisters would have, and because she didn't send me away she had less time with her music.

"Now I'm afraid she's forgetting what once made her happy. She's forgetting her secret self. The person she always wanted to be. I am afraid she is giving up. Giving up on her dreams. On herself. On life…"

The boy sighed heavily, shuffled a bit, and unwittingly kicked the bench behind him.

At the thud of a shoe hitting old, dry wood, Olivia stopped pattering her favorite reggaeton tune. She loved reggaeton. It was her latest musical craze and she spent all her free time listening to reggaeton on her little radio, which she also happened to use to eavesdrop on police talk, gossip, and dispatches.

Olivia scrunched her face and piqued her fuzzy, round ears to listen for more. She soon heard his sniffles echo through the empty church.

Hearing him, she instantly turned off her radio. Then she pulled back her thick, blue denim hood to free her ears and stuck one out of the one and only entrance to her home.

At the sound of more sniffling, this time louder, she poked her tiny little head out and peered out toward the Madonna. There she saw a boy kneeling in supplication.

OG LaFunk: Poor Little Church Mouse

When the boy turned slightly toward her for a brief moment, she recognized him. He had been here many times before. To pray. For toys, games, better grades... Things she wouldn't use her power for.

The boy's name was James, and Olivia knew he had a sister named Jenna.

She knew this because his mother had often spoken about and prayed for her children in the church, thinking she was alone, thinking no one was around to hear her. Not aware that a poor little church mouse was listening just a few benches away. Just like her son today.

It was strange to see him in the very same spot as his mother. Even stranger to hear him. He sounded so different. He sounded...a lot more like his mother and a lot less like the little boy who prayed and begged for toys.

In fact, today James not only sounded different, he was different. There was a distinctive change in his voice. And so...

You can imagine what Olivia needed to do next.

Olivia-the most curious mouse I have ever known-needed to find out more. So she prepared herself to leave the comfort of her tiny little home.

Olivia grabbed and wrapped a red piece of cloth around her blue denim robe and tightened it like a belt. She then snatched a matching blue denim newsboy cap, which like her robe, she had fashioned out of a discarded pair of blue jeans.

Olivia, you should know, did this with most of her attire, which mainly consisted of robes and hats and red sashes for belts. But it wasn't always this way.

You see, throughout Olivia's three hundred years of life she had made a habit out of wearing the clothes of dolls because it was...easier...much easier, I suppose, than fashioning her own clothes.

But the problem was she could never quite find a doll that matched her tiny little body just right. What's more, her wardrobe changed with the fads of the times, which didn't always impress her, inspire her, or fit her most dangerous, demon-fighting, angel lifestyle.

So around a hundred or so years ago she began to fashion her own wardrobe out of the discarded clothes she found in dumpsters. Her own suit, like any proper superhero.

She modeled her suit after a comfortable and sturdy monk's robe she had seen in Spain, which her tiny little brain registered and never forgot.

Her hat she modeled after the famous newsboy hat worn by the famous New York newspaper boys, which she loved ever so much for both the look and snug fit.

Her cloth of choice generally changed, but for the last fifty or so years it had been denim, blue denim, preferably dark. Tied, of course, with a piece of cloth, preferably scarlet.

Ms. Olivia Garcia La Funk could spend weeks, even months, sowing up a double stitched robe along with a matching newsboy cap. Even longer, though, and probably the most difficult part was finishing the suit with a little piece of graffiti.

You see, Olivia admired, appreciated and practiced, with little brushes, the art of graffiti.

After completing a robe and hat, Olivia would walk around the city searching for inspiration, something original, something challenging, something uniquely hers to paint on her uniform, which she used like a canvas.

Sometimes it could take months for her to find inspiration.

Sometimes it happened right away.

It all depended on how Olivia felt. But it just had to be perfect. For if there was one passion that could rival her passion for music, it was graffiti.

In all respects little Ms. La Funk loved to draw, paint and graffiti and would spend a good part of her day doing so. Over the years she had created dozens of these wonderful suits that were by all standards works of art.

Some of them, to be sure, were more than works of art.

Some of them, you could say, told stories much like a totem pole.

In fact, several of her suits told a story in one way or another about a special event or friend in her life. Someone or something she never wanted to forget.

But this particular hat and robe she wore today was still blank, freshly blue, still awaiting inspiration.

Soon inspiration would come, she knew. And soon she would be drawing and painting like a mad little mouse, giving this suit distinction, character, life. And, of course, her unmistakable OG 'tag'. Her unique signature. It was a human friend who had taught her the expression 'tag' several years ago. But that is another story and shall be discussed at some other time.

OG LaFunk: Poor Little Church Mouse

Now Olivia tightened her red belt and moved into the church. She made her way all the way to the boy and hid behind his running shoe without making the slightest sound, doing justice to the popular expression:

Quiet as a church mouse.

James continued:

"Ever since I can remember Jenna has been singing and writing music. It's as if she had been born with music in her blood."

Olivia smiled at this.

She, too, often believed she had been born with music in her blood. She loved any and all kinds of music, and had for as long as she could remember. She even made it a point to study all the musical movements and dance styles of the times and world.

Indeed, Olivia loved to dance, and she could make a wonderful musical instrument out of any gizmo, trinket, bucket or surface. Dancing, music, and percussion were her secret pastimes. And since the Radiance kept her young and strong, she had the time.

Olivia had learned hundreds upon hundreds of dances over her three hundred years of existence. She had also collected hundreds of tunes inside her tiny little library brain of hers.

Just then, thinking of a recent tune, Olivia lost herself in her musical brain and unwittingly pattered a small percussion tune on James' shoe, doing a great injustice to the expression:

Quiet as a church mouse.

At the slight pattering, James started.

The prayers stopped, and the sudden silence startled Olivia. She gasped, realizing her mistake and searched for somewhere to hide. And fast!

When James looked downward she was gone, hiding three rows behind him. He looked around, searching for something but not quite knowing what that something might be.

After a minute of staring around an empty church, he turned back to the Madonna, closed his eyes, knitted his hands together, and continued his prayer in a soft, quivering whisper:

"Ever since I can remember, Jenna has worked hard toward her dreams. Always happy, always joking, always making other people smile with her smile."

James paused, something in his throat thickened; he seemed on the verge of tears. Olivia edged closer to him ever so quietly, sensing his profound sadness. She understood his pain.

Olivia had had many close friends in her three hundred years of existence who had almost drowned in a dark, thick, lake of their broken dreams.

She, too, had prayed and hoped for their recovery despite the shadow aggies that kept them down with the ever-so-potent and damaging self-defeating suggestions only their subconscious could hear. Aggies, as you will soon discover, did whatever they possibly could to bring spirits down in order to keep theirs up.

After a moment, James cleared his throat and continued:

"But now, Jenna has lost her smile. She has lost faith in herself. She has given up and...and I am afraid I don't recognize her anymore. She always sleeps. Her blinds are always down. And when she is awake she is always sad..."

Olivia moved under the boy's chin and was startled when a silent tear splashed on her head and soaked her hat.

Olivia looked up at his wet eyes and felt his pain. She knew about his sister through her mother. She had heard about her several times a week. Her mother had come often to pray for her children.

Several years ago the family had experienced an unspeakable tragedy. There had been a robbery in their neighborhood followed by a shoot-out in the streets. The mother, walking home from a hard day at work, had been hit by a stray bullet. Jenna, being old enough to be considered an adult, had been given custody of her little brother.

"She never smiles, and nobody can make her smile. I don't recognize her anymore. I don't really know why I am here or if you can hear me...or what I am asking ...all I know is that if the right person heard her music...her hard work would be appreciated and she would have her chance. She would have her lucky break."

James paused for a moment, then continued in a trembling voice:

"If You or Your angels can hear me...please help her... She deserves a lucky break. She has done everything for me. I love her. I love her more than I can say. I want my sister back. The way I always knew her. Please..."

Olivia was touched by the boy's prayers.

James had often come in the church to pray. But this time it was different. This time he prayed for someone else. And that was all the difference.

OG LaFunk: Poor Little Church Mouse

So Olivia nodded and whispered:

"I hear you."

She knew that somehow she would find a way to help his sister. She also you knew that their home was most likely filled with aggies, and that the first step in helping Jenna was to clean her surroundings of all that kept her down in the dumps. That meant using the Radiance to send those terrible aggies back to the Shadowlands.

ॐ

And so, little Ms. La Funk followed James out into the rainy spring
morning, through the park, across the small basketball court, and through
a sunless alley. And as she progressed through the neighborhood streets
she watched carefully over her shoulder, trying her best to stay in the sunlight where aggies would shrivel up and vanish like vampires.

Olivia was quite aware that she was outside the protective walls
of the church. She knew that it wouldn't be too long before the aggies
would sense the magical and luring presence of the Radiance dangling
around her neck.

She also knew that aggies would do whatever they could to
secure the Radiance for their king. For these demons moved in distinctive
packs, almost like wolves, except they didn't quite respect territories, and
each pack tried to secure homes of chaos and sadness from one another in
wars for living space.

So Olivia carefully followed James to his rundown apartment
building and waited until he opened the front door with his shiny key.
The rain poured harder now, and each drop fell like pebbles against her
head. In any case, that is how rain would feel if you were little like
Olivia.

James turned the key, opened the door and walked inside.

Olivia waited a moment, timing her entry so no one would see
her. Just as the door was about to shut, she dashed and managed to
squeeze through. But not her robe. Her robe got caught in the door.

Olivia pulled and tugged and struggled to be free as she gazed
around nervously, making sure no humans were around, or any other dan-
gers for that matter. And just as she pulled herself free--

POOOW!

A crow smashed into the glass door sending Olivia soaring back
on her fanny.

Shaken, Olivia gathered herself and stood slowly. She looked out
the glass door and saw the biggest crow she had ever seen. The crow
stood on wobbly feet, a little disorientated, bewildered, wondering where
he was and what in fact he was doing there. It wasn't too long after spot-
ting Olivia on the other side of the door that he remembered.

OG LaFunk: Poor Little Church Mouse

Olivia gazed at him and sighed heavily. He had nearly made a meal out her, which made her instinctively scowl at the bird. But then she remembered a simple truth: had she been a crow she would have done the same.

For Olivia knew she was cheese to the crow. She also knew you couldn't blame a crow for being a crow. For that would be like blaming a raindrop for being wet. And you couldn't do that, could you?

Amazed he was still standing after the impact, Olivia watched the crow stagger left, then right. Then, stubborn as this crow was, he made another attempt for her.

The crow charged her with a yell and smashed the glass wall with a cry, followed by a moan. Then he fell backward on his feathery fanny.

Still not giving up--for this crow must have been not only stubborn but extremely hungry--he stood up again, moaning. He appraised Olivia. He pretended to walk away. Then, suddenly, he turned and made one final dash for her.

This time the impact was more than his feathery noggin could bear. He slammed against the glass and remained stuck there for a long moment. Then he slid down and sighed all the way down to the sidewalk where he fell into a deep, deep sleep.

Olivia caught her breath, shook her head at the crow, then turned and followed James up the creaky stairs to his apartment.

The building was quiet except for a cat in a nearby apartment meowing uncontrollably, scratching the door desperately, begging to be released into the hallway to investigate the sudden and unmistakable sent of a mouse.

Olivia didn't blame the cat. She supposed to this cat she smelled like...cheese. And she figured you couldn't blame a cat for being a cat. That would be like being upset with fire for being hot.

In the end, all Olivia knew was the outside world wasn't a safe place for an ordinary mouse. And she thanked her lucky stars she was anything but ordinary.

A cat she could handle. A cat she could use the Radiance to control and ride if she really needed to. But a gang of street cats...well, that's another story. This is something that has happened to her before, something we shall discuss another time.

Olivia followed James all the way up to his apartment.

When he opened the wooden door, the first thing she heard was exactly what no one else heard, and exactly what she expected to hear:

371

Jay Singh

Aggies. Hundreds of them! Screaming and laughing as they fed off the sadness and despair of a broken dream.

When the door shut, the laughter ceased at once. But Olivia knew they were still there. All of them. An army of aggies, behind that door, tormenting, laughing, basking in despair like bugs in a bakery. Aggies spewing subliminal messages of failure and messages of defeat into Jenna's poor, unsuspecting ears. Keeping her spirit down so as to keep their spirits up.

Olivia could sense them all right. They were powerful in this apartment. So powerful she imagined they had their king living with them. Something quite unusual for a king.

Usually aggie kings reigned over several apartments that made up their kingdom. But sometimes a home was so rich in chaos and negativity that the king would content himself with one single home. It was rare, but she had seen it before.

Indeed, shadow aggies and dirty homes were synonymous. Wherever you found one you usually found the other. Often people thought dirty homes led to or caused a despairing outlook on life. But that was not true. Olivia knew this all too well. She knew, as she often said:

"Dirtiness is next to agginess."

By which she meant a dirty home attracted aggies like flies to a pie. Aggies who would in turn whisper feelings of chaos and absurdity into inhabitants so that all they would ever want to do in their homes is sleep and watch TV.

Aggies were clever little demons. They always took things a step further, trying to completely break a spirit if they could. For they knew people who had given up on themselves had a habit of knowingly or unknowingly creating aggie paradises.

A dirty home and broken dream to feed off, that's all an aggie ever needed. And that is why they spent so much time keeping their benefactors down in the dumps.

Sad.

Depressed.

Hopeless.

All aggie doing!

373

And Olivia knew her job to help Jenna began with a total and complete clean up of aggies in her home. A clean up job no one would really notice, but one that made the difference. All the difference.

Yes, Olivia would have to contend with these aggies, but for now she would have to find a way in.

So she searched along the wall for a crack, a hole, an opening, any opening, but found none. For a moment she peered at the apartment door with a small feeling of defeat. She didn't know what to do.

She wondered for a moment what an angel would do in her situation. What Ashrualla would do. Probably, she thought, float right through the door and everything else that stood in her way. Angels were lucky in that way. Not having material bodies.

But clearly Olivia wasn't that kind of angel. She was a mouse angel with a real mouse body and would therefore have to find a real mouse solution.

After a moment of twisting her tiny little whiskers and pondering deeply, Olivia got an idea. Maybe, just maybe she could squeeze under the door like a dog under a wooden fence. She was, after all, a mouse, and mice could do these sorts of things. For her this was a practical mouse solution. And so...

She tried. She pushed her little head through the crack and hit a running shoe. She moved down toward the doorknob and tried again. But, again, she hit another shoe. She moved a little more and tried again... and...again she hit a shoe. This one harder than the last.

Now, to be fair, Olivia might have succeeded at squeezing under the door, but really there were too many obstructions on the other side blocking her path. Boxes. Umbrellas. Coats. But mostly...

Shoes.

Stinky old shoes.

Olivia needed to find another way in.

Again, she considered her options, then, after a moment, thought she could probably enter through an open window. She was sure they had left a window open somewhere in the apartment.

So Olivia climbed the plaster-peeling wall and made her way toward a cobweb-covered vent. She cleared the cobwebs with her tiny little hands, clambered into the dark vent and, moving toward a circle of light, made her way outside.

When she reached the mouth of the vent she stopped to see where she would go next. It was still raining and she knew things would be slippery out there. Then she saw a fire escape a few meters below and wondered if she could make the jump.

Thoughts soon became action. With a daring jump, Olivia landed on the edge of the fire escape and nearly slipped and fell to the hard, alley ground.

But Olivia quickly found her balance, gathered her wits, climbed up the ladder and stopped only when she reached Jenna's window.

Soaked, Olivia stood on the sill and stared into the closed window. She could see Jenna sleeping restlessly. Around her, hundreds of aggies jumped up and down on her bed as if they were on a trampoline. They played, laughed and danced around their big fat king who bounced up and down on Jenna's belly, barking silly orders at his subjects while he laughed a hideous laugh that only Olivia and the other aggies could hear.

It's a shame, Olivia thought, that people can't hear, see, or smell these aggies. If they could, they would surely keep their homes clean as sunshine.

Olivia gazed at the king. He was big, bigger than a shadow dragon. He had one of the fattest bellies she had ever seen, and she had seen many fat kingly bellies in her time.

As Olivia gazed around Jenna's room, she spotted a pile of envelopes and CDs scattered near her desk. She knew instantly. It could only be one thing. Her demo.

Olivia sensed and understood how to help her. She knew she had a way to make something happen for this struggling musician. If she could somehow find a way to put her demo in the right hands…

But who?

She pondered the people she knew or had heard about for a moment.

At last it came to her.

Donnie. She didn't know his last name but that didn't really matter. What she did know was that he was the owner of a nearby café bistro, and that he had given several young artists their first start. Their lucky break. Which was all Jenna really needed. An audience to appreciate and share her hard work.

But for now, Olivia stopped thinking about the demo or how she would get it in Donnie's hands. She had other problems to solve. Namely, how to get inside Jenna's apartment.

So Olivia focused only on the next step.

Jay Singh

How would she get inside?

She searched the brick wall for a pipe, a crack, a hole in the wall...

Then she saw it. The kitchen window. It was slightly ajar. Only problem was she would have to climb across the slippery bricks to get there.

But Olivia had done this before. Hundreds of times. And every time the experience was daring and intense, for one wrong move and...SPLAT! She would be a mouse pancake on the sidewalk. But that never happened because...

Olivia never thought of failure. She only focused on success. And because she only focused on success, success came to her.

And so, struggling against raindrops that fell like pebbles on her tiny little head, she swung, leapt, clutched and pulled herself from slippery brick to slippery brick like a little mouse monkey.

As you can imagine, it wasn't all smooth sailing for Olivia.

You see, just as she leapt and grabbed the edge of the window sill, little pieces of brick chipped away like rubble. Her fingers clawed desperately for something solid to hold on to. A moment later she fell six stories down with a loud cry like the end of the word.

And it would have been the end of her world had her tiny little mouse fingers not clutched and snatched a wobbly laundry line. Lucky for her she had fingers that thought for themselves. And thought quickly.

Olivia hung from the line and wobbled her tiny little legs in the emptiness below her where, to her chagrin, a soaked mutt jump, growled, barked, and chomped his big, ugly, salivating muzzle at her tiny little fanny.

Every time he jumped and chomped...Olivia swung her fanny left or right just in the knick of time.

Soon Olivia heard the music in her little musical mind. The dog would bark and leap. She would evade and sigh. The frustrated dog would chomp down on air. Teeth would smash teeth. Then he would yelp helplessly as he fell into a puddle with a thud, an ommph, and a wild splash.

Slowly, the mutt would clamber to his feet. He would shake the water off his body. Then he would stare at the mouse that gave him so much trouble and growl his humiliation; for failure was not something dogs took lightly. An instant later the percussion loop would start all over again while the persistent, ambient pattering of rain continued all around them.

    That was Olivia, all right. Always hearing music in the world when there really wasn't any to be found. She had what many musicians in the jazz bars she frequented called "The Ear", which basically meant she could hear what most of us missed every day. The symphony of life.

    Olivia didn't know how long she could keep up this little fanny dance, for her arms and hips were beginning to tire, but lucky for her, not as fast as the dog's pride.

    The mutt finally surrendered to the fact that he would not make a steak out of little Olivia. Besides, other dogs were beginning to watch him and their eyes made him self-conscious. They seemed to laugh at him.

    It was too much for his self-esteem. Especially when what he was after was a hundred times smaller and weaker than him.

    So the poor, defeated dog gave Olivia one last look, a searing look, barked his annoyance, lumbered away and hid himself in a small corner behind a garbage bin. The incidental symphony of danger, along with the hypnotic fanny dance, ceased almost at once. But not the ambient rain. That continued on, relentlessly.

    Olivia sighed when she no longer saw the mutt below. Now she could concentrate on scaling the wall to reach the open window.

    She narrowed her gaze and saw through the raindrops that she had a long and dangerous climb ahead. Which was not apple pie to her. Not in the least.

    You see, some mice are great at climbing. Some mice are great at jumping. Some mice are even great at swinging, leaping, twirling and all sorts of fancy acrobats. But Olivia wasn't really great at any of these things. But what she was great at was never giving up. And that, some would say, was a power greater than the Radiance.

    And so, refusing to give up, Olivia climbed up, up, up the building like a brave little mountaineer. Climbing up, she only thought about and focused on her next move.

    She didn't stare at the window, or think about the distance between her and her goal. Such thoughts would overwhelm her and merely lead to certain failure.

    Instead, Olivia merely focused on the next brick.

    One brick at a time, she would make it. There was no other way. And, sure enough, before she had time to be overwhelmed by the great climb ahead, she was pulling herself on top of the kitchen windowsill.

And there on the windowsill, Olivia laid on her back for a long, peaceful moment, staring at the sky, hoping to one day learn more about her power. To learn how to float and fly like an angel so that she wouldn't have to crawl and climb walls, doors, windows and vents like an ordinary mouse.

The Radiance helped her quite significantly when she called upon it, but there was only so much her tiny little mouse body could withstand. She knew that she had to choose her moments carefully. Choose the moments when she needed the Radiance the most.

Otherwise, the power would drain Olivia and she could find herself unconscious amidst a kingdom of aggies who would tear each other apart for the Radiance.

The aggies would be unstoppable if they ever gained possession of her necklace. It was a chance she wasn't willing to take. And so, for things she knew she could do by herself she would have no choice but to refrain from using her power.

After a reflective moment she stood on solid legs. She flicked her tail left and right like whip. Then she twirled her whiskers and gazed into one of the dirtiest kitchens she had ever seen.

Olivia breathed deeply and gathered all her strength as she prepared to bring down yet another shadow kingdom. Looking through the window, she could see a few aggies working together against James.

One by one they took turns whispering words of despair in his ears as he ate a honey and peanut butter sandwich. She knew very well that they wouldn't stop until they had broken both brother and sister. Two fountains of negativity contributing to their one glorious paradise!

As it was the aggies didn't like the fact that James was still sometimes cleaning up the apartment. For if there was one thing aggies could not stand it was a clean house. Which is perhaps why the easiest and most effective way to keep aggies out of your home was simply to keep it spotless.

At that very moment Olivia decided enough was enough! She would clean this apartment of aggies if it was the last thing she did on this planet.

So she did what she always did before she took on a kingdom of shadow aggies. She closed her eyes and visualized herself defeating them one at a time. When she opened her eyes, she was focused and ready. One aggie at a time, she would clean this home!

OG LaFunk: Poor Little Church Mouse

Slowly and quietly, Olivia moved toward the window. She waited ever so patiently for James to leave.

Being a mouse-angel, you understand, was far more difficult than being an angel-angel. For one thing people could see you. For another, people didn't like you. Most of the time the very people you tried to help tried to trap you, kick you, or broom you into oblivion.

The life of a mouse-angel was thankless, to be sure. More than once it had happened that poor Olivia had to run away from the very people she had been trying to help and protect.

Mice, for the most part, weren't well received in homes. For some reason-probably because of rats-mice had a bad reputation with people and elephants.

It was an attitude Olivia hoped to change one day. Though, deep down inside, she knew it would probably never change. Humans could be stubborn. Once they got an idea planted in the garden of their noggins they were hard like weeds to pull out.

And so, breathing deeply, Olivia watched James as he finished the last bite of his honey-dripping sandwich. Then she watched him stand up from the kitchen table and make his way to the living room. Olivia noticed the aggies were beginning to get to him. He had left a mess of crumbs and blobs of honey and peanut butter all over the table. If only he knew about the aggies, he would surely clean up the mess he left behind. Good thing Olivia was around.

Olivia made sure he was far, far away in front of a loud TV before she stepped out of the rain and onto a greasy kitchen faucet.

Not a single aggie noticed her.

Not a one.

They were all too busy with the mess James had left them, laughing and flinging scoops of peanut butter and honey at one another like snowballs.

Some aggies had even built honey and peanut butter forts and snowmen out of the mess. It was really quite a fun time for these unsuspecting demons who were about to be sent straight back to the shadowlands from whence they came.

At once, Olivia sprang off the faucet, landed on a pile of dishes festering and growing new life forms on the counter. Slowly, she rolled up her wet sleeves. Staring at the aggies, now completely covered in peanut butter and honey, she covered her head with her hood.

Jay Singh

Olivia never fully understood why she rolled up her sleeves and pulled up her hood. Ritual perhaps. Perhaps something more. In the end, she knew the act was more psychological than anything else.

Psychosomatic, or something like that, she had read in a magazine for athletes.

In any case, Olivia always thought she looked meaner and fiercer with her hood and sleeves up rather than down. Better for her self-confidence as an angel. It worked. That's all that counted. She gazed at the aggies and whispered to herself:

"Trust in yourself. Focus on success. Only success… One aggie at a time…"

She closed her eyes. Saw everything in her head first. Saw the entire battle in slow motion. Then, opening her eyes to a scene of pure decadence, she gathered the Radiance around her body.

Aggies wrestling in a mixture of yesterday's dinner and today's snack, all the while eating honey and peanut putter-covered pizza crust still hadn't noticed her.

She still had the element of surprise on her side.

Slowly, Ashrualla's power grew around her like a cocoon. She focused the power around her until her tiny little hands glowed with a dark, blue and white energy. Then, suddenly-

An aggie looked up and met her gaze. At once, he froze like a Popsicle. He couldn't believe his eyes. The great Olivia Garcia La Funk stood before him.

After a moment he shook himself out of shock and whispered: "Olivia…Garcia..."

And then, in a voice of sheer terror:

"LA FUNK!"

That was pretty much all he could mutter before Olivia cut him down with a fierce bolt of sizzling blue Radiance.

He flew back with a scream, knocking down a dozen or so other aggies in his path like a great big, unstoppable bowling ball. He repeated her last name in sheer terror, over and over again, as he flip-flopped all over the floor. Then he disintegrated into the void with a terrible shriek.

No sooner had he disappeared than Olivia was all over the aggies like ants on ice cream. She leapt into the air and blasted over a dozen frantic, honey-filled aggies before her tiny little feet even touched the ground.

When she hit the ground she instantly turned into an unstoppable tornado of blue lightning.

One by one, she cut her way through the aggies like a tornado through a forest.

One by one, she flung them and booted them in this direction and that direction, sending them shrieking back to the shadowlands with her power.

Olivia acted before she thought. She fought like a true soldier of the light and only stopped when the last aggie in the kitchen flip-flopped and properly disintegrated into the void.

"Return to the dark!" she commanded as she watched the last aggie in the kitchen disappear.

She lowered her arms to relax. She looked left and right and thought she was in the clear.

It was then she heard it.

The unmistakable shriek of a shadow dragon.

She turned slowly.

There in front of her was a shadow dragon the size of a basketball. And if there was anything Olivia hated more than aggie kings, it was their most beloved pets: shadow dragons.

The pitch-black shadow dragon shrieked at Olivia. He took two menacing steps forward. And she took two steps back in retreat. Then, loud as a tempest, he shrieked again.

Olivia shuffled back and readied herself for an attack. He would leap out at her; she could sense it, any second now.

They stared at one another for a moment that seemed like forever.

Olivia despised dragons. They were difficult opponents. Impossible opponents. And they always drained her of the necessary energy she would need should she want to overthrow a king.

Olivia knew more than ever that she would need to strategize. She would have to make this a short fight, a clean fight, a smart fight, as she could already feel her strength draining. She needed to save her power for the king. She would need it.

So Olivia gazed around the kitchen for something, anything, with her quick, calculating eyes.

Before she had a chance to come up with a clever scheme or strategy the shadow dragon, as if reading her mind, lashed out with sharp, knife-like claws, a mouthful of needle-like teeth, and red eyes glowing with menace.

381

Jay Singh

Olivia jumped back just as its vicious little claw ripped through the air and landed on the table. An instant later the dragon flew straight at her like a cannon ball.

She leapt out of the way just in time and landed on the floor as she watched the dragon crash straight into a pile of stinking garbage bags.

Lucky for her there was old pizza in the garbage.

Really old pizza.

Last week's pizza.

And lucky for her all creatures of the shadowlands love nothing more than really old, moldy pizza.

So for a moment, just a moment, the dragon completely forgot the little mouse as he became completely engrossed with a slice of pizza. The dragon chewed slowly and appreciated each and every bite as if he were eating, evaluating and criticizing gourmet food.

The older the pizza, like cheese, Olivia thought, the better. To each their own.

Olivia didn't wait for the dragon to remember her. She stepped back wisely and searched for something in the kitchen to trap the dragon.

She climbed up the counter and saw something in the sink. A dirty strainer still filled with last night's spaghetti. It would suffice.

Olivia loomed over the sink.

She closed her eyes and shut out the sounds of munching and moaning coming from the garbage bag.

She focused only on the Radiance. She gathered its scintillating power around her hands. Then she opened her eyes and released a powerful beam from her palms to the sink.

The beam reached out to the strainer and lifted it into the air. She then willed the strainer over the garbage bag and waited.

Waited for the munching to stop.

Waited for the moans to stop.

Waited for the characteristic burp that always came after a good old, moldy pizza meal.

As she had expected, after a moment all his grumbling and moaning stopped suddenly. A moment later there was a burp loud as thunder. Then the dragon scrambled out of the garbage with cheese and crumbs all over its black, scaly face.

No sooner did the dragon step out than Olivia let the strainer fall over him. He roared his surprise.

OG LaFunk: Poor Little Church Mouse

Olivia moved fast. Fast as lightning. She knew the strainer was only a temporary prison.

So she leapt from the counter to the chair. She released a bolt of Radiance across to the table, where she lifted an open jar of honey over the strainer-prison. She let the thick, sweet contents ooze out so that the golden cement could secure the strainer to the floor.

Then, inspired by the Radiance, she somersaulted from the chair to the floor and landed right in front of the dragon.

The dragon stared at her through tiny little holes that oozed honey. He shrieked at her and made every movement and gesture to intimidate her.

But Olivia wasn't intimidated.

Not in the least.

She merely pulled up her sleeves, which had fallen to her wrists again, and gathered the Radiance around her tiny little hands.

Seeing the blue energy scintillating around her open palms, the dragon went quiet and pale as a rabbit before a wolf. For now he knew this was the end. Olivia was about to send him back to the shadowlands.

And at that very moment, Olivia commanded:

"Return to the dark!"

And with those words she unleashed powerful bolts of lightning that fried the honey and pierced every hole of the strainer so as to blast the dragon back to where it came from.

The smell of charcoal filled the air as the dragon shrieked and shook frantically with the light. Then, all at once, the dragon vanished from our world as if he had never existed. And everything went silent.

Olivia lowered her palms and breathed deeply, sensing her strength beginning to wane. She understood her tiny little mouse body could only take so much of the Radiance. She understood she would soon collapse from exhaustion and that she would have to act now. And fast.

So she raced to Jenna's room and paused only to pull her sleeves up again as she readied herself to overthrow an aggie king.

With her sleeves rolled up to her elbows, she crept to the door and pushed it slightly open, careful not to make too much noise, or to lose the element of surprise.

Olivia then peered inside the room to make sure Jenna was still sleeping. Then, without a second to lose, she dashed inside and blasted aggies back to the shadowlands.

Jay Singh

There were too many aggies to describe each encounter. But the Radiance moved through Olivia like music and played every limb like a wonderful instrument of the light, so that within a minute hundreds of aggies were flip-flopping all over the floor as they vanished into the abyss with terrible cries and shrieks.

And all this, would you believe, before the aggie king had time to realize what was happening.

As Olivia coiled her tail around the king's very last subject and twirled him around the air gaining momentum, the king started. He instantly stopped his hideous laughing with the terrible realization that he was alone. All his subjects were gone. Olivia had toppled his aggie kingdom!

Olivia slammed his last subject against the floor like a dirty rug. She lifted him again and slammed him again. Once, twice, thrice! Then she flung him toward the ceiling and blasted him in mid-air.

The moaning aggie shattered like a plate and vanished before he realized what was happening to him.

At this the king roared in indignation. He swore he would make a mouse stew out of her by the time he was finished. The next instant he jumped in front of her and stood taller and fatter than any king she had ever faced.

He ran toward her and tried to squish her with his jiggling, fat belly. But Olivia saw him coming and jumped out of the way straight into a pile of dirty clothes.

Just in time.

When Olivia emerged, she was weak and wobbly. She knew she couldn't take much more of this incredible power flowing though her tiny little body. She felt her limbs trembling uncontrollably. She could sense her focus draining.

But Olivia Garcia La Funk wasn't one to quit. In fact, she never quit anything once she started. And so, weak as she was, she lifted her sleeves, raised her hood, took in a long, deep breath, and prepared to meet the king's every attack.

And attack he did!

The king narrowed his gaze on her and shook his chubby cheeks like a bulldog. He bared his teeth, pulled back his arms, stuck out his belly...and charged!

At the very last second Olivia dove out of his way as he careened past her with a terrible scream.

Realizing he had missed her, he stopped suddenly. Turned. Spotted her. Then attacked again. This time-

Olivia shoulder-rolled out of his way and laced him with a strong bolt of Radiance as she stood bolt upright. Which gave her just enough time to prepare her second attack.

And so, as the king shook uncontrollably with the light, Olivia leapt on top of a chair and concentrated and focused on the light, gathering around her arms the power of the Radiance.

This would be her last chance.

It was now or never.

If she missed the king, she wouldn't be able to withstand much more of Ashrualla's power flowing through her. Her timing and focus had to be impeccable.

And it was.

For just as the king regained his wits he did exactly what Olivia expected he would do. He stuck out his big, jiggly belly and, hoping to knock her off the chair, charged like a bull.

This time Olivia did not shoulder roll or dive away. This time Olivia ran across the chair, somersaulted into the air and caught the ceiling fan with her tail like whip. Then she aimed her tiny little palms at the king and unleashed a series of lightening bolts as he crashed through the legs of the chair and went tumbling to the ground.

At this the king yelled so loud she was sure all the demons in the shadowlands heard him.

Olivia didn't wait to feel his wrath. As he tried to stand up, she yelled:

"Return to the dark!"

And released one more bolt.

This time much more powerful.

Much more devastating.

To be sure, the bolt hit its mark-

Right across the king's noggin.

He flipped head over heels at least ten feet back, then shook uncontrollably on the dirty counter and vanished into the void as if he had never existed.

When Olivia was sure the king was no more, she unfurled her tail and, with a somersault, landed on her two tiny little feet.

For a moment she inspected the floor where the king had just disappeared.

Jay Singh

Just to make sure.

Then, satisfied with her work, Olivia pulled up her wet sleeves, which had fallen to her wrists again, and gazed through the window.

Breathing heavily, she realized she didn't have much time until the streets filled with darkness, and with the dark...

Demons.

Of all sizes, shapes and forms.

With a great sense of urgency, she ran to the desk and grabbed one of the many envelopes with the discouraging red stamp known to most aspiring artists:

Return-to-Sender.

She tore open the envelope, pulled out a CD, and holding it with one hand, she ran to the bedroom door. She then peeped her head out, making sure James was nowhere to be seen.

When she was sure the coast was clear, she charged into the kitchen, vaulted from the chair to the table, from the table to the counter, from the counter to the faucet and finally out the window into the now clear dusk of approaching night. As luck would have it--

There was a scruffy old, chubby pigeon searching for soggy breadcrumbs just a foot away from her.

With the grace and skill of a jockey, Olivia dashed toward the pigeon, leapt into the air and jumped on its back.

Before the pigeon realized what was happening, Olivia was using the last of her strength to control the bird's thoughts with the Radiance. The next thing the pigeon knew it was transporting Olivia to Donnie's café bistro.

＆

It took them no more than ten minutes to reach the bistro.

Normally Olivia would be subtler in her stratagems. But now she had no time for clever ploys. She was in a race against time, against the sun, against the night, and she would need to be as fast as possible.

So she watched the door carefully, waiting for just the right moment. When a patron walked out with a steaming cup of coffee, she commanded the pigeon down and made a bold entrance through a closing door that nearly made a pancake out of the both of them.

Even though Olivia was in a race against time, the first thing she noticed as she flew around the bistro was the distinct smell of freshly baked chocolate cake.

For a moment the smell made her lose wither grasp on reality as she dreamed about a world of chocolate and ice cream. She unwittingly followed the scent to the kitchen until she heard someone call out Donnie's name.

The name instantly snapped her out of her chocolate reveries.

Back on task, she flew around the bistro, searching for Donnie. Looking here, looking there, looking everywhere.

It wasn't long before she found him near the stage, testing the giant speakers for a late night show.

Like a true stunt pilot, Olivia circled the pigeon just above him. She waited for the right moment. Then, when she thought he was completely engrossed with a bundle of wires, she dove straight down and-

Slipped the demo into his thick, woolen coat pocket!

All Donnie noticed was a pigeon gliding away.

For a moment he tracked the pigeon to the kitchen, not fully believing his eyes. He was sure he saw...a mouse...atop the pigeon. He waited a moment. When the pigeon came flying out he swore he saw a mouse...a mouse with a big heap of chocolate cake in its tiny little hand.

Donnie watched a patron walk in, and Olivia fly straight out into the darkening sky. At once he closed his eyes, shook his head in disbelief, and thought he needed to get some sleep, for surely he was seeing things.

When he opened his eyes again, Olivia and the pigeon were nowhere to be seen. He shook his head again and returned to his wires. At

387

which point he felt a new weight in his pocket. Something he hadn't noticed before.

Donnie reached into his pocket and pulled out a demo. He inspected it, wondering. He had no idea how it had gotten there. For a moment he thought he was losing his mind.

But soon, very soon, Donnie would come to accept that other forces were at play here. He would finally conclude that the demo in his pocket was some sort of omen.

Soon Donnie would place the demo in his computer and listen to Jenna's song with unbiased ears and an open heart. Doing so, he would hear Jenna. Truly hear her. And he would gladly give her a lucky break.

Jenna would be given the opportunity to perform at his café bistro every Thursday and Friday night. The rest, as they say, would be history. But that is another story, Jenna's story, and shall be related at some other time.

As Olivia swallowed the last piece of cake and licked her tiny little mouse lips, she realized she was in a world of trouble.

Night was coming.

Fast.

Shadows grew darker.

Longer.

The sounds of night were already beginning. Intensifying with every second. The world was changing. Filling with the invisible and intangible.

Creatures she no longer had the strength to fight.

Creatures that would do whatever they could to posses her power.

Everything, that is, except venture into places of the light, where they knew they would meet the likes of angels and spirits.

Sometimes Olivia wished she was bigger and stronger. Then she wouldn't have to run away. She could face them all and send them all back to the great abyss without another thought.

Suddenly, Olivia heard something.

Something only she could hear.

When she turned around she gasped.

Dragons!

Hundreds of them!

Chasing her!

One approaching and snapping his ugly jaw closer and closer to her tail.

OG LaFunk: Poor Little Church Mouse

She hardly believed it. One minute the sky was empty. The next it was filled with dragons as though they had formed out of the darkness itself.

To make matters worse, Olivia could now see hundreds of aggies racing down below her, clambering over pedestrians who could not see or feel them as they stumbled, fumbled, and leapt off heads and noses of all sorts as they reached out toward the sky, yelling, crying, shrieking for the Radiance.

Olivia felt a whisk of air at her back. When she looked over her shoulder, a dragon was on her, snapping his terrible, salivating jaws at her poor, tiny little unsuspecting tail.

The dragon snapped his jaws to the right. Olivia flung her tail to the left. He snapped his jaws to the left. Olivia flung her tail to the right. Again, and again, this went on while at the same time she attempted to pilot the pigeon to the church.

A difficult task.

Some would say an impossible task.

But Olivia managed, somehow.

And as she tried to do two things at once she suddenly realized the dragons had caught up to her. There was one above her, one below her, and several on either side of her.

This, she thought, is the end. And just as she thought that the fiercest dragon of them all rammed into the pigeon with all his might. The pigeon tumbled through the air and sent Olivia almost falling off.

Lucky for her, Olivia grabbed the pigeon's back and she held on by a single feather.

She was nearly home.

Nearly safe.

Nearly.

For just as she approached the church steeple, a dragon--out of nowhere--rammed the pigeon again, like a bull, with his big, ugly forehead.

Olivia clutched the feather and held on for dear life. But the pigeon's feathers were still wet and slippery from the rain that had just fallen an hour ago. To make matters worse, the feather she held was loosening with every effort to hang on.

Then it happened.

With a small pluck--PLUCK--she fell with a gasp. But just as soon as she fell, she grabbed the pigeon's feet and dangled for dear life.

She held on with difficulty and watched as the pigeon carried her closer and closer to the church.

But then, just as they neared the church, at the moment she would have been safe, a dragon rammed her tiny little fanny. She fell down, down, down toward a sea of quick-moving shadows and demons--all of them screaming and jostling to be the one to catch her.

But none of them got that chance.

Just before she hit the ground something invisible and intangible caught her. Something she, or even the aggies, couldn't see for some reason. Something that had snagged her just a few feet above the claws of a rasping demon, for which she had no name and had never seen before.

For a moment that felt like forever, Olivia dangled in mid-air. Something held her safely in the air as aggies went hysterical trying to jump and leap and pull her down as they cried out her name over and over again.

Then, slowly, the mysterious force lifted Olivia high above them.

Not exactly sure what was happening, but desiring the Radiance, a dragon made a daring attempt for her.

No sooner did he approach her than a blast of white light sizzled him to smithereens, which sent a jolt of warning and fear to all other dragons and demons.

Dragons circled Olivia but dared not attack her for fear of a similar fate. They watched grudgingly as the mysterious force carried Olivia safely into the steeple.

Then the mysterious force placed her on a small, wooden bureau as Olivia drifted in and out of sleep, trying to focus and see who had helped her.

Olivia knew she had a spirit, or perhaps an angel looking out for her, just as she looked out for others. She had always felt a presence. She had yet to meet him, or her, or perhaps them.

She began to thank the mysterious force. But her lips and eyelids felt as if they had been filled with cement. And as she mumbled, her eyes closed and she fell asleep, despite the shrieks and cries of the demons gathering outside the church, crying out her name.

When Olivia woke up later that night the moon was full and bright in the sky. For a moment she thought everything had been a dream. But when she looked down at her neck and saw the Radiance she knew it hadn't been.

OG LaFunk: Poor Little Church Mouse

She gazed at the Radiance for a long while and breathed deeply. Then she stood on the bureau, which would one day be used by a writer to write inspirational stories about a tiny little hero who had saved his life. But that is another story, my story, and shall be related some other time.

Olivia yearned to be at her favorite place-the very summit of the steeple.

So she hopped from the bureau to the bell. Climbed a rope and chain to a beam. Walked across the beam to a small crack in the roof and slipped through like squishy cottage cheese.

She then climbed toward the summit of the steeple, ignoring the aggies that surrounded the church as they gathered from all corners of New York to beg and plea and cry for the power she possessed.

"Olivia... Olivia... Come down and play...come down, Olivia..."

By now most aggies knew her name, and whispered it over and over again in a futile attempt to befriend her and entice her to leave her place of refuge by her own volition.

Of course, Olivia ignored them all. Shut them all out of her mind like a bad memory as she continued up the steeple.

At the summit, Olivia lay on her back and watched the moon, dreaming of another time and place. She thought about England, about France, about Spain. She thought about friends and family. She wondered when she would see them again--if in fact she ever would.

And she wondered if she would ever find a way to free Ashrualla from her diamond prison. To break the curse. To free the Ashrualla like a genie in a bottle so as to free herself as keeper and protector of the Radiance. That was a dream, to live out a normal mouse existence.

The last two hundred and eighty something years had been the longest and loneliest years of her life.

Now all she wanted to do was serve the light and keep herself alone. Keep from getting too close to mice and people who she would only end up having to say good-bye to eventually. She hated nothing more than saying good-bye.

Yes, indeed, Olivia wondered if she would ever be free to one day live a normal mouse life. She longed to end this immortality. To free Ashrualla or find some other mouse or creature to take on her burden. To die and see everyone she had ever known and loved waiting for her in her tiny little mouse heaven.

391

But that, she knew, was only a dream.

And so, Olivia turned on her side, closed her glassy eyes, and simply remembered.

She missed them.

She missed them all.

Printed in the United States
by Baker & Taylor Publisher Services